The Keysha Diaries

Volume One

The Keysha Diaries

Volume One

A Keysha and Friends Collection

EARL SEWELL

HARLEQUIN® KIMANI TRU™

Recycling programs
for this product may
not exist in your area.

THE KEYSHA DIARIES, VOLUME ONE

ISBN-13: 978-0-373-09124-9

Copyright © 2013 by Harlequin Books S.A.

The publisher acknowledges the copyright holder of the individual works as follows:

KEYSHA'S DRAMA

Copyright © 2007 by Earl Sewell

IF I WERE YOUR BOYFRIEND

Copyright © 2008 by Earl Sewell

Printed in U.S.A.

CONTENTS

Feel free to send me an email at earl@earlsewell.com. Please be sure to put the title of the novel in the subject line. You may also follow me at www.facebook.com/authorearlsewell or at www.twitter.com/earlsewell.

Dear person who currently has my diary and is invading my privacy,

Were you so curious that you had to pick up my diary to snoop around? Is this something you do often? Since you're holding this book, I bet you can't wait to find out what fascinating secrets and scandals are in these pages. Come on! Admit it! I would think the same thing.

Because you obviously want to know more about me and I feel like sharing today, I guess I'll start by telling you a little bit about myself. You may want to find someplace quiet where you can focus and pay attention. A lot has happened in my mere sixteen years on this earth.

My name is Keysha, but you can call me Ke Ke. And as it seems, I have way too much drama in my life. Drama hovers around my head, as if it's my own personal storm cloud. Have you ever felt that way? Like one day, everyone wakes up and decides it is national hate on you day? The craziness I live with makes me want to scream.

My life isn't pretty:

My grandmother is incarcerated.

My mother is about to go to jail.

I don't know who my biological father is.

And I'm about to be shipped off to a state-run group home for at-risk teens.

And as if that isn't enough, I meet a girl in a situation similar to mine. I think she is my friend, but unbeknownst to me, she turns out to be a backstabber. Have you ever met a person who smiles in your face, but talks about you when your back is turned? I get angry every time I think about her. I'm serious. There should be a law against people like her.

On top of having to deal with that frenemy, there's a guy (with some serious issues of his own) who likes me. He steps to me with a line of poetry that he supposedly wrote for me, as if I would fall for that one. Well, maybe I do believe him, just a little.

Okay, I think that's enough for now. Are you ready? I am. Now turn the page, enter my world, and learn more about me in *The Keysha Diaries, Volume One*....

Keysha's Drama

"Anyone who has ever struggled with poverty knows how extremely expensive it is to be poor."

—James A. Baldwin

one

NO matter how hard I tried to get Ronnie's attention he wouldn't look at me. He avoided eye contact by toying with the ring tones on his cellular phone. His unwillingness to look me in the eye and speak directly to me annoyed me. Ronnie was seventeen and stood about five foot nine inches tall. He had brown skin just like mine and wore his hair French braided. That day he was wearing an oversize white T-shirt, baggy Sean John jeans and what appeared to be a new pair of Nike Air Force One gym shoes. We were standing on the sidewalk in front of the apartment building that he lived in with his mother. In the distance I heard the thud of music from a trunk amp bouncing against the air. Ronnie is my boyfriend, or should I say was my boyfriend until I caught him snuggled up with some girl inside of a movie theater. When I saw him and the other girl I decided to play it cool at first, you know, just to make sure that I wasn't overreacting. I discreetly positioned myself in a seat directly behind them so that I could keep a close eye on them. No sooner than the lights went down, Ronnie took off his jacket, hooked it around her shoulders and began kissing her. That's when I lost it. Before I could even think rationally, I began attacking them both. I slapped him on the head and pulled her hair. It wasn't long before two movie theater ushers rushed in to stop my assault as well as ask me to leave. At the time I didn't give Ronnie a chance to explain what was going on and who the girl was. To be honest, I really didn't care who she was. All I knew was that my boyfriend, who had told me at least twenty times he loved me the night before, wasn't acting like it.

The movie theater incident happened weeks ago. I hadn't seen or heard from Ronnie since that time because I had to move away due to a load of family drama that was going on in my life. During the time I was away, I cried a lot partly because of the situation my family was in and partly because I really missed Ronnie. Now that I'd returned to my old neighborhood, I thought for sure Ronnie had missed me at least a little. I also wanted to give him a chance to explain himself as well as see if we could forget about what happened in the past and start over. Besides, I'd heard that he was no longer with the girl he'd been caught cheating with.

I tried once again to get Ronnie to acknowledge me. When our eyes finally met, I could tell he wanted me to disappear and forget that we ever had anything meaningful.

"Why did you even come around here looking for me?" he snapped at me as if the very sight of me irritated him like a bad skin rash.

"Don't you bark at me like that," I shouted back at him. "I thought you'd missed me and I wanted to give you a chance to explain yourself. So, what happened between us, Ronnie?" I asked straight out.

"I've already told you. It's over between us. You're playing too many games, girl. I'm just not into you anymore."

"But why? What did I do?"

"You're crazy for starters," Ronnie said and then was silent for a long moment as I waited for him to elaborate. "Look, you just need to forget you even know me. In fact, just erase my name and face out of your memory."

"How can you say that to me? After all we've been through? You told me you loved me and no matter what we'd be together. You promised me, Ronnie, you promised me that you'd never hurt my heart." I raised my voice at him. I couldn't help it because my heart was hurting. It didn't matter that we hadn't seen each other in two months, my heart was still broken and I wanted an explanation.

"Look, girl!" he said, pointing his index finger at me as if it was a weapon.

"Oh, now I'm just some girl?" Whenever I got upset about something, no matter how calm I tried to be my voice would always express how I truly felt. "Get your finger out of my face." I quickly grabbed his index finger and tried to twist it off his hand. I wanted to hurt him at that moment. I wanted him to feel the heartache and pain I felt. We tussled for a moment before he broke free of my grip.

"You need to leave, Keysha. I'm not playing with you. Go on back home to your mama."

"So what are you saying, Ronnie?"

"Keysha, I'm through with you. What part of that isn't getting through your thick skull?"

"How can you just turn your feelings for me off like that? I mean, I thought about how I felt about you every day. I even called you after the incident and left messages for you asking you to call me back so we could talk but you didn't.

I even called you when I found out that I had to move away for a while. I thought for sure you'd at least want to know where I was being shipped off to but you never contacted me." I was pleading my case. I reminded him of my good-faith efforts to stick by his side. I was hoping that he'd feel some sense of guilt.

"Keysha, I'm just not feeling you like that anymore. You were cool for a minute but then you started smothering me. You called me too much, you didn't like it when I wanted to hang out with my friends instead of you. On top of that you're too bossy. I just can't get down with a girl that acts crazy and bossy all of the time. You need to roll out and leave me alone."

"Okay, I'll change. Will that help?" I asked, hoping to find the words he wanted to hear.

"No, just leave me alone, all right." Ronnie finally put away his cellular phone. "I've just erased your name, number and special ring tone from my phone. It's been real," he said and then turned his back and walked toward his building.

"I hate you, Ronnie!" I shouted out as loudly as I could. I wanted everyone within the sound of my voice to know how upset I was. I suddenly didn't care about making a public scene.

"Yeah, whatever. Don't come around here looking for me anymore," he said as he entered his building. At that moment rage pumped through my blood and I rushed into the building behind him. I grabbed a fistful of his pretty braided hair and tried to snatch it out of his head. He reached back and put his hand over my fist and tried to pry it away.

"Let go of my hair, Keysha!" he shouted out as we scuffled. At that moment I heard the door to his apartment open. Ronnie's mother came into the hallway above us on the next landing.

"Let him go before I call the police on you!" she screamed at me. Part of me didn't care if I went to jail but another part of me did. I held on to his hair for a moment longer and then yanked really hard, ripping his hair from his skull.

"Get out!" his mother commanded me. She was much larger than I was and for all my spunk I knew I was no match for her. "And don't let me catch you back around here any-more. Do you understand me?"

I rushed out of the building before Ronnie or his mother could come within arm's length of me. Once I got outside, I ran as fast as I could. I wanted to get away from them. In many ways, I wanted to run away from myself, but I knew that was impossible. When I finally stopped running, I was a good four blocks away. I decided to rest on a bus bench so I could catch my breath. I leaned forward and rested my el-bows on my thighs as I waited for my breathing to regulate. For a moment, I thought about crying but I couldn't sum-mon up any tears because I was too angry. My life was so messed up. I swear, sometimes I wondered if some mythical witch or wizard placed a curse on me. I swept my fingers through my hair as I mulled over my situation. My mother, Justine, was crazy as well as pregnant. I had to admit that it tripped me out when she admitted she was going to have a baby. Justine is a real piece of work. In fact, her brain should probably be donated to science because her thought process is completely twisted. My mom became pregnant with me when she was very young. She acts more like my girlfriend than my mom. She cares more about partying than she does about keeping a roof over our heads, a decent job or food on the table. Sometimes, well most times, we fought and argued with one another. I didn't like her because she didn't act her age and in some ways resented the day I was born. At least that's the way I felt.

A bus stopped in front of me, and the driver opened the door thinking that I wanted to get on. I looked at him for a moment and then waved him on. I sat upright on the bench and glanced at the green and white street sign. I was at the corner of Chicago and Laramie Avenues, which meant that I was in the heart of the hood. My mom and I were staying in a basement apartment a few blocks up. I hated the place. It was run-down, dirty and infested with roaches and rats. It was nothing like my Aunt Estelle's home. She had a beautiful high-rise apartment overlooking Lake Michigan. I used to live there with her husband, Dr. Richard Vincent, my Grandmother Rubylee and my cousin Nathan. It was nice living in such a grand place, but that all changed because my Grandmother Rubylee, who was crazier than my mom, was stealing money out of Richard's bank account. She got caught by the police and is serving time for her crime. Shortly after my Grandmother Rubylee was arrested, my Aunt Estelle passed away, and that pretty much ended the welcome of Justine and me in Dr. Vincent's home. All of that happened about two months ago, right around the time I caught Ronnie at the movie theater with some girl.

I decided it was time to get up off the bus bench before I started to look like a female version of Forrest Gump. As I continued on my way home, I thought about school, which would be starting soon, but I wasn't looking forward to it, especially since my mother didn't have money for back-to-school gear. I knew kids were going to talk about me walking around in last year's fashions. I was real self-conscious when it came to fashion and my appearance. My face was filled with pimples and my hair was overprocessed from doing one too many home perms. I thought my nose was too big, my butt was too big, my breasts were too small and my legs were too skinny. I was thinking about my situation and self-image so hard that I actually walked past my apartment building and had to turn around and go back. The building was a large red brick structure with three separate entrances. I had to walk down the block a little ways to the very last entrance, which was near an alley and vacant lot where alley mechanics liked to park their hoopty-mobiles and work on them while they drank alcohol. If they couldn't get their cars running they'd just leave them there until they could. From time to time, if the cars sat too long, eventually parts would come up missing. The entrance to my building wasn't secure at all. The landlord got tired of putting locks on the doors because tenants or their guests continually kicked in the door to gain entrance. I think people did that sort of thing because they didn't have much else to do. I was about to enter the vestibule of the building when I heard someone call my name.

"Keysha, hold on a minute." I stepped back out into the sunlight and saw Toya Taylor, a friend that I'd known for years. She lived in the apartment across the hall from me. Toya had a baby she was continually trying to get neighbors to watch for her while she roamed the streets trying to keep up with her baby's daddy. Toya is sixteen but the father of her baby is a few years older than her. Toya was also rather conceited when it came to her hair. She was one of those girls who had a finer grade of hair as opposed to a coarser grade. She loved to show it off and brag about its length. Today for some reason, she wasn't in the mood to show off her hair because she had it tied up in a black head scarf.

"Hey, what's up? Why do you have on that head scarf? It's hot as hell out here." I was being nosy. I wanted to know what was going on with her hair.

"Girl, my baby's daddy is tripping. He doesn't like for me to be outside by myself with my hair down so he makes me tie it up when I'm not around him."

"Well, if it makes him happy then I guess it is okay," I said, even though I didn't believe her for one minute. I think she did something to her hair and now it's messed up and she doesn't want to get ridiculed for having damaged it.

"Where have you been? I came over looking for you this morning but you weren't home."

"Girl, I got into a fight with Ronnie," I said as I sat down on the step. Toya sat beside me.

"What about? You told him that you wanted to give him a chance to explain himself, right?"

"Yeah, I told him, but it didn't matter. He still treated me like I was a fly at a picnic. I got so mad at him that I pulled out a patch of his hair."

"For real?" Toya's voice was now filled with excitement. "What happened next?" she asked, wanting to know every detail.

"His mother came out into the hallway where we were," I said as I scratched my arm.

"You fought his mother, too?" Toya asked, jumping ahead of my story.

"No. I didn't fight his mother. When I saw her I turned and ran out of the building."

"So, are you sad about the breakup?" Toya asked. "Because if my baby's daddy broke up with me, it would be on. I'd have to hurt him." I wanted to point out the fact that I'd heard that her so-called man had another girl he was dealing with, but I didn't want to go there with her. I just wasn't in the mood to fight with anyone else right then.

"So, what's next? What are you going to do? You've got to find a new man."

"Girl, I'm not thinking about boys right now. I'm thinking about school and trying to get through another year." I glanced up at a few billowy clouds and then down at my feet. My gym shoes had seen better days.

"I think I'm going to drop out of school," said Toya.

"Why do you want to drop out of school?" I asked, looking at her strangely.

"I can't find anyone to watch my baby. Do you know they want, like, eight hundred dollars a month to take care of my baby? I don't have that type of money. That's why I was really hoping that you were pregnant because we could've helped each other out. Maybe we could have gone to school part-time or something. While I was in class you could have babysat for me and vice versa. Our kids would've grown up together and been very close."

"You know, at first I wanted to be the mother of Ronnie's child because I thought it would bring Ronnie and me closer but now I don't. Especially after what happened today."

"Even if Ronnie wasn't around, you would've had me and we would've been close," Toya said but that didn't make me feel any better. Besides, I'm not sure if I would've ever left my baby with Toya. I mean, she did okay with her little boy, but I think caring for him was much more than she bargained for.

"So what are you going to do if you drop out?" I asked.

"I don't know. Probably sit around, play cards and collect a government check. I wouldn't have to worry about teachers or homework or anything. All I'd have to do is chill out." Toya began to bite her fingernails.

"Don't you think you'll get bored? Don't you want to make money and live in a big house, drive a nice car and have enough money to buy yourself some serious bling?" I asked.

"Girl, that's what a man is for. My boo is going to take care of me," she stated as if her life plan was rock solid. In her mind Toya had it all figured out. At times talking with Toya annoyed me because she didn't have any ambition. *At least I had that,* I thought to myself.

"I'm going to go inside. I'm starving," I said as I stood up.

"You want some company? Me and the baby could come over," Toya said.

"No, I'm cool," I answered her then walked inside of the apartment building. The last thing I wanted to do was hang out with Toya and her baby.

two

The apartment my mom and I lived in felt more like a big square box than a studio apartment. Once inside there really wasn't much to see. On the right wall was an old white stove that looked as if it'd come from the Stone Age. I was continually amazed that it actually worked. The refrigerator, which was next to the stove, was just as ancient. It was white with a chrome handle that had to be pulled toward your body before the door would open. There was one window at the back of the room. It looked out over the abandoned lot where the alley mechanics work and loiter. The window didn't have a curtain, just a dingy white shade. On the left side was the bathroom, which was long overdue for a makeover. Sometimes I was completely grossed out by the murky brown water that came out of the faucet. You had to let it run for a while before it changed color. Next to the bathroom was an oversize door, which was where the Murphy bed was located. That was about the only cool thing about the place. A bed that actually folded up into the wall was kind of neat. My mom slept on the Murphy bed and I slept on the sofa-sleeper, which was near the window. We didn't have any closets, only two large dressers that were positioned outside of the bathroom. We had one small television that sat atop one of the dressers, but it didn't have cable, so as far as I was concerned, it had limited value.

I went over and laid down on the sofa. I threaded my fingers behind my head and closed my eyes. I blocked out all of the sounds of the city—the wailing fire engine, the loud trunk amps and the sound of multiple conversations. My mind was flashing images of the events that had occurred over the past few months. Directly after the death of my Aunt Estelle and the conviction of my Grandmother Rubylee, my mother was arrested for driving around as a passenger with a friend of hers in a stolen car. While her case was being ironed out, Grandmother Rubylee got in touch with her father's relatives and convinced them to take me in for a little while. I hated living with them because they were mean-spirited people. They treated me like their maid, and if something malfunctioned or got damaged, it was my fault. Even if the utility bill went up, it was my fault. When the charges against my mother were dropped, I was relieved and excited to be back with her. It was clear that things were going to be hard for us, but I figured my mom would step up and make sure we were safe. At least, that was what I was hoping for.

Sometimes I fantasized about who my father was and what it would have been like living with him. I'd never met my father, but in a way, I'd always hoped that he'd magically appear and come and rescue me from my situation. But that was just a dream from the fairy tales of my imagination. I knew someone out in the world was my father, but I didn't know who, and Mother wasn't actually sure, either, or that was what she'd told me over the years. A loud knock at the door startled me back into reality.

"Who is it?" I asked aloud.

"It's me, Toya." *Dang, why doesn't she take a hint?* I thought to myself. *I just want to be alone right now.* I opened the door and she was standing there with her son perched on her hip.

"Girl, I need a real big favor from you," she said. I wasn't in the mood to give out any favors, but before I could tell her that, she unlatched her son, Junior, from her hip and handed him to me.

"I need you to watch him for about an hour," she said. I prepared to hand him back to her.

"Have your grandmother watch him," I said.

"Come on, Keysha, you know that she's going blind and can't see too good. I only left him in the house because he was asleep. I mean, she can watch him but it's not like she's really keeping an eye on him."

"Then why don't you take him with you? He's your son," I said.

"Girl, because I just got a phone call from my cousin telling me that my man is on her block all hugged up with some girl, and I need to go see what's going on with that." There was a long moment of silence between us. I wanted to tell her that she should take her baby with her because I just wasn't in the mood to deal with him right now.

"Come on, girl. I promise I'll only be about an hour." I sighed, and she took my grumbling sound as confirmation that I'd watch him.

"Thank you so much," she said, then left abruptly.

"Don't leave him here all night, Toya. I have to register for school in the morning," I yelled out behind her as she rushed down the corridor and out of the building.

Junior was quiet and didn't say much at all. I could tell that he was in some sort of deep thought. He was about fourteen months old and had beautiful eyes. I sat him down on the sofa and asked if he wanted something to eat.

"I don't have much, but I think I can whip up something that will hold you over for an hour," I said to him. Junior didn't respond. He only stared at me with sad eyes. I knew the sadness in his eyes all too well. I suppose in many ways he and I had something in common—a mother who wasn't ready, or equipped, to be one. I opened up the refrigerator and removed a package of bologna to make a sandwich. *I suppose he can eat this,* I thought to myself, uncertain of what he could and couldn't eat. I fixed him up the perfect sandwich and just as I was about to cut it into smaller portions, I noticed that he'd drifted off to sleep again. *This baby was still asleep when Toya woke him up to bring him over to me,* I thought. I placed the sandwich back in the refrigerator in case he wanted it later on. I went and sat down next to him and situated him so that his head was resting on my lap. I began to stroke his hair and think about what it would have been like if Ronnie and I would've had a baby. I wondered what his or her skin complexion would have been like. I wondered if the baby would've looked like me or him and if we would've made it in spite of all the obstacles that would have been in our way. Ronnie was my first, and I suppose in some ways I'd never forget him. I thought he loved me just as much as I loved him, but I was wrong. Ronnie was only interested in getting down with me and nothing more. It's hard when you don't feel loved. Now that I think about it, that was the reason behind sleeping with Ronnie in the first place. He kept telling me how much he loved me and I believed him. I mean, when a guy tells you that he loves you, he has to be serious about you, right? I mean, I can honestly say I'd never heard my mother tell me she loved me. Sometimes, I just wanted to be hugged. Even though I was a teenager, I still liked to be hugged, but my mother wasn't the hugging type. I felt like I was going to cry when I thought about how empty that part of my heart was. I stood back up and went over to the countertop, which was next to the stove, and retrieved some mail that I'd placed there. I gathered all of my school registration forms, found an ink pen, then sat back down on the sofa and filled out the forms. In many ways, going to school was the only thing that kept me sane. Now how sad is that for a teenage girl? I mean honestly, I didn't know of any girl my age who actually liked going to school.

About two hours later, Toya returned. When she knocked on the door, I was all set to snap out on her for taking so long. I'd gotten irritated trying to keep Junior entertained because he only slept for about forty-five minutes. Keeping his little bad butt entertained was no picnic. When I opened the door, I held my words because patches of her pretty long hair had been ripped out. The T-shirt she was wearing had been ripped and the side of her face and neck had clearly been scratched up.

"What happened to you?" I asked.

"It's a long story. Where is Junior at?" I turned around to call her son to the door but he was already making his way to her side. He gave her leg a bear hug.

"You got into a fight, didn't you?"

"I had to let her know not to sneak around with my guy," Toya said. As I scrutinized her more closely, it appeared that the other girl had got the best of Toya, but I didn't say anything.

"Well, tell me how it went down," I said, wanting to know every detail. I was about to step aside so that she could come in but she wouldn't.

"I don't want to talk about it right now, but I will tell you this. I found out that he has a baby with her, as well."

"Girl, stop lying." I didn't want to believe what I was hearing.

"I'm not—" Toya's voice cracked from all of the emotional energy she was trying to contain.

"I'll talk to you later," she said as she picked up Junior and walked across the hall to her apartment.

It was getting late, and my mother hadn't arrived home yet. When she left earlier that day, she only told me that she was going to take care of some business and would be back. I was hungry, so I pulled out the black skillet from the cupboard along with the rest of the bologna and cheese and fried myself up a sandwich. I loved fried bologna and cheese. I pulled down my mother's Murphy bed and turned on the television before I sat down. I flipped through the channels and finally stopped to watch a rerun of *The Fresh Prince of Bel-Air*.

"Why can't I live like Hillary Banks?" I said aloud. "Have a rich daddy, a goody-two-shoes brother and a crazy cousin who's always doing something that he doesn't have any business doing." The lifestyle that the characters were living seemed so phony and unrealistic to me, but I still enjoyed watching it. During a commercial break, I heard the key enter the lock in the door. A moment later my mom walked into the room. She opened the refrigerator and noticed that the bologna was gone.

"I know you didn't eat all of the damn bologna," she started snapping out on me. Her voice was loud and confrontational, which made me edgy and confrontational, as well.

"I was hungry. What was I supposed to do? Slit my wrists and suck my own blood for food?"

"If it fills you up, that's what you need to do," she shot back sneeringly.

"Whatever," I said, sucking air through my teeth and rolling my eyes at her.

"You better stop rolling your eyes at me before I knock them out of your head." I ignored her violent comment for the moment. She then moved in front of the dresser where the television was and began removing some of her clothes from the top drawer.

"Where are you going?" I asked.

"Out to a club," she answered.

"You know I register for school tomorrow and I still need supplies," I reminded her.

"And?" she replied as if my needs were not her priority.

"I need those school supplies," I answered her back loudly. I hated it when she acted as if I was unimportant.

"Borrow some supplies from a classmate. I don't have any extra money." She slammed the top dresser drawer closed and then opened up another one.

"But you have money to go to a club," I said, hoping to

make her feel guilty about her judgment. She turned and pointed her finger at me.

"Hey, what I do with the money I bring up in this house is my business. I don't have to answer to you for anything! If you want school supplies go get them yourself. I don't have time to deal with you. You're just dead weight on my shoulders, and you're slowing me down. As grown as you are you should be out on your own." Her attitude toward me really hurt, but I wasn't going to let her know. I wasn't about to allow her to get under my skin.

"So you don't care whether I drop out of school or stay in?" I barked at her. I really hated her as a person. At times Justine could be cold, like a pail of ice, and other times she acted as if we were the best of friends. That day, her mood was icy.

"You're only going to drop out and get on public assistance anyway. You didn't get pregnant this time but the next time you will," she said, referring to the time I thought I was pregnant by Ronnie. Thankfully it was a false alarm. "Pregnancy may not be the worst thing for you. At least you'll be able to bring a government check home." Deep inside I was yelling at her and wishing that horrible things would happen to her. Deep inside I wanted the power to strike her down with a bolt of lightning so her feelings would hurt as much as mine. The fact that I didn't have that type of power bothered me. Someday, I'd make her regret the way she treated me. My only wish was for that day to be today.

three

when I woke up the next morning, my mother hadn't
come home from her night at the club. *I swear, sometimes I fear
that the police are going to knock on the door and tell me she has been
killed or something,* I thought to myself. I knew a long time
ago that to a certain degree I'd have to take care of myself
early on in life, but at times I really just wanted to be a kid
with a normal life. I tossed aside my blanket, placed my feet
on the cold floor and then stood up and took a long stretch
to begin my day. I went inside the bathroom, took a shower,
got dressed and gathered up my school paperwork before
heading out the door. When I exited the building, I ran into
Toya, who was sitting on the stoop shuffling a deck of cards.

"Where are you headed to?" she asked, glancing at me.
Her face still looked pretty bad. Overnight a bruise had
formed on her cheek.

"I'm going to register for school. Aren't you coming?" I
knew that she wasn't but I thought I'd ask anyway.

"No, I don't have anyone to watch Junior. My grandmother is tripping. She told me to take him with me to registration."

"Why not? I mean, today is only the first day of registration," I reminded her.

"Girl, I have bigger things to deal with than registration and school. I'm trying to figure out when my man had time to have a baby with another girl. Plus my face and hair are jacked-up right now." Toya was quiet for a moment and I didn't say anything. "I mean, she's not even good-looking, Keysha. Her hair isn't as long as mine, her skin looks bad and she has a big gap between her upper front teeth. She pulled out my hair, Keysha. I swear, when I see that girl again, I'm going to cut her with this." Toya reached into her front pants pocket and pulled out a barber's straight razor. "Once I cut her in the face, I'll bet she'll think twice before messing with me."

I wanted to ask the obvious question, which was, "Why isn't she mad with her man for cheating on her?", but Toya didn't think like that. It was never her man's fault. It was always the other woman's fault.

"You'll have to tell me all of the details when I come back," I said, not wanting to listen to her issue at that moment.

"Why are you rushing off? You don't have time for me now? I listened to you yesterday when you talked about breaking up with Ronnie," Toya said, raising her voice at me. I felt guilty for a brief moment and was about to give her a little of my time, but then I glanced up the street and noticed my mother approaching with some guy. He appeared to be some stray man she'd picked up at the club to keep her company.

"Toya, I've got to go. I'll talk to you about this later." I wanted to leave before my mother made me greet her new friend.

"What the hell, Keysha? I thought you were my girl. I thought you cared about what I'm going through."

"I do, Toya, but I've got to get to school. Do you have your enrollment forms? If not I could pick them up for you."

"I told you, I've got better things to do. Why do you care about school, anyway? You're not an A student. You know that you don't want to be there listening to some boring-ass teacher. You'll have more fun sitting here with me all day playing cards. After that we could watch that television program where people get on it and start fighting. I love that show."

"I'm going to have to pass on that today. I don't want to go to late registration. Besides, this is a chance for me to get out of the house. My mother is coming with some weird-looking man." I nodded my head in the direction of my mother. "I'll catch you later," I said and moved past her. I crossed the street to walk down the other side so that I could just wave to my mother and keep on going, but she made me stop and cross back over to where she was. I took in a deep breath and prepared to deal with the nonsense that would fly out of her mouth.

"What's up, girl?" She greeted me as if she were my best friend instead of my mother. I didn't respond right away because I was scrutinizing her outfit. To put it mildly, my mother's outfit was a hot mess. She was too old for the style of clothes she was fond of wearing. She had her oversize be-hind stuffed into a pair of low hip-riding Phat Farm jeans, which were in desperate need of a belt. She had on a white belly top that exposed her pregnant chocolate tummy, her stretch marks and an old tattoo of a red rose. I'd tried on occasion to help her find clothes that were more appropriate, but she didn't like the fashions I'd picked out.

"I know, girl, I'm fine as wine," she said, mistaking my horrified expression for approval of the way she looked. "I couldn't take two steps without a car honking a horn at me. Isn't that right, Simon?" She looked to her friend to confirm the truthfulness of her statement.

"You know all the men want you, baby," said Simon. The way he was looking at me made me feel as if a thousand bugs were crawling on my skin—honestly, dude made my skin crawl as if I were watching an episode of *Fear Factor*.

"What's your daughter's name again?" asked Simon as he continued to rape me with his eyes.

"Keysha, fool. You know that," my mother answered him.

"Give me a break. I haven't seen this girl since she was a baby," said Simon. He looked over at my mother, and that's when I noticed a hideous scar that ran from his right earlobe, across his cheek and down to the corner of his lip. The site of the scar caught me off guard, and now I was the one doing all the eye raping.

"You don't remember Simon, do you, Keysha?" asked my mom.

"With a face like that how could I ever forget him," I said.

"I got this scar at one of the parties your Grandmother Rubylee used to host years ago. I was helping her collect a debt," Simon said as he continued to stare at me as if he were studying for an exam.

"Simon is an old friend of the family from around the old neighborhood," said my mother. "We used to hang out and

party together all the time. We had some good times together, didn't we, Simon?"

"Yeah, we did," he said, smiling at the memory.

"So you two used to date or something?" I asked.

"Something like that." Simon's answer was very vague.

"We ran into each other at the club last night. We got
to talking about the old days and the good times. Simon is
starting up a business," said my mother. "We're going to go
in the house and talk about it."

"Whatever." I rolled my eyes because I didn't care about
what her and Simon were really up to. One thing was for
sure, it wasn't about starting a legitimate business.

"Justine, she looks too damn familiar. Who's her father?"
Simon smiled at me and his teeth were as yellow as a lemon.
I cringed at the sight of them.

"Why do you want to go and ask me a question like that
in front of her?" Justine got irritated with Simon.

"You know why I'm asking," said Simon. "She looks just
like my cousin—"

"Look—" I cut him off because there was no way I was
related to anyone who looked like him.

"Wait a minute, Keysha, let me look at you one more
time," Simon said, studying the details of my every feature.

"Take a picture, it lasts longer," I said and rushed away
from them.

"Keysha, wait a minute." My mother chased after me.

"What? I'm heading off to register for school," I said.

"Hold on a minute." She grabbed my arm and forced me
to stop.

"Why are you just now getting home?" I asked with an

authoritative tone. "And why did you bring him with you, and why is he acting like he knows something about me?"

"Who the hell are you snapping at? I don't have to answer to you," she quickly reminded me. At that moment I noticed the unpleasant smell of alcohol and cigarette smoke that was pasted to her skin and clothing. The odor was choking the air between us.

"You need to start acting your own age and not like some teenager who can't control their hormones." I don't know why I said that; it just flew out of my mouth.

"Excuse you!" she barked at me. "Don't mess around and get a beat down in the middle of the street," she threatened me. I didn't say any more because my mother was crazy enough to knuckle-up her fists and fight me right where I stood.

"Why does he think I look like someone he knows? Why does he even think he knows who my father is?"

"Simon doesn't know what he's talking about, baby. He's just talking out of the side of his head. Don't pay him any attention."

"I'll be back later," I said, not wanting to speak with her anymore.

"Hold on a minute." She wiggled her fingers into her front pocket and pulled out a crumpled-up five-dollar bill. "Get yourself something to eat while you're out. I probably won't be home when you get back."

"Why?" I questioned her again. I'd gotten so tired of her being gone all of the time.

"Because I've got things to do. If things work out, I may be able to make a little money today."

"Doing what?" I asked suspiciously.

"I don't know. That's why Simon has come over. He's going to tell me about his business."

I didn't like her answer, and before I could stop my words I found myself interrogating her once again.

"Is it a legitimate job?" She didn't answer me. "Why don't you look for a real job, Mom?" I asked in a softer tone of voice.

"Because I don't have to. That's why I have you, so I can collect a check." She quickly turned icy on me. Her comment made me feel as if I had no emotional value to her. I was just a person she could get a welfare check for.

"You know that the back rent is due, and if you don't pay we could be put out again. I don't think the landlord is playing around."

"I'm not worried about it," she said and didn't offer up any type of comfort to assure me that everything would be okay. I wanted to scream and yell at her. I wanted to explode, but instead I just built a wall around my emotions for her. At the moment I refused to allow her to cripple me emotionally. If she didn't care, then I didn't, either.

"Have fun with your friend Simon," I said as I walked off.

"I will!" she yelled back at me as I rushed off down the street.

I thought for sure the lines for registration would be long, but they weren't. I was able to go through the process fairly quickly. One of the school administrative staff printed out my class schedule and handed it to me. I glanced down at it and noticed that I had math first thing in the morning.

"Nine o'clock in the morning is too early to have a math class. Can you switch it for me?" I asked the lady who'd printed out my schedule. She looked at me for a long moment, as if I'd lost my mind.

"I guess that means no," I said sarcastically.

She frowned and yelled out, "Next."

My biggest concern now was school supplies or my lack of them. I hated being unprepared but I really didn't have a choice in the matter. I'd have to recycle the folders that I had from last year and latch on to someone when I needed additional supplies. It was an embarrassment I'd have to contend with.

By twelve-thirty that afternoon I'd arrived back home. As I came up the block I saw Toya still hanging around the front of the building toying around with her deck of cards.

"What's up, girl?" I asked as I took a seat on a kitchen chair that Toya had placed on the stoop.

"How are you just going to walk up and take my seat?" Toya tried to sound angry, but I didn't take her seriously.

"My feet hurt from walking in these cheap shoes," I explained as I allowed my fingertips to massage my scalp, which had suddenly started itching. It was a telltale sign that I needed to wash my hair and oil my scalp.

"Do you want me to braid your hair for you?" Toya asked.

"No, I need to wash it before I do anything with it."

"So, how did registration go?" Toya asked.

"It went okay. It went quickly. I have to figure out how I'm going to get my school supplies because my mother—well, you know that I can't depend on her." A mischievous expression formed on Toya's face at that moment.

"You're right, Keysha. We can't depend on our parents because they aren't cut out for the job. What we need to do is look out for each other. Don't you agree?"

"Yeah, I can agree with that," I said as I scratched the dry skin on my left leg.

"Listen, I've been thinking of a way that we can help each other." Toya stopped shuffling her cards and focused all of her attention on me.

"Why are you looking at me like that, Toya?" I asked, sensing she was calculating something in her mind.

"I've got a plan. Junior needs some new clothes and so do you and I. My baby would look so cute in some baby Nikes and some new gear from Sean John. I want some stuff from Phat Farm, and I know that you do, as well. So here is what I say we should do. Let's go down to the mall and get what we need."

"You must have come into some money," I said, joking. She didn't say a word; she just looked at me and forced me to read her thoughts. Toya had a very serious expression on her face.

"You want to go out boosting again, don't you?" I knew that's what she wanted to do, but I wanted to confirm it.

"Yeah I do." She paused in thought for a moment. "I have got the perfect plan that includes you, me and Junior."

"Toya, you know you're my girl, and I'm all for heading out to the mall for a five-finger discount deal, but why do we have to drag Junior into this? Last time we went out you and I both almost got busted."

"That's exactly why we're bringing Junior with us. He'll

act as our decoy," Toya explained, completely convinced that bringing Junior along would work.

"I don't know, Toya." I had a very uneasy feeling about dragging her son along with us. Boosting is not as easy as it sounds. Whenever I go, I'm always on edge because I don't want to get caught.

"Keysha, you know we both need stuff. You need clothes just like I do, and you know that we can make money selling the stuff that we can't fit to the kids at school. You've done this before. Why are you acting as if it's a problem now?"

"I don't know," I answered her as I searched my mind for a reason as to why I was feeling the way I was.

"Listen, we'll put all of the stuff that we get in the bottom of Junior's stroller. If someone tries to stop us, I have a purse full of old receipts that we can use, okay? Trust me, it's going to work. This plan is foolproof."

"How in the world did you come up with that one?" I asked because Toya's mind was always working a mile a minute.

"I saw someone else do it like that," Toya said, going into more detail. "I went to the grocery store over the weekend for my grandmother. As I was walking past one of the aisles, I saw this woman tearing open a package and stuffing its contents into her baby's diaper bag. Once she was done, I watched her stroll right on out of the store without paying a damn dime. So I thought, *Damn, that's slick, because no one would ever suspect a woman with a baby in a stroller to be out shoplifting.* The security people aren't paying attention to people like her. She was dressed like someone's mother who was just out shopping. The security people are harassing the person who walks in the door looking like a thug. Do you see where I'm going?"

"Yeah," I answered as I began to understand her thinking a little better.

"So all I'm doing is improving on what I've seen. I'll take Junior with me and stuff merchandise into several diaper bags and the compartment at the bottom of the stroller. While I'm doing that, your job will be to distract the sales clerk. Of course, we're going to have to make a few trips to get everything we need, but hey, I think it's worth the effort. Don't you?"

"Yeah, it's worth it," I said even though I still wasn't comfortable with Toya involving Junior in all of this.

four

WE decided to go to Evergreen Plaza, which was on the corner of 95th Street and Western Street. Toya wanted to hit a mall where she was least likely to run into someone she knew. We had to catch two buses and the El train to get there. We had to hop on the Laramie bus and take it to the Lake Street El. Then we took the El to 95th Street. Then we took the 95th Street bus all the way down to Western Avenue. The journey was long and boring until we got on the bus at 95th Street. The bus was very crowded, which meant that some of the passengers had to stand in the aisle. Just as Toya, Junior and I got situated some younger boy dressed like a thug reject tried to step to me. He wasn't cute at all. He had tight nappy hair that needed to be cut, and his breath was so funky I could see the words coming out of his mouth. He had on a dingy white shirt and some baggy shorts that were pulled down so that they could hang low.

"What's up, girl?" He tried to add some bass to his voice but it cracked on him, and Toya and I busted up laughing.

"What's up, boo?" Toya answered as she continued to laugh in his face and bounce Junior up and down on her lap to keep him amused.

"I wasn't talking you. I was talking to your girl, here," he said with a tone of arrogance.

"Oh, well I guess I'll keep my mouth shut, hint, hint…" Toya continued her snickering as she covered her nose with one hand.

"So what's up, girl? Why don't you roll with a baller like me?"

"Maybe if a baller had a breath mint, a hair cut and looked better than you." I laughed.

"Oh, snap!" Toya blurted out. "I think that's your cue to leave, boo."

"I've got a car. It's in the shop right now," he explained, but I didn't want to encourage him.

"Yeah, whatever. You don't even look old enough to drive," I said, thinking that my comment would make him shut up and move on.

"Girl, I just look young. I'm seventeen," he continued.

"Well, you look like you're twelve," I shot back.

"Oh, damn," Toya blurted out once again. "You need to work on your macking skills."

"You know, somebody needs to put that attitude of yours in check," he said as if he were the person who could do it.

"Well, until that person comes along, I would suggest that you leave."

He made a hissing sound and then moved toward the rear of the bus and away from us. "Your ass is ugly, anyway," I heard him mutter. I wanted to say something mean about his mother but decided to let it go. The last thing I wanted was to get into a battle of wits with him. I just wasn't in the mood for it.

"Damn, girl, he was kind of cute," Toya leaned into me and whispered.

"No, he wasn't. That boy looked whack and had breath that smelled like the Crypt Keeper from that show *Tales From the Crypt.* Hell, all he needed was a coffin to complete the look."

"Why are you so mean?" Toya asked as she repositioned Junior on her lap yet again.

"He was on my nerves," I answered as I tried to focus on how we were going to get the merchandise we wanted without getting busted. In the back of my mind, I understood that if I got caught, my mother wouldn't be able to get me out of jail, and I had no one else I could really depend on to rescue me.

"We shouldn't do this today, Toya." I tried to stop her before we entered the mall through the Carson Pirie Scott entrance. My thoughts had gotten the best of me during the remainder of the bus ride down 95th Street.

"No, we're here now, and I didn't sit on that long bus ride just to turn around and go home empty-handed." Toya was being stubborn, and I didn't know how to break through and make her think. I glanced down at Junior, who was strapped in his stroller fast asleep.

"Keysha, sometimes you have to live for the moment and do stuff. We can do this and walk out of here with bags filled with all types of designer clothes." I released a big sigh as I held the door open for her.

When we entered Carson Pirie Scott, I stopped at the perfume counter and kept the saleswoman busy with questions while Toya walked around and removed several sample bottles from the display counter. Once she'd gotten what she wanted, she exited the store through the mall entrance. After I ditched the sales lady, I caught up with Toya inside the mall.

"Did you get some good stuff?" I asked.

"I got what I could," she answered.

"I'm surprised Junior didn't wake up," I said as I glanced down at him.

"That's why I was playing with him on the bus, to make him sleep," Toya said. "I told you. I've thought about every aspect of my plan. I'm about to go into that designer store right over there." Toya pointed to where she was going. I turned in the direction that she pointed.

"Do you see the cashier standing behind the counter reading a book?"

"Yeah, I see. She's reading *The Coldest Winter Ever*," I answered.

"Did you read it?" Toya asked. Toya didn't like reading nearly as much as I did. At times, especially when I'm feeling depressed, I'll go on a reading binge to escape from my reality. *The Coldest Winter* was read during my last escape from my reality.

"Yeah, I read it."

"I knew your ass was a closet geek."

"Shut up. That book was real good," I said.

"Really?" Toya smiled.

"Yeah, I mean, it was good from start to end." I was about to go on and tell her more but she cut me off.

"You can keep her busy talking about the book, while I go in there and rob her blind."

"You just make sure you get me some jeans," I said.

"I got you." Toya winked at me. "Now go in there so that she doesn't think we're together."

I walked into the store and pretended to be shopping for something. The salesgirl didn't even look up at me. I could tell she was lost inside the world the author had created. At that moment, I felt bad that I was about to take advantage of her because I identified with her. I began to think that if she's anything like me, a good book will have her in a day-dreamlike state for hours. Sometimes when I read, an entire day can go by without me knowing it. I didn't want to interrupt her reading because when I read, I hate to be interrupted. I glanced back outside toward the mall and saw Toya giving me a strange glare. I could read the expression on her face. She wanted to know why I wasn't talking to the girl. I wanted to tell Toya to hit another store, but I knew she'd have a fit if I suggested it because the setup at this store was too perfect.

"That was a really good book," I mentioned to the salesgirl as I approached the counter. "They should make that book into a movie."

"This would be such a good movie if they made it," said the salesgirl as she glanced up from the page.

"Who do you think could play the roll of Winter?" I asked her. She appeared to be distracted for a moment as she looked past my shoulder toward the front door.

"I'm sorry, I thought that lady over there with the baby needed help."

I turned and looked at Toya, who was reaching down for her diaper bag.

"Are you sure she doesn't need help? I could wait until you're done," I said, taking a huge gamble.

"No, that's okay. She'll probably just look at a few things and leave. That's what most of the young girls pushing a baby do."

"Okay, so if they turned the book into a movie, I think that girl from the television show *The Parkers* should play Winter." I paused as I tried to think of the actress's name. "You know that one that plays Kim Parker, oh, what is her name?"

"Wait a minute, it's coming to me," said the salesgirl. "She has a weird name, like, Count something." I immediately snapped my fingers.

"Countess Vaughn. That's her name," I finally said.

"I don't know if she could pull it off," said the salesgirl.

"You don't think she could play the part of Winter from the book?" I said, surprised.

"I think you need someone who looks a little harder and rougher. I think Vivica Foxx could play the part."

"She's too old," I quickly pointed out.

"I know, but she could probably pull it off," the salesgirl countered. For the next half hour, the salesgirl and I discussed and debated the character and situations within the novel. I'd gotten so caught up with talking about the book with someone who'd actually read it that I forgot all about meeting back up with Toya. When I finally realized how much time had gone by, I said thank you to the salesgirl and rushed out of the store.

"Hey, what's your name?" she asked before I got out the door.

"Keysha," I said and rushed down the hall before I heard

her tell me what her name was. When I caught up with Toya, she had an attitude.

"Dang, Keysha, I just said talk to the girl about the book not have a damn study lecture on it. You'd better watch yourself with all that geek nonsense. You and that girl were talking like the people in that book were real or something."

I wanted to defend myself and tell Toya I really enjoyed reading and it was cool to actually talk to another reader, but she wouldn't have understood. Toya and books just didn't mix on any level.

"Come on, nerd girl. Let's hit another store."

"Don't call me that," I snapped at her.

"All right, bookworm, don't go and get all sensitive on me." I wanted to scream at her for calling me names but instead I kept my mouth shut and followed her down the corridor to the next store. Toya and I hit three more stores and by that time the stroller was loaded down and Junior had awakened and was fighting to be set free from his stroller.

"I think we should head back now," I suggested as we approached the food court.

"Damn, I wanted to hit at least one more store. I haven't gotten Junior anything yet."

"Well, let me go to the bathroom first," I said. We walked into the food court, and Toya took a seat at one of the tables so that she could release Junior from his stroller before he started shouting.

I was about to exit the bathroom but needed to wash my hands first. As I placed my hands under the warm running water, two restaurant employees walked into the restroom laughing and talking loudly.

"Can you believe that dumb girl is down here stealing clothes with her baby?" I overheard one of them say.

"Then she pulled out a bogus receipt talking about how she'd paid for everything." The two girls started laughing uncontrollably. I rushed out of the bathroom and saw that three Chicago Police officers and mall security guards had handcuffed Toya to restrain her.

"Oh, damn," I said as I began to panic. I didn't know what to do. I was frozen with fear. Toya was yelling at one of the officers to put Junior down before she filed a lawsuit against them. Toya caught my gaze for a minute and motioned with her head for me to come over to where she was at. I started to take a step towards her but I stopped. I suddenly wanted no part of any of the drama that was going down. To my right there was an exit. Toya must have sensed what I was thinking and so she called out my name.

"Keysha!" she shouted at the top of her voice. As calmly as I could, I turned my back on her and walked hastily toward the exit.

five

MY stomach was doing flips during the entire journey back home. I was nervous, afraid and confused. I placed my elbows on my knees and my face in my hands and tried to think. I wanted to cry but I didn't. I was trying to figure out how Toya got caught. Everything was going so well. We'd moved in and out of stores without any problems. No merchandise alarms went off, and I know Toya was extra careful by making sure she was out of the sight range of the video cameras.

When I arrived home I found a big red notice stuck to our front door. It was an eviction notice. My mom and I had three days to either pay the rent or be set outdoors. *Oh, God, not again,* I thought to myself as I entered the apartment. I walked directly over to my sofa, rested my head on one of the cushions and went to sleep. I woke up in the middle of the night. My mother still hadn't come home, and I needed someone to talk to. The first person who came to mind was my ex-boyfriend, Ronnie. Even though I hadn't spoken to him in a while, I decided to call him hoping he'd be nice to me and listen to my problems. I gathered up some spare change and walked out of the apartment and onto the stoop. When I stepped out into the darkness I noticed that there were people just hanging out. Across the street, there was a group of kids I didn't know listening to music and dancing. To my right, there was a gathering of men sitting on make-shift crates drinking alcohol and talking loudly. To my left, I saw a woman wearing coochie cutter shorts, leaned over into the passenger window of a car talking with two men. Other men who were passing by her on the sidewalk stopped to ogle her behind. At that moment everything in my life seemed to be going wrong. Everyone around me seemed to be crazy, and they were making me crazy just by being around them. I calmed myself down as best as I could and walked up the street to the payphone. I called up Ronnie.

"Yeah," he said as he answered the phone.

"Hey, Ronnie, it's me, Keysha. What are you doing?" I asked.

"Why?" he shot back at me.

"Um…" I lost my nerve for a minute. "Do you really not love me anymore?" I don't know why I asked that question. I suppose in some sort of way I just wanted someone to care about me.

"You know I don't," he answered coldly.

"Do you want to come over? My mother isn't home. We could talk and stuff."

"Naw, I'm not even going to get down with you like that, Keysha. It's over. A baller like me has got to move on."

"You know what, Ronnie, I should come—hello, hello?" Ronnie had hung up on me. I slammed the phone against its cradle and started crying. I let go of my tears for a minute before I got myself together and headed back home.

The following morning, I got up and headed to my first day of school completely unprepared. I walked through the halls dazed and spaced out because I had so much on my mind. I was worried about Toya and Junior and didn't know what to do. I was worried about my mother and how she was going to deal with the eviction notice. I was worried about school because, even though it wasn't socially acceptable to say I enjoyed school on any level other than to socialize, I actually really enjoyed my literature class.

I had no idea of how I was going to make it through school, and the person I depended on would most certainly leave me hanging, just as she'd done so many times in the past.

I just entered my history class and took a seat at the back of the room. I was hoping the teacher, and everyone else, for that matter, wouldn't notice me. Once the roll call was completed, the course syllabus was handed out. Just as we were about to go over it, the principal and two police officers entered the classroom.

"Oh, shit," I whispered loudly. Toya must have tricked on me, and now the police were there to arrest me. I wanted to run out of the room but I couldn't because there was only one way in and one way out. The principal began searching the room, and I scrunched down in my seat as far as I could without actually going up under my desk. I was doing the best that I could to hide in plain sight. The principal finally found the student the police were searching for and I was thankful that it wasn't me.

"Dang, girl, you were trying to get up under the floor," said Lynn Jones, who was one weird girl.

"Yeah, whatever," I said to her.

"What did you do that has you afraid of the police?" she wanted to know.

"None of your damn business," I snapped at her for being nosy.

"Well, forget you, too. The next time the police come into this class I'm just going to start pointing my finger at you so they'll see you."

I leaned over in my seat and looked directly at her. "If you do that I'll put superglue on all of your clothes during gym."

"No, you wouldn't," she said, not believing me.

"Try me," I said, unafraid of her. She didn't say anything else to me so I dropped our conversation.

When I arrived home, I saw Toya's grandmother standing outside the building. She was wearing a one-size-fits-all flower-print dress, some run-over and worn-out looking brown sandals, her black sunglasses for the blind, and she had her white walking stick with the red tip. When I approached her I spoke.

"Hello, Ms. Maze." She turned to the direction of my voice.

"Who is that?"

"It's me, Keysha. Toya's friend," I answered her.

"Oh, how are you doing, baby?" she inquired.

"I'm okay. I'm just coming home from school."

"That's good, honey. I wish Toya was more like you and stayed in school." Ms. Maze hung her head low for a moment. "Oh, I don't know what I'm going to do with that girl."

"Um, where is she at?" I asked because I hadn't heard from or seen Toya.

"She's gotten herself and the baby into some trouble. I'm going to see what I can do about getting her out of jail."

"Oh," I said. I wanted to tell her everything but I couldn't. I just didn't have the courage. "Is she okay?"

"As well as to be expected," she answered me.

"Do you think she'll be getting out today?" I asked.

"I'm going to do my best to get her out," she said.

"Um, where is Junior?" I asked as I shifted my weight from one foot to the other.

"Oh, baby, I don't know." Ms. Maze got choked up and couldn't speak for a long moment.

"Keysha, are you still there?"

"Yeah, I'm here."

"Do me a favor, and stand here with me until the cab I called comes along. I'd like for you to help me get in the car."

"Okay," I said, feeling very bad about her having to go down to the police station to see about Toya. What made me feel even worse was the fact that she didn't know what had happened to her great-grandson, Junior.

When the cab arrived I made sure that she got in without any problem. I then turned to head inside. I was hoping that my mother had come home. When I walked up to our apartment I saw there was another eviction notice posted to the door. I snatched it down and walked inside. The notice said that we now had two days to either pay the rent or be put out.

"Mama!" I called out even though I knew she wasn't home. The Murphy bed was still inside the wall and hadn't been used.

"Damn!" I shouted because I didn't know what to do. I

paced back and forth across the floor trying to figure out where she'd gone and where she could be. It wasn't uncommon for my mother to disappear for several days at a time. Especially when we lived with my Grandmother Rubylee and my Aunt Estelle. I really didn't care about her disappearing then because I knew that either Aunt Estelle or Grandmother Rubylee would be around if I needed them. Now our lives were much different, and I had no choice but to worry about where Justine was. I was driving myself crazy trying to figure out what I should do. I finally decided that there wasn't anything I could do. I could only hope that in my hour of need, my mother wouldn't leave me hanging. I could only hope that by some miracle she'd manage to keep a roof over our heads.

---

when I woke up the following day, I was hoping to discover Justine had come home during the night. To my horror, she hadn't. I swallowed hard and tried not to panic. It was clear that she wasn't going to make it back home. I held on to hope that she'd be home by the time I returned from school, but in the back of my mind and deep in my heart I knew the chances of her returning were slim to none.

I walked over to the bed and got down on my knees. I peeked beneath the mattress and removed a small box filled with photographs. I opened the box and pulled out the first one, which was taken when I was about six years old. My Aunt Estelle took the photo. In the picture I was wearing my favorite blue dress. My hair was combed and braided beautifully. It was Easter Sunday and I was holding a stuffed bunny rabbit and smiling as hard as I could. I remember being so happy that day. It was one of the rare times that everyone was happy. I pulled out another photo of my Grandmother Rubylee and me. I was nine years old in this photo, which was taken at Rainbow Beach. My skin was so brown because I'd been out in the sun all day, and I had brown sand on my legs up to my knees. I was always pretending that my daddy lived in a real castle somewhere very far away and he was waiting for me to come and visit him. When my mother came over to see it, I told her that I thought my daddy lived in a castle like the one I was building. She laughed and said that I had been out in the sun too long and was becoming delusional. She didn't like to talk about anyone being my father. She always told me that she was both my mother and my father.

The final photo was taken at my eighth-grade graduation. I was standing in my blue and silver cap and grown. I'd graduated at the top of the class. I was a straight 4.0 student. I never missed a day of school, did all of my homework and studied hard because I wanted to prove to everyone that I was worth something. I wanted to feel validated in some way. I was so happy that day because I'd made everyone proud of me. It was one of the few times that I can remember where I felt good about myself. That day was perfect, well, at least as perfect as it could have been. Rubylee and my Aunt Estelle were there, but my mother wasn't. Rubylee insisted that she not show up and ruin my day. At the time of my graduation, my mother was in rehab for drug addiction. I remember wanting to do everything that I could to help her stay healthy, but my mother just kept getting into trouble. It was like trouble followed her as if it were a gray storm cloud on a mission to make her as miserable as possible. I didn't work nearly as hard back then. I thought good grades would somehow not only validate me but also motivate my mother to be more supportive and proud of me, but she didn't care at all. I figured, if she didn't care then why should I?

I put the box away because it was depressing me to look through it. I placed it in a bag with my other belongings and left everything sitting on my sofa. I got dressed and headed off to school, even though I really didn't want to be there. But in my mind, it was better than sitting around the apartment worrying myself into sickness. In many ways, school was where I escaped from my reality.

I didn't go directly home after school because I was afraid to. I spent an hour hanging around the basketball court at the park watching shirtless boys shoot baskets. It was cool for a while, but then a gang of girls who were there started making fun of me because of my bad skin and damaged hair, so I left. As I walked home I began to think. If my mother hadn't come home to pay the rent then I knew I'd have to leave, but I didn't know where I'd go. As I approached my building, I saw Toya sitting on the stoop with Junior's father. I was happy to see her, so I rushed up the street calling her name.

"Toya!" I shouted out. Toya gave me a nasty look that made me drop the smile from my face.

"What's going on, wench?"

"Excuse you?" I snapped at her.

"Give me a minute to deal with her," she said to her boyfriend. He glanced at me with judgmental eyes before stepping away to sit in his car, which was parked in the vacant lot near the building.

"Why did you leave me hanging like that?" Toya asked. Her voice was edgy and full of confrontation.

"Toya, I got scared. I didn't know what to do. The police were arresting you. You were yelling and hollering at them. What was I supposed to do?"

"You were supposed to have my back!" Toya pushed my shoulder and I backed up. She wanted to fight me. I could see it in her eyes.

"Toya, look. We just have a big misunderstanding here," I said, trying to calm her down. Other people who were just hanging out on the block started paying attention to our conflict. If we kept up our loud argument, it wouldn't be long before a crowd would form and encourage us to knuckle-up our fists and beat each other senseless for their entertainment.

"No, there is no misunderstanding. All I know is that I should kick your ass for what you did. Because of you, the department of family services took Junior away from me."

"They took Junior from you?" I was surprised by that.

"Yeah, and it's your entire fault," she said, absolutely convinced of her reasoning.

"How is that my fault? I told you not to bring that boy in the first place."

"I called you, Keysha, because I wanted you to come and get him for me. I didn't care about going to jail because I knew I'd get out. But I didn't want Junior to go with me. Instead of helping me, you ran your scary ass out the door."

"You know what—" I stopped backing away from her and stood my ground "—that is not my fault. I told you that if something went down and we needed to get away, Junior would be a problem. You should have thought about the consequences before taking him along with us. Plus, why are you always blaming other people when things don't go right for you?"

"No. That's not the way I see it." Toya pushed me hard and I pushed her hard back. "Everything that went wrong is your fault. We would have gotten out of there quicker had you not been lollygagging for thirty minutes with that salesgirl."

"Fight!" I heard someone on the street yell out. Before I

knew it there were people gathering to watch the outcome of our conflict.

"Toya, let's not do this," I pleaded with her. "We've been friends far too long."

"No, I'm about to open up a can of whup ass on you." Toya reached into a back pocket and pulled out the straight razor she'd shown me a few days earlier. I quickly backed up because I didn't want to end up with a facial scar like my mother's friend Simon. She opened it up and swung it at me but I was too far away from her.

"It wasn't my fault!" I shouted at her, hoping to get her to see my point of view. "Why are you always starting fights?" I asked but didn't get a response. I quickly scanned the ground in search of a weapon of my own but didn't find one.

"Come on, Keysha, you can't run. It's about to go down," she taunted me. I was a nervous wreck. I didn't know what to do. I couldn't turn and run because there was a crowd of people surrounding us; I certainly didn't want to step forward and risk getting split open by a razor.

"Toya, please," I pleaded with her, but she swung at me again. This time she aimed for my face.

"Somebody help me!" I shouted out, but someone from the crowed answered back.

"Help yourself!"

"Toya, how was I supposed to know that was going to happen, huh?" I asked. I figured that if I kept talking I might get through to her. "I mean, why would I want to see them take your baby from you?"

"Because you wanted a baby with Ronnie but you couldn't get pregnant," she snarled back at me.

"That's not true and you know it," I shouted back to her as she swung at me again. That time she almost got me on the neck. The circle of people surrounding us was getting tighter, and I had absolutely nowhere to go.

"If you want to fight then fight me fairly," I said, wanting her to put the razor down. She didn't answer me. We just kept circling each other cautiously, like two angry lions looking for the right moment to strike. She was much closer to me now and swung at me again. I held my hand up to protect my face. The flesh between my thumb and first finger got nicked by the edge of the razor.

"Damn it!" I shouted out as I made a fist to apply pressure in hopes of stopping the bleeding.

"Toya, this is crazy," I said. My voice was shaking with fear. "You've got drama in your life and so do I. I don't have a place to live. The landlord put an eviction notice on my door and today was the last day to pay rent or be put out." Toya suddenly stopped.

"Is that the reason why a strange woman is around asking all types of questions about you and is in your house going through your stuff?" I'd finally gotten through to her.

"What are you talking about? What woman?"

"It serves you right to be put out of the building, because your mother isn't anything but a whore, anyway. She hasn't paid rent because she's in jail. I saw her locked up when I was in jail last night."

"I'm going to give you a pass on that comment about my mother being a whore."

"Y'all are out here faking," I heard someone from the

crowd say. It wasn't long before people started moving away from us.

"Well, it's true. That's why you haven't seen her." I didn't want to believe Toya. I didn't want to believe that my mother had gotten into trouble yet again and left me out in the world to make it on my own. Now that the crowd was gone, I rushed past Toya and into the building. I walked down to the apartment door and found it open. I stepped inside and saw a woman dressed in a black business suit.

"Are you Keysha?" the woman asked but then noticed my bleeding hand. "Are you okay?"

"I'm fine. Who are you and how did you get in here?"

"My name is Maggie. The landlord let me in. I work with the Department of Children and Family Services." There was a long pause as I tried to understand what was going on.

"Your hand is bleeding pretty badly. You should let me take a look at it."

"I'm okay," I said. "Why are you here?"

"Your mother has run into some legal problems and she knew you'd need help. So that's why I'm here, to help."

"Help me do what?" I asked.

"Find a home," she said. I suddenly felt dizzy and light-headed.

"Find a home? It's true, I'm homeless now?" I asked, feeling anxiety, fear and emotional stress attack me all at once.

"There is a group home for teens in your situation that I can place you in."

"A group home." I repeated what she'd said as my vision became gray and blurry. I felt as if my legs could no longer support my weight. I felt them buckling beneath me.

"Sweetie, you're wobbling. Let me take a look at the cut on your hand." I tried to move away from her. I wanted to turn and run out the door, but I fainted instead.

seven

when I regained consciousness, I felt someone placing a cold washcloth around my face and neck.

"Mom, what happened?" I asked.

"You fainted. Your mom isn't here," said Maggie. "And your hand has been cut pretty badly. I called for an ambulance."

"I don't need an ambulance," I said as I tried to sit up, but Maggie placed her hands on my shoulders and held me down. She was a short, bony woman but strong enough to hold me down.

"You need to relax," Maggie reiterated. I didn't feel like struggling with her so I relaxed. I studied her features. She had caramel skin with dark brown freckles around her nose and cheekbones. She was attractive but I could tell by the deep lines beneath her eyes that she'd seen her fair share of heartache, drama and pain.

"Why is everything falling apart?" I started crying uncontrollably. I wanted Maggie to embrace me and tell me that it was going to be okay but she didn't. I wanted to feel safe, loved and wanted, but all I felt was alone.

When the paramedics arrived, they stitched up the deep cut on my hand and offered to take me to the hospital.

"I don't want to go to the hospital," I said.

"Honey, you really need to have a doctor look at your hand," said Maggie, who seemed to be concerned about me.

"I'm fine," I said as I looked at the bandage on my hand. "See, the bleeding has stopped."

"Will the stitches hold until I can get her to a private doctor?" Maggie asked one of the paramedics.

"Yes," answered one of the men as he began putting away his medical supplies. "But make sure she sees a doctor soon. Don't wait more than one or two days."

"Okay," said Maggie. She thanked them as they walked out of the apartment and down the hall.

Once the paramedics left, Maggie once again asked me how I got cut.

"What do you care?" I snapped at her.

"Okay, I'm just trying to help."

"You don't really want to help me. You're just doing a job," I said as I inspected the bandage around my thumb. She then showed me all of her credentials to prove who she was.

"You can't stay here," Maggie informed me.

"No shit, Sherlock," I said. "I suppose this means you want me to gather up my bags and go with you." Maggie didn't say anything; she just looked at me. I read her facial expression and deduced that was exactly what she wanted me to do. I walked around the room and gathered up my belongings. I took one last look around the apartment to make sure that I hadn't forgotten anything I wanted.

"What about the television?" Maggie asked. "Do you want to take it?"

"No, it barely works," I answered as I walked out the door.

When I stepped out onto the stoop of the building, I thought for sure someone would approach me and ask if I was okay. I mean, I figured that they had to have seen the ambulance and should've known that it was for me. No one looked in my direction or even thought enough about my well-being to ask me what was going on. Toya wasn't around, and I assumed that after she'd cut me, she got in the car with her boyfriend and drove away in case the police were called.

"That's my car over there." Maggie pointed to an emerald-green Oldsmobile. She hit the remote locks and the trunk of the car opened up.

"You can place your bags in the trunk," she said as she moved past me. I took a deep breath and then headed toward her car and my unknown future.

As I drove away with Maggie, I just stared out the car window and didn't say a word. I was angry at everything and with everyone. I was already making plans to run away from the group home. I'd rather take my chances living on the street as opposed to being forced to go into some home with a bunch of people I didn't know. I thought perhaps I could go back and talk with Ms. Maze, Toya's grandmother, and ask her if I could stay with her for a little while. I know the plan sounds crazy after Toya cut me with a straight razor, but I figured we were even now and we could move past that.

"I'm taking you to a facility for distressed teens that is on 114th and Western Avenue," Maggie said, interrupting my thoughts. I didn't want to say anything to her because I didn't like her.

"Has anyone explained to you what has happened?" she

asked. I wanted to answer her by saying, "Duh, no one has said a damn word to me," but I didn't. I just gave her the silent treatment.

"Okay, I'll take that as a no answer." She made a right turn and then continued. "There is no easy way to put it so I'm just going to tell you like it is. A few days ago, your mother was arrested as part of a police sting to clean up prostitution in poor neighborhoods. When she was picked up, she had illegal drugs in her possession." I could feel her looking at me, but I continued to look out the window at people who were waiting on the bus. For a brief moment I wondered where they were going, but Maggie continued talking.

"When Justine realized that she wouldn't be getting out anytime soon, she notified the officials at the jailhouse and informed them of you and your situation. Once it was determined that she was telling the truth, your case was assigned to me. If you allow me to help, we can work together on finding you a good foster home."

I felt as if I'd been kicked in the chest by a horse when she said the words, *foster home*. I never thought I'd end up living in a foster or group home for teens at risk.

"The group home I'm taking you to can be as comforting as you make it. You'll be staying with other teenage girls in a dorm-room setting. You'll be under constant supervision by the adult staff members. The facility works on trying to create an atmosphere of family so that everyone feels comfortable."

"How long do I have to stay there?" I asked with a nasty attitude. I didn't like the sound of the place she was taking me to one bit.

"Well, I'm not sure. I still have to speak with your mother about contacting your father."

"She doesn't know who he is," I said to her. "It could be any one. I could pass him on the street every day and never know it." I paused in thought. "You know her dumb ass is pregnant, don't you?" I tossed out the question because I wanted her to know that my mother suddenly meant very little to me. I had a very low opinion of her. If I saw her on the street, I'd turn and walk the other way. I wouldn't even acknowledge her.

"Yes. I am aware of the pregnancy. That case has been assigned to me, as well." I didn't say anything else because I was attempting to calm my nerves. I couldn't stop my hand from slapping my knee like a superball bouncing around recklessly. Maggie made a left turn and I noticed that we were going past a bookstore. I would have loved to stop so that I could get a few books to get lost in but I knew that wasn't an option.

"I'm going to be reaching out to a man who may be your biological father," Maggie continued. "She's given me the name of a man who she thinks is your dad."

"Well, how come she's never told me who he is?" I asked.

"Well, according to her, she didn't have a strong sense of who he was until recently. Her friend Simon helped her to narrow down the possibilities."

"Oh, God, please don't tell me I'm related to him."

"I don't know. We'll have to see if this man is willing to be tested. He may refuse testing or deny any type of relationship with your mother." I got so angry that I started slapping the dashboard of the car like I'd gone mad. My emotions were out of control. Maggie didn't say anything. I suppose she was used to sudden emotional outbursts.

"So if this dude takes the test and realizes he's my father then what?" I asked. "Do I get to go live in his castle and live happily ever after?"

"If he does agree to be tested and he learns that you're his child, I'm sure it would have an impact on his life," Maggie said.

"What if I don't want to go with him? What if he's some creep who's just as messed up as my mother? Then what?"

"Well, we'd never put you in a situation where you're in danger of being harmed. If your biological father has a criminal record or is unable to care for you, then you'd be able to remain at the group home until you turn eighteen years old. At that point, you'd be free to go forward and live your life."

"It sounds like a real jacked-up deal," I said as I wiped a tear from my eye. I was trying not to cry.

Maggie pulled into a gas station and turned off the car. She repositioned herself to look directly at me. I refused to make eye contact with her. I continued to look out the window at people who were walking by.

"If you're thinking about running away from the group home let me give you a few things to consider. The streets are very cold at night. You wouldn't know where you'd be sleeping or where your next meal would come from. You run the risk of being attacked or taken advantage of by people who don't have your best interests in mind. All I'm trying to do is help you. If the situation with your biological father doesn't end with 'happily ever after' then you still have the option of finishing your education and even going to college. Hang in there, get your education so that you can locate a good job and support yourself. You seem like a very nice girl who has been dealt a very bad hand, and I'd hate to see you crumble apart. Your situation is bad but I've seen worse," Maggie explained. I still didn't say anything to her.

"Look. All I'm asking is that you stay at the group home if things don't work out for the best."

"It doesn't matter. If this guy is anything like my mother, he doesn't give a rat's ass about me," I said sarcastically. "I don't care what happens to me anymore."

"Be positive, Keysha. Perhaps he will care once he's made aware of your situation." I finally turned and looked her directly in the eyes.

"No one has ever cared about me or loved me, with the exception of my Grandmother Rubylee, who is in jail. I might as well step in front of a bus and kill myself."

"Well, since you feel that way, maybe I shouldn't bother trying to contact this man," Maggie said as she started the motor back up and continued on.

We finally stopped in front of the group home, which was a brown brick bungalow-style structure. The screen door had black burglar bars on it, and the wooden banisters on the front porch needed to be repainted. The brushes around the property were overgrown, and the grass had been completely neglected. All the way at the top of the structure I noticed three small windows, which I assumed was the attic.

Maggie pressed the latch for the trunk and was about to get out of the car when I stopped her by speaking up.

"Contact him," I said. "Maybe fairy tales do come true."

"Okay," said Maggie.

eight

Maggie took me inside the group home and up to the attic, which had been converted to office space for the adult supervisors. I sat in a chair beside a desk and awaited further instructions. There was one girl who was about my age who was standing at the file cabinet filing. When she saw me she stopped working and glared at me.

"Why don't you take a picture, it lasts longer," I snapped at her. She continued to study me for a moment longer before continuing on with her work. It was noisy in the office. Old-fashioned typewriters were dinging, drawers were constantly being opened and closed and the phone rang constantly. The desks and equipment up there were very old and appeared to be secondhand. The metal desks and filing cabinets were all pea green. The setup reminded me of a police station. The floor plan was wide open, and you could see exactly what everyone was doing.

"Come sit over here," Maggie said, directing me to another desk. "Once I get you processed, we'll go over some general rules and then I'll give you a tour of the place."

"Rules?" I said. "I'm not following any rules."

"The rules are for your safety. If you break the rules there will be consequences."

"Yeah, whatever," I said, completely unafraid of consequences.

★ ★ ★

Thirty minutes later, Maggie gave me some basic rules for living in the group home.

"Boys are not allowed in this facility. There is a curfew of 6:00 p.m. on school nights and 7:00 p.m. on Saturday night. If you violate the curfew rule you will be placed in a secured facility. You must treat the staff here with respect. They're here to help and listen to you, as well as help you work through any problems you may be having or going through. Stealing will not be tolerated. Drug usage will not be tolerated. Fighting, inappropriate language or dress will not be tolerated."

"What *can* you do up in here?" I asked.

"Better yourself," Maggie said. I didn't respond to her comment because I wasn't sure exactly how I was supposed to do that.

"It will take me a day or two to get your school records and have them transferred to the high school in this area."

"What? I can't go to my old high school?"

"No. Each morning everyone will get on our school bus, and you'll be driven to school as well as be picked up."

"You're kidding, right?"

"No. I'm not," answered Maggie. "Come on. Let me give you a tour of the place and show you where you'll be sleeping."

The basement of the home had a small cafeteria and a common area with one television, a pool table, a combination bookshelf and magazine rack and three large tables, which were used for studying and doing homework. The main floor was where the sleeping quarters were. Everyone got a thin mattress and one small dresser with two drawers, and that was it. The main floor was also where the showers and bathrooms were located. After Maggie showed me the shower facilities, I followed her to another area where there was a group of lockers.

"This one is yours," she said as she handed me my combination lock. "Don't give your combination to anyone. You can keep your personal hygiene products and any other valuables you may have in here." I opened up the small, rusty locker and was immediately assaulted by an odor.

"Whew," I said aloud as I closed the door.

"I'm sorry about that. I'll have one of the janitors spray some disinfectant in there for you," Maggie said as I followed her back to the sleeping area. "Here is your cot," she said. "I'll let you get settled in. I'm sure the other girls will be along shortly to meet you."

"When are you going to make the phone call to that dude?" I asked. All I had was hope that my biological father was a decent man who wanted a troubled girl like me. I didn't want to stay in here any longer than I had to. In my mind, anyplace was better than where I was.

"I'll do it first thing in the morning," Maggie said.

"Why can't we do it now?" I asked. "I mean, can't you just call him up and say, 'Hey, did you ever have a sexual relationship with a woman named Justine from Chicago?'"

"It's a little more complicated than that. You're in the state system now and certain protocols have to be followed. It's going to take a little time."

"I don't have much time. I want to leave here." I was feeling crazy.

"I'll do everything that I can," Maggie said with a smile and then left.

I plopped down on my cot and placed my face in my hands. Everything seemed so unreal. I just couldn't believe this was happening to me. A short time later, I felt someone nudge the back of my shoulder with their fingertips. I glanced over my shoulder and saw a massive girl towering over me. She had to be at least six foot two and was very heavyset.

"What do you want?" I asked her.

"To look through your bags," she said.

"For what?" I asked, placing a very mean expression on my face.

"To see if you have anything that I want." I laughed.

"Honey, if you want to go through my rags to see if anything I have can fit you, then knock yourself out." I stood up and was about to walk away.

"Drugs," she whispered. "Do you have any?"

"No." I glared at her as if she'd lost her mind. Drugs just weren't my thing, especially after watching my mother struggle with addiction.

"They didn't give you any drugs for the cut on your hand? No painkillers or anything?"

"I have to wear the bandage to keep my hand from becoming infected. I don't have any painkillers for it," I said and headed down to the common area. When I got down there, some of the girls were watching an episode of *Jerry Springer.* I went over to the small bookshelf in search of something to read. I felt like escaping from the reality I was in. I didn't want to make friends at that point. I only wanted to be left alone.

The selection of books was very small, and some of the authors I'd never heard of. I picked up three books I thought would be interesting. There was *Lord of the Flies,* by William Golding, *To Kill a Mockingbird* by Harper Lee, and *The Women of Brewster Place* by Gloria Naylor. I picked *The Women of Brewster Place* and went back to my cot. I couldn't wait to mentally check out of the group home by getting lost in a book.

nine

I didn't sleep well at all my first night in the group home. I just couldn't sleep around a bunch of strange people I didn't know or in the strange surroundings. I stayed up most of the night reading. On top of that many of the girls snored loudly. The street lamppost provided just enough light for me to read by. I finally drifted off to sleep at around four o'clock in the morning. At seven o'clock I was awakened abruptly by the sound of someone screaming. When I sat upright, several of the supervisors were trying to restrain the oversize girl who'd asked me if I had any drugs.

"She's coming off of another bad hangover," I overheard one girl whisper to another one.

When they finally got her under control, they searched her belongings and found that she'd somehow gotten hold of some alcohol.

"That heifer is crazy," I heard yet another girl in the room say.

Once the supervisors found what she'd taken, they escorted her out of the dorm room. The other girls just sat and watched the whole thing go down without saying much more. It was strange watching all of this unfold. It was like being in a movie for the mentally ill. I felt as if I was watching things happen but not actually a part of it. In some ways the dorm room filled with cots felt like a ward at an insane asylum. Perhaps we were all just too emotionally empty to react to the madness that was going on around us. Perhaps we just couldn't cry or talk about our pain anymore. Whatever our reasons, none of us moved an inch as the girl was being removed.

Later, after everyone had gone to school, I took a long shower, got dressed and hung out in the common area. I was waiting on Maggie to arrive with my transcript so I could get registered at a new high school as well as take me to the doctor to have my hand examined. I picked up an old issue of *Vibe* magazine that was lying around and started reading an article on Usher. *God, if I had a boyfriend as fine and as rich as him, I'd be set,* I thought to myself. I'd just finished reading the article when I heard Maggie calling out my name.

"Oh, there you are," she said with a monotone voice. "Are you ready?"

"Yeah, I suppose," I said as I stood up and followed her. Maggie got me registered and I started school on the same day. *At least she thought enough to get me a book bag and plenty of supplies,* I thought to myself. I didn't know what my future held but there was no sense in worrying about what I couldn't control.

Several weeks went by, and I hadn't seen or heard from Maggie. I thought she'd left me hanging just like everyone else. I didn't make any waves, nor did I consider any of the girls to be my friend. At this point they were only acquaintances. I had a few conversations with some of the girls, and we even shared a few laughs but nothing real meaningful developed after that.

The adult supervisors had therapy sessions that they encouraged everyone to participate in. A group of us would form a circle and openly talk about our problems. Sometimes I participated and other times I didn't. It was depressing to sit and hear details about the situations some of the other girls came out of. Some were drug users, some were homeless teens from different states and others were selling themselves on the streets in order to buy food or purchase a bus ticket to a new town. It was sad, and downright horrifying listening to stories of sleeping in abandoned warehouses with rats and begging for money on the street corner. One girl named Africa, who was the same age as I was, talked about how she'd stand on the street corner and sing for money to get food. Her parents came to the United States from Haiti, but they both died in a fire when she was twelve. She was placed in a foster home but was abused by her foster mother, so she ran away. While living on the streets she had to constantly fight off men who tried to attack her while she slept on a mattress with a sickly stray dog she was trying to take care of.

"I named my dog Port-Au-Prince, which is where my family is from. He protected me during those times. No matter how sick he was feeling, he wouldn't let anyone get too close to me. He would always bark, even when it hurt to do so."

"What happened to Port-Au-Prince?" I asked her. Before she could answer, she started crying. "I was singing on a corner one morning trying to get enough money to buy him some food. He was lying down beside me, and when I'd finally gotten enough money I called to him, but he didn't move. He died while I was singing."

"What song were you singing?" asked another girl.

"An old song by Sam Cooke called 'A Change Is Gonna Come.' My mother loved that song." Africa sang for the group, and by the time she was done I was in tears. One thing is for sure, I didn't want any part of what I heard had happened to her to happen to me.

Early one Saturday morning, the group was scheduled to go for a fall outing to a local theater to watch a stage play. I had just boarded the group van but was pulled off of it by Maggie. I hadn't seen her in weeks. I followed her back inside and upstairs to the office where we'd be able to speak privately.

"I really wanted to go see that stage play, Maggie," I said to her.

"Well, we have to do something else instead. I have to get you over to a doctor for a blood sample."

"Blood sample for what?" I asked.

"I got in contact with the man that your mother said might be your dad. At first he said that he didn't recall who your mother was and that there was a mix-up," she explained. "I didn't hear from him for a few weeks and then, out of the clear blue sky, he called me back."

"Well, what did he say?" I asked, holding my breath on her every word.

"Apparently he has a cousin named Simon."

"The man that my mother got caught up with?"

"Yes."

"Oh, great. If my biological father is related to Simon, you can forget it. I'll just stay here at the group home."

"Well, hang on before you say that. Simon and the man who may be your father are as different as night and day."

"Go on, I'm listening," I said.

"Simon got in contact with his cousin through another family member and reminded him about a particular house party they'd gone to years ago when they were both young men. An encounter occurred between Simon's cousin and your mother."

"But Justine doesn't remember this, right?" I asked.

"I don't know what your mom remembers. Anyway, I got a phone call back from Simon's cousin and he has agreed to be tested just to make sure he doesn't have any children out in the world he's not aware of." I swallowed hard. I felt my heart racing and I couldn't calm myself down.

"So, we're going to head over to the clinic for a blood sample and let science tell us if we've located your biological father." I exhaled loudly. My feelings were somewhere between happy and terrified.

"I know this isn't easy," Maggie said.

"I'm afraid," I admitted as I swallowed hard.

Several weeks after my blood sample was taken, Maggie resurfaced again. I was in the common area playing Monopoly with Africa and a few other girls when Maggie rushed in and called out my name, "Keysha." I could hear the excitement in her voice. I captured her gaze.

"Come on, let's go upstairs into the office." I excused myself from the table and followed her. The upstairs office was as busy as it always is. The phones were ringing, the typewriters were dinging and there was a continuous hum of several conversations taking place at the same time. I took a seat in front of the desk where Maggie sat.

"The test results came back."

"And?" I asked, fearing the worst.

"We've found him," she said with a smile. I couldn't believe it. I suppose I should have been happy but I was actually mortified by this new information.

"Well, aren't you happy?" she asked.

"I don't know. I mean, who is he? What is he like? Does he even care about me?"

"His name is Jordan, and he's doing very well. He's married and has a son who is a few years younger than you." She paused in thought for a moment. "He and his wife have agreed to come and meet you."

"Come and meet me?" I began to feel a panic attack setting in. "How about coming to get me the hell up out of here?"

"Keysha, don't get upset. I mean, your existence is very shocking and unnerving to him. This has changed everything for him. He never knew about you."

"Well, he does now, and I don't understand why he just doesn't come down here and pick me up so that I can go!" I was emotional and shouting at Maggie. I didn't mean to shout at her but my emotions weren't in full control.

"Keysha, you have to understand the situation he's in, too. He had to explain you to his wife and the rest of his family. I mean, give him credit, he was man enough to admit he'd had an encounter with your mother. He and his family have yet to make a decision on what to do."

"Well, I'm part of his family. What about what I have to say?"

"Calm down, okay?" Maggie said, trying to get me to relax.

"Okay, I'm cool. When will they be here?"

"In a few days. His mother is coming into town, and he wants to wait until she arrives before he comes because she wants to meet you, as well."

"Well, what's his name?" I asked again.

"His name is Jordan," Maggie said. For a moment I felt good about knowing his name, but then random thoughts began dancing around in my head.

"What if they don't like me? What if they don't want me? What if—"

"Slow down, Keysha. Be patient. There are a lot of things that are still unclear, okay?"

"I can't be calm," I said, feeling my nerves buzzing.

"Keysha, whatever the outcome of all this is we're going to do what is best for you." Maggie smiled at me warmly. I didn't say anything else. I just tried to maintain my composure and hope that my father was the type of man who would understand me as well as get along with me.

ten

On the day I was scheduled to meet my biological father for the first time I was a nervous wreck. I wanted to look my best for him. I wanted to look perfect for him, but the clothes I owned made it impossible to look perfect. My hair was in horrible shape, my skin was full of pimples and I just felt completely inadequate. I was all set to just forego the meeting, but Maggie insisted that I at least meet him.

By 11:30 a.m. I was sitting in the office on one of the chairs awaiting their arrival. Finally, after waiting what seemed like an eternity, Jordan, his wife and his mother finally entered the room, and I was stunned into silence. They all looked so well and healthy. Jordan was impeccably dressed. Everything about him looked expensive, and I began to think that there had to be some type of mistake because there is no way that a man who looked like him would ever be involved with my mother or Simon. He was very handsome; he had smooth brown skin and eyebrows shaped exactly like my own. He didn't have any facial hair, and although his eyes appeared to be closed, I could tell that he was watching me and his vision was as sharp as a hawk's. Sometimes I hated my ability to read a person's thoughts through their facial expressions. My father did not look very enthused about being there. I stopped reading his mind and focused on his clothes again. He had on a gray pinstriped business suit with a very nice yellow satin shirt and matching tie. He had a gold watch on that was bling-blinging all over the place and some very expensive-looking shoes. My other grandmother looked very regal. She was tall and full-figured and had on a beautiful dress that flowed well with her body. Her hair was styled nicely and had beautiful streaks of gray running through it. She looked as wise as she was beautiful. When I looked into her eyes I could see pain in them. As I studied the two of them, I saw another part of myself that I hadn't known and for some reason I felt cheated. In my heart I knew we were connected, but in reality our relationship was estranged. Then there was Jordan's wife, Barbara. She walked into the room with her nose wrinkled up as if she smelled a foul odor. Everything about her—from the way she was dressed to her demeanor—said uptight, confrontational and mean-spirited.

"Come here, baby." My other grandmother summoned me to her once we made eye contact. I took a deep breath, stood up and walked over to her. She embraced me tightly and for a brief moment, the warmth of her hug felt beautiful and I got lost in the sweet scent of her perfume, but I didn't hug her back. I didn't know her like that.

"My name is Katie," she said, smiling at me. "I'm your grandmother." I looked into her eyes and somehow I felt as if she could see right through me. I wanted to say something but my words got trapped in my throat. These new feelings were foreign to me. I was looking into her eyes and felt like I knew her, but I didn't. I looked over at Jordan, and my heart started beating so fast that I thought it was going to smash through my chest.

"Hello. My name is Jordan," he said with a very commanding voice that made me nervous. Just hearing such a strong and unyielding voice made me swallow hard. We stared at each other for a long moment. Then without even thinking about it we both said, "You're reading my thoughts through my facial expressions." It was the weirdest thing that has ever happened to me. We had never known each other, but we knew each other in this bizarre way.

"It's okay. We're going to get you out of here," said Grandmother Katie. I backed away from my father because I didn't fully trust him. He was a total stranger, and yet he wasn't.

"Hello," I finally greeted him begrudgingly. I don't know why I had an attitude toward him.

"Are you okay?" he asked, trying to sound concerned, but I didn't truly think that he was.

"Does it look like I'm okay?" My tone of voice was filled with snake venom. Our eyes locked on each other again; he was trying to understand me just as much as I was him.

"Keysha, come here." Grandmother Katie once again summoned me to her side. "I know how you must feel but things are going to change, I promise," she said. I was so nervous at that moment I felt the urge to pee. I took a deep breath and began biting my fingernails.

"Hello, I'm Maggie Russo. I'm Keysha's social worker," Maggie greeted Jordan's wife, who looked like someone had just stolen her million-dollar lottery ticket.

"How did this happen?" Barbara asked Maggie. "We never knew about her."

"Jordan, if you, your mother and your wife would come over here we can discuss this situation a little more privately. Keysha, would you please have a seat over there in the manager's office." Maggie directed me to a small office that was just on the other side of the wall. I exhaled loudly and stomped over to a seat and made more noise than I needed to. I didn't go inside of the office right away. I hovered near the door where I could still hear their conversation. I listened to them talk about my case.

"Jordan, you can't deny that girl if you wanted to. She looks just like you," I heard Grandmother Katie say. "I know that you didn't know about her, but now you do. You can't leave her in this situation. She's your flesh and blood."

"Mom, please." Jordan wanted his mother to be silent for a moment. "I have a family," I heard him say. "I can't just move her in and make everything work."

"Can't you find a nice foster home for her?" I heard Barbara ask.

"At her age, it would be difficult for us to place her in a foster home."

"She has problems, right?" I heard Barbara ask another question.

"Problems that are not her fault," I heard Grandmother Katie argue back.

"Let me interrupt you guys for a moment," said Maggie. "Right now, Keysha is hurting emotionally. She's been through a lot, but she's nowhere near as bad as some of the other cases I'm dealing with. She's not pregnant, she still enjoys going to school and she's drug free. I have kids younger than her who are pregnant, drug abusers and prostitutes.

Many of them have been assaulted as young children and have self-esteem issues that you couldn't possibly imagine. In my heart, I know Keysha is a good kid. What she needs right now is a good, stable home with a lot of love and attention. Now, Jordan, biologically she is your daughter and responsibility. The state is overburdened, and a lot of kids fall through the cracks. However, it is understandable how this can be very disruptive to your current family. You have two options. You can agree to take your daughter with you, or you can sign over your parental rights and let her continue living here until she turns eighteen."

"What happens to her then?" Jordan asked.

"It's hard to tell. We do offer some assistance with college or job training, but it's a very hard road and only a small percentage of the kids actually make it. A lot of them end up falling into a life of crime or some sort of addiction."

"What about her mother? Did she sign over parental rights?" asked his wife.

"She automatically lost them once she was placed in jail," Maggie answered her.

"Will she get her parental rights back once she gets out of jail?" I heard my father ask. I felt so worthless when I heard him ask that question. I felt like he didn't see me as a part of him. I went into the office and sat down because I didn't want to hear any more of what he had to say, because I knew that in the end he'd leave me hanging just like my mother had.

About an hour later, Grandmother Katie came over and sat next to me. She draped her arm over my shoulder and hugged me once again.

"This is all going to work out," she reassured me but I didn't believe her words. "We're going to get you out of here. It's just going to take a little time though."

"You're kidding me, right!" I blew up because I figured it was all just a big lie. "You know what. He doesn't want me! You don't want me! His wife doesn't want me and neither does the state! Nobody wants me so I might as well just go and kill myself to make it easier on everyone!" I yelled at the top of my voice. When I quieted down, the entire staff was glaring at me through the office door, stunned into silence. I couldn't take the pressure so I ran out of the office and back to the sleeping area. I lay facedown on the cot and cried out loud into my pillow.

eleven

The following day, Maggie told me she would be meeting with my mother to discuss what the best options would be for the unborn baby she was going to have while still in jail. I told her I wanted to go with her because I wanted to see her. I had questions I wanted to ask her. When we arrived at the jailhouse it was scary. There were metal detectors and armed guards everywhere. We had to take off anything metal that we had on before going through the detector. Even after going through the detector, I had to be patted down to make certain that I wasn't sneaking in anything that I shouldn't be.

I went into a room with Maggie and sat at a long table that had partitions on each side for privacy. In front of me was a thick sheet of bulletproof glass and a black telephone. On the other side of the glass was an empty chair with the same setup. I had to wait for a long time before the guard brought Justine out. When I saw her, I was actually happy to see her, even though the circumstances weren't the best. I picked up the phone at the same time she did.

"Hey, Mommy," I said, noticing how tightly her hair had been French braided. I couldn't help the way I felt at that moment. My feelings were trapped somewhere between angry and uncertain.

"What's going on?" Justine asked.

"Nothing. I mean, a lot. Things are so chaotic right now. I'm living in a group home for teens and the other kids in there seem real crazy."

"Did that social worker get in touch with the man who might be your daddy?" Justine seemed to be indifferent about whether I found out the identity of my father. I think she was sensitive about the fact she really didn't know who he was after all of these years.

"Yes," I answered her.

"Did he come down to see about you?" she asked.

"Yes," I answered again.

"I didn't think he'd really show up after all this time, but Simon said he would." She paused in thought. "Well that's the best that I can do for you right now. Hopefully he'll take you in."

"I wouldn't count on it," I said, feeling my anger swelling up. "He doesn't want me."

"Well, neither did I, but you're here." Those words hit me like a wrecking ball slamming against a structure being demolished. I wanted to holler at her but I didn't. My heart just iced over and I realized that coming to see her wasn't such a good idea.

"You have to make it on your own," she told me. "I can't do anything more for you. You're old enough now to make your own choices. Hopefully, you'll make some good ones so that when I get out of here I can come and stay with you." What was that supposed to mean? I mean, damn! I can hardly take care of myself, and she's telling me to start preparing to take care of her. At that moment, I wanted nothing more to do with her. At that moment, I heard a little voice in the back of my mind telling me I was worthless and should disappear off the face of the earth because no one cared about me.

"Well, that's all I have to say," she informed me and then hung up the phone. I looked at her one last time and tried to read her thoughts but I couldn't. I got up and left the room. Maggie, who was waiting for her turn to speak with my mother, didn't say anything to me. I suppose the look on my face said it all. She went into the bulletproof room to speak with my mother without saying a word to me.

Three weeks had gone by since I'd seen Grandmother Katie and my father, Jordan. Just like always, I figured they had left me hanging and had no intention of coming to my rescue. I didn't expect them to return at all because, as I heard his wife put it, "I've got problems." Hell, in my mind, we've all got problems.

I was having a very difficult time concentrating on my schoolwork. I couldn't focus, especially after being rejected by my biological father and mother. I just didn't care about much of anything anymore. I didn't care about school, my grades, or the people at the group home or anyone, even myself. The only thing that kept me from going nuts was books.

One day when I was feeling particularly low and depressed, Africa came over to my bed and sat by me.

"You don't look so hot," she said.

"Things are just real jacked-up for me right now. My life isn't worth living," I said.

"Sure it is," Africa said, trying to reassure me, but her

words were of no comfort. "I know what it is like to feel the way you do."

"No, you don't," I snapped at her.

"Yes, I do," she snapped right back. "You look as if you want to just give up on everything." I didn't say anything.

"Yeah, that's what I thought. I've been there several times but I never had the nerve to go through with it. I guess I was too afraid to take my own life."

"So what kept you going?" I asked.

"I don't know. I just took one day at time. Some days were better than others, but I always knew that I'd find a way to make it through my problems."

"Don't you want to get out of this place? Don't you want to live with a family again?" I asked.

"Listen, when I was fourteen I joined this all-girl gang. For a while they served as my family, but the things we were doing—well, let's just say I have plenty of regrets about it. I barely made it out of the gang alive, but I did, and I'm thankful for that. Yes, I do want to get out of this place, but not right now. It's safe for me here, and it's much better than living on the street." I didn't say anything else.

"Hang in there. It will get better. It has to," said Africa, who then got up and left. It was thoughtful of Africa to try and cheer me up, but it didn't help because I still felt all alone. Maggie told me I should keep a diary of my feelings and share them in group, but I wasn't really sure how to do that. All I knew was I was hurting really bad and I wanted my mother and father to know how much I hurt.

During our Saturday trip to the library I came across a book called *The Diary of a Young Girl* by Anne Frank. At first

I didn't think I'd like reading some white girl's diary, but for some odd reason I sat down at a table with it. I opened the book and started reading it and got pulled into the story. I checked the book out and went back to the group home. I sat on my cot the rest of the day and read. I cared about Anne in a way that I have never cared before, and when I reached the end of the book, I cried for her. After reading what she'd gone through I decided that my life wasn't as bad as it could be. I mean, at least I didn't have to hide from soldiers inside a dark room and remain motionless and silent for hours on end just to save my life. I also didn't have to live on the streets like Africa had to.

The following Saturday evening, I was sitting on my cot reading another copy of *Vibe*. This time I was reading an article about how Beyoncé Knowles got her start in show business. Just as the article was getting good, I heard Grandmother Katie call my name. I looked up and saw her approaching me, wheeling a small suitcase behind her. Jordan and Maggie were with her.

"Let's start packing your things You're not staying here another night," said Grandmother Katie.

"What's going on?" I asked, confused.

"You're going to come live with me," said Jordan.

"What if I don't want to live with you?" I was being defiant.

"No, you're coming to stay with me. You have no idea of what it took to make this happen." Jordan spoke as if I had no real choice in the matter. He was serious, but I was suspicious. Inside I really wanted to be happy, but I wasn't.

Since I'd given up hope that anyone was coming for me, I'd gotten sort of comfortable living in the group home. Now I felt as if I were being uprooted once again and being carted off into the unknown.

"And you have no idea of what I had to go through just being here." My words were full of pain and contempt for him. I felt like fighting him, but I didn't know why.

"There is no need to be nasty with me. I'm your father and I want to help."

"Oh, now you want to be my father." Now I was really ready to fight. I'd shifted my body weight from one foot to the other and was about to unleash a verbal assault on him.

"Come on, now," Grandmother Katie's soothing voice cut the tension between us. "Now is not the time to have this conversation. Keysha, come with us. There is so much that needs to be said and understood. Now is the time for healing your bruised heart. It is not the time to create more wounds with angry words."

Grandmother Katie was good. She was very skillful in the way she defused the tension between Jordan and me. For the moment, I decided not to fight with him.

"Come on, start packing your belongings," Jordan said to me in a nicer tone of voice. *Here I go again,* I thought to myself. *I wonder what my life is going to be like now.*

twelve

I said goodbye to Africa and a few other girls that I'd gotten to know. We promised to keep in touch with each other, and I promised Africa that as soon as I got settled in I'd call her. We hugged each other for a long moment before I finally departed with Jordan.

During the long drive to my father's house, Grandmother Katie began asking me questions about my mother and our lifestyle.

"Has your mother ever held a job?" she asked.

"No, not one that I can think of."

"Have you been in touch with your other grandmother?"

"No," I answered her.

"What exactly happened to her? I know that she was mixed up in some type of mess with a bank, or at least that's what I've been told." I didn't want to talk about my Grandmother Rubylee. I missed her, and it was still difficult for me to talk about it because it made me think about my Aunt Estelle and how she passed away.

"Can we not talk about this right now?" I asked.

"Okay," said Grandmother Katie. "I understand. We can talk about it later." I remained silent for a long while as we drove down the highway. My father didn't say much but I could tell that he had a lot on his mind. I suppose we are alike in that sense. Whenever there is something eating away at us, we prefer to remain silent and think about the situation before talking about it. I know that my thoughts were all over the place. I was fearful, uncertain and confused. I felt like I was being forced on my father, and that made me feel as if I was some germ no one could get rid of.

"We have enough room for you," said Jordan, who only began speaking after I saw Grandmother Katie nudge him. "You also have a brother. His name is Mike."

"You'll be in the upstairs bedroom down the hall from him. He's a bit apprehensive about your coming to live with us. He's been the only kid in the house for a long time, and he now has to learn how to share." I didn't know what to say so I remained silent.

"I know you'll find living with me to be a lot different, but I know that it's for the best."

Whatever, I thought to myself. In the back of my mind, I was already thinking about running away. To where, I don't know. I just wanted to be alone and not be bothered.

We turned into this community where there was nothing but beautiful green grass and large homes. I took in everything. I saw both black and white people out mowing their lawns and planting flowers. A few younger kids were riding their bikes along the sidewalk. We finally turned into a driveway and I focused on the house.

"Here we are," said Jordan as he drove down a long driveway. My jaw dropped when I saw the home.

"This is where you live?" I wanted to be sure I wasn't dreaming.

"Yes, and now you'll be living here," said Jordan. The house was two stories tall. It was a soft shade of green with red roof shingles. The underground sprinklers were on. I noticed that there was a greenhouse attached to it that appeared to be filled with all types of flowers that were bursting with color. Once we reached the end of the driveway there was a large black iron gate. Jordon touched a remote that was in the car and the gates opened up. We drove in, and he parked the car in front of one of the doors of the five-car garage.

"Okay, we're here," Jordan said once again as he glanced into the rearview mirror to look at me.

"Do you like it?" he asked with a slight smile.

"It's all right," I said, not wanting to give him the satisfaction of knowing that I was completely impressed.

"It's just all right?" he asked again.

"Yeah, it's just all right," I answered him back.

"Jordan, why don't you give her a tour. I'll take her things up to her room and meet you guys up there," said Grandmother Katie.

"Is it okay with you if we take a walk around the property, Keysha?" asked Jordan.

"I guess it's not like I have a choice," I answered sarcastically.

We got out of the car and stepped into the bright sunlight. I heard a chorus of birds singing, and for the first time noticed all of the trees that surrounded the house. I counted a total of eight.

"This is the garage," Jordan said as he opened one of the

bay doors. We stepped inside. The garage was bigger than the apartment I lived in with my mother. Everything inside was organized and in its proper place. Items like bicycles, the lawn mower, leaf blower and hedge trimmer hung from hooks in the ceiling. There was plenty of shelf space and plastic color-coded and labeled containers on each shelf. To my right I noticed a car covered with a black cloth. Jordan noticed me staring at it.

"Do you want to see what kind of car it is?" he asked. Before I could answer he walked over to it and removed the covering. Beneath the cloth was a black sports car with an eagle painted on the hood.

"This is my 1979 Pontiac Trans Am," he said proudly. "I've spent a small fortune rebuilding it to its original condition."

"Do you ever drive it?" I asked. He looked at me strangely as if the thought of pulling it out of the safety of the garage would take an act of God.

"Rarely. This car is a classic. I drive it each year in the Memorial Day parade but that's about it." I looked around the garage a little more closely and saw that there was an additional door.

"What's in there?" I asked.

"Go ahead and take a look," he said. "I'll be along once I finish re-covering the car. I don't like dust getting on it." When he said that I quickly realized that his old car meant a great deal to him. I walked over to the other door and opened it up. Inside was a small workshop. It was tidy and well organized. On the shelves were various containers of paint, wood stain, tools and other items used for building and repairing.

"This is my workshop," Jordan said as he entered the room.

"You build stuff?" I asked.

"I restore things," he said. "Have you ever heard of the phrase, 'one man's trash is another man's treasure'?"

"No, I've never heard of the expression," I lied to him. I don't know why I did. I just did.

"It means that what one person tosses away, another person may find value in."

"Was the old-time car someone's trash?" I asked.

"Yes, it was. The man who had it sold it to me for only a few hundred dollars. It was just sitting on his property rusting away. I had it towed here and over the course of about seven years I rebuilt it." I was impressed but I didn't let him know it.

"So what do you build in here?" I asked.

"I restore furniture that I buy at garage sales."

"You're basically like the junk man who rides around in a raggedy pickup truck picking up everyone's junk on the street," I said as I found a way to identify with what he did. I could tell that he didn't like my comparison because he didn't respond to my comment. I wanted to laugh at him for being so sensitive but I didn't. "Where do those stairs lead to?" I pointed toward the back of the room.

"Come on, I'll show you," he said. I followed him through the work area and up the back staircase. When we got upstairs I was speechless at what I saw.

"This is the apartment above the garage. I had it converted to a workout gym," Jordan said as he flipped a few light switches so that I could take a better look. There were a number of machines positioned all around the room. There was a flat-screen television mounted on the far wall, and two treadmills were situated in front of the television.

"Do you know who this is?" he asked pointing to a mural on the wall. The wall painting was a life-size portrayal of two boxers. One had knocked the other one down and appeared to be towering above him yelling down at the other man on his back.

"That's that boxer man," I said, not remembering his name.

"His name is Muhammad Ali. He's fighting a man by the name of Sonny Liston. In this scene, Ali has knocked Liston down. Liston was the heavyweight champion at the time. Ali is yelling 'get up' to him."

"Why is he yelling at him?" I asked.

"Because Liston knew that he couldn't beat Ali so he tried to cheat by placing an eye irritant on his boxing gloves. So every time he hit Ali near his eyes, the irritation prevented Ali from seeing clearly. Once Ali's trainers realized what was going on, they washed the irritant away and Ali went back out to whip Sonny's behind."

"Oh," I said as I walked up closer to the mural. "Who painted it?"

"Your uncle did," Jordan answered. I looked back at him and noticed that he was just watching my every movement. His sharp eyes made me nervous. He made me feel as if he was mall security or someone watching and waiting for me to steal something.

"Don't stand behind me like that," I said, snapping at him.

"Stand behind you like what?" he asked.

"Like you're waiting for me to break or steal something."

"I'm sorry. I don't mean to make you feel that way," he said.

Next to the Muhammad Ali painting was a cabinet filled with track and field trophies.

"Did you win these?" I asked.

"No, actually most of them belong to my wife, Barbara. She was an exceptional high school and college track and field athlete. The three on the bottom shelf belong to your brother, Mike."

"Where is he?" I asked.

"He's out with his mother. They'll be home in a little while. You'll see him then."

I got tired of looking at the workout room and decided to walk back down the stairs.

"Come around this way," Jordan said, and I followed him around the side of the garage down a short brick path, which was lined with thick, neatly trimmed bushes. Once we got around the bushes I saw the in-ground swimming pool.

"Do you know how to swim?" he asked.

"No," I answered.

"Well, I can teach you how. It's real easy once you get the hang of it." I didn't answer him, I just looked at how pretty the water was. "We'll have to wait until next summer for swimming lessons though. I'm going to have to drain the pool for the winter next week."

We walked back down the short brick path past the garage and to the door at the rear of the house. I stepped inside and held the door open for Jordan. Upon entering he began talking.

"We'll start in the basement," he said and I followed him down a few steps. To the right there was a door, which he opened. It was his office. His computer, desk and photos of various entertainers were hung on the wall. I walked in and looked at one photo of him and TuPac.

"You knew TuPac?" I asked.

"I wouldn't say that I knew him but we've met before," answered Jordan.

"So what is that you do?" I asked.

"I'm the executive vice president for Hot Jamz 104," he answered.

"That's, like, the hottest radio station in the city," I said, sort of excited about the possibility of getting to meet a famous entertainer.

"Yeah, but our last rating has us as the number-three station in the city and I have to change that."

"Oh," I answered, not fully understanding what he meant. We came out of the office and went toward the rear of the basement. It was a typical basement. Gray concrete floor and walls. There was nothing exciting about looking at the laundry shoot or the washer and dryer.

"Over here, this is what I wanted to show you," he said as he opened another door, which led to the greenhouse. I stepped inside and saw an array of potted flowers blooming along with another door which led inside.

"It's pretty," I admitted and then turned and exited the room. I could tell that Jordan wanted to explain all of the flowers but I didn't care about that.

"I planted all of the flowers around the house," he commented as we walked out of the basement. "Gardening is something I've always loved. Have you ever planted a seed and then nurtured it into a flower?"

"No, and I really don't care to," I said with honesty. However, I suppose that my tone of voice made me sound rather snotty.

"This is the family room," he said as we walked out of the basement and up a few stairs. There was a large sectional brown leather sofa that looked huge enough to seat at least seven or eight people. At both ends of the sectional there were recliner seats. The oversize sofa even had cup holders and a compartment to keep ice cold. Another large flat-screen television was mounted on the wall along with a complete home theater system. He waited for a response from me, but I only nodded my head. From there we moved into the kitchen, which looked like it was out of a magazine. The refrigerator had a crushed icemaker, there was a center island where food could be prepared, and there was an abundance of cabinet and shelf space. From there it was on to the formal dining room. There was a beautiful wooden table large enough to seat eight people. The table was completely set but looked more like a display rather than a place to eat.

"Follow me and I'll show you to your room," he said as he opened yet another door, which I thought was a closet but it was actually a staircase that led to the upper level of the house.

"Damn, this is a big-ass house," I blurted out my thoughts.

"I'd prefer that you not use foul language. It's not becoming of a lady," Jordan said, and I looked at him like he'd just lost his mind. *I know that he didn't call himself putting me in check,* I thought to myself. *The last thing he has the right to do is discipline me.*

"Whatever," I said as I walked up the stairs. In my mind I didn't see myself staying in this house for very long. I felt like I was intruding on his space anyway. When I reached the top landing there were three bedrooms and a bathroom up there. Grandmother Katie was coming out of the bathroom as we were about to turn and walk down the corridor toward the bedrooms.

"Well, I see you two have finally made it up here," she said with a smile.

"I'm about to show Keysha to her room," Jordan said. I followed him down to the last door, which was closed.

"I think you should open it," he said as he stepped aside. I placed my hand on the handle of the white door, gave it a twist and opened it up. I was completely taken aback by the size of the room. It was huge. There was a beautiful vanity dresser filled with all types of cosmetic products. There was a queen-size canopy bed with linen that matched the curtains, a desk and chair were near the window, as well as a stand that had a small television with a VCR and DVD player built into it.

"I hope you like the room," Jordan said.

"Of course she likes it," answered Grandmother Katie. To tell the truth I felt like I was more like an outsider than I'd ever felt before. It all seemed so fake to me, and I feared that at any moment someone would come and tell me that there was a big mistake and I wouldn't be able to stay. So, in my mind, there was no sense in getting too comfortable, because I knew that dreams didn't come true, and at some point either I'd run away or get mixed up in some juvenile-delinquent mess just like I was expected to.

"Um, can I be alone for a moment?" I asked, turning to face Grandmother Katie and Jordan. Both of them had goofy smiles plastered on their faces. At that moment I felt as if I was the charity case of the century, and I didn't like that feeling.

"Sure, you can have some privacy, honey," said Grandmother Katie.

"Your brother will be home in awhile," said Jordan. That was another thing that was peculiar to me. Jordan spoke so clearly and flawlessly. He didn't sound anything like the men who hung around the empty lot near my old apartment building. He actually spoke like Carlton Banks from the program *The Fresh Prince of Bel-Air*. "Barbara will be home later. We're all going out for a nice family dinner tonight," he announced, and I cringed at the thought of sitting at a dinner table with them.

"I don't have anything to wear," I quickly said, confident that my excuse would get me out of having to go with them.

"Look in the closet over there, honey. Some nice clothes have been purchased for you," said Grandmother Katie, who still had a smile plastered on her face. I just knew that whatever they had purchased for me was all wrong. *Old people have no sense of style,* I thought to myself.

"If you need anything, we'll be down in the family room," Jordan said before he and his mother walked out of the room and shut the door behind them.

thirteen

I JUST stood in the center of my bedroom for the longest time, afraid to touch anything. Once I found the courage to move within the space, I went over to the vanity and looked at the products there. It was filled with Proactive Solution skin-care products, cotton balls, Q-tips and an assortment of nail polishes and other makeup items. I opened the top left drawer and discovered it contained feminine hygiene essentials, which I had to admit I was in desperate need of. I went over and sat down at the desk in the room and stared out the window. My view was of the backyard. There was a large tree directly outside of my window that blocked part of my view of the garage and swimming pool. I don't know how long I'd been sitting there but I was startled out of my trance by a knock at the door. I didn't say anything, so the person knocked again. This time a little louder. I got up, moved to the door and opened it.

"What's up, son?" A young boy was at my door. He had caramel skin, a thin trace of hair on his upper lip and an athletic build.

"You're Mike, right?" I asked, trying not to laugh as I studied his appearance more closely. He had a white scarf wrapped around his head, which I assumed was more for fashion than it was for hairstyle. He had a Band-Aid positioned under his left eye, which made him look like a Nelly wannabe. He contorted his face and puckered his lips into an expression he considered to be thuggish, but it only made him look as if he were sitting on the throne with a bad case of constipation. He had on an oversize Akademiks T-shirt with matching Akademiks Armor jeans and a pair of Akademiks gym shoes.

"What? You see something funny?" he asked as he crossed his arms across his chest and tucked his fingers in his armpits. He appeared to be attempting to flex his chest and arm muscles, but he didn't have enough muscle to flex.

"Boy, you are not hard, so don't even try to act like you are some thug with a reputation and a criminal record."

"You don't know me. You don't know the things I've done. I'm a straight gangster. You're in my world now."

"Well, you're the first thirteen-year-old hardened gangster I've seen," I said, thinking he was joking.

"I'm going to be fourteen in a minute," he said, making a gesture with his fingers. It was then that I realized he was serious about the charade he was putting on.

"Whatever, fool," I said and was about to slam the door in his face.

"Girl, why are you hating on me? Is it because I'm so iced-out? Is it because of my grillz?" He smiled at me, and I peeked at his teeth.

"That is not a grillz in your mouth, those are braces," I said. "Who do you think you're trying to fool? Your money is not long, and you are certainly not a baller." I'd suddenly become annoyed with him. I studied him closely for another moment and could tell he was up to no good by the way he shifted his eyes from left to right.

"Okay." He lowered his voice to a loud whisper. "I may not be a baller or a thug but listen up, because I'm only going to say this once. If you want to get along up in here, all you need to do is stay out of my way, mind your own business and don't be up in here trying to act like daddy's little girl. Do you understand what I'm saying, son?" He stepped closer to me as if he wanted to knuckle-up and fight. I wasn't afraid of his scrawny behind at all. I made a sudden move as if I were about to hit him and he flinched with fear.

"Yeah, just what I thought. You're just a little spoiled-ass punk!" I said with a vicious tone in my voice.

"Well at least I don't have a face that looks like pimple paradise. I mean, damn girl, did every zit in the nation take up space on your forehead?" Before I could stop myself, I swung at him. Mike saw the punch coming and quickly moved out of my reach.

"Hey, you don't want to throw down with me. I may not look like it, but I know how to fight," he said as he backed away. I could tell that I'd scared him because his voice trembled.

"You see that I'm not scared, don't you?" I snarled at him, feeling a deep hate for him growing each second that ticked by. "Here is a word of advice for you, Chicken Little," I called him out of his name. "You have to bring some ass in order to kick some ass. If you come at me sideways again, I will beat you down like a crackhead who stole my last two dollars." I gave him the meanest, most threatening glare that my face could form. He didn't say anything, only continued to back away. He went back to his room and shut his door. I went back inside my room and shut the door, as well. I didn't feel good about being in this house at all, but until I could find a place to run away to, this would have to do.

I decided to just chill in the room and pass the time by watching television. I was watching a movie called *Save the Last Dance* starring Julia Stiles. It was about this rich girl who lost her mother and then had to go live in the hood with her father. I suppose I identified with the movie because my situation was reversed. I had to move from the hood with my mother and live like some stuck-up girl in the rich suburbs. The movie was excellent, and I enjoyed watching all the dance moves she and the other characters did in the movie. The movie was just about to reach its climax when I heard Jordan's voice.

"Keysha." I didn't answer him because I was trying to figure why it sounded as if he was in the room with me.

"There is an intercom on the wall next to your closet door. Go over to it and press the 'talk' button to answer me." I looked over at my closet door and noticed the intercom. I did as he instructed.

"We're going to be going to dinner in about a half hour, so start getting ready. We're going to the Outback Steakhouse so jeans will be the appropriate attire to wear."

Appropriate attire, I thought to myself. *He sounds all nerdy.*

"Okay," I answered him back and then sat back on the bed to continue watching my movie. I was dreading looking in the closet at the clothes my grandmother had picked out because I knew they'd be a throwback to the sixties or seventies. After the movie ended I opened the large walk-in closet and flipped the light switch.

"Damn," I spoke aloud. "This closet is big enough to put a bed in." There were two dressers inside the closet along with plenty of shelf space for shoes and other accessories. There was also a large dressing mirror inside. The other thing that freaked me out was each drawer had a small label on it indicating what item of clothing was on the inside. I opened the drawer that said "jeans." To my surprise, Grandmother Katie had pretty good taste. Inside were several pairs of Baby Phat blue jeans.

"This is all right," I said to myself as I opened up other drawers and located tops, underwear and other items. This entire change in my life was like magic. It was like living in a fairy tale, and it just seemed too good to be true. I matched up an outfit that was acceptable to me. I then went into the bathroom and got ready. About fifteen minutes later, I stood in front of my mirror fully dressed, fussing with my hair because I was trying to make myself perfect, but my hair wasn't cooperating. Months of neglect and bad styling decisions couldn't be erased in a matter of seconds. I decided to put on my night hair scarf to cover it up just like Toya was so fond of doing. It would just have to do for now until I could get something done with it. I had butterflies in my stomach because I was about to go down and really meet Barbara, my stepmother, who made me feel very uncomfortable. I decided if she was going to be mean to me, then I'd be just as mean to her. I finally got my nerves in order and walked downstairs and into the family room where everyone was sitting and waiting on me.

"It took you long enough, I started growing a gray hair waiting on you," Mike said sarcastically.

Grandmother Katie smacked him on the back of his head. "Watch your manners, Mike." I looked around at each of them and felt as if they were all judging me.

"Why does she have that head rag on, Jordan?" Barbara tried to whisper in my father's ear, but I heard her. She acted as if I wasn't there and couldn't hear her. I felt as if I wasn't good enough for them. I felt as if I just didn't measure up.

"Just forget it. Y'all go out by yourselves. That's what you want anyway," I said as I rushed back up to my room. I shut the door and began to pace the floor again. I tried to focus my thinking and determine what to do next. The only thing that came to mind was to pack my things, steal any money lying around and take my chances out on the streets.

"Baby, come on and go with us. She didn't mean anything by what she said." Grandmother Katie had just opened my door.

"She doesn't like me," I said. "It was written all over her face."

"Give it time, Keysha. Your existence is news to all of us. We all have to make some adjustments and make room in our lives for you." I plopped down on the edge of the bed and placed my face in my hands.

"Keysha, I really want you to have dinner with us," said Jordan, who was now in my bedroom, too. I looked up at him and saw a part of me in his eyes. For a brief moment I felt some sense of a connection and wanted to hug him but I didn't. I just felt angry with everything and everyone.

"Can I sit down next to you?" he asked.

"It's your house," I answered.

"When I look at you, I see myself," he said. "I see a part of me that I feel like I should know but I don't, and that hurts. Perhaps I'm moving too fast, but I want to give you all of the things that you've never had. I want to make up for that. I can give you a decent place to live, nice clothes and some sense of stability. What I can't give you is the time we've lost. There is so much to learn and understand, but we have to give things time."

"He's right, you know," said Grandmother Katie. "There are so many things about me and our family that you need to know, learn and understand. I want you to have that sense of belonging, but I know it's not going to happen overnight. A sense of belonging comes from within, and when you get that feeling hold on to it, because it also means that you're beginning to feel loved." It's just downright frightening how Grandmother Katie could read me.

"Let me see your hair." Grandmother Katie walked over to me, and I allowed her to remove my scarf.

"It's not so bad, honey. We just have to let it grow out a little and take care of it better," she said as she took a closer look at my hair. "We can just brush it back and you'll be fine." Grandmother Katie picked up the brush that was sitting atop the vanity. She sat down at the foot of my bed and asked me to sit on the floor between her thighs.

"I want you to know that I'm always here for you, Keysha. I want you to be able to come to me and confide in me. I want you to know about my history just as much as I want to know about yours. I don't even know what your favorite color or food is. Just like you've missed out, so has this family," Grandmother Katie explained as she continued working with my hair.

"She hates me, doesn't she?" I asked, referring to Barbara.

"No, she doesn't hate you at all. She just has to adjust to this change in her life," said Grandmother Katie as she brushed the other side of my hair. Her brush strokes were soft and comforting.

"There is a lot that you have to understand. One of which is that we've always wanted two children, a boy and a girl. We were able to have a son together but medical complications have prevented us from having additional children," said Jordan.

"Life is like that sometimes," Grandmother Katie continued. "You can plan out the perfect life for yourself, but if your plans don't match God's plan, then I'm afraid that you're setting yourself up to deal with a lot of heartache."

"I wonder what God has planned for my mother?" I spoke aloud as I thought about what Grandmother Katie said. No one could give me an answer to my question. The room was silent for a moment, and then Barbara walked in.

"Listen, why don't we just order pizza tonight," she said, refusing to make eye contact with me. "I'm not feeling too good, and I just want to lie down."

"Are you okay?" Jordan asked as he draped his arm around her shoulder.

"I'm just not feeling good. Come help me lie down," she said, and Jordan escorted her to her room. At that moment I felt jealousy raise its ugly head. I mean, for the first time I was actually starting to feel some sort of connection to my father, and she came up and took him away from me. She'd had him for years and I couldn't get twenty minutes alone with him without her interrupting us. I hated her for intruding on my time with him. It wasn't fair.

fourteen

The following morning, I woke up and for the first time in ages I felt very well rested. The bed I was sleeping in was the most comfortable bed I'd ever been on. It was just right; the linen smelled fresh, and the pillows were soft and fluffy. Just as I was enjoying my blissful moment, I was startled out of my mind by the presence of Barbara sitting in the vanity chair staring at me. It freaked me out because I didn't know what to think or what was about to go down.

"What's going on?" I asked as I quickly sat upright in my bed.

"Did you sleep well?" she asked with a wicked undertone in her voice and an evil glint in her eyes.

"I slept fine. Why are you in my room?" I didn't like the invasion of my privacy one bit.

"This is my house. I can go into any room of my choice." I couldn't argue that point with her so I didn't.

"You and I need to have a little girl-to-girl chat," Barbara said as she leaned forward in the seat and locked her gaze on me.

"You're Jordan's daughter, there is no denying that. You look more like him than Mike does. And since you were obviously conceived before Jordan and I were married, I can't hold your existence against him. Especially since he didn't know about you. But that's not what I'm here to talk about."

"Well, get to the point," I snapped at her. I didn't like her attitude or the way she was talking to me and I wanted to let her know it. It was bad enough that I didn't measure up to her standards but now she was about to reinforce my shortcomings.

"Yeah, we need to get some things ironed out. According to your social worker, Maggie, you're sexually active." I twisted my lips and rolled my eyes at her.

"Yeah, I know about it." She paused briefly. "There are some rules and boundaries we need to get ironed out. You will not set one foot back in this house if you go out and get yourself knocked up. I don't care if you are Jordan's daughter, getting pregnant out of wedlock is not acceptable."

"Jordan knocked up my mama out of wedlock," I reminded her.

"That was then, but this is now. I expect you to do well in school. Failing grades will not be tolerated and will be dealt with accordingly."

"You know what, I'm not even trying to hear you. You don't know anything about me and you're not trying to, either. So you can just talk to my hand." I held my hand up in front of her face.

"Do you know why I feel this way, little girl?" I didn't answer her question.

"Because I think you're going to follow in your mother's and your grandmother's footsteps and become a jailbird and a failure."

"Whatever," I snarled at her. "I'm not even trying to go

to jail," I said to her, even though I felt as if some situation would befall me and I'd end up in juvenile court for one reason or another.

"Then prove me wrong," she said. "Prove me wrong by shocking the daylights out of me."

I looked up at the ceiling because I didn't want to listen to her anymore.

"No boys are allowed in the house without an adult present."

"So does that mean that Mike can't come in when I'm here all alone?" I was being a smart-ass because I didn't like her rules at all.

"You know what I mean. I don't want any of your male friends from your old neighborhood visiting this house," she said, raising her voice at me. I could tell that my indifference and lack of fear were irritating her. I was getting a twisted joy out of it.

"So what are you trying to say? You think that just because I'm from the inner city that all of my friends are thugs, prostitutes and dope dealers?"

"Let's just say I wouldn't be surprised if they were." She moved my hand from in front of her face.

"I guess you don't know or see that Mike wants to be a thug. His pants were sagging more than anyone I've ever known."

"He's just going through a phase, that's all. As long as he continues to be an honor student, I can live with his temporary fascination with hip-hop culture."

"You have an answer for everything, don't you?"

"You know, Grandmother Katie will be going home

soon." She stood up. "And when she does, it will just be the two of us. And you should know I'm the only queen in this house."

"Is that all?" I asked, glad to see she was about to leave. It was now very clear to me that we would never get along.

"For now. I'm sure we'll have future conversations, because I know you're going to mess up." After that comment, she walked over to the door but stopped just before exiting.

"Oh, by the way, Grandmother Katie is taking you to my hairstylist so that your hair can be taken care of. I can't have you walking around looking bad about the head because it makes me look bad." When she turned her back again, I stuck my tongue out at her in a gesture of defiance.

I really liked my Grandmother Katie. She had a way of knowing just what to say and how to say it without being offensive or mean-spirited. I also liked her because she didn't judge me. She accepted me for who I was and saw me as a young lady who was very badly bruised. I fell in love with her for understanding me in ways that I didn't understand myself. I enjoyed talking to her more than I did Jordan, my snotty brother, Mike, and my wicked stepmother, Barbara. What made her even more special was that we'd read some of the same books and had fun talking about them. Grandmother Katie said that once she returned home she'd ship me a few books that she thought would interest me. She was planning to leave on Wednesday, which I was rather sad about because she was the only person I felt comfortable talking to.

Late Sunday evening, I was sitting in my room with my back resting against the headboard of my bed. I was feeling rather sad because I had gone to the hairstylist and she'd had to cut most of my hair off because it was too damaged. I was also missing my mom and wished she and I could do things like going to get our hair and nails done. Grandmother Katie knocked on my door and asked if she could come in.

"How are you feeling this evening?" she asked. That was another thing that I liked about her. She seemed to be genuinely concerned about me.

"Kind of sad," I said.

"Do you want to talk about it?" she asked. I moved my feet so that she could sit on the bed with me.

"All my hair is gone, and I just miss my mother a little," I admitted.

"Well, darling, your hair is nice. I bet in time you will grow to like it. And if I were you, I think I would miss my mother, too. You should take some time and go see about her."

"I'm not ready. I mean, the last time I saw her she was mean to me, and I just don't feel like getting my feelings hurt again."

"It wasn't easy for you growing up, was it?" she asked.

"I guess not. I mean, I never thought that we had it bad or anything like that. Things were just the way they were. I thought it was normal."

"Tell me something about you that you really like about yourself."

"What do you mean?" I asked because I was confused by the question.

"Tell me something about you as a person that you really like about yourself."

"Nothing. My hair is whacked out, my skin looks like volcanoes are about to erupt on it, my butt is like my mother's, it's too big for my body and guys are always making me feel self-conscious about it."

"Those are all of the things on the outside. Tell me what you like about you, the person?" she asked.

"No one has ever asked me that question before." I paused in thought. "I don't know what I like about me. I feel like I'm just here."

"Well, I've only known you for a short time and let me tell you what I see. You're a very smart and shapely young woman who has been able to survive on her own with very little adult supervision. That's a sign of character. You have a strong mind that guides you and hungers to learn, and to me that's a sign of a very intelligent young woman. Keysha, I want you to work on the mental voices in your head that feed you negative information about yourself. You don't need to be your own worst enemy. When you hear the voices of doubt and self-defeat, you have to quiet them with more positive things about who you are and what you can do and accomplish. If you belittle yourself, you only open the door for others to do the same."

"Wow, how are you able to do that?" I asked.

"Do what?" she asked. I began trying to express myself with my hands as I spoke.

"You have a way of getting around me and my barriers. You know how to go directly to my fears without me telling you. What are you, gifted or something?" Grandmother Katie smiled at me.

"I listen with my heart and soul," she said, which confused me even more.

"No one has ever called me intelligent before," I admitted, holding my head down. "Everyone has always expected me to mess up. When my mother and other grandmother thought I was pregnant, they were happy because it meant more money would be coming into the house." I swallowed hard because I was embarrassed by that fact. "I love my Grandmother Rubylee, but all she ever does is try to steal from people. I don't want to be like her or my mother. I don't want to rip people off, but that's all people expect me to do. Even Barbara doesn't think much of me."

"Listen, baby. Let me tell you something. You don't have to be like your mother and grandmother at all. The choices you make are your own, and if you choose *not* to follow in their footsteps then you will not. You are in control of what you do, not them, not me and certainly not Barbara."

"Tell me honestly, why doesn't Barbara like me?"

"Barbara cares more than you think. She just has a different way of expressing it. She may be rather blunt and frank, but she means well. You wouldn't have made it into this house if she had not agreed to it. Give her credit for that. She may be stern—"

"And stuck-up," I interrupted her. She smiled and nodded her head.

"She has her moments. I think that once you and Barbara get past this odd time you'll discover that you guys aren't as different as you might think you are," she said, being sure she'd selected the right words.

"What about my daddy? What was he like growing up?" I asked.

"Oh, your father was a mischievous and a curious young man," she said, chuckling as she thought about Jordan as a young man. "When he was around eight or nine, he'd heard from somewhere that you could dig your way to China. So he went into the garage and got a shovel and dug up all of my flowers because he wanted to see if he could dig to China." I laughed at the silliness of my father's logic. "I made him replant every flower he dug up. As quiet as it's kept, that's probably why he likes gardening so much. Your father is a very loving and generous man, but he also likes control and can be stern and hard. However, if you're ever in a jam, he'll never leave your side."

I didn't really believe everything she said, but I took it for what it was worth. "What about Mike? What's your take on him?" I asked.

"He's just a typical teenaged boy trying to find out who he is. He's at a very impressionable age."

"So the thug thing is just an act?" I asked, looking for confirmation.

"Mike is just imitating what he sees rappers do on the television. He's lived a privileged lifestyle, and as far as I know, has never been near a bad neighborhood. His mother sees to that." I was quiet for the moment because once again I was feeling jealous. I just couldn't understand why he ended up with everything and I ended up with nothing.

"Listen, I'm going to leave my phone number with you. I want you to call me if you ever need anything or just need someone to talk to."

"Okay," I said.

"Keysha, can you do me a favor?"

"What?" I asked.

"Smile for me. You don't smile much and you have such a beautiful and warm smile."

"I really haven't had much to smile about. Smiling would mean that I'm happy and that everything is going okay, but it's not."

"It's not going right, even just a little bit?" she asked.

"Well, yeah, on the surface all of this appears to be perfect, but at times I wonder if it's too good to be true and what did I do to deserve this?"

"You see, that's the negative voice you need to work on. You shouldn't say what I did to deserve this. You should say 'I do deserve to live where I feel safe and loved.'"

"Okay, I'll work on that," I said.

fifteen

jordan and Maggie took care of the details regarding
getting my records transferred to Thornwood High School,
which was my new school. Going to a new school as a new
kid is never easy. In my case, going to two new schools in
such a short time was even more difficult. I didn't know anyone—well, I knew Mike, but he was a jackass. I didn't know
exactly where my classes were, and I didn't know which
teachers would be mean and difficult, so on my first day I
was very nervous. I was worried about the way I looked and
how people would perceive me. I was worried about my new
haircut because I knew girls talked about other girls with
short hair. I was paranoid that someone would say something mean about my pimples, which actually were looking
a lot better since Grandmother Katie had shown me how to
use Proactive Solution. But still I had some concerns about
self-image.

Thornwood High was within walking distance of the
house. I thought for sure Mike would at least walk with me,
but he had football practice at 6:00 a.m. on my first day. As
I approached the school, I saw kids hanging out in the school
parking lot. Kids were pulling up in Mustangs and BMWs,
which was unheard of at my other schools. I looked over at a

group of girls who were standing next to a silver Mercedes. I listened as they sang the lyrics to a Missy Elliott Song.

"Why don't you just take a picture, it lasts longer," said one girl who noticed me studying them. It was clear that I'd annoyed her. I walked away quickly before I ended up getting into an altercation on my first day. I walked through a set of large brown doors and searched for a sign that would point me in the direction of my guidance counselor's office. I had to stop and meet my guidance counselor, some dude named Mr. Sanders, to pick up my class schedule. I didn't see any signs so I asked a guy who was passing by.

"Excuse me, can you tell me where the guidance counselor's office is?"

"Go all the way down the hall and make a left," he said and continued on his way. I followed his directions and a short time later entered the guidance counselor's office.

"Excuse me," I said to the receptionist. "I'm here to see Mr. Sanders."

"Do you have an appointment?" she asked.

"Yes, I'm a new student. He's expecting me."

"Name," she said without looking at me.

"Keysha Wiley, I mean, it's Keysha Kendall now."

"Oh, yes. We've heard about you." I quickly caught an attitude.

"What have you heard?" I asked. She didn't answer, only looked at me as if I'd offended her.

"Are you Keysha?" A very tall Caucasian man with a round belly and thick glasses appeared from one of the offices.

"Yes," I answered.

"Well, come on in," he said with a pleasant voice. I entered his office and sat down. He shut the door and took a seat behind his desk, which was very junky. There were papers piled up everywhere.

"You'll have to excuse my desk. My student assistant is out with the flu," he said as he searched through the mountain of papers and folders on his desk.

"Here we go," he said once he found my file. He leaned back in his chair and studied it for a moment before speaking.

"The scores that have come in from your other schools aren't very impressive, that is with the exception of your literature grade. You did well in that subject." I wanted to explain the reason I did so poorly was because my mother never prepared me for school and how I was expected to become pregnant and bring a welfare check into the house, but I didn't think he would care to hear my drama.

"We're going to monitor your progress and see how well you perform academically. This is a tough school, Keysha, and the teachers here expect nothing but the best." He glanced up at me. I didn't know what to say. School for me was just a place I could go to get away from my mother. I hadn't paid attention to my grades since middle school. After I saw that my mother couldn't care less, I stopped putting forth an effort. Mr. Sanders exhaled loudly.

"Here is your schedule." He handed me a sheet of paper and began to explain it to me.

"Your math scores are very low so we've placed you in a remedial class." I cringed when I heard that. "Now this doesn't mean you have to stay there. If you can prove yourself, we'll move up to a basic math class, and if you do well there, you can move on to a class that's at the correct level.

Math is the first class that you have. Second period you're in a basic science class because your other school didn't offer a science program. Third period you have gym, fourth period you have study hall, then lunch, social studies and finally literature. Is that okay?"

"Do I have a choice?" I asked.

"No, you don't," he answered me honestly. "But I'll tell you the same thing I tell all of my other students. School is what you make of it. If you don't put forth an effort, you're going to get poor results. You're responsible for the decisions you make regarding your education."

"I understand," I said.

"Come on, I'll show you where your locker is and then walk you to your first class so that you don't get a tardy slip."

When I walked into my math class, everyone stopped what they were doing and looked at me. Mr. Sanders spoke with the teacher briefly, and then I was instructed to sit next to this chick who was wearing all black. I mean, she was the strangest-looking white girl that I'd ever seen. Her hair was raven black, her eye shadow was black, her lipstick was black and her fingernail polish was black. She had multiple piercings in both ears, her bottom lip was pierced and all of her earrings were black. The girl looked like the daughter of Morticia from *The Addams Family,* but she was nowhere near as sexy or as cool as the character Morticia. I cautiously sat next to her because I didn't know if she was diseased or something. Shortly after Mr. Sanders left, the teacher gave me a math book and opened it up to the section we were going over. She told me to follow along, so I took out my math notebook and a pencil. The class was studying basic addition and subtraction.

"Hey, girl," whispered the chick wearing all black. I nervously glanced over at her. She stuck out her tongue and flicked it back and forth against her lips, making an odd noise. Her tongue was pierced, as well. *This chick is crazy as hell,* I thought to myself. I looked at her clothing more closely. She had on a black top, with black jeans and black combat boots. At that moment, I told myself that my problems weren't so bad.

"This class totally sucks," she whispered but I didn't respond. "I know you can hear me," she said but I continued to ignore her.

"Ahhh, you're a new chick," she said. "I'm going to have to break you in, girl." I was horrified at the thought of exactly what she meant by that.

The bell rang and I pulled out my course schedule to see what room my science class was in.

"Let me see your schedule," asked the girl. I hesitated.

"Come on, let me see the damn thing. I'm not going to eat it." I was still hesitant.

"Look, you're new, right?"

"Yes," I said.

"That means you don't have a frigging clue as to where you're going. Let me see your schedule and I'll tell you which way to go." I handed it over to her. She began to bob her head up and down.

"Oh, cool. We have the next four classes together."

"You're kidding, right?" I asked.

"Nope. Looks like that jackass Mr. Sanders thought you

were going to be a problem child so he stuck you in all of the classes with problem kids."

"How do you know that?" I asked.

"Because only the problem kids get low test scores and end up in a classroom full of rejects. Like you and me." I looked at her like she was crazy.

"I'm Liz." She stuck out her hand for me to shake it. It was the first time I'd noticed that all of her fingers had black rings on them.

"I'm Keysha," I said as I shook her hand.

"Come on, stick with me. I'll make sure you get to your classes." We walked out of the room and into an overcrowded hallway filled with students. As we made our way through the crowd I heard other students boldly degrading Liz.

"Aaaaaa—It's God-Lizard," said some basketball jock.

"Aaaaa—It's Hillbilly Bob from Hillbilly Heaven," Liz quickly fired back.

"It's the Lizard Wizard," said another student.

"Ooh, it's Loser Lou," Liz said as she gave him the middle finger.

It was strange watching how Liz maneuvered through that crowded hallway and through all of the teasing and wise-cracks. I felt bad for her and began to think that she was misunderstood, just like me.

We entered the science room and I followed her to the back table and sat next to her on one of the stools. We were the first students in the class.

"Look, I need a lab partner, so what do you say? You and

I can be partners." I was hesitant at first because I wasn't sure that I even wanted to be around her.

"Look, you're new. No one is going to pick you and since I don't have a partner, the brilliant science teacher is going to pair us up anyway. So let's just cut the middleman and be partners."

"What's up, Lazy Liz?" said some guy who had just walked in.

"Bite me! Groovy Grover," Liz shot back.

"Groovy Grover?" I laughed out loud.

"Yeah, that's Garret Groover. He's a complete idiot. Don't pay him any attention."

"Girl, I'm not trying to get any of your fleas," said Grover. Liz gave him the middle finger and stuck her tongue out at him.

"Look, just sit someplace else. If you don't want to be my partner then I don't care. Just go and sit someplace else and leave me alone," said Liz.

"No," I said. "I'll be your partner." I felt sorry for her.

"Cool, we can both flunk the class together." She laughed and so did I.

sixteen

"SO where are you from?" asked Liz. We were now on the way to lunch together. There was nothing feminine about Liz. She walked like a man and talked like a man and had a very strong presence about her. Regardless of the nasty comments a few students made about her, Liz couldn't have cared less, and I suppose I was drawn to her because of her strength. She was strong in ways that I didn't think I was.

"Chicago," I said.

"Really? What side of the city?"

"South side," I answered her.

"Cool. I used to live on the north side a few years back. Up in the Ravenswood area. I still have a lot of friends in that part of town. They're much cooler than these stuck-up rich kids out here." We turned left down another corridor and I could see the cafeteria ahead of us. "So how did you end up at this school?"

"It's a long story," I said.

"Hey, I've got nothing but time," Liz said as she held the cafeteria door open for me. The place was noisy and packed with kids.

"Come on, the line is over here." I followed Liz and stood in line.

"The pizza sucks. Never eat it because I think they spit on it. The fries and burgers are good but never, under any circumstances, eat the fish sticks. If you do, you'll spend the afternoon with a bad case of the runs."

"Eeew," I said.

"Exactly," Liz responded. "The people in this school are so lame. The cheerleaders are way too damn catty. The jocks, or the jockstraps as I call them, are completely into their bodies. They're all brawn and no brains, if you know what I mean."

"Yeah, my brother is like that," I said, thinking about the incident I had with Mike yesterday.

"You have a brother who goes here?" Liz asked.

"Yeah, his name is Mike Kendall."

"You're kidding me?" Liz asked completely surprised.

"No. Why did you respond like that?"

"The kid is only a freshman, and he is one of the most popular kids on campus. He came into the school and broke the sprint record for the fifty-yard dash. The old record was 5.5 seconds and he ran it in 5.3 seconds. The football and track coaches were on him like flies on shit. I heard that he's the only freshman on the varsity football squad."

"I don't know much about all of that," I admitted.

"Well, just FYI for you. He thinks everyone likes him, but it's only because of his speed and the fact that your dad works for the hottest radio station in town. People have been blowing his head up because they're hoping to get some free concert tickets or something."

"Does he know kids are just using him?" I asked.

"I don't know. Maybe he does and maybe he doesn't. Either way, the guy is popular. It's practically unheard of to be a freshman and playing football on the varsity squad."

Once we got our food, I followed Liz around the cafeteria to a table filled with other students who were dressed like Liz. Everyone had piercings, spiked and multicolored hair, and damn near all of them wore black.

"Yo, listen up." Liz got everyone's attention.

"This is Keysha, she's new and is going to be hanging out with us." I said hello to everyone and they just nodded.

"So what's your story?" Liz asked as she dipped a few of her French fries in a small cup of ketchup.

"My story is real jacked-up."

"Hell, honey, I've already figured that one out. Give me details." Liz leaned forward so that she could hear me clearly.

"My grandmother was arrested for bank robbery and is serving time in prison. My mother is also serving time. When she got arrested, I had to live in a group home for a while."

"Oh, man, you too? I knew that I liked you the moment I saw you. Which whacked out facility were you at?"

"I was at a place on the south side. You were in a group home too?" I asked.

"Hell, worse. I was at Sunnyville."

"Sunnyville?" I asked, confused.

"You know, the nuthouse. They wanted to evaluate my mind for a while," she said, bugging her eyes wide open as if her mind was some great mysterious phenomenon. I was intrigued by her story and wanted to know more.

"My dad was my world. I was his princess." I read Liz's expression and I could tell that what she was about to tell me was deeply personal. "He and my mom got divorced a few years back. I can't stand my mom because she's such a bitch, so I asked to go live with my dad. He was the coolest dad a girl could have. He was a soldier in the army. When the whole Iraq War thing broke out he was called to duty. To make a long story short, his unit was escorting a supply truck and they were ambushed. He was killed."

"I'm so sorry to hear that," I said, feeling really bad. I knew that it had to have been hard to know her father all of her life and then lose him.

"Anyway, when I got the news I didn't take it very well," she said, and then she just stopped talking. I waited for her to continue but she didn't. It was as if she'd locked up her feelings about it or something.

"So that's why you wear all black, because you're in mourning, right?" I asked. She suddenly slapped the palms of her hands down on the table, making a loud sound that startled me.

"See." She pointed her finger at me. "Why is it that you can see that but my all-knowing mother thought I'd flipped out and shipped me off to the damn nuthouse where a weirdo tried to fry my damn brain?" Liz was very passionate as well as angry.

"So, you're back at home with your mother?" I asked.

"Yeah, and her new boyfriend, who has moved in with us. I don't like him at all. He keeps telling my mother that I'm headed for trouble and blah, blah, blah." I didn't ask Liz any more questions because she appeared to be on the edge and I didn't want to push her. *Hell, and I thought I had it bad,* I thought to myself.

I met Liz after school, and since her house was in the same

direction as mine, we walked home together. I wanted to know more about her dad so I asked another question.

"So, what was your dad like?"

"He was cool. If I said, 'Hey, dad, can I get fifty bucks to go shopping with,' he'd give me sixty and say get something to eat, as well." Liz continued, "He was always around whenever I needed him. If my bike was on a flat, he'd fix it for me. When I wanted to learn how to swim, he'd spend his Saturday mornings teaching me how. When I was selling Girl Scout cookies, he made sure that my order sheet was always filled. I loved him. I could always depend on him for anything. He was the type of dad who always bought me something when we went shopping. Even if it was the dumbest toy ever made. He'd buy it for me because I wanted it."

"What do you miss the most about him?" I asked.

"His smile, his laugh and his scent." Liz paused in thought. "I suppose the thing I miss the most is him coming into my room at night and tucking me in. I know it sounds corny, but I'd lie in the bed and he'd wrap me up like a mummy and then hug me. That was the best feeling in the world." I saw Liz wipe a tear away from her eyes. I felt her pain so I hugged her.

"Ew, you're hugging Lesbo Liz," said a group of guys who were walking past us. I didn't care what the other kids thought. I just felt she could use a hug, and she accepted it.

"I hate this damn war," Liz said as she backed away from me. "I'm sorry for dumping on you like this."

"It's okay," I said. "I can understand how you must feel." We walked a little farther and finally reached my house.

"Nice house," Liz said. "It's big."

"Maybe you could come over sometime. We could sit around and listen to music or something."

Liz laughed. "Or we could get online and hang out in a chat room and see what kind of perverts are out there."

"I'm not too sure about that one," I said, laughing.

"Well, don't knock it until you try it. It's kind of fun and exciting to talk with someone who is in another part of the country or the world."

"Well, I'd better go. I'll see you tomorrow," I said. Liz said goodbye and continued on her way. I walked down my driveway toward the house feeling good that I'd met a nice person, even though she was kind of odd.

seventeen

Once I got closer to the house, I saw my father in the greenhouse planting flowers in a clay pot. He saw me and waved and I waved back. Since he was alone, I thought it would be a good time to go and talk to him. I walked across the grass and entered the greenhouse through the side door. There was a small black radio with paint spots on it on top of a small furnace that was built into the glass of the greenhouse. A song called "Quiet Storm" by Smokey Robinson was playing on the radio. I remembered the song because Grandmother Rubylee played it often.

"Hey," I said.

"Hey, how was your first day at school?" he asked as he looked over his shoulder at me.

"It was okay. It went better than I thought it would. So why aren't you at work?" I asked.

"I wanted to be here when you got home so I took off early today. I want to make sure things go well and that you get settled in and used to being here. Do you like the school?" he asked as he turned the radio down a little.

"It's okay. It's just a school," I said as I took a seat on a small chair that was near me.

"So what are you planting?" I asked.

"Mums, for the fall season," he said. "Do you want to help me place them in these pots?"

"No," I answered. The last thing I wanted to do was play in the dirt.

"Are you sure? It's very relaxing."

I chuckled because being relaxed about anything was foreign to me. Everything in my life thus far was drama and tension.

"You know, I would imagine you have a lot questions." He stopped playing in the dirt and looked directly at me. "I'll answer any questions you have, Keysha. No matter how trivial or adult they are. You have a right to know, and I'm here for you," he said. I wasn't used to someone speaking to me with a calm and soothing voice. I was accustomed to shouting and yelling to get my point across. He smiled at me, and I felt funny because his smile reminded me so much of my own and it was weird to see it on someone else's face. I was quiet for a long moment as I tried to organize all of the questions in my head.

"Let me start. I want to tell you that as a man, and your father, I'm always in your corner. I'm always on your side, and I have your best interests in mind. I want you to know that about me," he said. I swallowed hard as I thought about the first question I wanted to ask.

"Go ahead," he said. "No question is too tough."

"How did you meet my mother?" I wanted to know. Jordan pulled up another chair and sat down directly in front of me so that we could look at each other.

"I know you may find this hard to believe, but I was the

nerd in the family," he said, and I started laughing because he was a nerd to me through and through.

"I was the straight-A student who actually loved school. Unlike some of our family members, I grew up in the suburbs as opposed to the inner city. At family gatherings my other cousins, who were much worldlier than I was at the time, made fun of me. They criticized my intelligence, called me a sellout and teased me about my lack of street sense. My cousin Simon was the ringleader, but for some reason I envied him, because no matter how crazy and cocky he was, he seemed to always be able to get the prettiest girls. By the time I was twenty-one years old, I was a college student with a healthy appetite for a good party. I'd been square all of my life and going away to college helped me out of my shell. I'd only gone to a few parties, because at my core I was an overachiever who couldn't stand getting anything less than a superior grade. Anyway, during spring break that year, your grandfather gave me five hundred dollars for being a straight-A student. Your grandparents loved to brag about that sort of thing, and Simon heard about the bonus money and convinced me to come and hang out with him. He said that he knew of some great parties where there would be plenty of girls. He assured me that I'd have a great time. Simon was true to his word. He took me to a jumping party. In true Simon fashion, he was able to hook up with some of the prettiest girls there. And in my true fashion, I struck out with every girl I spoke to. Eventually, Simon came up to me and said, 'There is a girl over there who wants to get to know you better.' He pointed her out to me and I thought, Wow, she's a nice-looking girl. 'Don't blow it this time by acting all nerdy,' he said. I walked over to the girl and introduced myself. I was so nervous that when I went to shake her hand I inadvertently knocked her drink out of her hand. I was a complete klutz. After I cleaned up the spill, she told me her name was Justine. I asked her how old she was and she told me that she was eighteen. A few more drinks, a little conversation and several dances later, we were really enjoying each other. One thing led to another, and we had a fling that same evening."

"So, I'm just a lust baby," I said, feeling really bad about myself. I suppose that in some weird way I was hoping that there was at least some type of relationship between him and my mother.

"Keysha, you have to understand that my mind-set at that time was much different than it is now and don't call yourself that. You're a beautiful young lady."

I wanted to say, "yeah, whatever," but I didn't. I just listened.

"The next day I woke up in Simon's spare bedroom with a massive hangover. As I got dressed, I searched my pocket and I noticed that all of my money was gone. I thought perhaps Simon was holding it for me, but as we talked about what happened the prior evening he began laughing at me. He told me, 'Fool, you never take that type of money to a house party in the hood. You let that young girl get you for five hundred big ones.' He blamed me for the loss of my cash. I got angry and demanded that he call Justine so that I could get my money but he refused to do it, stating he couldn't be responsible for getting me cut or beat up. I was so disgusted by everything that I left Simon's apartment and came back home. A few months later at a family holiday gathering I ran into Simon. Myself and a few other male cousins were hanging out in the garage shooting the breeze. Simon let it slip that he and Justine had actually set me up and split the money that your grandfather had given to me. To humiliate me even more, he announced that Justine wasn't eighteen years old, she was much younger than what she led me to believe. It was then that I realized that not only was Simon petty, but he was actually jealous and envious of me. Simon and I fell out after that. I never trusted him again or went to any other parties with him."

"So what happened after that?" I asked.

"I wanted to forget about the entire episode so I left the garage and went back into the house. I went on with my life, Keysha. I summed up the incident with Justine and Simon as one of life's lessons. I just wanted to have a good time. I wasn't thinking about the consequences of my actions. I never knew your mom had gotten pregnant that night. I was never told about it, and I don't know what the circumstances were with your mom at the time that left doubt in her mind as to who your father was. I made a bad judgment call that night. I never thought that my mistake would lead to your birth."

"So I guess I'm the poster child for unprotected sex." I was being both sarcastic and truthful.

"You're not the poster child for anything. Keysha, none of this is your fault."

"What?" I asked, not sure if I'd heard him correctly.

"I said none of this is your fault. What I did was beyond your control. I'm so sorry that I wasn't available to you as a father. I'm so sorry for anything that you've had to go through as a result of my absence." When Jordan said that I felt better.

"Tell me something about you?" I asked. "I barely know you. Like, what's your favorite color, and what is your favorite food?" Jordan smiled at me, and I smiled back at him.

"I'm not sure that I have a favorite color but my favorite food is macaroni and cheese." Jordan laughed again. His laugh made me laugh.

"I know how to cook. I could make you some if you'd like," I said.

"I'd like it very much if you made me some."

"Okay, I have another question," I said, feeling butterflies dancing in my stomach. At that moment I felt the little girl within me come forward and ask questions that I never could.

"Have your ever sat at the beach and built a sand castle?"

"I used to build them all the time when I was a boy. I learned how to do it from a guy on the beach in Miami, Florida. We used to vacation there every summer. I used to build them and pretend that I was riding up to it on my horse."

"Really?" I asked, filled with excitement.

"Yes," he answered.

"Let me ask you a question," Jordan said. "Are you happy that you know who I am now?" I didn't know how to answer that question. I had to think about it for a minute.

"I guess a part of me is glad that I can put a face and name to my father, but another part of me just isn't very sure about you."

"Okay, I can understand that. I have another question. Tell me something that you really enjoy doing."

I was about to tell him about all of the books I'd read and

how much I loved reading, but Barbara walked up and interrupted us.

"Jordan," she spoke directly to him without so much as saying a word to me. "I need to speak with you."

"Give me a minute," Jordan said, wanting to continue our conversation.

"This can't wait. I need to speak with you right now, in private." I rolled my eyes at that heifer. She didn't want or need to speak with him. She just couldn't stand the fact that I was spending time with my daddy. Barbara locked her gaze on me for a moment, and I could tell that she didn't like the fact that Jordan and I were spending time with each other. I felt as if I was competing with her and I was ready to fight her. It wasn't fair in my mind. She'd known him for years and wasn't willing to give me one hour alone with him. I began to think of mean things I could do to her. In my mind I felt there wasn't enough room for the both of us.

"I need you to help me go over my campaign literature."

"Campaign literature?" I said aloud.

"Yes, I'm running for re-election as president of the school board. There is no need for your help. It's a little too complicated for you."

Oh, no, she didn't just say that to me. I was about to snap the hell out on her, but Jordan didn't let me.

"We'll talk some more later on, okay?" Jordan said, looking at me. "I promise. I have so much more that I want to share with you. I need to tell you about the history of our family." I calmed down and agreed that it was okay with me if we spoke later on.

eighteen

Later that evening, I was sitting in my room at my desk listening to an Alicia Keys song. I loved her voice and her style. I was thinking about my Grandmother Rubylee and decided to write her a letter. I was about to pull out my notepad and begin when there was a knock at my door. I looked over my shoulder and Mike was standing in my doorway holding his football uniform. There were green grass stains all over it.

"What's up, son?" There he goes calling me out of my name again. I swear I was going to beat him down for that, I thought.

"My name isn't son," I reminded him.

"So are you into girls or what?" he boldly asked.

"Excuse you." I contorted my face into an angry expression.

"Yo, I heard that you were, like, all out in the open hugging up on Lesbo Liz. I just want to know. Are you into girls or what?"

"Go away, Mike," I said, not wanting to answer his dumb question.

"You certainly know how to pick a friend. Liz is a real whack job. She's crazy. I've heard all kinds of crazy stories about her."

"All of the stories you've heard are probably all false," I said as I got up and moved toward him.

"No, I don't think so. That chick isn't working with a full deck, you know what I'm saying?"

"No, I don't know what you're saying." I was now standing in front of him. He looked me up and down as if I repulsed him.

"Well, you two deserve each other. And just so you know, I got people watching you, girl. One false move and I'm going to hear about it." I slammed the door in his face. *Damn jackass,* I thought to myself. I went over to the radio and channel surfed until I found a station that was playing music that reflected the somber mood I was in. I sat back down at my desk and began to write my letter.

Dear Grandma,
I don't know what it's like for you being locked up but my guess is that it's no fun. I miss you. I miss hearing your voice, even though you yelled and shouted a lot. I miss lying in the bed with you and your cooking. I guess I'll never fully understand why and how you ended up where you are, but I wanted you to know that I still love you. I'm not sure if you've heard yet, but Justine is back in jail. She was arrested on some drug-related issue with an old friend of hers. When she got locked up, I ended up having to live in a group home. Being there was no picnic and I was really afraid most of the time. I was afraid of being left all alone like that. I didn't know anyone in the place, and I sort of got to the point where I didn't care what happened to me. A good thing that happened is I found my biological father. How I found him is a long story but I live with him now. He has a big house in the suburbs and I have my own room. Can you believe that? I've never had my own

*room before. Getting to know him is both easy and hard. I'm
really trying hard to let our relationship develop naturally, but
at times I get angry and mad that my life wasn't as perfect as
it could have been.*

*I have a stepbrother named Mike. He's a suburban boy who
wants to be a thug. Let me tell you, that boy doesn't have an
ounce of thug in him. I know he and his mother don't like me
very much. I don't know why they don't like me. I mean, I
haven't done anything to them. Anyway, I hope to save up
enough money to come and visit you one of these days. When
I get enough money I'll let you know. I hope you're doing well
and I hope that you write me back soon.*

Love, Keysha

I filled out an envelope and placed my perfectly folded
letter inside of it. I sealed it and placed it in my duffel bag so
that I could mail it in the morning while on my way school.

Early Saturday morning I was sitting next to Jordan in
his office. He'd pulled up a bunch of pictures on his computer screen for me to look at. The first photo was of him
as a young boy.

"I think I was about six months old in this photo," he
said. The photo was of him sitting on a bed holding a bottled
filled with milk. The only garment he was clothed in was
a white diaper. He was staring directly at the camera when
the photo was taken.

"That doesn't even look like you," I said, laughing.

"Well, that's me," he said. He clicked the mouse and another photo popped up. The next photo was of him and his
father. They were on the beach. Jordan was standing next to

a very large sand castle. His entire body appeared to be covered with brown sand. Also in the photo was another very tall and slim man pointing to Jordan.

"I was about nine years old here. That's your Grandfather Quinton. He and I actually built that sand castle."

"Wow," I said, completely amazed that we had that in common. "What happened to him?" I asked.

"He passed away in his sleep shortly after I graduated from college."

"Are you sad that he's gone?" I asked.

"Yes. He was a good man and I wish you could've known him. He would have loved and spoiled you to death. He loved kids and was a mentor in the church and at the local Boys and Girls Club. Dad was a professor who taught history."

"He sounds as if he was very smart," I said, studying the photo.

"He was the smartest man I've ever known. He loved to read. He'd read anything and the library of books he had was incredible."

"Really?" I got excited. "What happened to all of the books he read?"

"Grandmother Katie has them. When you go visit her I'm sure she'll show them to you."

He clicked the mouse again and another photo came up. This photo was a very old one. It was of an old black man wearing overalls and a hat. He was standing in a prairie field next to two mules.

"Who is that?" I asked, studying the photo. The man's skin looked like soft brown leather.

"That is your great-great-great-grandfather, Roy Tommie."

"He looks worn out," I said.

"Roy Tommie had a hard life, but he did well for a black man during that time period. He was an uneducated but very skilled man. He was a farmer and a carpenter. He helped build houses for emigrants coming in from the Netherlands in the late 1800s. As a young man he worked on an onion farm for a Dutch family who were abolitionists."

"What's an abolitionist?" I asked. I'd heard the word before but I didn't remember exactly what it meant.

"Abolitionists were people who opposed slavery. Have you ever heard of the Underground Railroad?"

"Yeah, sort of. That's the thing where people were running in the middle of the night, right?"

"Something like that. You see, abolitionists were generally people who had a strong belief that slavery was wrong. They helped slaves escape to northern states through a network called the Underground Railroad."

"Oh, okay. I understand now. So, Roy Tommie used to work for these people who were against slavery."

"Yes. Roy Tommie was born into slavery but his family ran away just before the outbreak of the Civil War. He was around six years old at the time. His parents were captured by bounty hunters. He had to survive in the wilderness on his own for five days. He continued to run north until a Dutch abolitionist family named Faulkenberg found him sleeping in their onion field. They took him and kept him well hidden from bounty hunters who came looking for him. After the end of the war, Roy Tommie stayed with the Faulkenberg family, and from them he learned how to become a skilled laborer as well as a farmer. Roy Tommie worked hard and saved up enough money to buy some land from the Faulkenberg family. He built a house on the land he'd purchased and farmed it for years. This is a photo of him around 1925. He was well into his sixties and still farming."

"Wow," I said, completely fascinated by the story. "So what happened to the land and the house?"

"Very good question. It's still in the family. The land has been passed down through the generations, and now Grandmother Katie has a house that's on the land."

"She has all of the land?" I asked, pointing back to the photo.

"No, she doesn't have that much anymore. My grandfather, Willie Curley." He clicked the mouse button again and another photo came up. It was of a man standing, in a suit. He wasn't smiling and looked as mean as the first man.

"In the late 1950s developers wanted the land to build new homes, so Willie Curley sold a large portion of it to them and used the rest of the money to build a new house and put your grandfather and my father, Quinton, through college."

"Wow," I said, feeling a sense of connection. Jordan pulled out a CD and placed it into the CD drive of the computer.

"This CD contains some old eight-millimeter film that I had converted so that I wouldn't lose it. The footage goes back to the 1950s." My dad and I sat there and watched the film. He explained who the people were and what had become of them. I was hungry for more information and more stories. He clicked on a file from the 1980s. When it opened up, a video of my dad with long, greasy hair appeared.

"Oh, hell to the no, you look stupid on this video," I said, laughing as he turned up the sound.

"Hey, back then you weren't cool unless you had a Jerry Curl."

"What are you saying?" I asked, trying to listen carefully to the video.

"I was singing the song 'Rapper's Delight' by the Sugar Hill Gang."

"Oh lord," I said, laughing hysterically as I listened to him try to string all of the words together. "So that's where Mike gets it from," I said, laughing again. I studied the clothes he was wearing.

"What kind of jeans are you wearing?"

"Those are my Sergio Valente jeans. Everyone was wearing them back then. These fashions are still around, you know."

"Why are they so tight?" I asked, but then started cracking up again when I saw him trying to do the pop lock, which I knew as a popular dance from back then. "You couldn't dance, either."

"What are you talking about? I was doing it right." He laughed.

"You're offbeat. Even I can see that—and what's up with those sunglasses?"

"Hey, those sunglasses cost me twenty-five dollars, and I looked good in them."

"You needed fashion help," I said just as the video clip ended. We laughed for a moment, and then I stopped. A feeling of sadness blanketed me. Although Jordan was a complete nerd, he seemed happy. He seemed to have a family who loved and took care of him. I loved my grandmother and mother, but they were con artists and that wasn't cool.

"What's wrong? Why do you look so sad all of a sudden?"

"Can I ask you another question?" I glanced at my hands and began to wring them. I wasn't sure if I wanted to hear the answer to my question.

"Ask," he said.

"How did you find out about me—I mean, why did you even take the blood test? You could've continued on with your life without me." He sighed before he spoke.

"Look at me," he said, but I couldn't. He tilted my chin up and I looked into his eyes. It was hard for me to do that. I felt like what he said next would determine whether I wanted to live or die. Just as he was about to answer my question, Barbara once again barged in on our private time.

"You have to get Mike to his football game. I can't do it," Barbara said. She didn't look at me or acknowledge my presence, and that really irritated me.

"Why can't you do it?" Jordan asked. He seemed surprised by her request as well as her intrusion.

"Hello," I said just so she'd look at me. Our eyes locked on each other, and I could see utter contempt for me flowing through them.

"Excuse us for a moment, Keysha. Jordan and I need to speak privately."

"What about?" I snapped at her. At that moment I wanted to fight her again. I wanted to scratch up her face and pull all of her hair out. I wanted to hurt her for not giving me time with Jordan.

"Listen you little—" She caught her words.

"Little what?" I sprang to my feet ready to set it off anytime she was ready.

"All right, that's enough. Keysha, excuse us," Jordan said.

"What the hell for?" I yelled out. "I'm tired of her always barging in when I'm trying to talk to you. She doesn't barge in on you when you're talking to Mike and neither do I. So, what's that all about, Barbara?" I worked my neck and pointed my finger in her face. She worked her neck, as well, and was about to say something that I was set to make sure she regretted but Jordan stepped between us.

"Keysha, I'm only going to say it once more. Step out of the office."

"You know what? This isn't working out," I said and left. I went into the family room and found Mike packing his duffel bag.

"What are you looking at?" I barked at him like a vicious dog.

"A little lost ghetto girl," he said and then laughed at me. That did it. I had to put him in his place. I marched into the kitchen and grabbed the wooden broom. I rushed back into the family room howling out like a woman who'd gone mad, and whacked him so hard that the broomstick snapped in half.

nineteen

"What's wrong with you, girl? Have you lost your damn mind?" Mike hollered at me as I stood before him with the broken broomstick. He wasn't hurt because of all the football gear he was wearing.

"Say another word and I swear I'll stab you in the neck with this damn broom!" Both of my hands were clutched around the broken broomstick and I desperately wanted him to say something else. I was on edge and was angry enough with him, my situation and the world to do it. At that moment I just didn't care about the consequences of my actions. I just wanted him to give me a reason to kill his spoiled ass.

"Keysha!" Jordan's voice was like a sonic boom in the room. He quickly snatched the broom out of my hand.

"Daddy, that girl is crazy!" Mike squealed like a baby.

"Keysha, go to your room now!" Jordan commanded me.

"He had it coming!" I screamed out. My words were as poisonous as a snake's venom.

"Get up to your damn room before you make me get ugly with you." I looked at the expression on Jordan's face, and I knew he wasn't playing with me. I did as I was told, but in the back of my mind I wanted to kick Mike and his mama's asses for being so mean to me.

★ ★ ★

I got grounded for a week for attacking Mike. He didn't get in trouble at all for provoking me, and I didn't like that. I felt like he and his mother could get away with treating me like I was Cinderella, and Jordan didn't notice it or refused to notice it. Jordan took away my television and radio. I could have lived without the radio, but the television really hurt.

Sunday night I was in my room because I didn't want to be bothered. I was perfectly fine being by myself because I was used to it. I was lying on my bed with my eyes closed. On the walls of my mind I saw my mother and me. I was visualizing one of the rare times that I was happy to be with her. It was a summer day and it was very hot. My mother and I were on the bus, which was overcrowded with people. I can still smell the stale odor that was wafting through the air. We were going downtown for the Taste of Chicago Food Festival in Grant Park. When we arrived, we walked around all day sampling all types of food. We had ice cream, barbecue turkey legs, pizza, fried chicken and shrimp gumbo. My stomach was so full that day. At sunset we stood near Buckingham Fountain. It was the very first time I'd seen the fountain. I found a penny on the ground, made a wish and then flicked it into the water. My wish was that my mother would be nice to me all of the time instead of just some of the time.

There was a brief knock on my door and then Mike opened it up. I looked over at him.

"What do you want?" I was still pissed off with him.

"I just wanted to let you know that my father will never love you the way that he loves me."

"Kiss my ashy black ass, Mike," I snapped at him.

"Only in your dreams," he shot back. "By the way, you should know that my mother is working on getting you kicked out of here. She feels that you're a psycho for attacking me with the broom, and I agree with her." He placed a sinister grin on his face and I felt rage flowing through me. I sprang to my feet and raced toward him. Mike quickly turned and ran away from the door just like I knew his punk ass would.

The following day at school I was telling Liz about my situation and how ticked off I was with my stepbrother and stepmother. Liz listened to me vent about it during lunch hour, and I really appreciated her for doing that.

"Do you know what I do when I feel like the world is against me?" Liz asked.

"No, what?"

"I party, girl. I mean, I really party. Sometimes you've just got to do something crazy and insane just to free yourself of all the bullshit that people shovel at you. There is a party at this teen nightclub called Tricked Out that's going on this Friday night. You should come."

"Girl, I'm busted. How am I going to go?" I asked.

"Come on, Keysha, do I have to spell it out for you?"

"What? Sneak out of the house? How am I going to do that?"

"You mean to tell me you haven't figured out how to sneak out of the house yet? Come on, Keysha, you're kidding, right?" Liz asked, surprised that I hadn't mastered the art yet.

"No, I haven't figured it out yet. I just got there," I said, defending myself.

"Okay, let me school you a little. The best way to get out of the house is from your bedroom. Don't walk around the house. You run the risk of waking someone up. Also, don't leave your party clothes in your room. Leave them in the garage inside of a duffel bag. You can change clothes once you get to another bathroom."

"You sound like an old pro at this."

"Let's just say I've learned a trick or two over the years," Liz said as she took a gulp of her soda. I guess she thought that she'd mapped out the perfect plan for me to get out of the house.

"Liz, my bedroom is on the second floor," I said. "What do you suggest I do? Jump off the damn roof?" I laughed.

"I've done it before," Liz said as if it were no big issue.

"Liz, I'm not about to jump off the roof and possibly break my damn leg in the process."

"Okay, plan B. Act like you've fallen asleep in another part of the house." Something clicked for me at that moment. I remembered that the greenhouse had a door that led outside. I snapped my fingers.

"I just figured a way to get out and back inside the house," I said.

"Cool, then you're going to come to the party, right?"

"Yes," I said, feeling as if I deserved to go out and have a good time. In my mind, I truly believed that. After all I'd been through in the past several months, going out and having a good time was exactly what I needed.

"Now, Liz, there will be cute guys at this club, right?" I

wanted to be sure Liz wasn't taking me to some alternative lifestyle hideaway.

"The place is going to be crawling with guys from our school as well as other schools in the area. I'm telling you, Tricked Out is the spot. If you can't pull a guy or girl, depending on how you get down, then you need to go and live in a cave for the rest of your life."

"I am only into boys," I clarified my orientation for her.

"So." Liz leaned in closer to me. "You're not a virgin are you?"

"No," I answered. Liz placed a sinister smirk on her face. I could tell she was about to fire off a bunch of questions. She wanted to get all up in my sexual history as if she were studying for an exam.

"How old were you when you first did it?"

"Last year when I was fifteen it was my first time."

"You ever give a guy oral sex?" she asked. I guess she thought her question would shock me or make me feel uncomfortable but it didn't. My ex-boyfriend Ronnie and I had done a lot of things.

"Yes," I said, glaring at her. I wanted her to read my facial expressions well. I wasn't afraid of her questions.

"Has a guy ever gone down on you?" she asked.

"Yeah, plenty of times," I answered her. But now I had a question for her.

"My turn," I said. "You ever got down with a girl before?"

"I've done both," she answered.

"So, which do you prefer? Guys or girls?" I wanted to know.

"I consider myself to be bisexual. I like what both sexes can do for me.

"Have you ever been with a girl?" she asked. I placed an angry expression on my face.

"Oh, hell to the no, I just don't get down like that," I answered.

"Have you ever considered it or thought about trying it?" Liz asked, pressing the issue.

I was about to answer with a resounding "no" but I stopped and thought about the question before I answered. "Well, the thought has crossed my mind but I'd never act on it." Liz smiled at me.

"You're going to have a damn good time at the club Friday night."

"I plan to," I said boldly. At that moment the bell rang and we had to go to our next class. As I walked out into the hallway I thought about going home and standing in front of the mirror so that I could work on my dance moves. After all, it had been a minute since I'd gone out, and the last thing I wanted to do was hit the dance floor looking all stiff. I laughed to myself as I continued on. *I'm going to look hot out on the dance floor. I'm going to burn the memory of my hips and sensual movements into the minds of all the boys at the club.*

When I got home from school, no one was there. I hadn't been in the house a good five minutes when the phone rang. I answered it. It was Jordan.

"I see you made it home," he said.

"Yeah, I'm in here," I answered him.

"Are you okay? You're not afraid are you?"

"No. My mother started leaving me in the house alone when I was eight or nine," I answered him condescendingly. He was quiet after I said that. I guess he didn't like hearing the truth.

"Okay, Barbara will be there in about a half hour."

"Whatever," I said.

"I want you to work on building a better relationship with her," Jordan said.

"I don't see why. She wants me to disappear and you know it." He was silent again for a long moment.

"Listen, if we're going to make this work, we've all got to be willing to put forth an effort."

"I'm not the one you need to be telling this to." I couldn't help speaking my mind to him. I mean, he was coming at me like I was the damn cause of all the drama. I came to the house being as nice as I could be and both Barbara and Mike came at me all twisted.

"We'll talk when I get home," he said and then hung up the phone.

I walked upstairs and noticed that the door to Mike's bedroom was open. I walked toward his room and peeked inside. To my surprise his room was rather clean. In fact, it was too clean. Mike was a neat freak. As I glanced around his tidy room, I noticed that his computer was on. Since no one was home, I decided to see what Web sites he'd been to. I sat down at his computer and hit the button for Internet Explorer. I looked at his favorites list and saw that he had a personal Web page on MySpace. I opened it up and saw that he had a photo of himself without a shirt on. Next

to the photo was a little information about him. It said that
he was eighteen years old, which was a lie. He listed his city
and state correctly. Under the heading "About Me" it read:

Im a gangsta u c. Im Mad funni two. I Lov two go out
and party—drinking and smoking ain't my scene-hey
I'm doin' my thang, sun. Da Gurlz luv err thang I got, I
gotz dat six pac cuz i workout err day. i play football im
fine az hell an I keepz ma pockits full of kash. Soo im
sayin for all ya cuties out dare if ya think ya can handle
da kid holla @ me.

Under the heading of "Favorite Movies" it read, *Scarface,
Carlito's Way, Boyz n the Hood* and *Menace II Society.* I noticed that he also had a blog. When I saw that, I felt an exquisite rush of vindictiveness pulse through me. I decided
to post a new blog to all of his friends. The title of it was,
"I'm a spoiled punk-ass suburban boy who is only thirteen
years old."

After I posted a real ignorant blog, I scrolled down to the
bottom of his page and peeped that he had close to three
thousand friends linked to his page. I decided to click on the
first picture that I saw, which was of some guy from Philadel-
phia. When his page came up, the song, "Hot In Herre" by
Nelly began to play. I noticed that he'd posted a video on his
page. I clicked another button to turn Nelly off and clicked
the button for the video. The boy had videotaped himself
dancing in his bedroom without a shirt on. I watched him
as he sensually and rhythmically moved to the song "Con-
fessions" by Usher.

"Damn," I said aloud. "He is so fine." I watched the video

several times before I'd had my fill. I copied his Web address and e-mailed it to myself so that I'd be able to find his page again.

I went into my bedroom and shut my door. I pulled out several outfits and finally settled on some Phat Farm jeans and a belly top that exposed my flat and sexy chocolate stomach. I placed the clothes and some accessories in a small duffel bag and rushed out of my room to hide it in the garage so that I'd be able to get it once I'd sneaked out of the house on Friday night. I decided that it would be best to play the role of daddy's little girl and apologize to Jordan and explain that the reason I snapped out on Mike was because I wasn't raised properly. My plans centered on making him feel guilty for not being around during my childhood. I didn't see any harm in using guilt to my advantage. In my mind, I knew that I could pull it off. After all, my mother and grandmother were some of the best con artists around. I wasn't going to mention the party because I didn't want him to get the idea I was pulling one over on him. I wanted him to think I was genuinely sincere, even though I wasn't.

My guilt-trip con worked better than I thought it would. By the end of the week, I had Jordan apologizing to me. It was such a rush to know I'd pulled one over on him. Friday during school, Liz and I mapped out our plan. I told her that I probably wouldn't be able to escape from the house until around eight o'clock in the evening. Once I got out of the house I was to grab my duffel bag and go over to her place. From there we'd head out to the club. I hung out in Jordan's office all evening pretending to read a book. Before he went to bed, he came into his office to say goodnight.

"Are you still reading?" he asked.

"Yup, I love reading. I've never read *Moby Dick* and so far it's really interesting."

"So, what do you think of Captain Ahab?" he asked me. I hadn't actually read the book so I didn't know who the hell Captain Ahab was, but the name sounded crazy as hell, so I took a huge gamble.

"That fool is crazy," I said, smiling at him. I must not have been too far off because he smiled back at me.

"He had an obsession with that whale." He was about to go into details but I stopped him.

"Don't tell me the story, Daddy. Let me read it first," I said, smiling at him really hard. He once again fell for my con, hook, line and sinker.

"You got it," he said. He walked over to me and kissed me on top of my head. "Goodnight," he said and went back upstairs and into his bedroom. I looked at a clock situated on the bookshelf and noticed that it was eight-thirty.

"Damn," I said. "I hope she hasn't left yet." It was hard for me to tell if Liz had given up because Jordan had taken my cellular phone. I had to give it to him when he said that my privileges were going to be taken away for a week, and he meant a full damn week.

Once I was confident that he and Barbara had gone to bed, I skillfully moved toward the inside greenhouse door. Once I opened it and was inside of the greenhouse, I moved through it quickly and exited out the outer door. I rushed across the driveway to the detached garage. I opened the door, grabbed my duffel bag and rushed off toward Liz's house. Once I was a good distance away from the house, a car pulled up beside me.

"Are you looking for a ride, girl?" I looked to my right and saw Liz driving a black PT Cruiser.

"Girl, where did you get this car?" I asked, walking around to the passenger side. She unlocked the door and let me in.

"Don't worry about it," she answered.

"Do you even have a driver's license?" I asked.

"No, but I drive very well," she said, laughing as we sped off into the night.

"Seriously, Liz. This car isn't stolen, is it?" I asked nervously.

"Now do you honestly think that if I was going to steal a car my first choice would be a goddamn PT Cruiser?"

"Hell, I don't know," I said.

"Well, for the record, if I were going to steal a car, it'd be a Jaguar or something like that," Liz said as she merged over to make a right-hand turn.

"Okay, once again. Where did your crazy ass get this car from?"

"You're such a nervous broad." She chuckled.

"I'm waiting for an answer. I'm not trying to go to jail with you."

"Girl, relax." She placed her hand on my thigh. I looked at her hand and then she removed it.

"It's my car—well, it's really my dad's, but my mother said that I could have it. When I get my license this will be my car. Do you feel better now?" Liz asked.

"Yes, much better," I answered.

"We can go back to my house so you can change clothes."

"What about your mom? Isn't she going to freak out about you driving this car without a license?"

"She's working the night shift and doesn't get home until about one o'clock in the morning. By the time we get back she'll never know that it was even out of the garage."

"What about her boyfriend?"

"What about him? When she works the night shift he hangs out."

About an hour later, Liz and I arrived at the nightclub, which was packed with partygoers. We paid our admittance fee and walked down a long, dimly lit corridor. The walls were painted black and had various concert posters of popular recording artists matted to the walls. Once we arrived at the end of the corridor, we made a sharp left and entered a room as large as our school's gymnasium. Rapper Kanye West's voice was blasting through speakers.

"Come on, let's walk around the club to check out the action." I could barely hear Liz over the noise but I understood her enough to follow her through the dense crowd of people. It was exciting being around all the dancing and music. I felt like I'd been missing out on so much, but I was definitely about to make up for lost time. Club Tricked Out had some seriously fine-looking boys. I felt a lot of eyes on me as I moved around the club, and a few times the boys would get close and whisper things like, "Let me get your number" or "Can we hook up?"

"Look, there is an empty table that we can grab," Liz said

as she pulled my hand and led me to the table. Now that I was seated, I looked around and took in the decor in more detail. The bar was on my left. Suspended above the bar was an iron cage with a girl dancing inside of it. She wasn't moving all that well, and I began to think to myself that if I were in there I'd put on a pretty good show. The DJ booth was to my right. Next to the DJ booth was the mechanical bull thrill ride. I watched as some guy tried to hold on for as long as he could until he was tossed safely off onto a heavily padded mat below the machine. Directly in front of me was a large dance floor filled with bodies dancing in wild abandon and brushing against each other sensually. The place was a beautiful spectacle of youth, beauty and untamed energy. You could feel a sense of magic in the air. I was ready to dance and was eager for someone to ask me. Then within a matter of moments a cute boy walked over to where we were sitting.

"I know I'm the one you're looking for," he said as he undressed me with his eyes. I felt a bolt of sensual energy tickle my nerves in the sweetest way.

"What are you? A mind reader or something?" I smiled at him.

"Come on, Keysha, let's dance," Liz said, pulling me away before the guy could even respond back to me.

"Damn, Liz, slow the hell down. That boy was fine," I shouted, but she couldn't really hear me because we were now directly under the speakers. Once I was out on the dance floor, I looked into her eyes and waited for an explanation of her behavior. She drew herself closer to me and spoke purposefully in my ear.

"His girl just walked in with her crew," she said. I looked back in the direction of the cute guy and sure enough he had his arm looped around another girl.

"She and her girls would've been all over you for talking to him. I've seen them in action before," Liz said. "He loves it when his girls fight over him. I almost got into a fight with the girl with the short hair. I could have easily kicked her butt but she backed away."

"Damn, good looking out, girl," I said. "The last thing I need to be involved in tonight is a fight."

"Come on, let's find another seat." Liz and I looped around the club several times before we finally found a seat near the mechanical bull.

"This placed is packed tonight," Liz said, smiling at me. I smiled back, and for the first time took a good look at what she was wearing. Of course she was wearing all black. She had on a short black skirt with a cute matching black V-neck shirt that hugged her body. Her legs were long and muscular and were in need of a pair of stockings, but Liz still looked attractive.

"Girl, I'm so glad that you told me about this place. I'm going to be here every weekend," I proclaimed as I got caught up in the energy of the atmosphere. I focused my attention back on the dance floor and watched as some girl worked her behind in front of the guy she was with. I could tell he was impressed by the way she moved. I thought I could move better than she could and was looking forward to teasing the imagination of the first cutie who asked me to dance.

"She isn't all that." Liz was apparently looking at the same girl. "She isn't even doing the booty bounce right. It's supposed to go like this." To my surprise, Liz had a whole lot of rhythm for a white girl.

"Girl, where did you learn how to move like that?" I asked with a teasing smile.

"What, you think white girls can't get down? Please, I can do my thing with the best of them." She chuckled. "Hold still for a minute," Liz said as she fixed a strand of my hair that was out of place. "I'm going to get something to drink. Do you want anything?"

"A soda is fine," I said. I was about to give her some money but she quickly told me that she'd pay for it. When Liz stepped away, I turned my attention to the mechanical bull. I watched as a guy and girl rode it together. The girl was holding on to the guy and the guy was holding on to the bull. The machine jerked and twisted them around until they both fell off of it, laughing.

"Do you want to try it?" asked Liz, who had just returned with my drink. I took a few gulps of it before I answered.

"I'd love to try it," I said. "Let me see how much it costs?"

"Don't worry. There is no charge. It's free to ride. Come on, we'll go stand in line." We watched as two other people enjoyed the thrill of the ride.

"Either I'm thirsty as hell or this drink is just damn good," I shouted so that Liz could hear me. I drank the rest of my soda then began to groove to the rhythm of the group Black Eyed Peas.

"Okay, it's your turn. Have fun," said Liz. I took off my shoes and walked out to the bull. I had a hard time mounting the apparatus, but when I finally did I felt a sense of freedom and independence I'd never felt before. Just as I was positioning myself for the ride of a lifetime, Liz hopped on behind me and locked her hands around my waist.

"Liz, what are you doing?" I shouted out but she couldn't hear me. The ride started and I had to hold on. We were spun around in circles and then the bull began shaking violently and I could feel my behind giggling violently. It was an embarrassing, yet wonderful feeling. As we spun around in a different direction I noticed that a bunch of guys were cheering us on.

"Wooooo!" they howled out at the sight of Liz and me riding the bull together. I couldn't help but laugh and smile as Liz clutched my waist harder. I thought for sure I was going to fall off but Liz somehow kept me balanced and on the damn thing. Around and around we went until we were flung off and thrown into the pit. I landed on my back and Liz landed on top of me. We were both laughing hard as the guys continued to shout and howl.

"We gave those guys one heck of a show, now didn't we?" Liz said as she maneuvered herself to her feet, pulled her skirt down and then helped me up.

"No wonder they were howling out. Your underwear was showing," I said.

"And," Liz said as if it were no big deal.

"Never mind," I said, not really caring. I was too busy enjoying the buzzing that was rushing through me. I suddenly felt very alive and as if every nerve in my body was being strummed gently like a harp. It was such a sweet feeling I'd never felt before.

"Girl, that bull ride did something to me," I said as we left the bull pit.

"Yes, it does awaken the senses," Liz admitted. At that moment the song "Bootylicious" by Destiny's Child came blaring through the speakers, and Liz went wild.

"I love this song." She began dancing around slowly and sensually. She moved her body up and made her behind bounce.

"You are so crazy," I said. I looked up at the dancing cage, which was empty, and suddenly I wanted to get inside it and act wild. I wanted to see and tease every guy in the place. I wanted them to see me and want me but not be able to reach or touch me. Without even thinking twice about it, I moved over to the bar and asked to get inside. One of the very muscular and very strong bouncers lifted me up and helped me get inside the cage. He was about to close the door, but then Liz joined me.

"Come on, we're a tag team," she said, and I laughed. I was pleased that she followed my lead and wanted to continue to act crazy and wild.

"You are so insane but I like that about you," I shouted over the noise of the music. We were both lifted up and suspended in the air. I clutched my fists around the bars of the cage and popped and jerked my body and moved like I'd never moved before. I was completely lost in the music, when suddenly I began to feel incredibly aroused. I don't know if it was the exhibition I was putting on or the cheers from all of the guys below glaring up at me. I'd never been so turned on in my life. Then the room seemed to be moving in slow motion. I wanted to be touched so I began to touch my stomach and tug on my clothes as if I were going to take them off in front of everyone. I don't know why, but I felt like a seasoned exhibitionist. The next thing I knew, Liz had placed her hands on my shoulders and I felt as if I was melting. I couldn't believe that I was aroused by a girl's touch. I suddenly felt very confused. I removed her hands from my shoulders and kept dancing. A moment later, Liz placed her hands on my hips and pressed her body against my back. An exquisite sensation washed over me that was both titillating and perplexing. A wisp of her breath blew on my neck, and goose bumps leaped up on my skin. Guys continued to howl out, and I knew that they were enjoying the impromptu show. I glanced down at all the boys and froze up when I saw my brother, Mike. He was glaring at me with eyes that were asking a thousand questions. I gathered myself as best as I could and pushed Liz off me. I felt very strange. I felt as if something wasn't exactly right with the way I was feeling. The way my body was responding to Liz's touch frightened me. I turned around to face Liz. My vision started getting blurry on me. I thought I was about to faint again. Liz was moving very seductively and for some reason her movements started making me feel dizzy.

"Liz," I called to her and she approached me. I wanted to tell her that I wasn't feeling right but my words got trapped in my throat. She thought that I was encouraging her to keep it up. She was all over me, and I felt horrified by it because I liked it. At that moment, I felt as if I was not me. I felt as if I was out of my body looking at myself doing things that I never thought or believed I would do. I finally spoke in Liz's ear.

"I need to get out," I said.

"Why? This is so much fun. Come on, you're into it," she

said and kept dancing. Thankfully the song was ending and we were let back down. Once we were back on solid footing, Liz said, "Woo, girl, you're so hot!" She was glancing at me as if she wanted to kiss me. I didn't understand myself at that moment.

"I need a drink," she said and excused herself. I found an empty seat and sat down. My brother came up to me.

"What are you doing here? You're grounded until tomorrow." I just looked at him with an incoherent glare.

"When Dad finds out he is going to go through the roof. You're so busted," he said. I could hear his words but I felt as if I had trouble fully understanding him. Something was definitely out of place. I touched him, and his skin felt really silky. It was a wonderful feeling.

"Wow, you have such soft skin," I said. Mike studied me for a long moment.

"You are so smashed," he said. "What are you on?" he asked, but I couldn't answer him. At that moment I only wanted to find Liz. I was missing her and needed to know her whereabouts.

"Where is Liz?" I asked. Mike didn't answer me.

"You need to leave," he said.

"Where in the hell is Liz!" I shouted at the top of my voice.

"I don't know," he said. I got up and walked around to search for her. I don't recall how long I'd been walking or at exactly what point I exited the club, but somehow I ended up sitting on the hood of someone's car. I placed my face in my hands to try and pull myself together. I was having difficulty remembering why I came outside in the first place. I got up and started walking deeper into the parking lot.

"Hey, baby, you looking for a party?" I heard someone behind me ask. I turned around and there were three guys glaring at me.

"What party?" I foolishly asked.

"We're having a party right here in the parking lot," he said. I didn't care about his party. I only wanted to find Liz, so I began walking again. Off in the distance I saw two silhouettes. One silhouette appeared to be strangling or choking the other figure.

Whoa, I thought to myself as I tried to wrap my thoughts around what my eyes were seeing.

"Did you get the job done?" I heard a male voice ask as I got closer.

"Yes," I heard a female voice say. I think it was Liz.

"Come on, girl, you want to party with us." The guy grabbed my arm and started pulling me away.

"Am I supposed to go with you?" I asked. My mind was in a fog. "Liz, baby, why did you leave me in there? Don't you know how much I need you?"

"Yeah, girl, my name is Liz. That's right, keep calling me Liz." I heard a bunch of guys laughing.

"What's so funny?" I asked, but before I could get an answer I collapsed.

"Damn it. It's the first day on my new legs," I said.

"Open your legs," I heard a male voice say.

"Why?" I asked. I managed to get back to my feet. I couldn't see clearly and my vision was very blurry. I started walking again but I'd only taken about three steps and collapsed to the ground again between two cars. For some reason the ground felt as soft as a pillow and I was suddenly sleepy. I lay down and rested. I last thing I remember was someone yelling, "Get away from her!"

twenty

when I woke up, I was in my bed fully clothed, and I had no idea of how I'd gotten there or why I was sleeping with all of my clothes on. I felt as if someone was inside my head smashing the walls of my skull with a sledge hammer. I had a migraine headache that was out of this world. As I became more aware of my surroundings, I could hear muffled voices arguing.

"What in the world happened to me?" I said aloud as I sat up in my bed. I looked around my room and, for a brief moment, I recalled sneaking out of the house to hang out with Liz. I knew that we went out, but the last thing I remembered was riding the mechanical bull with Liz. All of my other memories were very vague and unclear. The urge to puke was strong so I got out of bed and made my way to the toilet just in time. I remained on my knees puking for a good five minutes. I felt as if I'd been kicked in the gut by an angry horse.

"You know, I've never heard them fight like this before. If my parents get a divorce because of you, I swear I'll kill you my damn self," Mike said angrily.

"Get away from me, Mike, I'm not in the mood today," I said as I tried to remember what day it was. I puked again. I scratched my scalp with my fingertips and tried to remember what happened. I kept seeing flashes of myself riding the bull with Liz, but nothing more. I moved over to the faucet and turned it on so that I could wash my face and brush my teeth.

"You do realize how very wrong things could have gone for you last night?" Mike asked.

"Gone wrong?" I asked, confused.

"Last night," he said as if I should've known. "You don't remember, do you?"

"Remember what?" I looked at him, confused. There was a long moment of silence between us.

"What do you think happened to you?" he asked. He appeared to be fascinated with me for the moment.

"I know that I went out with Liz. I'm assuming that I snuck back in the house and was so tired that I didn't take off my clothes," I said. It sounded like the most logical explanation. I looked into his eyes and saw that my account of events was way off. I suddenly felt as if I were in a dream, falling backward into darkness.

"Aww, man, you were so fried, you don't even remember what you were doing?" Mike had a perplexed look on his face. "You have no idea of how much trouble you've gotten yourself into or how you—"

"You can't scare me, Mike, so don't even try it," I interrupted him. My stomach started doing flips and I had to puke once more.

"Here, let me help you," Mike said, handing me a warm face cloth.

"Thanks," I said.

"You looked like you were doped up last night."

"Doped up? What the hell are you talking about? I don't do drugs."

"Sure, you don't do drugs." Mike didn't believe that I was telling him the truth. "Whatever you were on, it had you all whacked out. I'm the one who brought you home and Dad is the one who put you in bed. You were so out of it that you thought Dad was Estelle."

"Estelle," I said, wondering why I would have thought that.

"I think you were hallucinating. By the way, who is Estelle?"

"My aunt. She passed away earlier this year."

"Oh, sorry to hear that."

I paused in thought for a moment as I tried to remember what happened to me. Again, I could only see quick flashes of what had gone down. I did remember feeling very aroused, and I didn't understand why.

"Mom and Dad know about you sneaking out of the house and your dope problem."

"I don't have a dope problem," I said as I exited the bathroom.

"Yes, you do, and you'd better get help for it because that just isn't cool." Mike didn't say anything else. He just went into his bedroom and shut the door. I began walking down the stairs but stopped midway so I could sit and listen to Jordan and Barbara argue about me.

"You gave it a shot, okay. I'll give you credit for trying to correct a mistake, but at this point you have to toss in the towel, Jordan."

"She needs help, Barbara. She doesn't need another person to turn their back on her," Jordan argued.

"You can't save her, Jordan. She's too far gone. If she stays in this house, she's going to ruin everything we've worked so hard for. She has to go."

"And where do you suggest she goes? She has no other family."

"I don't care where she goes as long as she leaves this house. We can call that social worker back and tell her that we tried but we can't deal with her. Let her go back to the group home until her mother can come for her."

"Barbara, I'm not sending her back there. She's been through enough already," Jordan countered.

"And what about us? Huh? What about what she's putting Mike and me through? She's using drugs, Jordan. My God, are you fully comprehending what this means? We're going to have to hide all of the valuables. She may let her drug dealer break into our home. Anything could happen."

"I know that she has some problems, but I felt as if I was getting through to her. I felt like we were able to connect last week. She's a part of me, Barbara, and I can't change that."

"She's playing you for a complete fool, Jordan, and you're too damn blind to see it."

"I'm not blind," he snapped back.

"Jordan, she acted nice to you all week so that you'd let your guard down, that's all. I'll bet you she planned how she was going to manipulate you in order to sneak out of the house."

"She wouldn't do that to me," I heard him say.

"She already has, Jordan."

"Look, I'm going to put a special lock on the basement doors so that she can't sneak out at will. There are going to be severe consequences for what she's done, but I'm also going to look into getting her some help."

"Why don't we just send her back, Jordan?" I could tell that Barbara was pleading with him.

"Because it's not her fault. It's my fault," he answered. I was like, whoa, when I heard that one. I couldn't believe that he actually felt that responsible for me.

"If she does one more thing, Jordan, I swear to you, our marriage is going to suffer because of it."

The next thing I heard was hard footsteps and a door slamming. I swallowed hard and then stood up. I wanted to defend myself and let Jordan know that I didn't do drugs and how I didn't understand what had happened to me. It was the first time that I really wanted to open up to him and explain myself. Hell, I even wanted to apologize to him for manipulating him just as Barbara knew I had. I'd never seen nor heard anyone stand up for me like Jordan had.

I walked down the rest of the stairs and into the kitchen. I stood at the archway between the kitchen and the family room and stared at my father. He was sitting down on the sofa glaring directly at me. His eyes were red with rage, his jaw was tight and his chest was still heaving from the confrontation he'd just had with Barbara. I wanted to tell him that there was just a big misunderstanding about me and that I didn't mean for things to happen the way that they had. I tried to speak but my words wouldn't come out of my mouth. My father's hardened gaze put the fear of God in my heart.

I felt that at any moment he was going to snap at me in a way that would scar me emotionally for the rest of my life.

"Go back to your room and don't come back down here until I tell you to."

"But—"

Jordan sprang to his feet, rushed over to me and locked his hand around my wrist. He hauled me back through the kitchen into the dining room to the staircase.

"This is not a damn game I'm playing!" His voice roared like thunder and was filled with hell's fury. It was the very first time that I felt afraid of him. I began to cry as I rushed back upstairs to my room. I wished that there was a way I could explain everything and make him believe that I was telling him the truth.

twenty-one

I didn't have any appetite, so I didn't eat dinner that night. I remained in my room and started reading *Moby Dick* to escape from the pain I'd caused. The next morning I woke up very early. I was awake before anyone else in the house. I opened my door to go to the bathroom but stopped when I saw an envelope sitting outside of my door. I reached down to pick it up and saw that a letter from my Grandmother Rubylee had arrived. I went back inside my room and shut the door. I sat down on my bed, ripped the envelope open and read her letter.

Dear Keysha,

It has taken me a while to get my thoughts together enough to write you. Prison life isn't easy, but I'm making the best of it. I'm working on my getting out of here so that I can have my freedom back. The prison guards in here aren't very nice, and the food is nasty. At night I sleep on a hard bed with bedsheets that have a sour odor. The bedsheets smell like they've been inside of a Dumpster filled with spoiled food. Adding to my misery are the large spiders that chew on me all night while I'm asleep. Sometimes I don't sleep at all. I just stare up at the ceiling and try to make myself believe I'm not in here. The prison guards tried to break my spirit but I won't let them. I'm too strong, too smart and too tough for that to happen.

I was trying to think of things you'd want to know about my life as it is now. The best I can do for you is to describe a typical day and what it's like on the inside of this place. I'm not in a prison cell like you see on television. I'm in a dorm room setting. Everyone is in a big room with a mattress and a locker. You can't hang any posters or pictures because the walls are solid white brick. The floor isn't carpeted, it's gray and made of concrete. Let me tell you, it gets bone-chilling cold in here during the winter. Prison is supposed to be about rehabilitating a person so that they can go out and function in society. However, I've run into more corruption in here than I ever did out on the streets. I've got myself a little trading hustle going on in here. One of the girls in the stockroom and another one in the cafeteria used to run the streets with me back when I was messing around with Stanback. I'm not sure if you remember Stanback. He was your grandfather but he was killed a long time ago. Anyway, my girl in the supply room makes sure that I get extra toiletries in my weekly care package so I can trade them for cigarettes or other things I may need. Believe it or not, you only get one roll of toilet paper every seven days. If you run out before then you're up shit's creek without a paddle. So women come to me when they need hygiene products and I give my girls a percentage.

When I wake up in the morning I have at least two or three women putting in orders with me. When I go to the cafeteria for breakfast, I give my order to my girl who is serving food and she gets it to my girl in the supply room who then makes sure that my weekly toiletry bag is filled with all of the right stuff.

After breakfast I head to the break room where I sit and talk to people while playing cards or some other game to take my mind off of where I'm at. Around one o'clock we get an

*hour of free time out in the prison yard. I mostly walk around
and talk to people but you have to be careful about that because not everybody around here gets along. You could easily
end up in a fight and if you get jammed up you have to go to
a hearing in front of a prison judge who then disciplines you
by adding time to your sentence. So far, I've had four alter-
cations and I've had seven months added on to my time. I've
taken on the meanest and baddest women in this place and
have whipped them all. You can't walk around this place with
fear in your eyes because the women in here will take advantage of you. From two o'clock to six o'clock, I'm in the library
shelving books. The small amount of money I make is placed
on the prison books. The money is supposed to help me start
over when I get out. It's nice doing that type of work but I
don't think it's going to serve me well when I get out of here. I
just do it to pass the time. After that I go back to the cafeteria
and eat dinner, which isn't very good. After dinner they usu-
ally have a movie for us to watch, and then after that I go back
to my locker and fill my orders. After that's done, I lie on my
back and try not to let the spiders chew on me.*

*I'm not sure how you found out who your real daddy is.
Your mama was out running the streets with so many guys
during the time she got pregnant. It sounds like your father is
a good, quality man with some money. Money is what makes
the world go around, Keysha, even in prison. So when you
do come to see me make sure you have some money for me. In
fact, I want you to send me any allowance money that you get
so that it can be put on the books for me. Since you're living in
high society now, I know you can afford to send your Grandmother Rubylee some money. In fact, I know I shouldn't be
writing this because sometimes the guards read your mail, but
I'm going to risk it. Look around your daddy's house and see
if you can find his bank account information as well as his so-*

cial security number. If you can get that information to me, I know some people who can make sure that you and I both can reap all of the benefits of a man with good credit.

Let me know when you're coming my way.
Your Grandmother,
Rubylee

I was sick after I read her letter. I couldn't believe she had the nerve to ask me to rip off my own father. I buried my face inside my pillow and screamed as loud as I could before I began crying.

twenty-two

AS I walked through the hallway to my locker on Monday morning, guys were gawking at me, and I didn't know why. I couldn't wait to see Liz so I could find out what I did, because I still couldn't remember much. I didn't see Liz in the hallway but thought for sure I'd see her in our first-period math class. When I walked into our math room, one of the students, named Lou Lopez, spoke to me.

"What's up, cage bird?"

"What's that supposed to mean?" I wasn't in the mood for any nonsense.

"Let's just say I now know why the caged bird sings." He along with several other students laughed at me, and I didn't know why. I didn't like being ridiculed because it didn't feel good at all. I didn't see Liz at all during the day so I assumed that she didn't come to school. I couldn't call her because my phone privileges had been completely taken away.

After school I had to go to the football stadium and sit in the bleachers and wait for Mike to get done with football practice so we could walk home together. Since my parents didn't trust me, I couldn't enter the house without Mike. When practice was over I walked home with Mike, who refused to speak to me. He'd recently checked his MySpace account and realized that I'd posted a very mean-spirited blog about him.

When I first posted it I didn't feel bad at all, but after learning that he actually made sure that I got home safely Friday evening, I felt like crap for doing what I did.

"Mike, I said I was sorry. How many times do you want me to apologize to you?" I asked. Mike didn't say anything, he just kept walking in front of me as if I didn't exist. When we got to the house he immediately went to the phone and called Jordan to let him know that we were both safely in the house. Mike was now my personal watchdog who was just itching for me to screw up again so that he could tell Jordan and Barbara. I went into the family room with my duffel bag, sat down on the sofa and removed my homework from the bag. Mike came into the family room and turned on the television. News reporter Angela Rivers was supplying the known details about several teenagers who became very ill after taking the hallucinogenic drug Ecstasy while at the Tricked Out teen dance club.

"Police officials are saying at this time several Thornwood High School students had to be transported to area hospitals for treatment. One of those students is said to have suffered brain damage from taking the drug," said the reporter.

"Did you hear that?" I asked Mike but he didn't acknowledge me.

"Police are saying that there is an ongoing investigation as to how students obtained the illegal drug. Police are working with the school and school district officials. We'll be reporting more on this story as the details become clearer." As Angela Rivers concluded her report, Mike glanced at me for a long moment, but didn't say a word. I could see the suspicion in his eyes.

"What?" I asked.

"I hope you're not involved in that mess," he said.

"I'm not," I quickly answered. "I don't know anything about that." I was insulted so I gathered up my belongings and went upstairs to my room.

The following morning at school, I was removing my science book from my locker when Liz finally surfaced.

"Hey, girl, I have something for you," Liz said, returning my duffel bag to me from Friday evening. I took it and stuffed it inside my locker.

"Where have you been?" I asked.

"Hell, I felt like ditching school so I did," she answered as if it were no big deal.

"What the hell happened to you Friday night? Why did you leave me?"

"Leave you? Huh, that's a laugh. You disappeared on me." At that very moment I remembered going out into the parking lot to search for her.

"No, I went looking for you, Liz." My memory was still kind of hazy.

"What's going on, love birds?" Lou Lopez teased us as he walked by. I glared at Lou with hate as he passed.

"Ooh, what's that nasty look for?" Liz asked. I focused my attention back on her.

"Look at you," Liz said, adjusting a loose strand of my hair. I didn't like her touching me and she must have sensed it. "Come on, don't be like that. You were so into it Friday night."

"Into what? I swear I barely remember anything that happened that night. Then on the news I heard about students who got sick because someone was passing around Ecstasy. My father doesn't trust me, my stepmother hates me, my brother despises me, my mother is in jail and my Grandmother Rubylee wants me to rip off my dad and take him for everything he's got. I swear, my life is so screwed up right now that I don't know what to do."

"Jeez, look on the bright side. At least the cops aren't searching the school looking for you."

"Why would they be?" I asked as I exhaled and slammed my locker shut.

"The police are here doing an investigation involving that Ecstasy scandal," Liz said. She tried to touch me again but I moved.

"I don't like it when you do that, Liz."

"What? I didn't do anything." She laughed at me as if she didn't take me seriously.

"Whatever," I said and headed toward our science class. As soon as we sat down the teacher announced that there was going to be a pop quiz.

Damn it, I thought to myself, *I haven't been following along or keeping up with reading the textbook like I was supposed to at all.*

"It's okay, we can flunk it together," Liz said. I just rolled my eyes in annoyance at her. She didn't seem to care about what I was going through, and I didn't understand why. I mean, when she was talking about how much she missed her dad, I was there for her, but now that I have a problem, she thinks my situation isn't important. As I looked at the questions on the test I knew right away that I was going to flunk it because I didn't know any of the answers. I didn't have even the slightest clue because I had a "who gives a damn" kind of attitude, just like Liz. As I sat there staring at the page, the principal and two uniformed police officers walked into the classroom. My heart began to pound and I didn't know why. Liz was summoned to go with them and my heart damn near stopped. Liz captured my gaze as she got up. Her eyes were asking a thousand questions that I didn't know the answers to. Liz never returned to class. I thought I'd see her in our next class but I didn't. There were reports and rumors all around the school about how the police and the principal were pulling students out of their classes. Then, during my lunch hour they came for me.

"Keysha Kendall," I heard an officer call my name just as I was about to sit down. I swallowed hard.

"Yes," I answered him.

"You have the right to remain silent. Anything you say can and will be used against you in a court of law." *Oh, damn, I'm being arrested, but for what? What did I do?* I felt a panic attack consume me. I began to breathe hard and wring my hands.

"What's going on?" I asked.

"You're under arrest," said an officer as he removed his handcuffs. I felt dizzy, and the next thing I knew I fainted.

twenty-three

FAINTING didn't help my situation at all, because once I was revived, I was placed under arrest and taken to the principal's office. I was so nervous that my bottom lip trembled uncontrollably. I wanted to call my mother but I couldn't. I could've called Jordan but I was too afraid to because he was so angry with me, and I knew that an episode like this would land me back at the group home for sure. I knew that Barbara would see to it this time. The two police officers left me in the care of my guidance counselor, Mr. Sanders, while they went and searched for another student.

"Keysha, you're in some very serious trouble," said Mr. Sanders. "This is what the police found in your locker once it was opened." He pointed to a large clear plastic bag with a load of pills in it.

"That's not my bag," I said.

"It was in your locker, Keysha. How did it get there?"

"I don't know but that's not my bag or pills." Mr. Sanders exhaled slowly and looked at me with judgmental eyes. I read his facial expression and knew right away that he didn't believe me one bit.

"Look, I'm just trying to help. Just tell me where you got it from?"

"I'm telling you that I don't know," I shouted at him. He picked up a file from his desk and opened it up. He didn't say anything for a long moment.

"So your mother has been arrested and is currently serving time until her court date. Your grandmother was arrested and convicted of bank robbery and—"

"Don't you bring them into this," I snapped at him. "I am not them, and I don't appreciate you trying to insinuate that I'm a criminal, because I'm not."

"Okay, Keysha. Have it your way. The police have returned, anyway. I've tried to help you but I can't if you are unwilling to help yourself."

"Her locker is the only one that had the drugs in it," said one of the officers.

"That's not my stuff," I told him.

"Does anyone else have the combination to your locker?" asked the officer.

"No," I answered him.

"Then how did this bag of drugs get in there?"

"I don't know—I have no clue." I wanted him and everyone to believe me but I saw by their expressions that they didn't.

"Come on," said one of the officers who helped me stand up. I was then escorted out of the building between classes so everyone saw me. I was placed in the backseat of the squad car, and hauled off to the police station.

Once I arrived at the station I was taken into an interrogation room for further questioning and processing. The interrogation room was very small with solid white brick walls. It reminded me of the room my Grandmother Rub-ylee described in her letter. There were no posters, no art-work or anything of that sort on the walls to give the room any life. The room felt like a tomb, and the police officers were there to seal my fate.

The police officials left me in the room all alone for a long time. I was a little feisty when I'd arrived because I knew that I was innocent and that all of this was some huge misunderstanding. They left me alone in my tomb until I calmed down. I felt as if I had no one I could depend on. I felt as if no one would come to defend me or speak up for me. I began to think about my Grandmother Rubylee's let-ter and how she described prison life. I felt my tears swelling up because I didn't want to go to jail. My body just started trembling all of a sudden and I couldn't control it. I felt as if I were coming unglued. I felt as if my mind couldn't take or comprehend what was going on.

In all honesty, I felt as if I'd just reached my crossroads. I could turn left and go down the crazy road or turn right and try to fight to prove my innocence. At that moment, the crazy route was the road I was leaning toward. In my mind, it offered me a sense of peace that I wouldn't get anywhere else. I wouldn't have to talk to anyone and I would be able to live inside of my own world, with my own rules and laws. At the very moment I was about to make my choice, I heard the door open. I looked over my shoulder and saw my father. Never in my life had I been so happy to see him, even if he did have a crazy look on his face.

"Daddy?" I said, bursting into tears. I couldn't help it. I stood up, locked my arms around his neck and buried my face in his shoulders. I was so happy to see him. I was so happy to know he cared enough to come when I thought he wouldn't. Jordan hugged me back, and being held by him for the very fist time made me feel safe.

"I didn't do it, Daddy," I said through my tears. "This is all some big mix-up."

"All right, we'll get this all sorted out," he assured me. "First I need you to calm down, okay?"

"I just want to go home with you," I said, refusing to unlatch myself from his embrace. "Please take me home," I pleaded. "Please make them leave me alone." Jordan didn't say anything, he just stroked my hair and kissed the top of my head. I cried some more. I didn't realize I had so many emotions stored up inside of me. I cried so much that I wet up the front of his suit.

"I'm sorry," I said as I finally lifted my face. He wiped the tears away from my cheeks, and we locked our eyes on each other. I wanted to tell him that I loved him. I wanted him to know that deep in my heart I truly loved him for taking the test and saving me from the group home, but a boulder was in my throat blocking my words.

"I'm going to ask you this one time and I want a straight answer. I don't care if you're guilty or innocent. All I want is the truth." I felt more tears surfacing, but I didn't take my eyes off of him.

"Were you planning to sell and distribute Ecstasy to the students at your school?"

"No, Daddy, I wasn't." My voice trembled. I could feel my lips quivering as I found the strength to answer him.

"Have you ever used or been addicted to any type of drug?"

"No, Daddy, I've never used anything. My mother and grandmother did a lot of things that just turned me off. I never wanted to be like them. I've always wanted a better life for myself, and I never thought I could until you came into my life." He searched my eyes and face for the truth.

"That is the truth, Daddy," I said, still looking him directly in the eyes. "I don't know how that stuff got inside of my locker."

"Okay, I have an attorney on the way. We'll get through this," he said.

"Do you believe me?" I asked, because I needed to know. I wanted and needed him to know that I wasn't using or manipulating him in any way.

"I'm your father, and whether you're right or wrong, I'll always be here for you," he said. "And yes, I do believe you."

twenty-four

several hours later, I learned that I was being charged with possession of a controlled substance with the intent to distribute it. Asia, a woman of Chinese descent whom my father went to undergrad school with, was the attorney he hired. Asia informed us that it was going to be a long, hard fight, especially if the batch of Ecstasy found in my locker was linked to the batch that caused a severe reaction in the people at the Tricked Out dance club. And especially since one kid actually got brain damage from the stuff.

"If she's found guilty, you should expect a civil lawsuit from the parents of the child with brain damage to follow," said Asia.

"But I didn't do it. That's not my stuff," I said.

"I know and I believe you. We just have to make a judge believe you. We do have several things in our favor. You don't have any criminal history and there is no medical file that indicates you've had addiction problems. I'm going to be honest with both of you. The prosecution is under pressure to bring someone to justice. Apparently, according to police, there has been a recent invasion of Ecstasy in this community, and they want to stop it."

"But I don't even know where to get the stuff," I said.

"That's another thing. The prosecution contends that they have a witness who says that they saw you with a man named Trinity Neophus Friday night at Tricked Out. Police say he has strong ties to the drug world."

"I have no clue as to who that is. And whoever this witness is they've found is flat-out lying."

"Were you at this club last Friday evening?" asked Asia.

"Yes, I was there, but I don't remember everything that happened. I got sick and fainted. My brother had to bring me home."

Asia exhaled. "Look, we're free to leave now. Bail has been posted, and we'll be notified of a court date in the coming weeks. Keysha, it is very important that you don't talk to anyone other than me, your father or mom about this case. Anything that you mention to friends at school can be used against you in court."

"So I need to keep my mouth shut about all of this?" I asked.

"Yes. And under no circumstances should you speak with the media. That's my job as your attorney."

"Okay," I said, feeling as if I'd somehow gotten myself into something that was way over my head.

When we arrived home it was around six-thirty in the evening. No sooner had we set foot in the house, than Barbara began snapping out on Jordan.

"Do you see now, Jordan? She's too much," Barbara began talking about me. Before, she would at least wait until I was in another room, but now she just didn't care whether I heard what she said or not. "This girl is going to rip us apart!"

Jordan sat down on the sofa in the family room. Now I wanted to be there for him. I wanted to defend and fight for him the way he'd done for me.

"I'm not trying to rip you apart," I said. Barbara's eyes became slits in her face.

"Listen, you little—"

"That's enough, Barbara," Jordan cut her off. She took her attention off me and focused back on Jordan. I went and sat down next to my daddy.

"We are going to stick together on this," Jordan said. "We're going to get through this storm—"

"You believe her, don't you?" Barbara had a shocked expression on her face. "Jordan, how can you be so blind?"

"I'm telling the truth," I said, hoping she'd understand.

"Okay, hang on a minute," Barbara said. She marched out of the room and returned with the letter that Grandmother Rubylee had written me. "I didn't want to have to do this but I guess you have to see it for yourself." She handed him the letter. "Read the highlighted part." Jordan looked down at the letter. I glanced over at it and saw that Barbara had highlighted Rubylee's request for money and bank account information.

"Do you see now, Jordan? The girl and her grandmother are plotting to clean us out! For all we know, Rubylee could be running a narcotics ring from prison, and if we're linked to it we could lose everything. The house, our lifestyle, everything!"

"Grandmother Rubylee is crazy, okay?" I said because I didn't want my daddy to think I was playing some kind of game with him.

"Why would she ask you to do something like this?" Jordan asked me. I looked into his eyes and saw nothing but pain.

"Daddy, I don't know. All I told her was that I'd found you and that you had a nice house."

"Well, now she has our address and can probably send a hit squad or something over here to take us all out," Barbara insisted. She was very passionate about her position.

"It's not like that at all," I said. "You have everything all twisted."

"Keysha, I want you to go upstairs while Barbara and I talk."

"Yeah, get upstairs, because you have a lot of work to do." Barbara's anger toward me was teetering on turning into violence.

"Come on, let's go take a ride," I heard Jordan say to Barbara.

When I got upstairs, Mike was waiting for me on the landing. We locked eyes for a moment. He didn't say anything and neither did I, but I could tell that at that moment he didn't like me very much.

"My life was sweet until you came along," he finally said. "Why are you doing this to us?"

"I didn't do anything, Mike," I said sincerely.

"I've never seen my mom go so crazy," he said, pointing to my bedroom. I looked down the hall toward my bedroom. It looked as if a tornado had gone through it.

"What did she do?" I asked as I rushed into my bedroom.

"She really lost it when she found out about drugs being

found in your locker. She demolished your bedroom," Mike said. My bedroom was a complete disaster. Every dresser drawer had been pulled out and dumped out. All of my clothes were turned inside out, and all of the pockets were hanging out of them. She even cut open my mattress and pulled out the foam. As my mind processed all of this I felt weak. I placed my back against the door frame and slid down to the floor. I closed my eyes, and placed my face in my hands.

"Why is my life such a mess?" I spoke aloud. "Why can't things ever go right for me?"

twenty-five

The following day I didn't go to school because I'd been suspended. I didn't sleep well, my stomach was sour and I felt as if I were coming down with the flu. Around midmorning I turned on the television to catch the news and to my surprise and horror, reporter Angela Rivers was doing a follow-up story on the Ecstasy problem in my neck of the woods.

"Tonight school board officials in District 411 will have to face residents who are angered and outraged that the student charged with possession of the drug Ecstasy has only been suspended and not expelled from the school. Many residents say that their quiet close-knit suburban community now has a black eye because of the drug scandal, and many of them are not happy about it."

Angela paused briefly while video interviews played of residents talking about how they wanted school officials to get rid of any student who was involved in any way with the drugs. My heart began to beat very fast and I began to panic and hyperventilate. I couldn't believe how serious the residents were about kicking me out of the neighborhood.

"The school board meeting begins at seven o'clock tonight, and many of the residents I spoke with said they planned to be there to express their views and concerns."

Angela concluded her report, and I turned off the television. I now felt sicker than I ever had before.

That evening I sat in the family room with Mike and watched the school board meeting on our local community cable channel. The meeting was held inside the high school cafeteria, and it was packed with parents and students from not only my high school but other high schools within my district. I watched as they talked about issues regarding building repairs, school supplies and funding for extracurricular activities. Everything seemed to be going fine and no one mentioned anything about the drug problem until they reached a part on the agenda that called for open comment. Then, all hell broke loose. Parents were yelling at the board members about protecting their children. One person even wanted random searches of student lockers. Then some lady stood up and attacked Barbara directly.

"Mrs. Kendall, I've heard that this drug problem didn't seem to appear until your stepdaughter began attending Thornwood High School. It is also rumored that she is the one actually behind all of this. In light of this, don't you think it would be wise for you to step down as school board president?" My heart dropped when I heard that lady ask such a mean question.

"Oh, go to hell, lady," Mike shouted at the television screen.

"Why would she ask a question like that?" I asked Mike. I

didn't like Barbara very much but I certainly didn't wish for her to be put on public display. In my mind I knew that she was going to say something negative about me and I didn't know if I could take hearing it. Barbara repositioned herself in her seat before speaking into the microphone.

"To place such a heavy blame on my stepdaughter would be unfair. Let's keep in mind that what you've heard are only allegations. She has not and never has been convicted of a crime."

"So are you saying that she didn't have the drugs in her locker?" The woman pressed the issue.

"No, what I'm saying is you're asking me about a personal situation with my family that I feel is inappropriate to bring up at this meeting."

"Get her, Momma," Mike shouted out. It was the first time that I realized just how strong Barbara was.

"However, to ease your concerns I will tell you that I believe my stepdaughter has been wrongly accused and that I do not believe she has or ever did intend to become a dope pusher. My family and I stand united with her, and we will have our day in court where her innocence will be proven beyond a shadow of a doubt."

"That's right, Mama, you tell them. They just can't push us around." Mike continued to taunt the television. My jaw hit the floor. I couldn't believe Barbara actually defended me. I was speechless and didn't know what to think. I looked at Mike, who pressed the mute button on the television.

"So do you believe me?" I asked him.

"My mom went through your bedroom like a mad woman. She thought for sure she'd find a hidden stash of something, but she didn't. This morning on my way to school she shared a family secret that I never knew about. Her older sister used to be on drugs, and she watched how it destroyed her and my grandparents. Eventually she got help, but not until after a whole lot of emotional damage. Anyway, she was glad that she didn't find anything. The fact that she didn't gave you credibility in her eyes. You have to understand something, Keysha. I may have been mean to you but I never wanted any harm to come to you. Even after you hit me with the broomstick, I wasn't mad at you because I knew that I had it coming. When I saw you at the dance club I knew something wasn't right. You weren't yourself at all. After you left me I tried to find Liz because I wanted to know what the deal was. I wanted to know why you were acting so differently. When I couldn't find her I started searching for you again. One of the guys on the football team told me you were out in the parking lot and several guys were taunting you. By the time I got back out there with the guys, you had fallen to the ground and they were about to have their way with you. That just wasn't cool. Even if I did fight with you all the time, I wasn't going to stand by and watch them violate you."

Mike paused in thought and I suddenly saw him as a completely different person. He'd actually come to my rescue when I needed help. Now that I was thinking clearly, I saw that the entire family was standing by my side. No one was going to leave me hanging.

"Thank you," I said and remained quiet for a moment. "What about you? Do you believe me?" I held my breath as I awaited his answer.

"Yeah, I believe you," he said as he turned the volume

back up. I wanted to hug him. I wanted him to know that it meant a great deal to me to have his support.

"I'm so lucky to have a kid brother like you," I said. I draped my arm over his shoulder and gave him a big hug. It felt so good to have a family who cared about me. I wanted to cry again, but I didn't because I knew Mike would think that I was way too emotional. I enjoyed that moment we had with each other and looked forward to having more of them because I knew that I'd need them, especially once the trial began.

twenty-six

shortly after dinner I went upstairs to my bedroom, which was still messed up from Barbara's tirade. I started picking up a few of my belongings but stopped because the clean-up job was overwhelming. Instead, I rested on my bed, which wasn't very comfortable but I still tried to find a good position that didn't feel too awkward. As I relaxed on my back with my eyes closed, the image of being hand-cuffed and taken to jail kept flashing in my mind. I thought I'd fall asleep easily but that just wasn't the case because my mind wouldn't shut off. Another image of a judge slamming down a gavel and saying, "You're guilty," kept replaying itself. Even though I knew I was innocent I felt that I was hexed and everything that could go wrong would go wrong during the trial and I would be hauled off to jail for a crime I didn't commit. I attempted to calm my nerves by taking several deep breaths but it had no impact whatsoever on my paranoia.

After tossing around and slapping my forehead with the palm of my hands a few times, I developed a headache and concluded that no matter how hard I tried, my bed just wasn't going to feel right. I decided to go into the spare room and sleep on Grandmother Katie's bed. Once I entered her bedroom, I relaxed my tortured body on her soft bed. I know that this is going to sound strange, but as soon as I rested my head on the pillow I felt very relaxed and my headache faded away. I think it was because the pillow coverings still had a hint of her scent, which for some reason had a soothing effect on me. I think Grandmother Katie has a presence, which lingers long after she's left. I know that sounds strange but it's true, at least in my mind it is. I closed my eyes and a short time thereafter, I drifted off into a peaceful sleep.

When I opened my eyes again it was morning. I was surprised I slept all through the night without waking up. As I became more alert I could hear the sound of raindrops splashing against the windowpane.

"It's raining pretty hard. The wind is rather high, too." The unexpected sound of Barbara's voice made me jump out of my skin. Once again she was sitting in a chair positioned in front of me waiting for me to wake up. I assumed she was waiting so that we could get into another catfight first thing in the morning. The fact that Barbara got some sort of twisted pleasure out of watching me sleep was very creepy and it made my skin feel as if there were a thousand ants crawling all over it. It was unsettling the way she could sneak up on me without my being aware of it. She was like a cat stalking a mouse. I sat up on the bed and looked at her. I didn't say anything because I didn't know what to say. I wasn't sure if I should thank her for standing up for me or prepare myself for a vicious exchange of words. Lord knows I didn't feel like fighting, but if she was looking for a confrontation, I was ready to do battle with her.

"This isn't easy for me." Barbara finally shattered the silence. "I like to have order in my life. I don't like a lot of drama and I have a difficult time dealing with change. I don't tolerate ignorance or attempts to destroy the life I've worked so hard to build and protect." Her calm tone of voice caught me off guard. I wasn't expecting her to be civil. I coiled my knees up to my chest and listened. "I destroyed your bedroom because I was certain that I'd find a stash of pills or something that would indicate you had a problem. I was also determined to prove that you were on a crusade to destroy everything I've worked so hard for."

"I'm not like that," I whispered to her.

"My heart knows that but my mind and logic are overriding what my heart knows to be true. You have to give me a little more time to adjust." There was another long and awkward moment of silence before she spoke again.

"I owe you an apology, Keysha."

"You do?" I asked, surprised.

"I judged you before I got to know you. I'm sorry I did that to you. You see, I've lived in a home with a drug user before. I know all about how abusers play tricks and how deceitful they can be."

"I'm not a drug user or a drug seller," I said, wanting to reassure her.

"I know you're not. Because if you were, by now I would have stumbled across your supply somewhere in this house or been able to detect your addiction problem." Barbara stood up and drew back the curtain and watched the raindrops fall before she spoke again. "During my freshman year of high school I looked up to my older sister, who was a junior. She was one of the most popular girls on campus. She was the party-girl type and I was pretty much a tomboy who loved sports. We had a pretty decent life. Our parents loved us, we lived in a good suburban neighborhood and we did well in school. All of our normality changed the summer before my sister was to become a senior. During that summer, she met this college guy who was attending the university that was near our home. My sister loved to brag about dating a college boy." Barbara cleared her throat. I could tell that what she was telling me was something deep and very emotional. "Anyway, my sister started hanging out at frat parties with this guy and sneaking out of the house at night to be with him. It wasn't long before he introduced her to drugs."

"Why did she take them?" I asked. "If you guys had cool parents, a nice home and weren't struggling to make ends meet, why would she want to do drugs?"

"Peer pressure I suppose. I think she really wanted to fit in with the college crowd. She started off with pills and when that wouldn't get her high enough she began using harder drugs. It got to the point where she began stealing money from my parents in order to supply her habit. When my parents discovered the awful truth, it changed everything. They placed my sister in rehab and became overprotective of me."

"Did your sister ever get clean?" I asked, wanting to know what happened.

"Eventually, but not before damaging our relationship to the point that I refused to speak to her for one full year."

"What did she do?" I asked.

"The night before my junior prom, my sister had somehow gotten out of the rehab center and came home. She arrived at our door and began begging for money. When my father refused to give her money she became irate but eventually calmed down and pleaded with my parents to let her sleep in her own bed. She begged them to let her stay and not send her back to the rehab facility. She won their trust along with mine and she was allowed to stay. The following morning when I woke, I discovered that she'd stolen my mother's car along with other things she thought she could sell, including my prom dress."

"She stole your prom dress?" I asked, completely shocked.

"Yes." Barbara exhaled loudly.

I didn't know what to say after hearing that. I could only imagine how she must have felt.

"Anyway, there were other times that my sister conned her way back into the house. I eventually picked up on her tricks and where she hid her drugs."

"So when did she stop?" I asked.

"Around the age of twenty when she almost died from an overdose," said Barbara. "That was her wake-up call. She eventually got the help she wanted and needed but she took the family down a difficult road that I never want to go down again."

I took in everything that she'd just shared and concluded that perhaps she and I aren't so different in the sense that we've both been deeply wounded by people we love.

"Can I ask you a question?"

Barbara looked at me. "Yeah," she answered.

"If you had discovered that I had a problem, would you have kicked me out of the house?" I swallowed hard as I awaited her answer. She didn't take her eyes off me, not even for one second. As I read her expression I knew what her answer was before she gave it.

"No. I would have worked with Jordan to find help for you." I exhaled. It was such a relief to know that she wasn't as evil as she first appeared to be.

"I'm sorry, too," I said. "I only lashed out at you because you always seemed to be out to get me. I also want to say thank you for standing up for me in front of all those parents who were at the school board meeting. No one has ever stood up for me like that." Barbara smiled.

"Well, I think it's about time that you start benefiting from the strength of a family that cares and sticks together. We're also going to prevail in court and get to the bottom of who is trying to destroy our happy family." I swallowed hard because my heart was doing something weird. It was filling my body up with an emotion that was foreign to me.

"Um." I paused because my voice was shaking. "So you're saying that you consider me to be a part of the family?"

"Yes, I do," Barbara answered. I put my face in my hands and started crying tears of joy. Barbara came over and draped her arm around me and held on to me until I pulled myself back together.

"I'm sorry. I don't mean to be so emotional."

"It's okay to cry. Listen, I've brought up some cleaning supplies and trash bags so that we can clean up your room."

"You mean you're going to help me?" I asked, wanting to be sure I heard her correctly.

"Yes," she said with a smile.

It took a good portion of the morning for Barbara and I to get my bedroom back in order. We had to use the mattress from Grandmother Katie's room temporarily until my mattress could be replaced, but I didn't mind one bit. When we were finished I fell in love with my room all over again.

twenty-seven

Later that afternoon I went to the garage and upstairs to the workout room. Jordan was just finishing his run on the treadmill. I sat down on one of the weight machines and watched him as he wiped sweat from his face with a towel.

"Can I ask you a question?"

"Yeah," Jordan said as he stepped down from the treadmill and took a seat at another weight-lifting machine, which was next to me.

"When the results came back and they told you that I was your daughter, why did you come for me? Why didn't you just let a judge sign me over to the group home permanently and leave me there?"

"Sweetie, when I learned that you were my baby there was no question in my mind as to what my next step would be. I couldn't turn my back on you. You are my responsibility." Jordan paused for a moment and then placed his hand over mine.

"I feel cheated, Keysha. I've been cheated out of watching you enter the world, cheated out of your first steps and your first birthday. My heart is hurting about this in ways that are unimaginable. Trust me, had I known about you, believe me when I say that life for you would have been very different."

I swallowed hard because my next question was a real tough one to ask. I glanced down at the floor.

"Do you—" My words got trapped in my throat. "I mean—what I'm trying to ask is, even though all this crazy stuff is going on, do you think you'll ever be able to love me?" Jordan got up from his seat and kneeled down before me.

"Look at me. Look into my eyes," he said. "I don't want you to ever think for one minute that I don't love you or that I will stop loving you."

"But I've screwed up so badly. I didn't mean to but somehow everything just went crazy," I said. I was trying to tell him how sorry I was for causing so much drama.

"You are my daughter and nothing on this earth will ever change that or the way I feel about you. Do you understand?"

"But what if we don't get a chance to really get to know each other?" I asked nervously. My worst fear was that I'd be convicted and end up in prison. "I mean, this entire drug thing doesn't make me feel good at all."

"This family is going to get through this and no matter what happens, I'm going to be there for you." I don't know why his words went directly to my heart but they did. I leaned forward, rested my head on his shoulders and hugged him.

"I love you, Daddy," I said.

"I love you, too," he answered, and hearing him say those words to me made me feel more loved and cared for than I ever had before.

READING GUIDE QUESTIONS

1) What does Keysha want the most?

2) What are Keysha's flaws and how do you think she got them?

3) What are Keysha's strengths?

4) Is Keysha a leader or a follower?

5) What is Toya's motivation for trying to pressure Keysha to consider dropping out of school?

6) Why does Keysha still care about her mother, Justine, even after she's left her in a desperate situation?

7) While in the group home, Keysha hears stories from teen kids who were homeless and living on the streets. Discuss what you think it would be like to live on the street without food, shelter or someone to love you.

8) Discuss why you think Mike wanted to be viewed as a hard-core gangster as opposed to a clean-cut young man.

9) Discuss how and why Liz was able to connect with Key-sha and get her to trust her.

10) Why do you think Jordan is willing to risk everything for a daughter he didn't know he had?

TEXT ME LIST

Favorite female artist: Alicia Keys

Favorite female group: Pussycat Dolls

Favorite female rapper: Missy Elliott

Favorite young female actress: Julia Stiles

Favorite Teen Movie: Take the Lead

Favorite Song on my iPod by a female artist:
Hips Don't Lie by Shakira

Favorite female track and field athlete:
Florence Griffith Joyner

Favorite male artist: Usher

Favorite male rapper: Yung Joc

Favorite young male actor: Mark Wahlberg

Favorite guy movie: Four Brothers

Favorite male athlete:
Muhammad Ali (the greatest of all time)

Favorite Song on my iPod by a male artist:
Justin Timberlake (SexyBack)

Favorite online site I'm hooked on for the moment: ww.myspace.com/earlsewell

Most interesting and informative Web site: www.americaslibrary.gov

Favorite cartoon: The Simpsons

Favorite food: Banana Pudding

Favorite football team: Da Chicago Bears

Favorite basketball team: Da Bulls

Favorite baseball team: Da White Sox

Favorite season: The Fall

Favorite city to visit: Miami, FL

Favorite romantic DVD: The Piano

If I Were Your Boyfriend

one

Wesley

"YOU look like you're a smart-aleck with a dishonest heart who wants to say something really stupid." The brawny police officer had singled me out to make an example of. She was eager for me to challenge her in some way so she'd have the authority to use force against me. She was much taller than I was and had a solid-looking jaw, a fierce and unyielding glare and appeared to be powerful enough to crush my skull with her bare hands. It was obvious that she spent all of her spare time at the gym, pumping iron. She was as tall as a tree in the rain forest and at any moment I thought she would howl out a battle cry like Xena the Warrior Princess.

I'd just walked down a ramp from the back door of a bus with about five other guys who were restrained. The bus had been converted into a transport vehicle to move detainees from the local jailhouse to a facility specifically designed for juveniles. Along with the five other guys, I was now standing outside in the pouring rain, and I wasn't happy about my Nike sneakers and clothes getting soaked.

"Come on, say something. I can see everything you're thinking." A pellet of saliva flew from the officer's mouth and landed on my lip just below my nose. For a brief moment I could smell her tart breath. I didn't respond to her verbally. Instead I looked at her and elected to answer her with silence and a smart-aleck facial expression. When she reached the conclusion that she couldn't provoke me beyond my facial contortions, she moved on to the guy who was shackled up in front of me. He asked how long we had to stand out in the rain and she shouted at him so viciously that his composure snapped like a twig and he began crying tears of sadness. Punk was the first thought that flashed in my mind when I saw his chin take a nosedive into his chest and his shoulders slump forward. His body began jerking violently as his emotions took control of him.

"You are not to speak to each other!" She tapped the butt of her revolver with her index finger. The officer smirked at him as if she'd accomplished a particular goal. She then roared out instructions like a lion in the wilderness.

"You are to march into the building and line up with your backs against the wall and await further instructions."

No one said a word or uttered a single sound except for the guy who wouldn't stop crying. I wanted to smack him on the head to make him shut up, but I couldn't. I didn't know about everyone else, but I felt a very strong anxiety attack swelling up within me. As we marched into the building, I found it difficult to move because the steel shackles the police placed around my wrists and ankles were ratcheted on very tightly and were gnawing deep into my skin. I was doing my best to control my renegade feelings from surfacing and making me do something stupid, but it wasn't easy trying to contain an emotional swell that was like a wild beast buckling iron bars. I tried to reposition the steel bracelets into a more comfortable position, but I only made my situation worse. I felt as if the armor I was being restrained with were sawing straight through to my bones.

Once inside we lined up against the wall as we were instructed to do. A few moments later a handful of police officers appeared and stood by each one of us.

"Come with me," said a male Hispanic officer with a slight smile. His eyes and skin were brown and his black hair was freshly cut and styled. He had a medium build and walked with presence and purpose. He escorted me through a series of giant and impenetrable doors.

"So, what are you in for?" he asked. The tone of his light Spanish accent seemed friendly and caring. His demeanor was nothing like the madwoman who had escorted me off of the bus.

"I don't know," I answered.

"Come on, man. There's no need to be angry with me. I'm not the one who put you in here. You did that all on your own." He was right. I didn't have any reason to have an attitude with him. He was just doing his job.

"Alcohol abuse among other things," I said.

"So, you have a drinking problem? You're too young to toss your life away over alcohol, *amigo*."

I didn't say anything because he didn't understand anything about what I was going through. And I certainly wasn't his friend.

"I'm Officer Sanchez. You've been assigned to my unit. I'm going to process you into our system," he said. Officer

Sanchez escorted me into a small room and sat me down in front of a desk with a computer.

"Give me a moment, I'll be right back," he said, and then exited the room, making sure to lock the door. It was so quiet in the room that the silence seemed loud. Maybe it was because I could hear myself thinking. I could hear my thoughts lying to me, telling me that everything would be okay and that I'd be released. I looked around to try to distract my mind. The room was cold and uninviting. The walls were made of solid brick and were painted white and the floor was gray like a rain cloud. Ten minutes passed by before Officer Sanchez came back and sat at the computer. He took a deep breath, then began typing. He stopped pecking at the keyboard with his two index fingers and began talking.

"Wesley Morris, why were you driving a stolen car while you were drunk?" he asked. I couldn't tell if he was actually concerned or just asking an obvious question.

"The car wasn't stolen, it belongs to my mother."

"When you take a car without getting permission, that's called stealing, even if it is your mom's car."

"How is that stealing when I was going to bring it back? Last time I checked, true car thieves don't return a car after it's stolen." Officer Sanchez threaded his fingers together behind his head. His chair groaned as he reclined back. We looked at each other for a long moment before he asked another question.

"What's your relationship with your mother like?"

"I don't know," I answered.

"Do you guys get along?" he continued questioning me.

"Obviously we don't since she said I stole her car."

"Hey, I'm just trying to understand what happened here, okay?"

"I don't even know why I'm here. I didn't really do anything wrong." Officer Sanchez was silent again. It was clear that he could see right through me, but I didn't care.

"Do you want me to call your mom right now?" he asked.

"No, I'd rather be locked up in here than be around her," I answered truthfully.

"Why?"

"Because it's probably better for me here. I'll be away from her and all of her bull."

"Do you think your mom is too hard on you?"

"I don't want to talk about my relationship with her anymore. Besides, it is what it is," I said as I once again tried to adjust my wrists so that the handcuffs felt more comfortable.

"Well, as a matter of procedure I have to call her," said Officer Sanchez.

"Whatever, man," I uttered.

Officer Sanchez pressed the speaker button on the phone and then dialed my mom's phone number, which I'd provided earlier. I sat in my seat, shackled up and glaring at the phone as it rang. I heard my mom answer.

"Hello, Ms. Carter. This is Officer Sanchez from the County Juvenile Detention Center. How are you today?"

"I've seen better days," my mom answered through the speakerphone. The sound of her voice made my blood pressure rise. My mother and father were divorced. Their marriage was always on shaky ground, but when my mom refused to stop drinking, that was the breaking point. After my mom won the bitter court battle for custody over me, she started using her maiden name. She didn't want any association with my father.

"I can understand that. It's not easy for a parent to go through this sort of thing." There was a short moment of silence and then Officer Sanchez continued. "Ms. Carter, I have here in the room with me your son, Wesley, who said he wanted to speak to you." Officer Sanchez motioned with his hands for me to speak at will. I really didn't have anything to say to her, but he insisted that I speak.

"Hey," I said.

"Wesley, why are you doing this?" my mom asked.

"I didn't do anything," I insisted.

"You are just making things harder than they have to be. You're going down the wrong path, Wesley, and that hard head of yours is going to keep getting you in trouble if you don't change."

"You know what, I wouldn't be in trouble if you weren't always on my back and pushing me so much. I mean, you don't like me, you pick your boyfriends over me and on top of that you're offended by my very presence. So you can save your little speech for another time."

"Wesley, you know that's not true," she said, defending herself.

"Then why did you report your car stolen when you knew that I had it? You knew your car wasn't stolen. Did one of your boyfriends suggest that you do it?"

"Don't twist this around on me, Wesley!" The anger in her voice flooded the small room I was sitting in. "Why are you drinking again?" she asked.

"You know what, just forget it. I can't believe you have

the nerve to ask why I'm drinking. Now I know for sure that I'm better off here." I leaned back in my seat and refused to say anything more.

"Wesley, I want you to think about what you've done while you're in there. Do you understand me?" she asked.

"Whatever," I answered her just so she'd shut up. At that moment Officer Sanchez stepped back into the conversation.

"Ms. Carter, will you be at Wesley's upcoming court hearing?"

"Yes, his father and I will be there," she said. After sharing a few pleasantries, Officer Sanchez hung up the phone.

"Why is your relationship with your mother so poisonous?" he asked.

"Like I said, it is what it is, man. She doesn't care about me and I don't care about her."

I suppose Officer Sanchez didn't know how to respond to my comment so he didn't. He went about the business of processing me into the system. After I signed several documents regarding my personal belongings, Officer Sanchez walked me through another series of doors and into a small shower, which was about the size of a tiny fitting room at a clothing store.

"There is shampoo and soap over there on the shelf." He pointed. "I need you to get undressed and hand me your clothes."

"What? While you watch?" I asked, horrified at the thought of him looking at me while I undressed.

"*Amigo*, this is the way it goes down in here. These are the rules you must follow." He removed my shackles.

"What if I refuse?" I asked.

"Trust me, you don't want to do that." Our eyes locked and I knew he was dead serious about what he'd just said.

"Fine, man," I said, then got completely undressed and handed over all of my clothes.

"The shower is on a timer. By the time it stops I'll be back with our standard inmate gray jogging pants and sweatshirt. All of the detainees wear them. After you get dressed, I'll take you through orientation so that you'll know the rules and what is expected of you while you're here. After we're done with that, I'll show you your sleeping quarters and then take you to the common area where the other detainees are."

Officer Sanchez shut the door and locked me inside the tiny shower. I pressed a white button on the wall and the water came on. I stepped under the showerhead and got goose bumps as the water splashed against my skin. It was freezing cold at first but then adjusted automatically. I preferred nice long hot showers, but since there were no sill valves on the wall to adjust the temperature I had to live with bathing in water that was barely warm. I closed my eyes, punched a wall a few times with the side of my fist and then thought about how I was going to survive. The shower turned itself off and I moved over to the door to open it but I couldn't. I stood at the door, naked, wet and cold, searching for any signs of Officer Sanchez. When I didn't see him I took a few steps backward and placed my back against the wall. I folded my arms across my body, exhaled and tried to keep myself from going completely insane.

two

Keysha

"Wake up, Keysha, we're almost there," said Grandmother Katie. I opened my eyes just as she turned off Main Street and onto Church Street. I stretched out my body and released a loud yawn. She and I had been driving several hours from my dad's home to her house in the country. I tried to stay awake and keep her company during the long journey, but once the landscape changed from picture-perfect suburban homes to farmland, barns and smelly cows, it was all too easy to fall asleep from visual boredom.

"Where are we?" I asked as I brought myself back from the land of the sleeping.

"We're just about there. I live on this street," she said as we drove past a neighborhood playground. There was a Little League football game going on and I briefly watched as a young boy ran about ten yards for a touchdown.

"This is it," she announced as she brought her car to a hard stop directly in front of her home.

"It's a beautiful home," I complimented as I studied the yellow two-story frame house. The white picket fence, which was in need of a fresh coat of paint, outlined the boundary of the property. I noticed the porch swing that was swaying back and forth and could hear it squeaking.

"I just love this time of the year. It's so pretty to see the season change from summer to fall," she said as I studied several auburn leaves billowing downward from trees that were around her property.

"I pay the young man who lives a few doors down to rake up the yard for me. He does a good job and he's reliable. Next year he'll be heading off to college and I'll have to find a new person who is willing to do the work for me." She paused for a long moment, so I turned my attention to her. She was smiling at me as if I were the most precious thing she'd ever seen. Her smile, her eyes and her spirit made me feel warm all over.

"Well, come on, let's get all of your belongings inside." Grandmother Katie pressed the trunk release button and we both got out of the car. I removed my belongings from the trunk and followed Grandmother Katie up the pathway toward the house. I wrestled with my suitcase as I pulled it up the front porch steps one at a time. Once on the porch I looked to my left through a window and saw Smokey, who was Grandmother Katie's black Labrador retriever. We talked about her dog during the journey to her house. Smokey had tucked his head beneath the drapes and was greeting us with loud barks.

"Hey, Smokey." Grandmother Katie waved to her dog as if he were a real person. Smokey responded to her greeting by whining and then barking again.

"It's okay, Keysha, he's not going to bite you. If anything, he'll try to lick on you."

"Being licked by a dog would not be cool," I said. As soon as she placed her door key in the lock tumbler, Smokey barked even louder. When the door finally opened, Smokey rushed up to her, wagging his tail, wiggling his body and sniffing her clothing.

"Did you miss me, Smokey?" she asked as he petted him on his head.

"He loves it when you pet him," she said. "I'm afraid that I've spoiled him."

Smokey came over to me and I let him sniff my hands, my clothes and my luggage. Once he approved of me, he rushed back inside the house. I listened as his paws clicked against the hardwood floor.

As I entered her home the first thing I noticed was all of the photos on the wall. There were pictures everywhere of her, my grandfather, my dad, her parents and my grandfather's parents. One entire corner of the room felt like a visual history book. I was about to ask some questions, but she interrupted my train of thought.

"Bring your suitcase along and follow me. I'll show you the room where you'll be sleeping." I followed her up the wooden staircase that groaned the moment we began climbing.

"You can sleep in here," she said as she opened a door to one of the bedrooms. I wheeled my suitcase to the center of the room and plopped down on the bed. The yellow paint on the walls was a little too bright for my taste. There was an old dresser in the room, a desk with a sewing machine and a built-in bookshelf on the far wall. The lime-green bedding complemented the curtains and the pictures of fruit hanging on the walls. The room was very clean. In fact, it was too clean and looked as if no one had slept in it for a long time.

"Well, is the room okay with you?" she asked. I turned and smiled at her.

"Yes, the room is perfect," I answered. I then stood up and moved over to the bookshelf to see what was there. All of the books appeared to be about sewing and knitting. They were definitely books for a grandmother.

"Well, go ahead and get yourself settled in," she said. "I'm going to head downstairs to let Smokey out in the backyard and take care of any accidents he had while I was gone. Come on down the back stairs when you're done. The stairs lead to the kitchen and that's where I'll be."

"Okay," I said as I moved toward the window to see what was outside. When I drew back the curtain, I could see the park and the football field. The game was still in progress but not for long because I noticed that the scoreboard said that there was only two minutes left in the fourth quarter. As I moved away from the window, I noticed Smokey sniffing around a tree. I thought he was about to unearth something, but I quickly realized that he was only searching for the perfect spot to raise one of his legs.

It took me about twenty minutes to unpack all of my belongings and explore the other rooms. Once I'd finished snooping around I did as Grandmother Katie asked and walked down the back staircase and into the kitchen. I found her sitting at the table with an assortment of vegetables on a silver tray. She'd just placed a carrot in the vegetable shredder and I watched as the machine spewed out long cords of carrots into a stainless-steel bowl.

"Hey, what are you making?" I asked.

"A big salad for dinner. Have a seat," she said, nodding at the empty chair on the opposite side of the table.

I took a seat and looked around the kitchen, which was very clean, organized and built for cooking fabulous meals. It was nothing like the kitchen in the small studio apartment I lived in with my mother. I focused my attention on the platter of food. Grandmother Katie was making a salad that included cucumbers, lettuce, green and black olives, mushrooms, beets, cheese and sunflower seeds.

"Do you know how to cook?" asked Grandmother Katie.

"I know how to cook for myself," I answered.

"What do you cook well?" she asked.

"I'm pretty good at making tacos, spaghetti and my lasagna is the bomb, or so I've been told."

"Well, I think I'll let you cook tomorrow evening's dinner, then," she said as she adjusted the setting on the food shredder before placing the cucumber through the slicing mechanism.

"It's been a long time since I've made anything," I admitted. "I'll need some help." I smiled at her. She smiled back and the warmth of her smile made me feel loved the way the sun loves a flower.

"Well, that's what I'm here for, to help—I want to help you, Keysha."

"I shouldn't need that much help, only—"

Grandmother Katie interrupted me. "That's not what I meant, baby. I want to help you get through the trouble you've gotten yourself into."

I stopped smiling and craned my neck down toward the

floor in shame. I didn't want to talk about my pending court case, my suspension from school or my strained friendship with Liz Lloyd.

"Hold your head up, honey. There is no need to feel as if I'm attacking or judging you. I just want to listen to you, understand what's going on and offer suggestions to help you make better choices, okay? You've got a good head on your shoulders. You just have to use it to its full potential."

I wanted to hold my head up and look her in the eye but I couldn't because I felt as if I'd caused everyone a lot of grief over my mistake.

"Everyone makes mistakes, Keysha. It's just a part of living and that's a true fact. Even some of the most intelligent people can have a lapse in judgment from time to time."

"Yeah, but the mistake I've made is a colossal one."

"Oh, honey, your mistake isn't all that bad," she attempted to assure me.

"How can you say that? I have a court case. People think I'm a drug dealer and I might go to jail for it."

"Well, are you a drug dealer?" Grandmother Katie asked.

"No," I answered.

"Then as I see it, the only mistakes you've made are selecting a bad friend and bowing down to peer pressure, and anyone can make that mistake."

"Well, to me they feel like the mistakes of the century," I said, releasing a nervous sigh.

"Do me a favor and boil some eggs for me. I want to slice up some eggs to put in our salad."

I stood up and went to the refrigerator and removed a carton of eggs.

"How many should I boil?" I asked.

"Four should do it. You can use the pot that's sitting there on the stove," said Grandmother Katie.

I removed the eggs, poured water in the pot and placed the pot over the flame. For a brief moment I stared down at the white eggs floating in the water.

"You know, your friend Liz may be jealous of you." Grandmother Katie pulled me out of my trance.

"I don't see for what," I said, sitting back down.

"It doesn't take much for a person to be jealous of you. Jealousy is an ugly trait and can show its hideous face over something as simple as a new outfit. I think young folks call jealous people 'the haters' these days."

I laughed.

"Look at you, trying to be all hip and stuff." We both laughed together for a moment, but then Grandmother Katie began to share some of her wisdom.

"You know, when I was fourteen, there was a girl who had a problem with me even though we were friends. Her name was Willie Mae Smith."

"Willie what?" I laughed at the name.

"Willie Mae. It's an old southern name."

"What did she look like?" I asked.

"I remember her skin being very dark and beautiful, but I think she viewed her pretty dark skin as a curse. Her hair was short, she was overweight and her family was extremely poor. Willie Mae's mom attended my father's church and that's where I met her. We became friends and were always with each other."

"So, why was Willie Mae jealous of you?" I asked.

"You're going to laugh when I tell you this but Willie Mae couldn't articulate her words or express herself the way I could."

"So she was jealous of you because you could talk better? That seems dumb," I said.

"To you it may seem that way but to her it was a huge deal. Willie Mae's problem stemmed from her lack of understanding. She always got her words twisted around. She would say things like 'I'm going to be a confessional when I grow up.'"

"What in the world is a confessional?" I asked.

"You're missing my point. She really meant to say the word 'professional.'"

I cracked up laughing when I heard that.

"I would laugh at her too but I also tried to help by correcting her. I was always correcting her, speaking up for her and finishing her sentences for her. Especially when we were around other people."

"So, how did you find out she was jealous of you or had a problem with you? It sounds as if you guys were good friends."

"Willie Mae and I sang in the youth choir together at my father's church. During choir practice a situation arose with another girl who was making fun of Willie Mae's shabby clothes, big nose and dark skin. The other girl, Nicole, was a mulatto with fair skin, a thin nose and a fine grade of hair. Willie Mae had trouble locating the right word she needed to express her feelings. I knew the word she was looking for so I acted as her liaison as I'd done countless times. I guess this particular day she'd had enough and hauled off and slapped me during choir practice. I was stunned and hurt at first, but those feelings quickly turned into anger. Before I could stop myself or ask why she'd slapped me, I slapped her back. The next thing I knew we were on the floor fighting."

"Wait a minute, you were fighting while in church?" I asked for clarification.

"Yes, and my father had a fit. He marched into the choir stand and broke up our fight and tanned my hind parts for fighting in the house of the Lord."

"I can't imagine you in a fight," I said.

"Well, I've had my fair share of them."

"So, what happened after that?" I asked.

"My father made me apologize not only to Willie Mae but to her mother, Lonnie. It wasn't until I apologized to Miss Lonnie that I realized she had a speech impediment. She couldn't articulate or enunciate a single word. Miss Lonnie got through life by mumbling her words. It was the strangest thing. I'd met Miss Lonnie plenty of times, but as I thought about it, I realized that whenever I ran into her she was always with someone who spoke for her and the most she'd ever said was 'okay' or 'that's right.'

"Later that evening during dinner my father explained that Miss Lonnie and her family were from a small Island off of the coast of South Carolina. Miss Lonnie was a Gullah woman and spoke the Geechee language."

"The gee what?" I asked.

"The Geechee language," she restated.

"Come on. That sounds made up. You're pulling my leg." I laughed.

"No, it's not made up, Keysha. Hang on a minute, your grandfather has books about the Gullah people in his library."

Grandmother Katie got up and told me to follow her. We walked into another part of the house that was filled with shelves of books. It was one big library. Grandmother Katie began searching the shelves until she found what she was looking for. She opened the book and flipped to a page featuring several enslaved blacks.

"See?" Grandmother Katie pointed and began reading the passage below the photo. "It says, 'The Gullah are blacks who live in the Low Country region of South Carolina and Georgia, which includes both the coastal plain and the Sea Islands. Historically, the Gullah region once extended north to the Cape Fear area on the coast of North Carolina and south to the vicinity of Jacksonville on the coast of Florida; but today the Gullah area is confined to the South Carolina and Georgia Low Country. The Gullah people are also called Geechee, especially in Georgia. The Gullah are known for preserving more of their African linguistic and cultural heritage than any other black community in the United States. They speak an English-based Creole language containing many African loan words and significant influences from African languages in grammar and sentence structure.' It wasn't until my father explained the culture that I understood why Willie Mae resented me for constantly correcting her."

"Oh, wow. So she was doing the best that she could with what she'd learned from her mother," I said.

"Yes, and on top of that she was speaking a language that had survived slavery. However, when you're young, these sorts of things seem strange, especially if you perceive them as something abnormal. So in my mind at the time, Willie

Mae suffered from the same speech problems as Miss Lonnie although it wasn't as severe as her mother's."

"So Willie Mae was jealous of you because of how you could articulate."

"Yes, and she was also angry about people making her feel bad about being Gullah."

"Well, I don't know why Liz would be jealous of me," I said. "We haven't even known each other that long and I haven't done anything to her." Grandmother Katie was about to put the book back on the shelf.

"Can I read that?" I asked.

"Sure," she said. She handed me the book and we went back into the kitchen.

"Liz could have a beef with you for any number of reasons," Grandmother Katie said as she checked the stove. "The eggs are ready now," she added as she drained the water off of them. I sat back down at the table and searched my mind trying to identify any warning signs I may have missed with Liz, but I couldn't locate any.

"So, how do you know if your friend is really your friend?" I asked, because I was puzzled as to what a true friendship looked and felt like.

"Your friends should reflect who you are. They should feel like a part of you. Good friends always have your best interest at heart and will tell you the truth even when you don't want to hear it. Good friends don't put you down or call you stupid or dumb in an effort to make you feel as if you're beneath them. A good friend will not try to convince you to do something that you know in your heart is not right or good for you. Good friends are never, ever, fake," she said.

"But how can you tell if your friend is fake?" I asked.

"You'll feel it," she said. "Something inside you will guide you. Most people call it intuition."

"Oh," I said. "I had a friend named Toya who I knew in my heart really wasn't a good friend and I knew that she didn't have my best interest, as you put it, at heart. She was the type of girl who liked getting into trouble. She had a way of making me feel bad whenever I didn't want to do all of the crazy things she wanted to do. But I wanted her to be my friend, so I went along with whatever she wanted to do." I paused. "One thing is for sure. I knew that our friendship was over when she split open my hand with a straight razor."

"A straight razor?" Grandmother Katie screeched.

"It's a long story. But all I'm tying to say is that I should have listened to my intuition because Toya was and probably still is rotten to her core."

"Here's a bit a' knowledge I want you to keep with you always. When someone isn't good for you, leave them because you can do bad all by yourself. As you mature, you will find it a little more difficult to separate yourself from people who are no good for you. You may discover that your worst enemies are the people who are the closest to you. A husband, a child, a coworker—"

"A crazy mother," I interrupted. She had a slightly baffled look on her face when I said that, but then she made the connection as to what I meant.

"You see, that is why you're so smart. You've learned some of life's most important lessons on your own and that is one of the things that makes you very special, Keysha."

When Grandmother Katie told me that I felt validated.

I felt as if I wasn't crazy and I also felt something inside me change. I felt love for her. I felt as if I could be myself, open up and talk to her about anything, and I'd never really felt that way before about any of the adults in my life.

"Okay, this salad is just about ready," she said.

"After we eat can we read some of this book together? I want to know more about these Geechee people," I said.

"Absolutely," Grandmother Katie said as she smiled at me.

three

Wesley

I'd just finished putting on the gray sweat suit and was standing by the mirror giving myself one last glance over. The sweats were huge and I had to pull the drawstring to its limit in order to keep my pants from falling down. The water at the detention facility was very hard and as a result my skin got very dry and had begun turning white. I exited the shower area and found Officer Sanchez waiting for me.

"Do you have any lotion? My skin is all dry," I said.

"Yeah, I do," he said. "Hold out your hand."

I did as he instructed me to do and he squeezed some lotion that he had gotten off of a countertop that was nearby into my hands. Once I finished applying the lotion to the exposed parts of my skin he took me into the main group area where the other detainees were sitting around talking, playing cards and chilling out. I found a spot to sit down and just watched everyone, feeling slightly afraid and a little paranoid. In my mind I knew that I didn't belong. I wasn't this type of person. I didn't consider myself to be a trouble-maker or a criminal. I just made a mistake, that's all. A lot of guys looked evil, hard and mean. It wasn't difficult to tell which dude had a street reputation and thug credibility.

Those type of guys had a certain persona and presence about them. Their body language spoke for them. *This is a drag,* I thought to myself. Just sitting around waiting for the day to end was enough to drive me crazy if I let it.

"What's up?" asked this guy who sat down next to me.

I looked at him and studied him for a moment. I knew him from somewhere but I couldn't exactly remember where we'd met. He was slender with large almond eyes. His hair was combed out on one side and braided up on the other.

"Nothing," I answered.

"I know you," he said. " You don't remember me?"

"I sort of remember your face but I don't remember your name."

"It's Deon, man. You hang out at Tricked Out Nightclub with that chick Liz Lloyd, right?"

"Yeah, Liz and I are cool," I said.

"I also partied with you at a house party a while back. You and your boy had scored some alcohol and everyone at the party got completely smashed."

"Oh, yeah, I remember you now," I said, feeling better that I knew someone.

"My name is Wesley," I reminded him.

"That's right, Wesley." He snapped his fingers. "So, what are you in for?"

"Stupid stuff, what about you?"

"I was at a party celebrating with my basketball team. My school team had just won a big tournament and I shot the winning point at the buzzer. It was a sweet shot too. I got the rebound, got around two defenders and dribbled the ball hard up the court. I glanced at the shot clock real quick and noticed that I only had two seconds left. I arrived at the three-point line, to find Joey, another defender, waiting on me. I faked him out as if I was going to take the ball to the hole. When he went for the fake out, I launched myself high into the air. Joey tried to come back and block the shot, but it was too late. I released the ball, watched as it soared through the air and then whoosh, nothing but net, baby. The buzzer sounded, indicating that time had run out, and I tossed my arms up in the air to celebrate the victory. Unfortunately, Joey got nailed in the face during my moment of jubilation. Before I had an opportunity to apologize, my teammates swarmed me." He paused for a moment, a look of regret crossing his face. "Anyway, getting back to the party, it got out of control when Joey showed up with a few of his teammates. I apologized to him, but Joey wasn't there to receive an apology. He wanted to fight."

"His boys probably hyped him up to battle on the way over," I stated.

"Joey and I got into a shouting match and then he swung on me and nailed me right on the jaw. I wasn't about to get my butt whipped so I tackled him, got him on his back and unloaded on him. The next thing I knew guys from my team were fighting with the guys from the other team. It became a full-blown brawl within a matter of moments. The entire situation snowballed out of control. A lot of screaming, furniture was being broken and people getting bloody knuckles and split lips. I don't know how long the brawl went on because I was caught up in the moment. I came to my senses when I heard someone shout, 'The cops are here!' Everyone scattered at that moment. I tried to get out before the cops came in, but they cornered me and then took me into custody."

"But what for? You were only defending yourself. Did you explain that to them?" I asked.

"Yeah, I explained everything to them, but since I had alcohol in my system I was brought in on charges of disorderly conduct and underaged drinking. Joey went to the hospital because I'd knocked out one of his teeth during our fight. I heard that he's been released already and is doing okay."

"Well, did the cops arrest him?"

"Nope."

"Well, why didn't the cops bring him in for disorderly conduct too?" I asked.

"That's what I'd like to know," Deon answered as he shrugged his shoulders. "This entire situation is real jacked up." He leaned back in his seat. "I'm worried about going in front of the judge and what this is going to look like on my record."

"It probably won't be bad," I tried to reassure him.

"No, it is bad, man. My coach came to see me yesterday. He told me that two college scouts had come to see me and he had to tell them that I was in here. On top of that I'm going to miss four games that I know college scouts planned on attending. Man, I just feel as if I've blown my scholarship opportunities over something really stupid. Colleges look at this sort of thing, you know. This is my senior year, dude, and I may have just blown it." Deon released a sigh of frustration. I could hear the fear and anxiety in his voice. "If Joey had just accepted my apology, none of this would have happened."

"Have you ever gotten into a brawl before?" I asked.

"I've had my fair share of fights but nothing major," he answered. "Say, have your parents been here to see you yet?" he asked, changing the subject. I could tell that reliving events that landed him in this place was causing him more stress than he had anticipated.

"No, and I really don't want them to come." I repositioned myself in my seat. "I especially don't want to see my mother because we don't get along. I get along better with my father."

"Well, my parents came here and, man, I'm telling you, it was hard for me. I feel as if I've disappointed them. I didn't want them to see me in here dressed like this." Deon stopped talking. Judging by the look in his eyes, I knew he was hurting but trying not to show it by acting macho.

"Everything will be fine. This is no big deal. Is this your first offense?" I asked.

"Yeah," he answered. "I've never been in trouble like this before."

"I think the judge will probably go easy on you. It's not as if you're a repeat offender or anything," I said.

"This isn't me, man. Being in here is the last place I ever expected to be. It's cold in here. I don't like the single rooms with the hard mattresses or the stainless-steel toilet. This will be the last time that I ever mess up. I'm hoping that the college scouts will look at this as a small mistake and nothing more." Deon ran his fingers through his hair and then met my gaze. "Come on, Wesley. Tell me what you're really in for," he inquired.

I didn't answer Deon right away because I was trying to

figure out a good starting point. There were so many events that had led up to my being locked up.

"Hey, man, if you don't want to talk about it, I understand."

"No, it's not that I don't want to talk about it. I'm just trying to figure out where to start."

"Well, for starters do you like being in here?" asked Deon.

"You know, at first I didn't but now that I've had a chance to calm down and relax, this place isn't so bad. In fact, it's okay because I can hear myself think."

"Man. If you like this place, things must be pretty bad at home."

"'Bad' isn't the word for it. 'Chaotic' would be a more accurate description," I said. I relieved some of the tension in my neck by rotating it in a circular motion until it cracked. "I'm tired of all of the constant screaming matches that I get into with my mom. At least in this place I get a chance to escape from her. In here she can't touch me, or tell me what to do or belittle me. Now that I think about it, I'm actually in a pretty good mood," I said.

"Is it really that rough?" asked Deon.

"Dude, you have no idea," I said, and was silent again. "When you get out of here you'll probably go back to a loving family," I continued. "Your family will probably look at this as a learning lesson and all will be forgiven."

"Don't get it twisted," Deon corrected me. "My dad is not happy about me being here. And when I do go back home, I know that things are going to be different."

"Yeah, but your parents care and understand, right?" I asked.

"My dad sort of understands but my mom couldn't even talk when she saw me in here. She just cried. It was hard for me to see her so hurt." Deon swallowed hard.

"That just means that she cares, man, and that's a good thing. My mother will come in here and raise hell with me. That's how she is. She'll remind me how all of this is my fault and I deserve what I'm getting. I swear, sometimes I wonder if she's really my mother."

"Come on, let's walk around a little," said Deon.

"Walk where, man?" I asked, looking around. "This place is like the inside of a bank vault."

"I know it is but the moving around helps to keep me from going completely nuts. By moving around I feel like I'm going somewhere."

Walking around was cool with me, so Deon and I slowly strolled around the outer walls of the common area. No sooner had we begun moving about than he started pretending that he was shooting jump shots. "They have a gymnasium in here for us but the floor is being fixed." Deon shared more information with me but I couldn't have cared less about the gymnasium.

"Okay, go on. What's the deal with how you ended up here in prison paradise?"

"Saturday night I took my mom's car while she was asleep and drove myself to Tricked Out, the teen nightclub. When I got there, a line of people was wrapped around the building waiting to get in. I parked my mother's car next to a black Chevy Caprice that was filled with people. When I got out of the car, one of the guys recognized me. They'd scored some alcohol from a nearby convenience store and asked if

I wanted a drink. I joined them and hammered down a few beers and a few wine coolers. There was no need to go inside the club because the party was right outside where I was. The guys said that they were going to go get some more alcohol and asked if I wanted to come with. I said no, because I wanted to catch up with some more folks who were inside the club. I went inside and hung out with Liz Lloyd and the crew. I was feeling great when all of a sudden I felt as if the room was spinning around. I knew I was feeling that way because of all of the alcohol I'd drank. At that point I decided that it was time to head home. So I walked back out to the parking lot and got in my mother's car. I knew that I was too buzzed to drive so I got in the passenger seat, pulled the seat lever and lowered it into a reclining position. I then drifted off to sleep. The next thing I knew cops had surrounded the car and had their flashlights beaming in my face. They were yelling and shouting, 'Get out of the car!' I had no clue as to what was going on. I got out of the car and was detained and placed in the back of a squad car. Several officers searched the car but didn't find anything unusual. Then an officer comes over and opens up the squad car door to talk to me. He says, 'The car you're in has been reported stolen.' At that point I got ticked off.

"'Get real,'" I said, snapping at him because I thought he was on some racial-profiling power trip. "'Look, man,' I said to him, 'I have keys to the car. I didn't steal it.'"

"What did the cop say then?" asked Deon.

"He said that it didn't matter as far as he was concerned because I was inside a vehicle that had been reported stolen.

Then he asked me if I'd been drinking. I refused to answer his question.

"'Did you hear me?' he asked once again. 'I said have you been drinking alcohol?'"

"At that point I'd gotten irritated and wanted to smash anything that I could because nothing was going right. I wanted to lie to him about the drinking, but I didn't. I told him that I had a few drinks but not that many. I told him that I was a really good driver and I was resting in the car because I didn't think it would be a smart thing to do if I drove after having as many drinks as I had. He said that he appreciated my honesty but wanted to see if I could pass a few simple tests. I got out of the squad car and he took off the handcuffs. The officer told me to spread my arms out like an airplane and then touch the tip of my nose with my index finger one at a time. I tried to do it but I got dizzy and almost fell to the ground. Then he asked me to close my eyes and count backward from one hundred. I couldn't believe I'd failed that simple test. No matter how many times I tried to count backward my numbers got twisted and came through out of sequence. At that point the other officers agreed that I'd had one too many and needed to be taken into custody."

"Why didn't you call your mom? Didn't you have a cellular phone on you?" asked Deon.

"No, I didn't have my phone with me. When I got to the jailhouse they called my mom but I refused to speak with her. I was too angry."

"Well, did she report the car stolen?" Deon wanted to know.

"What do you think?" I answered sarcastically.

"Man, that has to be hard." Deon was now sympathizing with me.

"So now you know a tiny slice of my story. I'm in no rush to go back home because I can't stand it there."

"Yeah, but you can't stay here forever." Deon once again pretended to shoot a jump shot.

"I know that. What I really want to do is live with my dad. If I can go and live with him, I know that my life would be so much better than it is now," I said as I noticed how everyone in the common area began lining up.

"What's going on over there?" I asked.

"Feeding time," Deon answered. "They're about to take everyone to the cafeteria for some food that is sure to give you diarrhea."

"I'm not hungry so I'm just going to chill over at one of the tables," I said.

Deon laughed. "Dude, you don't have a choice here. You have to go. Come, I'll show you what's safe to eat and what isn't."

I followed Deon and lined up with the rest of the detainees and stood in silence as I thought about how I could convince my mother to allow me to live with my dad permanently.

four

Keysha

ON Sunday I woke up very early in the morning because I couldn't sleep. I got out of bed and walked down into the kitchen, opened up the refrigerator and poured myself a glass of cranberry cocktail juice. I was wide-awake and knew that I wouldn't be able to fall back to sleep, so I went into the family room and turned on the television. Flipping through the channels, I located MTV. A program was on that talked about the lives of Tupac and Biggie Smalls. I got engrossed in the program along with their music and fast-paced lifestyles. It was appealing to me to have fancy cars, loads of jewelry and to be the center of attention. I also liked Tupac and his thuggish looks. To me he looked untamed, masculine and gentle all at the same time. And his voice, I loved the sound of his rough and jagged voice. I was so involved in the program that I didn't notice that Grandmother Katie had gotten up and had just entered the room. I quickly clicked off the television.

"Good morning," I greeted her.

"Good morning. What were you watching?" she asked.

"Nothing," I answered. I didn't think she'd approve of me watching the life story of Tupac and Biggie.

"Yes, you were. You were watching something. What was it?"

"It was nothing," I said once again.

"Let me see the remote," she said. I reluctantly gave it to her. She clicked the power button and the program was on the part were Biggie Smalls had been murdered.

"Is this what you were viewing?" She looked at me disapprovingly.

"Yes, ma'am. I couldn't sleep so I came in here to watch television." I told her the truth because I had a difficult time lying to her. Grandmother Katie sat down on her recliner and continued to watch the program.

"Who is this about?" she asked.

"Biggie and Tupac," I answered her.

"Oh, yeah. The two young men who were murdered."

"You've heard of them?" I asked, utterly surprised that someone her age even knew of them.

"Yeah, I've heard of them. We've talked about them before at church," she answered.

She and I watched the remainder of the program together, and at its conclusion, Grandmother Katie turned off the television.

"What a waste," she said. "All of that beautiful creative talent gone to waste. Perhaps if their energy could have been focused in a different direction their lives would not have been so short."

"But they had it going on while they lived," I said. "I mean, they had everything. Cars, a house and money. They were doing it," I said, excited about their lifestyle.

"Honey, money, cars and a home will not make you happy.

Having purpose in your life can make you happy. Doing for others can make you happy. Giving—" Grandmother Katie stopped talking and there was a perplexed look on her face.

"Keysha, did your mother and other grandmother ever take you to church?"

I laughed.

"Are you kidding me?" I laughed again. "We never went to church. Grandmother Rubylee said that the church was full of sinners pretending to be sanctified."

Grandmother Katie's mouth fell open and she glared at me as if she were completely bewildered by what I'd just said.

"What are you thinking? What's wrong?" I asked because I was beginning to think that I'd traumatized her.

"Has Jordan taken you to church yet?" she asked. My grandmother was referring to my father who we called by his first name, Jordan. I had recently discovered my father and his side of the family a few months ago. My mother, Justine, and I were struggling to make ends meet in our old neighborhood in Chicago. When she got busted by the police for passing bad checks, I ended up in foster care. I had never met my father until I wound up in the system. Because I shared the same last name as Jordan, the social workers were able to locate him.

Jordan never knew of my existence before that time. He invited me to move into the house he shared with his wife, Barbara, and son, Mike. Jordan and Grandmother Katie were always kind to me, but Barbara and Mike really resented my presence those first few weeks.

"No. He said that we were going to go but I think he first

wanted to build up our relationship. I'm positive we were about to go, but then I sort of complicated things."

"I want you to go upstairs and get ready for church," she said.

"What?" I asked.

"We're going to church this morning. I was going to go to the afternoon service, but I think it would be better for us to go to the early-morning service."

I rolled my eyes. "It's going to be boring," I protested.

"You're bored sitting here now, so your being bored at church will not harm you."

I was ready to snap back with an ugly comment, but I held on to my words before my mouth got me into trouble. Still, the last thing I wanted to do was listen to some old sweaty preacher talking about sinners and heathens.

When we arrived at church, everyone there knew my grandmother Katie and everyone seemed to want a moment of her time to speak with her. I don't know why I got jealous about sharing her but I did. Someone asked her about organizing a health day at the church for people who didn't have medical insurance. Someone else asked her if she could find some hours to assist with the adult-literacy ministry. She graciously acknowledged everyone's plea for her assistance and she said that she would see if she could find some time in her schedule to volunteer.

"Dang, why are these people all over you like that? Can't they do stuff for themselves?" I asked with an undertone of irritation that Grandmother Katie sensed immediately.

"Get your attitude in check, young lady. You're in the house of the Lord and your nasty mood will not be tolerated in here." Grandmother Katie gave me a look that I knew instinctively not to play with unless I wanted my life to end right where I stood. I released a big sigh and wanted to follow it up with a snide remark. But out of respect for her I held my words.

"To answer your question, along with other members of our family, I have done a lot of community service in this town and for this church. It's not about people wanting me to do stuff for them. It's about giving and helping those who are in need. That is my passion. Doing this kind of work is what fills my spirit with joy and gives my life meaning and purpose."

"How are you doing, Miss Katie?" A young man in his late twenties approached us. He was gorgeous. I mean, *stop what you're doing and smile at him as hard as you could* gorgeous. I knew he was too old for me, but still, he was too fine for words.

"I'm doing fine, Erin." Grandmother Katie embraced the gentleman.

"How are Kayla and the baby doing?" she asked.

"They're doing wonderful."

"That is so good to hear. I've very proud of you. Oh, Erin, this is my granddaughter, Keysha. Keysha, this is Erin, our youth pastor."

"I didn't know you had a granddaughter. It's nice to meet you, Keysha," he said, smiling at me.

"Hi," I greeted him back, but the word came out all wrong. I sounded as if I was completely lame.

"Is this your first time here?" Erin asked.

"Yeah," I answered, smiling hard. I couldn't help it. He

looked like an older version of the singer Neo-Yo. And Lord knows I've fantasized about being Neo-Yo's wife on a number of occasions.

"Have you met anyone in the youth ministry yet?"

"The answer to that would be no." I extended my arms out as if I were taking a long stretch. When I did that my breasts rose up and jutted forward toward him. For a brief moment Erin's eyes fell downward and danced all over my breasts. A delicious twang of energy consumed my mind and body. It excited me to know that I could tempt an older man. It excited me to know that he lusted for something he couldn't have. I was about to do the move again, but I felt Grandmother Katie's laser-beam eyes all over me.

"I mean, I'm visiting my grandmother for a few days and this is my first time here so I haven't had an opportunity to meet anyone yet." I tried to cover up the naughtiness of the little temptress inside me.

"Well, sit up front and after the service I'll introduce you to some of the kids in choir."

"We will, Erin," Grandmother Katie said. We then said goodbye for the moment as we made our way to the front of the church. As soon as we sat down Grandmother Katie snapped at me.

"Little girl, don't you ever pull a stunt like that again!" Grandmother Katie's face was masked with scorn.

"Do what?" I played dumb. We locked eyes on each other as if we were having a staring contest. But Grandmother Katie wasn't toying around. She did something to me with that glare of hers. I felt as if she read every impure thought I had in my head. Grandmother Katie was admonishing me without saying a single word, and that frightened the hell out of me. No one had ever done that before. I broke eye contact. I felt as if she'd just entered my soul and found the temptress inside me and set her straight.

"Erin is a very bright and intelligent man." She began to speak. "He's a great leader and has inspired a number of young people to come off of the streets and join the church."

I wanted to say, *whatever,* but I didn't. A few moments later the choir stand began filling up with the members of the youth choir. The choir began to sing a popular gospel song by Kirk Franklin. The choir was well trained and sounded very good. The live music, the energy and the spirit of fellowship quickly filled the air around us. The young music director encouraged everyone to stand on their feet and clap their hands and sing along. Grandmother Katie stood on her feet and allowed the music to consume her. She turned toward me as she sang and I saw a completely different person. Her facial expressions, her voice and eyes were all completely filled with joy. It was amazing how quickly she changed. I'd never seen anything like that in all of my life. When the pace of the music slowed, everyone sat back down and Erin, the youth minister, stepped up to the podium.

"A lot of adults look at youth today and the only thing they see is a headache and a problem. They complain about the negative energy in the music youth listen to, they complain about the way they wear their clothes and violence they commit against each other. It would appear to many our youth today have completely lost their minds. But I'm here to tell you that it's not all about the youth and what they're doing. Some of it is about the parents and what they are not doing.

You see, as a child you come into this world knowing very little. And it is up to the parents to program the child with good information so that he or she can function and be all that God intended them to be."

"That's right," I heard Grandmother Katie say in agreement.

"When I was a young man coming of age my family wasn't rich, but we weren't poor either. We were just broke all of the time. And what I mean by that is there was always enough money to take care of the household but rarely was there enough left over for luxuries. Today, we call that 'living from paycheck to paycheck.'"

Everyone in the church laughed together because they understood where the pastor was coming from.

"When I needed new clothes for school or church my mother would always take me to a discount department store called Value Smart. And she would always take me to a shoe bin in the middle of an aisle where the shoes were connected together via their shoestrings and tell me to find my size. And I would always say, 'Dang Mama, why can't we ever go to the regular department store instead of coming here to Value Smart?' And do you know what she said?"

"Tell us what she said," Grandmother Katie said.

"She said that we don't go to those stores because I want you to understand that your value is not linked to the clothes on your back or the shoes on your feet. She told me that my value was the light that was inside me. She said my value was linked to my intelligence. She said that my value was linked to the content of my character. She said that my value was linked to how I feel about myself and not about how I look."

Wow, I thought. I felt as if Erin was speaking directly to me. I listened to the rest of his sermon, and what I thought would most certainly be a completely boring time actually turned out to be interesting.

As promised, Erin introduced me to members of the youth choir. They were all very nice and welcoming and one girl even suggested that we catch a movie during my next visit.

After church Grandmother Katie and I went to the mall. We stopped at the bath-and-body shop and she said that I could pick out some scented lotion and bubble bath for myself. I walked around sniffing a variety of scents but finally settled on a body lotion that smelled like peaches. We stopped at the food court, got something to eat and then headed back home. It was during the drive home that I got brave and decided to share the reasons behind why I gave myself to Ronnie.

"The sermon was really interesting today," I said.

"Yes, it was," Grandmother Katie agreed as she merged with the traffic on the expressway.

"All of the talk about being valuable was kind of new to me. Why do guys make girls feel as if they're valuable or special just to get what they want and then dump you?" I swallowed hard because that was a tough question for me to ask.

"Well, what is it that guys want?" she asked, and I couldn't believe that she was going to make me spell it out for her. I swallowed hard again. It wasn't easy for me to ask adult questions.

"You know, when they want you to give it up. They'll tell you how much they love you and want to be with you and say all types of things to make you feel special. And then, when you finally say yes and they get what they want, then it's like they treat you differently." I tried to make sure that my question was a broad one so that she'd believe that I was speaking about girls in general and not myself, even though I was.

"Oh, okay." Grandmother Katie was silent for a moment. "Well, young lady, first off, a young woman should never offer the honeypot to a man just because he says he loves you or makes you feel good about yourself. You should already feel good about who you are and you should love yourself. When a young woman has good self-esteem, a boy or man will not be able to come along and offer her something she already has. The second thing is, and I know this is going to sound old-fashioned, but you shouldn't do adult things and not be married. You shouldn't give a boy privileges without being in a devoted relationship, and young ladies around your age are much too young to deal with those kinds of feelings and emotions. Young people need to enjoy being young because being young only happens once."

"Okay," I said, analyzing what she'd just told me. She released a big sigh and then continued to talk.

"Keysha, young men around your age are not serious. They're too young to be seriously in love. It's a game to young men. The idea is to be as charming and as clever as you can to get a girl to lower her guard. Once they get what they're seeking, they may become bored and search for a new challenge. The other side of the coin is that once a girl gets a reputation for being active, other boys will come buzzing around like flies at a picnic in search of an opportunity to use their wit and charm to get some honey."

"Yeah, I've seen guys do that before. Okay, so how does a girl control her urges? I mean, it's not all about the boy wanting to do something. Girls have those feelings too."

"Keysha, you must understand that a woman is carrying paradise. And you can't let every ship you see dock on your shores. It is okay and normal to have urges but you're in control of them. You choose when, where and how to turn them on or off. Remember, being intimate with someone is a very special gift and should not be given away because of an urge. Urges come and go but love lasts a lifetime."

"But what if a boy doesn't like a girl because she isn't active?"

"Then he never saw the value of you in the first place."

Wow, I thought to myself. I was amazed at how Grandmother Katie connected our conversation back to the church sermon.

"Do you have any more questions?" she asked. "Come on, it's okay. You can ask whatever you want."

"No," I said. "I think I'm good for now. But if I have more, I will definitely ask you," I told her as we exited the highway and continued on our journey home.

five

Wesley

when I awoke the sun was just peeking over the horizon. A sense of peace washed over me as I watched the sun prepare to greet the world. I felt rejuvenated because I'd gotten a good night's rest. I was happy because my mom couldn't rush into my room during the night, shouting and screaming at me. Nor did I have to listen to her accuse me of doing things that I did not do. I sat upright on my bed, pressed back against the cold brick wall and peered out of the narrow window that was in my holding cell. I wanted to cry about my situation, but I fought off the urge by thinking about stuff that made me angry. That was a unique trick that I'd taught myself. It was my way of covering up just how badly my feelings were hurting. My mom has made my life a living hell. She doesn't trust me, she's suspicious of me and she makes up stories about how horrible I am as a son. She thinks I'm violent, disrespectful and has hated me since the day I was born. At least that's the way I think she feels. One time she sent me to a therapist because I told her that I'd rather run away and live on the streets than live with her. I cringed at the memory of having to go a therapist.

Spending a lot of brain energy thinking about my mom

was driving me nuts, so I decided to lie down for a while longer or at least until the guard opened the door to let me out.

Later that same day I was sitting around the common area killing time listening to Deon talk about how he'd met his girlfriend at a regional cheerleading competition.

"My buddy Jerry and I went to the competition to see how lucky we could get," Deon said. "Fifteen different schools were represented and the girls were a perfect ten."

"Yeah, right," I said, not fully believing him.

"Dude, I'm telling you. Every girl in the gymnasium that day was a hottie. It was like being at a Miss America pageant and the Playboy Mansion all at the same time."

"Okay, with all of the perfect models there, how did you manage to pick just one?" I asked.

"I don't know. It just happened. I was sitting in the bleachers watching her and her team compete for the regional title. My eyes were just drawn to her. I liked the energy she had and she never stopped smiling even when the pyramid her team tried to create collapsed because a move wasn't executed right. Right then I knew that I wanted to meet her and learn everything about her."

"So, what did you say when you got your chance to meet her?" I asked.

"I caught up to her out in the gym hallway at the water fountain. She was humped over, sucking up water like a fish. I stopped for a moment and studied her long brown legs and the way they disappeared behind her red cheerleader skirt. I studied the shapeliness of her legs and the way her calf muscles contracted to form a perfectly shaped heart. Man, she has some awesome legs." Deon momentarily became lost in his thoughts until a batch of new detainees who'd just entered the common area moved directly past us. "Anyway, our first meeting didn't go so well. I said to her, 'Hey, tough break, you'll get it next time.' She stopped drinking water and looked at me as if I'd just spit on her."

"She said, 'There won't be a next time. You'd know that if you were a true fan of the sport.'"

"Oh, snap. She treated you like that?" I asked, laughing because I could visualize him standing in the hallway with a clueless look on his face.

"Yeah, she called me out on that one. But I did try to recover because my game was tight. I know how to charm a girl. I told her that she was right. And asked her if she'd be willing to help me learn the sport. At that point she told me to get lost and rushed into the girls' locker room."

"You struck out," I said. "So, how did you guys end up dating?"

"A few weeks later I had a game at her school. When I saw her again, I was still in awe of her. She was just so perfect for me." Deon leaned back in his seat. "I took another leap of faith and actually introduced myself to her again after the game. I told her my name, where I was from and asked her if there was any chance for me to get to know her better. She smiled at me and said, 'Possibly.' And the rest, as they say, is history. What about you, Wesley? Do you have a girl?"

"No. Not right now. My last girlfriend played too many games. She liked dating several guys at the same time. The final straw came when I almost got into a fight with this guy over her. But then I realized that she really wasn't worth fighting for, so I let her go. I was cool with it, though. I wasn't terribly upset over it." I was about to tell Deon about another relationship, but Officer Sanchez called my name.

"Wesley, come here," he said. I stood up and walked over to him.

"What's up?" I asked.

"Come with me. You have a visitor," he said.

"Who?" I asked, even though I already knew the answer. My mother had arrived to cast judgment upon me.

"Your mom is here," he answered.

I suddenly felt ill. "Look, man. Do I have to go and see her? Because right now, I really don't want to. My mother is Puerto Rican and African American and has the temper of a grizzly bear."

"Yeah, you have to see her," said Officer Sanchez. "You're lucky that you have someone coming to see about you."

I grumbled loudly as I followed Officer Sanchez to the visitors' room.

I walked through a series of doors and entered the visiting area, which was set up like a large high school cafeteria.

"Okay, here are the rules." Officer Sanchez captured my gaze. "There is no touching, no yelling and no use of profanity. And don't get up from your seat until you're told to do so. Break any one of the rules you will be placed in isolation for five hours."

"Dude, please don't make me talk to her. Tell her I'm in detox right now," I pleaded.

"Have a seat right here," said Officer Sanchez, completely unmoved by my cry for mercy.

I sat at the table for a few minutes feeling anxious and jittery. The moment I saw my mom enter the room, my stomach did a somersault. The very sight of her shot my blood pressure sky-high and made my skin itch. My mom is a tall hefty woman who is fond of wearing oversized wigs and too much make-up. She absolutely refuses to allow the big hairstyles of the 1980s to die. Today she has on a sandy brown wig that is tilted too far to the right. She is wearing a long-sleeve V-necked dress that is showing too much cleavage. When my mom finally spotted me, she walked over and sat down on the opposite side of the table. I had a hard time looking at her because not only was she an embarrassing sight, but I was angry with her.

"How is it going?" she asked.

"It's going fine," I answered her.

"Are you in a cell by yourself?" she asked.

"Yeah, and it's great because I don't have to worry about you charging into my room in the middle of the night shouting at me."

"Wesley, I'm here to help. I had to do something. You're out of control and this was the only way that I could get your attention. You left me with no other choice."

"Oh, no, you don't. Don't you even try to twist this around. You had a choice. You didn't have to report your car stolen. You knew where I was going," I said to her.

"Wesley, you took my car without my permission," she said.

"No," I cut her off. "You gave me permission to take it."

"No, I didn't," she fired back at me.

"Yes, you did! You know what?" I raised the palms of my hands up. "Let's just stop now. I'm ready to go. I don't want to talk to you."

"Wesley, you have to listen to me. I love you, but I don't know what to do with you. You're lucky that the police found you before you drove home. Your alcohol levels were past the legal drinking limit. Do you know how dangerous it is to drink and drive?" she preached to me.

"Well, I had to learn how to drink and drive from some place." I looked in her eyes to see if my words hurt her, and they had. For some twisted reason hurting her feelings made me feel good. "So don't come up in here acting like the pot who called the kettle black."

"I don't do that anymore, Wesley." She tried to defend her drinking problem.

"Yeah, right. You practically come into my room every night sloshed. Yelling at me and making my life miserable."

"I need you to hear me, son. I want to help you," she said. She looked as if she wanted to cry, but I didn't have any sympathy for her at all.

"Are we done?" I asked. "Because I don't have anything else to say."

"I'll see you in court," she said, and then stood up. "I hope you fix your attitude by then."

"Yeah, whatever! I'll see you when I see you," I said as she walked out of the room. I remained seated for about fifteen minutes before Officer Sanchez reappeared. He told me that I could get up so I did and followed him back to the common area.

"Hey, *amigo,* it's not cool to be so disrespectful to your mom."

"Well, if she did some of the things to you that she's done

to me, you'd fully understand why things are the way they are."

"But she's still your mom and you have to respect her no matter what," said Officer Sanchez.

I didn't respond to him because I didn't fully agree with what he was saying to me. In my mind, my mom was crazy and if I didn't get away from her soon, I'd go crazy too.

"So, what are you going to say at your court hearing tomorrow?" asked Officer Sanchez.

"Whatever it takes to get the judge to see that I don't want to go back to my mother's house," I answered.

"Where do you want to go?" he asked.

"With my dad," I said.

"You and your dad get along well?"

"Yeah. Me and my dad are real cool. We don't have any problems. I'd go live with him in a heartbeat, but my mother won't let me."

"Why not?"

"Because she sees me and the child-support check as a way to support her drinkng problem. And that's the truth, man."

"Is that how you started drinking?" asked Officer Sanchez. "By watching your mom?"

"Something like that."

"*Amigo,* you're only sixteen. You shouldn't be drinking to solve your problems. How long have been doing this?"

"About three years. Since I was thirteen."

"Do you think you need help?" asked Officer Sanchez.

"Dude, right now I'm in the best place in the world. So, as far as I'm concerned, my call for help has been answered."

"That's twisted, man. You don't want to be here. This is not a place to live," said Officer Sanchez.

"Well, for now it suits me just fine," I said as he opened the door for me to head back to the common area.

Later that evening I received a phone call from my dad. I was happy to hear from him because I knew he'd understand everything that I was going through.

"Hey, Wesley, how is it going?" he asked me through the phone.

"Well, things have been better," I admitted. "I can't wait to get out of here."

"Yeah, I know, son. I heard that your mom came to visit you today. How did that go?" he asked.

"Not so good," I answered him truthfully.

"Was she sober when she came to see you?"

"Yeah, she was sober, but we still got into a little bit of a shouting match." I began bitting my fingernails. "Hey, Dad."

"Yes?"

"I want to come and live with you. I don't want to be in Mom's house anymore and I'm going to let the judge know that."

"Well, don't you worry about that, Wesley. I've got a lawyer coming with me tomorrow and together we're going to get all of this mess straightened out, okay?"

"Okay," I answered.

"Now, you get some rest. You've got a big day tomorrow and you're going to need all of your strength."

"Okay, Dad, love you," I said.

"Love you too," he responded.

SIX

Keysha

I was standing at the kitchen sink with my head underneath the water faucet getting my hair washed by Grandmother Katie. She was massaging shampoo into my scalp and the strokes of her fingertips put me in such a relaxed state that I felt I was going to sleep.

"All right, I'm going to rinse this shampoo out now," she said as she carefully and skillfully guided my movements so that all of the shampoo was washed out.

"My grandmother used to wash my hair like this all the time when I was a young girl," she said. "I loved the feeling of her strong, soft hands."

"What was your grandmother like?" I asked as I stood erect, and began the process of drying my hair so that Grandmother Katie could blow-dry and curl it for me.

"Your great-great-grandmother Lorraine was a very tall woman. She stood around six foot one or two. She had a very difficult life, though. You see, her mother passed away when she was only twelve years old. And her father was as mean as a pack of wolves. When I was a little girl, he used to own a corner newspaper stand. He sold the daily paper, soda pop and candy every day. One particular day I'd found myself four pennies while outside playing. I walked to the corner where his newspaper stand was and asked for a piece of hard candy. I stood on my tiptoes and placed my four pennies atop a stack of newspapers and waited for my candy. Do you know what that low-down snake-in-the-grass man said to me?"

"No, what did he say?"

"He told me that hard candy costs five cents. I looked at him perplexed because I knew he'd let me get away with being a penny short. That mean man glared nastily at me and said, 'Now, git on-way from round here. And don' come back till you got all yo' money.'"

"You're kidding, right?" I asked.

"No. I'm not," said Grandmother Katie.

"That was mean," I said. We went upstairs to her bedroom so that I could sit on a small stool while she blow-dried my hair.

"Why was he so mean?" I asked as I sat on the stool. Grandmother Katie draped a towel over my shoulders.

"I think he'd seen a lot of things in Mississippi as a young man that made him very bitter and mean-spirited. As a result of his experiences I was told that he placed an iron wall around his heart so that he wouldn't have to deal with his pain. My grandmother told me one day, someone would come along and break through his iron wall and help him deal with all of the vaulted emotions he'd been hiding. For a long time I thought I could fix his broken heart, but I was wrong. He died an old, lonely and bitter man."

"Don't you get lonely being in this big house by yourself? I mean, this is a big house for one person," I said.

"No, not at all. I have plenty to keep me busy and from

being bored. Besides, Smokey keeps me company. I was lonely and sad for a while after the passing of your grandfather. He would not have wanted me to stop living, so I grieved and moved on. I see life so differently now. I feel that my purpose is to help others any way I am able."

"Well, lately I've been thinking about my situation," I said. Grandmother Katie turned off the blow dryer so she could hear me. I figured since she wanted to be of service, it couldn't hurt to share my thoughts.

"Go on, I'm listening," she said.

"I know that my friend Liz is behind what has happened to me. I know that she set me up but I don't know why. I don't know why she pretended to be my friend and then turned around and stabbed me in the back. It just doesn't make any sense," I said.

"Have you talked with her since all of this madness began?" asked Grandmother Katie.

"No," I answered. Grandmother Katie took in a deep breath and then exhaled. I could sense that my situation was heavy on her heart.

"I'm going to find out, though," I said. "When I go back home tomorrow, I'm going to confront her and just ask her straight out. Why did you do me like this?"

"Well, if you ask and she doesn't give you an answer, don't push it. The truth will come out in court," said Grandmother Katie.

"But I don't want to go to court. I want her to own up to what she's done. I mean, setting me up like that was just low down." I started feeling myself get emotional about being framed.

"Remember, Keysha, you don't want to get yourself into any more trouble, okay? You have your entire life ahead of you and I don't want things to spiral out of control."

"But this entire situation is stupid. All of the charges can be dropped if she'll just admit to what she's done."

"Maybe she won't talk because she's protecting someone," Grandmother Katie said. "I'm not defending her actions, I'm just trying to think of a reason as to why she'd do it."

"If Liz is protecting anyone, it's her own self. But I don't care about her need for self-preservation, I just want my life back," I said to Grandmother Katie.

"And you will get it back. I promise you that," she said.

I was silent for a long moment because I was lost in thought. Grandmother Katie turned on the handheld dryer again as I continued to visualize my confrontation with Liz. If she didn't own up to what she'd done, I planned to beat her down until she did.

seven

Wesley

OFFICER Sanchez entered the common area and asked the detainees that were assigned specifically to him to form a large circle with the chairs. We were about to have a group discussion about the reasons why we were being detained and what changes we were going to make once we got out.

"I wanted to take some time to talk about what you can do to change your life so that you don't end up back here or in a maximum-security prison. Yesterday during visitation I noticed that Wesley here—" Officer Sanchez nodded his head in my direction "—was being very disrespectful to his mother. He was so disrespectful that when she left she was in tears. Wesley, why were you being so insolent to your mom? And second, does anyone in the group feel that it is ever appropriate to be rude to your parents?"

"You all just don't understand the things my mom has put me through," I said as my stomach began doing flips. I didn't think that I'd have to defend my ill feelings toward my mother.

"Well, tell us." Officer Sanchez encouraged me to open up to the group, but I wasn't about to spill my guts to a bunch of guys I didn't know. I'd look like a complete punk if I did that.

"Let's just say she doesn't do the things that a mother is supposed to do," I answered, and wanted the conversation regarding me and my mother to end.

"Hey, man, that's your mom," said Santiago, a short Latino guy with thick black eyebrows whom I'd spoken to only briefly during lunch break. At the time of our greeting we only said hello and asked each other what we were in for. I learned that he was here for vandalism. However, he certainly didn't know me well enough to be offering up advice about my situation. "I know that I don't know you all that good but it's your mom, man. You're going to need her before she needs you. In my opinion, you need to settle whatever beef you have with her."

"You don't have a clue," I answered him, feeling as if he was sticking his nose in my private business. "That woman has done things and said things that no mother should do or say."

"Like what?" asked Officer Sanchez.

"Forget it, man. Move on to someone else. I don't want to talk about my problems right now."

"But it's your problems that got you here, cowboy." Santiago kept running his mouth and I didn't like it. "Don't you think that having a bad relationship with your mom has led to you being here?"

That did it. I felt rage starting to flow through my veins.

"What about your mom? What's your relationship with your mother like?" I snapped at him. I locked my gaze upon him so that there was no mistaking my anger.

"Man." Santiago dropped his eyes and focused on the floor before him. It wasn't the reaction that I was anticipating. "I wish I could have a relationship with my mom. She's gone. She left me with my elderly grandmother when I was two years old to try to make it big as a singer in Las Vegas. She left Chicago with a suitcase, a bus ticket and a big dream. She ended up on the streets, selling herself. Eventually, her life-style took her life. So I'm talking to you from the perspective of someone who would've loved to have one more day with my mother, regardless of how much I disagreed with her."

I leaned back in my seat because I didn't know how to respond to that. All I knew was how I felt. My mom bruised my heart in such a way that I vowed to never allow her to get close to me again, and when I made that commitment, I shut my emotions toward her off. Right now I just didn't see any way to change my animosity toward her.

"You have your court hearing tomorrow," said Officer Sanchez, speaking to me. "When you go before the judge, what are you going to say in your defense?"

"I'm going to tell her that I don't want to live in my mother's house anymore and that I want to go and live with my dad. Life is so much better with my dad. We get along very well and I just think everything will be much better than what it is now," I said.

Officer Sanchez looked directly at me, searching my eyes for sincerity.

"Okay, perhaps living with your dad will be much better for you. Do you respect your father?" he asked.

"Yeah, I respect him."

"Do you argue and yell at your dad?"

"No, he isn't going to put up with me shouting at him. I just don't have a reason to be angry with him," I said.

"That's good," Officer Sanchez said. He was satisfied with the answers I'd given him. Officer Sanchez shifted his attention to Deon and began speaking about the fight he'd gotten into and how he could have prevented the brawl.

A few hours later I found myself hanging out with Santiago and a few of the new detainees. Deon had already gone before the judge and I'd received word that the judge released him to the custody of his parents. I heard that he got off with twenty hours of community service. The news of his release sparked conversation between Santiago and me. "Who is the judge in your case, man?" asked Santiago.

"I got Judge Hill," I answered briefly, wondering when and where I'd run into Deon again. I was thinking that he could've at least come back to say goodbye, but then I realized that he probably couldn't.

"Aw, man. She's tough. I've gone in front of her before. She doesn't play around. I know when she sees me again, she's going to throw the book at me."

"You've been in here before?" I asked, sort of surprised.

"Yeah, I'm kind of a repeat offender. I saw Judge Hill about five months ago on a trespassing case. This home construction company was building a new subdivision near my home. Some friends and I waited until after the construction workers left for the evening and jumped the fence. We ignored the giant No Trespassing sign and wandered around to check out the new homes. Some nosey neighbor saw us jump the fence and called the cops. When the police arrived, my friends and I scattered, but I was the only one they caught. I was arrested and they booked me on trespassing charges."

"She's really not going to be happy about seeing you brought in this time on vandalism charges."

"I know. Judge Hill is going to scream at me, I just know it. She gave me three months' worth of community service for trespassing and she'll probably triple my sentence for vandalism." Santiago paused in thought. "I had to get up every Saturday morning and go down to the homeless shelter and work like a slave. I'm being real with you. If she doesn't sentence you to community service, she'll fine your parents, or worse, she will leave you locked up, especially if she thinks for a second that you haven't learned your lesson."

I didn't say anything because I was at a loss for words. I also didn't feel good about going before a tough-as-nails judge. I suddenly wasn't so sure if she'd see my side of the story or at least be willing to listen to what I had to say.

"So, what do you suggest I do when I see her?" I asked. I wanted to get a better sense of what to expect.

"Hey, man, just don't be disrespectful and tell your side of the story. Maybe she'll understand," said Santiago.

About a half hour later Officer Sanchez and several other security staff members came toward me, carrying handcuffs and shackles for my ankles. I was still sitting at the table with Santiago, playing a card game.

"Okay, *amigo,* I need you to turn around and kneel down on the floor with your hands behind your back."

I took a deep breath and did as Officer Sanchez said. He placed my ankles and hands in the shackles. Officer Sanchez helped me stand on my feet and then escorted me out of the common area and over to the court building.

"Your parents have already arrived," he told me as we walked down a long corridor.

I didn't say anything because my emotions were swelling like a water barrel about to overflow. I was trying to contain them as best I could, but it wasn't easy. We stopped in front of a wooden door that said Courtroom Nine, Judge Nancy Hill. I swallowed hard as Officer Sanchez opened the door. I stepped inside and awaited further instructions.

"I'm going to take off the handcuffs. You are to have a seat over there next to the attorney your father has gotten to represent you." Officer Sanchez pointed to a bald-headed African-American man who wore glasses similar to those that fictional character Harry Potter wears. I said okay and did as I was told. As I moved deeper into the courtroom I saw my dad and acknowledged him by nodding my head in his direction. My mom was sitting as far away from him as possible. We made eye contact but did not exchange greetings through body language.

"Hi, I'm Rick Waters," the attorney said as he shook my hand. "I've been talking your case over with your father, who has filled me in on some of the problems you've been going through with your mother. I want to ask you a few questions before the judge enters the courtroom."

"Okay," I said. Mr. Waters asked me a series of questions about my relationship with my mother and my father. His tone was serious as he inquired about where I'd gotten alcohol from and how long I had been drinking. He also asked me how I was introduced to alcohol and how often I drank. I answered his questions openly and honestly. Just as we were finishing up, the judge entered the courtroom. Everyone had to rise to his or her feet when she entered and then sat back down after she did.

"Okay, I've read over the circumstances involving this case and I want to start by asking a few questions of Ms. Carter," said Judge Hill. "Ms. Carter, would you please have a seat up here next to me on the bench?"

I watched as my mom took a seat next to the judge. I could tell that she wasn't comfortable.

"Ms. Carter, can you explain to me what happened and why you reported your car stolen?"

"Yes." My mom paused for a second as she cleared her throat. "I was taking a nap and when I woke up to run an errand, I noticed that my car was gone. I didn't know what happened to it. I figured that it must have been stolen because my neighbor's car was stolen a few days earlier."

I held my head down in disgust. I could tell that not only was my mother telling a lie, but also by her speech patterns, she'd been drinking.

"Ma'am, do you allow your son, Wesley, to drive your vehicle?" asked Judge Hill.

My mother repositioned herself in her seat. Her body language was giving her away. Now it was not only clear to me that she'd been drinking, but Judge Hill was also suspicious. "You know, I let him drive sometimes. Around the neighborhood or to the— What do you call it?" My mom began snapping her fingers because she couldn't recall the word she was trying to say. "Oh, dammit, what's the damn word I'm searching for? You know the word." She looked at the judge for an answer.

"No, I don't know the word." Judge Hill appeared to be

irritated with my mother. "And I ask that you refrain from cursing in my courtroom."

"The place where the kids go and buy clothes." Mom raised her voice to Judge Hill. "The mall." The word finally came to her.

"Ma'am, are you under the influence of any prescription medication or perhaps a narcotic?"

"I'm no damn drug addict," my mom snapped at Judge Hill.

"Ma'am, one more outburst like that and I will fine you," Judge Hill barked back at my mother. "Now answer my question. Are you under the influence of anything?"

"Okay." My mom began trying to explain herself. "I was just a little bit nervous." She squeezed her thumb and index finger closely together to emphasize her point. "So to help calm my nerves I had a little something to drink."

A very stern and dissatisfied expression washed over Judge Hill's face. She looked at her watch. "Ma'am, do you realize that it's only 10:30 a.m. and you're already intoxicated?"

"I'm not intoxicated," my mom snapped back at the judge. There was no way she was about to admit that she'd had one too many.

"Ma'am, have you ever given alcohol to your son?" asked Judge Hill.

"Who, Wesley?" My mother asked the question as if she'd never heard of me. "You know, it's better if he does that kind of thing at home with me where it's safe." My mom looked to the judge for approval of her rationale, but she didn't get it. "Look, I'd rather that he be in the house with me drinking than being out in the streets. At least I'd be able to monitor him." My mom began raising hell because she wasn't getting the response she wanted from Judge Hill. "Sure, I've let him have a glass of wine around the holidays and other special occasions." My mom finally admitted that she had introduced me to alcohol.

"Do you realize that in this state that is considered to be child endangerment?" asked Judge Hill.

"Come on, it's just a sip of wine from time to time. It's nothing serious." My mom downplayed the significance of her error in judgment.

"I have no further questions," said Judge Hill as she began jotting down some notes. "Mr. Waters, do you have any questions?"

"Yes, Your Honor, I do," said Mr. Waters. "First, I'd like to state that the problems between Wesley and his mother go back several years. Now, Ms. Carter, would you like for Wesley to go home with you today?"

"Yes, Wesley needs to be at home with me. His dad is too irresponsible to take good care of him like I do."

"Do you feel that providing a minor with alcohol is a good standard of parental care?"

"Look, it's not as if I gave my son a bottle of Jack Daniel's after school and said 'drink up.' It was just a few sips of wine every now and again."

"Ms. Carter, do you keep alcohol in your home?"

"Of course I do. Everyone does," my mom answered.

"Ms. Carter, are you aware that when Wesley was picked up by the police, he had a blood-alcohol level that was above the legal driving limit?"

"Yes, I know about that."

"Where do you think Wesley got the alcohol from?"

"I don't know, out in the streets somewhere. He probably got it from one of his older friends. Now, that's who you should be after. The one who gave him the hard stuff." My mother wanted to get the focus off of her.

"Ms. Carter, is it fair to say that your protection of Wesley from drinking outside of the home has failed and that, in fact, you have been encouraging your son to drink with you other than on special occasions?"

"No, that's not true!" my mom howled out. "Listen, mister! Don't you go trying to twist my words around! I'm a good mother and I love my son. He's all I've got. I can't be with him everywhere. If he gets alcohol out there in the streets, that's not my fault! You need to go out and find the criminals who got him intoxicated. If I knew who did it, I'd go and make a citizen's arrest myself!"

"Your Honor, I have no further questions," said Mr. Waters.

"Okay, I want to hear from Wesley," said Judge Hill. "Please approach the bench."

I stood up from my seat and approached the bench near Judge Hill. I was nervous but happy because I was finally going to get a chance to tell my side of the story.

"Wesley." Judge Hill looked at me.

"Yes, ma'am," I answered.

"Who would you like to be released to today?" she asked.

"If I had a choice, I'd really like to go and live with my dad."

"Why is that?" she asked.

"Because." I paused to select the right words. I had wanted

to be fearless with my criticism of my mother, but when I looked at her I began to feel sorry for her. "I mean—my dad and I get along well and me and my mom don't. We haven't gotten along in a very long time. My life was great until I turned thirteen." I sniffled. "Aw, man." I felt myself tearing up as I was about to speak the truth and bare my soul to Judge Hill. "As far as I know, the reason my parents got a divorce is because my mom accused him of physically abusing me. And that just wasn't true. When she divorced him, she forced me to sit down and have a drink with her to celebrate their separation. She was happy about it, but I was miserable. My heart was so torn up over the divorce."

I stopped talking so that I could wipe the tears away from my eyes. "Man, this is harder than I thought it would be." I swallowed hard and took a few deep breaths to calm my nerves and manage the adrenaline that was flowing through me. "The first time I got drunk was that day with my mom. Once I recovered from being sick and managing my hangover, I made a vow to myself to try and get them back together so that we could be a happy family again. But that all changed when her boyfriend moved into the house just one week after my parents' divorce. That hurt me so badly that I just didn't know what to do." I stopped talking because my words were imprisoned in my chest.

"Wesley, why are you telling these lies on me?" my mother blurted out from the rear of the courtroom. I looked into her eyes and saw nothing but defiance in them. At that moment, I sucked up my emotions, got angry and barked back at her.

"What I'm saying is not a lie! It's the truth and you know it! You ruined everything! You ruined a great home and a great life all for some jerk that was cheating on you. My dad is a good man and you treated him like scum. You made it seem as if everything was his fault. But it wasn't his fault at all! You wanted a divorce from my dad so that you could be with some jerk. You're a big liar and you're a drunk, Mom!"

Judge Hill slammed down her gavel.

"Okay, that's enough," she said, and I calmed myself down. There was a long moment of silence. I noticed that Judge Hill was scribbling down something on a notepad.

"Wesley, has your dad ever abused you?" asked Judge Hill.

"No, ma'am, never," I answered.

"Okay, I have no further questions of you. I'd like to hear from your dad now. Mr. Morris, would you please have a seat up here on the bench next to me?" Judge Hill pointed to the seat beside her. My dad got up from his seat and did as Judge Hill asked.

"Mr. Morris, do you live in Illinois?" asked Judge Hill.

"Yes," answered my dad. "I live about eight miles away from Wesley."

"Mr. Morris, what do you do for living?"

"Right now I work as a claims adjuster for an insurance company."

"And how long have you had that job?" she asked.

"I've been an adjuster now for about six years," answered my dad.

"Do you have room for your son?" asked Judge Hill.

"Yes, I do. I've always had room for him and he knows that he can come and stay with me anytime."

"Would you like to have primary custody of your son?" asked Judge Hill.

"Yes, I would," answered my dad.

"Is there anything additional you'd like to tell the court?"

"I'd just like to say that I know that Wesley has been struggling with a lot of things and that I know he hasn't had any peace since the divorce. I have really made an effort to be a part of his life, but at times his mom has alienated me from him and has done a lot of things to keep us apart. If Wesley were to come home with me, we'd work out whatever problems he's having. There will be ground rules that he'll have to follow in order to keep him out of trouble, but honestly, Wesley isn't a bad kid. He's just a kid in a crisis situation."

"Do you have any questions of Mr. Morris, Mr. Waters?" Judge Hill looked at the attorney my dad hired.

"Mr. Morris, are you behind on your child-support payments?"

"No. I'm actually three months ahead," answered my dad.

"I have no further questions, Your Honor," said Mr. Waters.

"Okay, you may step down and go back to your seat," Judge Hill instructed my dad. Once he sat down, Judge Hill began to speak.

"Okay, let's cut to the chase here. Today this court is going to reduce the charge of auto theft down to joyriding. This court is also going to find probable cause that Wesley needs crisis intervention to address his addiction to alcohol. I am mandating that he get treatment at the Mayville Rehab Facility. This court is also going to order that this child be released from the custody of this facility into the custody of his father." Judge Hill slammed down her gavel, indicating that her decision was final.

I leaned back in my seat and exhaled a big sigh of relief. *That was intense,* I thought as I closed my eyes for a brief moment. When I opened them back up, Officer Sanchez was standing next to me.

"Come with me," he said. I followed Officer Sanchez past Judge Hill.

"Wait a minute," I said, stopping. "I just want to say thank you. I am so glad you listened to me."

"You make sure that you do right by your father, stay sober and don't let me see you in here again or else." Judge Hill glanced at me for a brief moment before opening up the file folder to her next case. I walked out of the courtroom feeling a sense of relief.

eight

Keysha

I was fussing with my suitcase as I tried to pull it up the stairs to my bedroom. My luggage was much heavier because Grandmother Katie and I had gone shopping for fall clothing. Grandmother Katie had purchased two winter coats, several turtleneck sweaters and a variety of other necessary clothing for Chicago's harsh winter season, which would be arriving soon. I jerked so hard on the suitcase that the strap snapped off and the suitcase tumbled down the stairs.

"Mike." I called out my brother's name. I needed him to come out of his bedroom and help me.

"Mike, I know you hear me, boy!" I said with an irritated tone because he didn't answer me right away.

"What?" he shouted out.

"Can you please come help me with this suitcase?" I asked.

"No. I'm busy revamping my MySpace page," he hollered out to me.

"That's okay, you're going to need me for something one day and I'm going to be just as inconsiderate to you as you are being now." I walked back down the stairs and tried to pull my suitcase up the stairs once again. Several moments later Mike came out of his room wearing his blue pajama pants and a Bernie Mac T-shirt that had the phrase I Ain't Scared of You in bold letters just below the image of Bernie's face. Mike had been spending an enormous amount of time in the gym and in the workout room above the garage. His biceps, triceps and chest were noticeably bigger. Although I hadn't been gone very long, Mike seemed to have gotten a little taller and his voice seemed a little deeper. I hated to admit it, but he actually had all of the tools to be an irresistible man. But I wasn't going to tell him that. I didn't see the need to inflate his head or ego any more than it already was.

"I'll get it," he said as he maneuvered around me.

"What for? I'm almost there now," I said with a wise attitude.

"Look, do you want some help or not?" he asked. He finally grabbed my luggage and hauled it up the remaining steps.

"Jeez, what do you have in here? A dead body?" Mike complained.

"Come on, use your man strength, I'm sure all of your bulking muscles can handle my small suitcase."

Mike gave me a sarcastic look. "Whatever," he said, and then left the suitcase at the top of the landing before heading back into his room.

"Thank you, Mike," I said aloud. I rolled the suitcase into my room and unpacked all of my clothes. Just as I was about to hang up my new winter coat, Grandmother Katie and Jordan, my dad, entered my room. My dad would be turning forty soon but could easily pass for a man in his midthirties, especially if he dyed his hair to hide the gray. He's tall and has the same chocolate brown skin as me. He has broad shoulders and sizable arms. Although he has a little bit of a tummy, it doesn't droop over his belt.

"Okay, baby, I'm going to head back home now. I've got a long drive ahead of me." Grandmother expanded her arms so that I could step into her embrace for a giant hug. I know it sounds silly and probably a bit childish but I loved getting hugs from her.

"Now, you remember what we talked about, okay? And if you need anything, just pick up the phone and call me."

"Okay, I will," I said.

"Now, let me go down the hallway and fuss at Mike for not coming out of his room to say hello to me." Grandmother Katie exited my room and headed down the hallway toward Mike's room.

"So, how was your visit?" asked Jordan.

"It was good," I answered as I scanned my room in search of my television remote.

"Just good? Did anything happen?" Jordan pressed the issue.

"No, nothing happened," I said, not sure why he was grilling me. "Anything happen here?"

"No. Nothing happened while you were away. How do you feel about spending time with your grandmother?"

"It was cool. It was nice to get away from all of the madness. I had a chance to clear my head and think about my situation."

"Is there anything new you'd like to share with me regarding your situation?" asked Jordan.

"No," I answered. I wasn't ready to tell him that I knew

what Liz had done. I wanted to wait until I got an answer from her as to why she'd set me up.

"Are you nervous about going back to school tomorrow?" he asked.

"No," I said. "In fact, I can't wait to get back. There are a lot of things I need to get straightened out."

"Like what?" Jordan asked suspiciously.

"Just school stuff. You know, working on improving my grades and stuff like that," I lied to him. The only thing that was really on my mind was confronting Liz. I thought about calling her but changed my mind because we needed to talk face-to-face.

"Well, I'll let you finish getting settled in. I'll be down in my office, working, if you need me," he said, and then left my room. Once he was gone, I shut my door and turned on my radio. A popular song by Destiny's Child came blaring through the speakers. I rocked my head to the melody as I sang "I'm a Survivor."

The following morning at 6:00 a.m. my alarm clock began buzzing loudly.

"Dang," I said as I looked at the clock, which was sitting atop my desk on the opposite side of the room. I tossed back my bed linen and dawdled over to the desk and slapped the off button so the loud noise would stop. The alarm clock was normally situated on the nightstand next to my bed, but my stepmother, Barbara, moved it because I kept hitting the snooze button instead of getting out of bed.

I was about to get back in bed and lie down because I really wanted to sleep a little longer, but I heard a knock at my door.

"Who is it?" I asked.

"You know who it is." Mike didn't wait for me to invite him in. He opened the door.

"What's up, son?" he greeted me.

"Mike, I am not a boy, would you please stop calling me son!" I think Mike enjoyed irritating me. Mike was already dressed. He had on a pair of Girbaud blue jeans and a matching button-down blue jean shirt. He had a black do-rag on his head so that his hair would appear wavy and smooth once he removed it.

"How was your visit with Grandmother Katie?" he asked.

"It was okay, I was bored at times but overall it was a nice visit," I said to him as I sat down on the edge of my bed. I yawned but covered my mouth so that my breath wouldn't assault the air around us.

"So, what's been going on around here?" I asked.

Mike looked at me for a long moment before speaking. "It's been a trip. This whole drug thing you're mixed up in has everyone talking. The rumors that are going around are very ugly."

"Rumors?" I asked. "What rumors? Jordan said nothing new went down."

"He doesn't know about the rumors. People believe you're a straight-up drug dealer, girl. There are rumors about the Ecstasy being made in this house. Rumors about some girl named Toya Taylor who you used to get high with but then ratted out to the cops because you wanted to have a relationship with her but she rejected you."

"What!" I almost puked when I heard that. "Where are these ridiculous rumors coming from?" I asked.

"The rumor mill!" Mike said sarcastically. "I don't have a clue as to where they're coming from. I do know the rumors have messed up my reputation at school. People are saying that I'm helping you sell it because I've been defending your name."

"Sit down here next to me." I patted a spot on the bed. Mike came over and sat down.

"It's Liz," I said. "Liz is responsible for all of this drama, Mike. I got a chance to do some thinking when I was at Grandmother Katie's house and I realized that Liz is the one who planted the drugs on me."

"We'll have to get her to confess that before you get put in jail."

"Put in jail? What are you talking about? I thought we were going to fight this and win?"

"Well, I probably shouldn't tell you this but I overheard a conversation Dad had with your lawyer, Asia. And from what I could tell, the police feel as if they have a slam-dunk case against you. They're not even looking for the real criminals."

"That's crazy." My voice trembled with nervousness. "I didn't do anything. This is all Liz's fault. This is her doing. Why can't they see that?"

"I don't know," Mike answered. We were both silent for a moment because we were at a loss for words.

"I can't go down for something like this," I said. "It's not fair." I stood up and began pacing back and forth. I was trying to focus my thoughts on what to do next. "If my grandmother Rubylee were here, she'd get all of this mess straightened out in no time flat. She wouldn't even be stressed out over it." I turned toward Mike.

"Well, what do you think your other grandmother would do in a situation like this?" asked Mike.

"Who, Rubylee?"

"Yeah, Rubylee. What would she do?"

"She would tell Liz, 'I'm about to kill you cemetery dead' and then shoot her where she stood," I answered. "But killing her is not an option for me. I need her alive."

"I say kill her anyway." Mike laughed a little bit.

"My grandmother Rubylee doesn't play around," I said as I raised my index finger to my teeth and began chewing on my fingernails. "I've already made up my mind to confront Liz and ask for an explanation and a confession." I focused my attention on Mike. I was searching his eyes for support.

"What if she doesn't confess?" he asked.

"Then I'll have to make her," I answered with absolute resolve. "Let me finish getting dressed. I've got a big day ahead of me. I've got to deal with all the rumors, confront Liz and clear my name."

"That's easier said than done," Mike said as he stood up and walked out of my room.

"Yeah, I know," I mumbled to myself. "But I have to do what I have to do. Some days are just born ugly, and this day is shaping up to be a very ugly day."

nine

yesterday, after the judge rendered her decision, I walked out of the courtroom and was escorted to a holding area. After I'd waited for about twenty minutes, Officer Sanchez entered the area with a box that contained all of my belongings.

"This is it for you, *amigo*. You make sure that you do right by your father."

"Oh, you don't have to worry about that," I said as I opened the box and removed my jeans.

"I don't want to ever see you back here, you understand?" Officer Sanchez was about to leave the room to give me some privacy.

"Trust me, I'm never coming back to this place. I hated being locked up," I said, even though I hadn't wanted to admit it when I arrived.

"No, you told me that you liked it here, remember?"

"Yeah, I remember what I said. This place was better than where I was at, trust me on that one. But staying here permanently would have driven me crazy."

"Make sure that you do great things with your life. You

seem like a smart guy. I hope my perception of you is correct."

"It is and I will," I said. Officer Sanchez instructed me to place my prison clothes in the box once I was fully dressed and to leave them in the room.

"You'll have to stop at the front desk to fill out some paperwork. After you've completed it, you're free to go."

"Hey, thanks," I said, extending my hand for a handshake. "Thanks for helping me get through this."

"No problem. You take care of yourself." Officer Sanchez said his final goodbye and then left.

I never thought putting on my own clothes could feel so wonderful and liberating, but it did. I followed Officer Sanchez's instructions and filled out some paperwork at the front desk, which was nothing more than a sheet of paper that confirmed I received all of the belongings I had when I arrived. Once I did that, I walked through a series of doors until I saw my dad sitting on a chair waiting for me. When he saw me, he stood up. I walked over to him and gave him a big hug.

"Man, you've got to go on a diet," I said as I patted his belly, which was as round as a barrel. He tried to suck it in, but that couldn't hide the years of bad eating habits and lack of exercise.

"Yeah, well, when you get to be my age your metabolism slows down quite a bit," he said, chuckling. My dad is slightly taller than I am, he has broad shoulders that slope downward and he leans forward when he walks. His skin complexion is almond brown and he has a bald pattern shaped like a horseshoe on top of his head. I've been trying to get him to completely shave his head, but he refuses to do it. He keeps saying it might grow back, but the chances of that ever happening are extremely slim.

"Are you all set?" asked my dad.

"Yeah, where is our attorney, Mr. Waters? I want to thank him."

"He walked me through some paperwork I had to fill out but then headed back to his office. He's a busy man. I'll be sure to let him know how much you appreciate his hard work."

I was silent for a moment as I stood in the presence of my father. On the inside I was jumping up and down, but on the outside I was just trying to be cool about everything.

"Come on, let's get out of here," said my dad.

"You took the words right out of my mouth." We walked out of the facility together and into the bright sunlight. I felt renewed and I was certainly overjoyed with the fact that I'd been given a second chance.

Being able to live with my dad was the best thing that could've ever happened to me. Now I wouldn't have to worry about being in an environment where there was constant yelling and shouting. I no longer had to worry about my mother's mood swings, her lies, her temper or her manipulating ways. I was so thankful that Judge Hill was able to see and understand that I was in crisis and needed an exit out of my situation.

When my dad and I arrived back at his house we sat out on the patio so we could relax and have a very serious conversation. As I sat I mentally prepared myself to listen.

"Here." My dad handed me a can of soda as he walked through the large patio door.

"I know that it hasn't been easy on you," my dad started. "Neither you nor I have known a moment of harmony since the divorce. I'm so sorry that your mom has been encouraging you to drink, which has led to your bad decisions." My dad paused and then looked directly into my eyes.

"I knew there was something going on but—how serious is your drinking problem?" He asked the killer question.

I swallowed hard as I tried to find an answer to his question. I didn't know what to say so I remained silent.

"Okay, let me try getting my answers another way."

"Where have you been getting alcohol from?" He asked another killer question.

I leaned forward in my seat, stared at the ground and began tapping my foot against the pavement. His questions were making me nervous. I felt that if I answered them, he might not want me. I feared that he'd ship me off to some orphanage or some reform school for kids who were really messed up.

"I just want the truth, Wesley," he said.

Again, I swallowed hard because I didn't know where to begin.

"Answer me." My dad demanded a response.

"I, um." I choked on my words. "I know that I have a problem. But I want to fix it. I don't want to be like Mom. She did this to me. She made me drink with her. The first time I drank with her I got so sick and I hated that feeling. But then when I told my friends that I got sloshed with my mom, they all thought she was the coolest mother in the world. Since my friends thought it was cool, I just went with the flow. At first I was a light drinker. I'd have a beer every now and again, but when I entered high school, I hooked up with a group of kids who loved to party. They could get their hands on anything through this adult guy named Neophus and his student contact, who is a girl named Liz."

"Why didn't you tell me about this? Why hasn't anyone reported these people to the police? With all of this information everyone could be charged with child endangerment, including your mom." My dad was shocked and troubled by what I was telling him.

"No one wants to be a snitch, Dad. Besides, I wouldn't feel right turning in my own mother. I don't think I could live with the guilt that I'd feel in spite of all she's done. Besides, everyone was having a great time and no one was getting hurt."

"Well, it may be too late for your mom. The cat is out of the bag and Judge Hill didn't like the fact that your mother gave you alcohol. I'm almost positive that there will be consequences for her actions."

I didn't say anything because I suddenly felt numb. I didn't like my mother, there was no question about that, but to see her convicted of a crime wasn't on my agenda either.

"The consequences? Did any of your friends ever stop to think about the consequences of their actions?" he asked.

"No. We were having fun. We don't think about stuff like that, especially when we're partying."

My dad leaned back in his chair and brushed his hand across his lips. I could tell that he wanted to know more, but he was thinking about how to phrase his words.

"Okay." He inhaled and then exhaled. "So, how often do you drink?"

"Every day," I answered truthfully. "But I want to change," I quickly added. "You've got to believe me. I really want to change."

My dad stood up and began pacing back and forth. He was thinking very hard. I could see the worry and concern written on his face. He rubbed the tension out of his neck as he processed his thoughts.

"I'll do whatever it takes, Dad." My emotions started getting involved. I felt as if my father didn't want to know the truth and I began to panic. "Please don't put me out like Mom used to do. I hated it when she did that. She'd come home, start a fight with me and then force me out of the house." I swallowed down my anxiety because I didn't want to cry. I was sixteen years old and way too mature to be crying like a baby, so I began using the angry and bitter feelings I had for my mom to squash the crying spell I felt I was about to have.

"When she did crazy stuff like that, I wanted to tell you but I didn't know how. I didn't know where to begin or even how to express my pain. I thought everything was my fault, your divorce, her unhappiness and even her drinking problem. Somehow she made me feel as if I was the root cause of everything that was wrong in her life. I took her B.S., Dad. I dealt with it every day and it wasn't easy."

"Come here." My father placed his hands on my shoulders. "Look at me," he said.

I raised my eyes and looked directly into his and saw his pain.

"I'm never going to turn my back on you. Do you understand me?" I nodded yes. "We're going to work together to break through the invisible bars of addiction. You are my son. And whatever it takes to get over this is what we'll do." My dad embraced me and it felt so good to be in the arms of someone who truly cared.

ten

Keysha

I walked to school at a brisk pace because I couldn't wait to walk up on Liz and confront her about what she'd done. I wanted an explanation. I wanted to know why she doped me up at the teen nightclub. Why she planted drugs on me and why she was spreading vicious rumors around. The more I thought about what she'd done, the angrier I became. Honestly, what she'd done was grounds for a good old-fashioned beat-down if not more. As I came to the four-way stop sign other students who were also heading to school joined me. That's when all the judgmental glaring and whispering started.

"That's her, the drug dealer," I heard someone whisper. I tried to ignore the whispering but it was difficult. I continued on my way more determined than ever to set things right and to clear my name. Finally I arrived and entered the school through the gymnasium doors. The girls' basketball team was still having early-morning practice. As I walked across the gym, the entire basketball team stopped dribbling their balls and focused on me.

"Hey," I heard one of the girls call out to me. I glanced in the direction of the voice and noticed five girls approaching me. I suddenly felt very uneasy. I felt as if something major was about to go down and I didn't want to be a part of it.

"I hear you're the one who has given our school a bad name and reputation," said this girl who was extremely tall. She had on pink sweatpants and a pink T-shirt with the words Don't You Want to Take Us Out? written across her bosom. The other four girls were dressed similarly but were not as tall.

"Excuse me?" I asked, not understanding what she was talking about.

"Come on." She leaned into me and spoke in a loud whisper. "Everyone knows you're the supplier. Everyone knows that you're going to be going to jail soon. And from what we've heard, going to jail would be like going to a family reunion for you."

I couldn't believe it. This girl, whom I'd never met before, had approached me with a nasty attitude and had the nerve to talk about my family.

"You'd better get away from me before you get dealt with," I threatened her, even though I had no intentions of fighting her.

"What, you think you can take me?" She began flailing in a violent manner. "Do you know who I am? I'm Dorothy Pam Pinkerton and I'll put you in the hospital! You think you're big and bad enough to jump on me. Come on with it, then. We can do this. Because of you, all of the other schools in the conference believe that our school is filled with drug addicts and losers. Because of all the negative publicity you brought to this school, the college basketball coach who had planned to come watch me play canceled her trip. You may have ruined my chances of getting a scholarship. I've just been waiting to see you," she snarled at me. Anger and waves of rage were in her eyes. The other four girls closed in around me. I looked into the eyes of each girl and all I saw was hatred.

"Look," I said to Dorothy, "I don't know what you've heard, but it's not true. I am not some dope dealer, okay? I'm sorry that your scholarship opportunity got messed up."

"Sorry just isn't good enough," she said, then lowered her eyes to slits and moved forward. She was very close now and looking down at me. My heart began to race like a herd of wild stallions galloping across an open prairie. I wanted to run but I couldn't.

"Make your move." She pushed my shoulder.

"Did you just hear what I said?" I gave her a nasty look. "I told you that whatever you heard just isn't true. Your missed opportunity isn't my fault!" I hollered out loud, hoping that someone would hear me and come to my aid. I quickly scanned around for the coach but didn't see him. The girl pushed me again and my duffel bag fell from my shoulder.

"Coach Sanders is in the bathroom and he'll be there long enough for me to jack you up! So, what are you going to do now? I'm all up in your face."

"You need to back up off of me, Dorothy," I said, trying to sound tough. I didn't want to fight, especially not on my first day back from being suspended. She pushed me a third time but then I pushed her back. She tried to grab me but I fought her off. The other four girls began shouting all at once. Dorothy swung at me but I ducked and caused her to miss her mark. Instinctively, I drop-kicked her and nailed her on the thigh. I was about to swing on her but the others girls grabbed me from behind.

At that moment I heard a man's voice ask, "Ladies, what's going on over there?"

It was Mr. Sanders, my guidance counselor and the girls' basketball coach. I exhaled a sigh of relief. I was happy to see him.

"This isn't over yet, Keysha," said Dorothy as she limped away. Mr. Sanders approached.

"Keysha, I should have known you were at the center of the controversy. What was all that about?" he asked.

"Nothing," I answered as the pace of my heartbeat began to return to normal.

"Well, wait for me in my office. I have to give you a permission slip."

"A permission slip for what?" I asked.

"Students who are returning from a suspension need to have a permission slip from their guidance counselor indicating that their suspension period has concluded."

"Dang," I fussed at him.

"Get your attitude in check, Keysha. Getting another suspension would not look good to the judge when your case is finally heard." Mr. Sanders threatened and advised me all in one swift tongue-lashing.

"Whatever," I answered as I continued on toward his office.

Sitting in Mr. Sanders's office, waiting for him to return and type up my permission slip took forever. I had bigger things to concern myself with. Before being delayed, I had planned to catch Liz at her locker, but now I'd have to wait until first period before I saw her. When Mr. Sanders arrived at his office to meet me, he took his sweet time filling out my permission slip. He finally finished just as the first-period bell rang.

"I'm going to be late for math class," I said.

"Relax, I'll walk you to class so that it doesn't get marked."

I sighed impatiently and tapped my index finger against his desk repeatedly. My unconscious tapping must have annoyed him because he stopped what he was doing momentarily and looked at me.

"You know, Keysha, it's no picnic down at the juvenile detention center." *Oh, boy, here we go. Another lecture,* I thought to myself. "I've been there many times and none of the students have ever said that they loved being there." I glared at Mr. Sanders because I had no clue as to what he was talking about. "If you get convicted, the judge is going to place you at a maximum-security juvenile detention center. Your freedom will be completely taken away from you. The judge can sentence you to twelve months or longer. The jail cells are cold, the food is horrible and the guards will not put up with any nonsense or foolishness."

I didn't say anything to Mr. Sanders. I just shifted my eyes around the room and focused on everything but him. I didn't want to listen to him. I didn't want to even think about being locked up against my will for something I didn't do.

"Don't get into any trouble, young lady," he scolded me.

"Yeah, whatever," I answered sarcastically. He'd gotten on my nerves.

"See, that attitude of yours is going to get you into deeper trouble." He pointed out what he perceived to be a character flaw.

"No, it's not!" I snapped at him. "Why does everyone assume that I'm guilty? Huh? You're not in my corner, Mr. Sanders, so don't even try to act like it. When the police came for me, you automatically assumed that I was responsible for everything. Well, I'm here to tell you that I'm not."

"I am here for you, Keysha. I want to help in any way that I can. You say that you're not responsible, then tell me who is."

"Forget it. I just want to get to class," I said.

"You're only making things worse on yourself by not talking about it." He tried to convince me to open up to him.

At that moment I made sure every word that came out of my mouth next was filled with damnation.

"The lawyer that my daddy got for me told me not to discuss my case with anyone and that includes you." I folded my arms across my chest.

"Okay, that's fair enough," said Mr. Sanders as he pushed himself away from his desk. "Come on, I'll take you to your class now."

When I walked into my math class, the first person I scanned the room for was Liz. I saw her sitting and talking to another student. The student she was talking to directed Liz's attention to me. When our eyes locked upon each other I was shooting artillery and missiles with mine. Liz winked at me. She was toying with me the way a cat toys with a mouse. I took my seat on the opposite side of the room and waited for the period to end. When the bell rang, I sprang from my seat and marched toward Liz but was stopped cold in my tracks when Ms. Allen called me.

"Keysha, please come here. I need to see you," she said.

"Dang." I stomped my foot against the floor. Liz didn't even look in my direction. She just walked out of the room as if I were a complete stranger to her. She didn't say hello, or how is it going or anything. I was so infuriated by this that if I'd had a blowtorch on me she would've been toasted beyond recognition.

"Keysha, you need to take a make-up test," Ms. Allen informed me. I huffed and she mistook my irritation with Liz as an attitude problem with her.

"I don't have to give you a chance to take this test, you know?" She pulled a pencil out of her desk drawer.

"No, I want to take the make-up test," I answered.

"We covered a lot of ground while you were out. So you'll need to spend time catching up. If you need a tutor let me know." Ms. Allen opened up her lesson book.

"Keysha, Keysha, Keysha," she repeated. "You're a borderline *D* in my class. If you don't pull it together, you will fail."

"That's because I haven't really been applying myself," I answered truthfully. "I can do better."

"I hope so because this class is the lowest math class this school offers. You can't afford to fail."

"Okay. I'll do better," I said.

"I'll give you two days to take the make-up test. You'll need to come into this class early on Wednesday morning. Understood?"

"Yes," I answered as the students in the second-period

class began taking their seats. She focused her attention on the students who were entering.

"Mr. Wesley, long time no see. Please come up here and see me." Ms. Allen began talking to one of the boys who'd just entered the room. I looked at Wesley briefly but was distracted when I heard the second-period bell ring.

"Dang it. I'm late now."

"I'll give you a pass," said Ms. Allen, and began filling out a late slip.

"What's up?" Wesley spoke to me.

"Hi," I said. I didn't study Wesley because I was in a hurry to get my slip and head off to science so that I could catch up with Liz.

"Are you new here?" Wesley asked.

Before I could answer, Ms. Allen interrupted. "Mr. Wesley, this is not a place to pick up girls. It's my math class."

"Oh, sorry about that, Ms. Allen, I didn't mean to be so disrespectful," Wesley apologized.

"Here you go, Keysha. Remember, first thing Wednesday, you need to be in here taking that exam. I will not accept any excuses. If you're not here I will fail you."

"Okay," I said, and rushed out of the room.

When I entered my second-period science class I gave my tardy slip to Miss Eisner, who was my teacher.

"Welcome back, Keysha." I was all set to go take my seat next to Liz, who was my science partner, but there was someone else sitting in my seat.

"Who is your science partner?" asked Miss Eisner.

"Liz Lloyd," I answered.

"Oh, yes. I had to give her a new partner since you were out. You are now with William Baker, opposite side of the room and toward the back."

I grumbled. I did not want to be lab partners with William Baker, whose body funk was strong enough to wake the dead at a morgue. I swore that boy had no idea of what soap and water is.

"Oh, and you need to see me after class to discuss how you plan to make up the assignments you missed."

I grumbled once again as I caught Liz glaring at me. She placed a silly smirk on her face. It was as if she was laughing at me, and I didn't like it. The more I looked at her, the more I wanted to strangle her.

I didn't get a chance to confront Liz right away because all of my teachers kept me after class to talk about all the assignments I had to make up. I knew I'd get my chance to talk to Liz during lunch, so I wasn't too upset. As I was making my way to the cafeteria, Mr. Sanders spotted me in the hallway and asked me to step inside his office for a moment. Once again, I rolled my eyes and huffed out of frustration. I spent twenty minutes of my lunch hour talking to Mr. Sanders about my failing grades and how, if I didn't get my act together, I'd end up in summer school or repeating my junior year.

"Keysha, I just got your grades from your teachers. Right now you have four *D*s, one weak *C* and one *F*. You've got to pull these grades up. If you don't earn your credits you will be in summer school."

"I know, okay? I'm going to do better."

"A lot of kids tell me that just because they think it's what

I want to hear." Mr. Sanders paused and then showed me an envelope that had been opened.

"Do you have any idea of what's in this envelope?" he asked.

"No," I answered.

"It's a request from the court for a transcript of your grades. It appears as if the judge who has been assigned your case wants to know what kind of student you are."

My heart began racing once again.

"I'm a much better student than what those grades are showing," I argued. The last thing I wanted was for the judge to think I was completely lame.

"Documentation beats conversation, Keysha. The proof is on paper, not in your words," said Mr. Sanders.

Even though he was only telling the truth, I still wanted to scream at him because I hated his smug attitude toward me.

"I'll be forwarding a copy of your grades to the judge and your parents, as well. It's kind of like my little insurance policy that you'll change your ways."

"Fine, I don't care." I looked him directly in the eye. "Can I go to lunch now?" I asked.

"Yes," he said, and I got up and rushed out of his junky office.

I didn't have enough time to get any lunch, so I walked directly over to the lunch table where Liz and the crew were hanging out. I rushed up to the table and slammed the books I was carrying down on the table in front of Liz.

"Why did you do it, Liz?" I was angry and restraining myself from calling her every word in the book.

"Do what? I didn't do anything to you." She treated me as if I were delusional.

"Liz, you're the one who set me up! You're the one who planted that crap in my locker!"

"Sweetie, you need to bring your voice down a notch or two." Liz was mocking with her fingers.

"I know you're not trying to tell me to be quiet! Girl, I will beat you down up in this cafeteria and this school if I don't get an answer!" When I made that statement, everyone at the table began to give us space.

"Hold up, ya'll," Liz said with a smirk on her face. "I want everyone to know that Keysha has flipped completely out. It sounds as if that Ecstasy you're hooked on has killed one too many brain cells because you're talking like a psychopath."

"I want answers from you, Liz, and I want them right now, or else!"

"Or else what?" Liz was defiant.

"Yeah, or else what?" said Courtney and Brittany, who were sitting next to Liz.

"If you fight Liz, you'll have to fight all of us," said Courtney.

"You see, Keysha, I have friends and you don't. I have people who will vouch for my character and you don't. I have a lot of things that you don't. I'm smarter than you, I'm prettier than you and everyone knows that my style is much better than yours."

I was so angry I felt as if I were about to explode with rage. Then it happened, something in my mind clicked and I heard a voice tell me to beat her down. I swung at Liz but she moved out of range and immediately sprang to her feet.

Earl Sewell

"Come on! I'm not afraid of you," Liz said as she removed her earrings. Everyone sitting at the table suddenly jumped to their feet.

"Fight!" someone cried out. Just as I was about to leap up on the lunch table and punch Liz and her goons in the face, my brother, Mike, appeared out of nowhere.

"Keysha, come on," he said as he hooked his hands on my shoulders and held me back.

"No, she has it coming, Mike! Let me go!" I shouted out and wrestled to free myself from his clutch.

"What's wrong? Your brother has to come to your aid and fight your battles for you?" Liz continued to antagonize me. In that moment whatever thread of a friendship we had ended. Liz had just become my frenemy.

"Let me go, Mike!" I tried to jerk away from him, but he was much stronger than I was. He grabbed my arm with one hand and picked up my books with the other and pulled me out of the cafeteria. His clutch was so tight I felt his fingernails tunneling into my skin.

"Why did you stop me, Mike? I was about to kick her—"

"You can't afford to get suspended again, Keysha! Think about what you're doing."

"Let me go!" I snarled at him like a wild monster.

"Keysha, calm down before a hall monitor comes and nails both of us," Mike snapped at me.

"Okay, just let me go," I said. Mike wasn't sure if he should.

"Please, just let me go," I pleaded, and finally Mike released his grip.

Mike and I argued during our walk home from school.

He was talking to me as if I had no business starting trouble with Liz.

"You've got to calm down, Keysha. You just can't go around getting into fights."

"Why not?" I barked. "She had it coming, Mike. She's the source of all the drama that's going on in my life."

"I know but you've got to think about the consequences of your actions."

"I wasn't thinking about consequences. All I wanted to do was to beat the truth out of her. I mean, who does she think she is? When I came to this whacked-out school, I didn't know anyone and she was the first person who acted as if she wanted me as a friend. Then she turns around and stabs me in the back?" I growled. "I want to know why she's doing this to me. I want to know why she's treating me like I'm some psycho who doesn't know up from down."

"Look, I'm not saying that she didn't have it coming. What I am saying is that you can't get involved in a fight. You have two strikes against you already. You have a court case and you've been suspended. One more mishap and who knows what will happen? If a hall monitor had come you'd have gotten suspended again, then what?"

"At least I would've felt better knowing that I'd gotten suspended for seeking the truth."

"Ahhh, why can't you see what I'm saying, Keysha?" I was frustrating Mike because I refused to agree with him.

"No, Mike. Why can't you see what *I'm* saying? If I go down for this, they're going to ship me off to a juvenile detention center and I can't deal with that, okay? You have no idea of what it's like to be in a place like that."

"They're not going to ship you off to a juvenile detention center." Mike didn't believe me.

"You want me to leave, don't you?" I snapped out on Mike. "You never did want me in the house. You and Barbara really want Jordan all to yourselves. Come on, Mike, say it?" I punched him on the arm. "Come on! Say it." I hollered at the top of my lungs. "Say it, you jerk!" I felt tears of anger swelling up inside. I didn't want Mike to see me cry but I couldn't help it.

"Say it! I know that's what you're thinking!"

"Keysha." He tried to calm me down but his words didn't offer me any comfort.

"You hate that I know you?" When Jordan discovered that I was his daughter a few months ago, Mike gave me such a hard time. He was suspicious that I was trying to take advantage of their family, and probably felt I was a no-good hood chick.

"Keysha—"

"Whatever, Mike!" I said as I ran ahead of him so that I could completely let my tears go.

When I reached the house, Jordan was home. I gave him an ugly glare before rushing in the house and up to my room. I slammed my bedroom door so hard that several items on my desk fell over. Picking up one of my pillows, I began slamming it against the walls of my room. I'd lost it. I didn't understand why everything had to be so complicated. In the middle of my display of rage, Jordan walked into my room without even knocking on the door and that ticked me off.

"What do you want?" My words were poisonous.

"First of all, you need to put yourself in check when you're speaking to me."

"What for? You really don't want me here and I know it. You want me to go away. You want me to disappear. I can feel it. You never wanted me in this house. You never wanted me to be around you or Mike. You only took me in because you felt sorry for me. I know it's true so you might as well say it so that I can move on with my life."

Jordan closed my bedroom door and leaned his back against it. He folded his arms across his chest and just looked at me.

"I'm going to say this one more time, young lady, and if I don't get the results that I want, you're going to see just how ugly I can get. Lower your voice and sit down on the bed."

I didn't like being told what to do one bit and I was about to let Jordan have it. But something deep inside me told me not to make things worse for myself. Forcing myself to sit down on my bed, I focused on a spot on my wall. I didn't want to look at Jordan and right now I certainly wasn't in the mood for one of his speeches.

"Tell me what's going on with you," he asked, but I remained silent.

"Answer me, Keysha." Jordan raised his voice at me, which made feel worse. The sound of his displeasure with me hit my heart like a flaming arrow and I began to cry.

"Nothing," I lied.

"No, something is going on and I want to know about it." His voice became calmer.

As I continued to look at the wall, my tears continued to overflow. I hated the fact that I'd lost command over my emotions.

"Mike probably already told you what happened." I sounded as if I had several frogs lodged in my throat.

"I want to hear your version of what happened," Jordan said.

"It was nothing." I paused.

"Keysha, tell me. We can talk about this. You know that I care."

"No one has ever really cared about me. No one has ever really cared about what I did or didn't do. So why do you care?" I asked.

"Because that's what dads do. We care about our children."

I took a few deep breaths and tried to calm myself down. "I almost got into a fight today," I answered.

"A fight! Mike didn't tell me anything about a fight."

I was surprised that Mike hadn't. I automatically assumed that he would.

"Mike arrived in the nick of time and stopped me," I said. "Please don't raise your voice at me. It upsets me when you do that."

"Who were you fighting?" Jordan wanted to know.

"I don't want to tell you because then you'll get mad at me," I answered. Jordan was silent for a moment.

"That girl. What's her name?" He began snapping his fingers, trying to recall her name.

"Liz." I told him the name that had eluded his memory. "She's the girl responsible for all of this mess. I went to talk to her today but she treated me as if I was a complete outsider. She made me feel dumb and worthless, so I was about to make her eat her words."

"Keysha, look at me."

I slowly blinked away more tears from my eyes and then craned my neck toward Jordan.

"Under no circumstances are you to be up at the school fighting."

"She had it coming, Jordan."

"I don't care whether she had it coming or not. Fighting is not an option, especially with your court case pending."

"She's the very reason why I have the case, Jordan."

"That may be. However, we're going to let Asia, the attorney, deal with this."

"Asia doesn't know Liz like I do. Liz is a two-faced—"

"Keysha," Jordan interrupted, "fighting is bad for several reasons. You could seriously hurt someone or they could seriously hurt you, or even worse, if things get too far out of hand, someone could lose their life. I'm not saying don't defend yourself if you're being assaulted. What I am saying is that I don't want you initiating any physical confrontations with this Liz girl."

I placed my face in my hands.

"She's ruining my life and she doesn't even care," I said. "I can't let her get away with that."

"And she's not. We're going to prove our case in court," Jordan assured me.

"How, when everything points to me? How are we going to do that without any evidence? We need evidence or a confession or something. All I was trying to do was to save time, money and a big effort. If I get locked up at some juvenile detention center, you're not coming back for me and I know it." I stood up and began pacing the floor. I was trying to think of ways I could torture a confession out of Liz.

I was thinking about my grandmother Rubylee and what she'd do in a situation like this. She knew how to make Liz talk like a bird singing in a tree.

"Keysha, I'm not going to leave you," Jordan said.

"Yeah, you say that now. But I know the minute I get locked up, you're going to disappear."

"Why do you think that?" he asked.

"Because everyone has always left me hanging," I answered.

"Keysha, who came and got you when the police pulled you out of school and took you to the station?"

"You did," I answered. Jordan was making me remember and think rationally.

"If I didn't leave you then, what have I done to make you think I'm going to turn my back on you now?"

"Nothing," I uttered. Jordan stood up, approached me and placed his hands on my shoulders.

"Look at me," he requested once again. I looked into eyes and listened to the words coming from his heart.

"I will always be there for you. I know it's hard to accept given the fact that we haven't really known each other very long, but I need you to place more trust in me."

"It's hard for me to trust adults," I answered honestly.

"I know it is, but you've got to place a little faith in me."

I studied his eyes for a long moment before breaking the connection. Not wanting to have another weird Grandmother Katie moment.

"I don't want you making things worse for yourself. Fighting Liz at this stage would send the wrong message to the judge and the prosecution. Not to mention it may draw more negative publicity to us."

"I just want to hit her one good time, though." Once again I was expressing how I felt.

"I know you do, but that's not the solution to our situation."

"I'll try not to beat her down but I can't make any promises," I said.

"Then I'll help you stay out of trouble. I want you and Mike to be together as much as possible."

"What?" I was confused.

"You heard me. I want him to be around you as much as possible during the time you're not with the family. I want you to walk to school together."

"But Mike has football practice twice a day sometimes."

"Then I want you to be at those practices with him."

I rolled my eyes.

"You can't be serious," I said.

"Yes, I am serious." Jordan stood his ground.

"I don't even like football," I whined.

"It's not about what you like or don't like. It's about keeping you out of trouble."

I huffed at the idea of being with Mike so much, but I agreed with him for the moment.

"So, what's going on with the case?" I asked.

"Things are still in the preliminary stages. The case has been assigned to Judge Nancy Hill, who has requested a transcript of your school records."

My heart sank.

"What's wrong?" Jordan asked. "Why do you have that look on your face?"

"It's nothing," I said as I began to think about what my guidance counselor told me.

"No, it's something. Now, what is it?" Jordan pressed the issue.

"Why does Judge Hill need my school records anyway?" I had gotten anxious again.

"It's not uncommon. It will help the judge make a determination about your character."

"Huh, she'll end up throwing the book at me," I said sarcastically. "Right now my grades aren't in the greatest of shape."

"Yes, I've heard," Jordan said. "Today I received a number of e-mails from your teachers explaining your poor performance to me. We have to address that as well."

"I can do better," I quickly let him know. "I'm smarter than what my grades say."

"Then prove it to me. Turn your grades around and show me who the real Keysha is."

"Okay, I'll do what I need to do in order to pull my grades up," I said.

"Just saying okay is not enough. To make sure that you do what you're supposed to I'm going to be on your back. And don't worry about this court case. I'll deal with that, understood? You focus on your education."

"I understand," I said, and sat back down next to him. Jordan sat with me and draped his arm around my shoulder. I locked my arms around his waist and we hugged each other. At that moment, hugging him was one of the best feelings I'd ever known.

eleven

Wesley

Three weeks had gone by since I was released from juvie and moved in with my dad. He and I followed up with the Mayville Rehab Facility as instructed by the court and I now had to go to meetings in the evenings on Monday and Wednesday and all day on Saturday. Parents were allowed and encouraged to come on Saturday so that they got a good sense of how they could help keep their loved ones on the road to recovery. I must admit that I thought going to rehab would be a real drag, especially on a Saturday, but it wasn't so bad. A lot of the kids in my group had the same addiction as I did and some had worse addictions. The thing that we all had in common is that we came from troubled homes. During one group discussion on Saturday I really opened up because I wanted my dad to hear how I truly felt.

"It was very difficult for me," I began. "My mom would always tell me that she loved me but her actions wouldn't reflect her words. I felt valueless to her and I felt no matter what I said or how hard I tried to do everything she wanted me to do, it was never enough. I felt that all the things she was showing me went against who I was. It was as if she thought that just because she was a heavy drinker that automatically made me want to be one, as well. I felt as if she'd given me a label and an identity that I had to follow no matter how incongruent it was with who I truly was."

My father interjected his thoughts after he'd listened to what I'd said. "I would imagine that what you went through was like trying to wear a pair of shoes that belonged to someone else or didn't fit your feet."

"Yeah, Dad, that's kind of what it was like. Every day I felt hurt or abused in some way by my mom. I felt as if I was cursed and had no real way out of my situation. All of my friends and those within my crew were seasoned drinkers, drug abusers and could be certified as insane. I mean, some of the stuff I did with them was so outrageous and dangerous that I still wonder how and why I'm still alive." I was quiet for a long moment as I thought how many times I'd almost seriously injured myself by doing some dumb stunt to prove how cool I was. One of the worst stunts was driving down a pitch-black farm road at a high rate of speed with no headlights on. "It was as if I was chasing death because I thought it was a way to exit my misery." My dad draped his arm around me. I was silent again.

"If it's too hard to talk about right now, it's okay," said my dad. "I'm going to be with you every step of the way, okay?"

I nodded my head in agreement. It was strange how just talking about my problems had such an impact on how I felt. It was almost as if I were getting rid of the monstrous person I'd become. Others in my group opened up, as well. One guy got hooked on pot when his uncle introduced it to him. A girl in the group got hooked on antidepressants because the kids at school ridiculed her to no end and yet another girl was recovering from heroin that her boyfriend got her hooked on. After hearing some of the problems the others had, I didn't feel horrible or alone.

I got all of my belongings out of my mom's house and got settled into my permanent life with my dad. My dad set boundaries and expectations that had to be met. His biggest concern was my grades. He demanded that I improve so that I wouldn't flunk out of my junior year of high school. His other rule was the harshest. No parties or free time until further notice. That rule would kill my social life, but I could deal with that because under no circumstances did I ever want to go back with my mom.

My first day back at school was interesting because I was cleaning out my friends' closet and getting rid of people who were bad for me. The first person on my list was Ed Daley. He stopped by my locker between first and second period to see me and welcomed me back.

"Aw, man, they finally let you out," said Ed, who was a short and stout Irish kid with red hair, freckles, braces and a speech problem that caused him to sound as if he was slurring his words.

"Yeah, Ed, I'm out." I began working on my combination lock so that I could get my book for science out.

"Hey, man, I hear that Liz Lloyd has been looking for you. I think she's got a little release present for you." Ed laughed at the idea of alcohol being my present.

"Release present?" I asked as I stooped down to pick up my science textbook.

"You know," Ed whispered, "she got you some booze,

man, so that you can celebrate." Ed began guffawing again. He was goofy like that. "When she gives it to you, let me know so that I can help you kick off the party." Ed waited for me to laugh along with him, but I didn't.

"What's wrong with you?" he asked with a perplexed expression.

I swiveled my head from right to left.

"Liz can keep her present," I said. "That's not who I am anymore, Ed."

"What's that supposed to mean?" Ed was confused by my response.

"I don't drink anymore," I answered.

"What the hell, man? What are you talking about? You're Whiskey Wesley. You'll drink anything. Do you remember the time we got hammered and then went for a swim in Lake Michigan? Remember you almost drowned and—"

"Ed," I interrupted. "That's not who I am anymore. I'm sorry."

"Aw, man. What did they do to you at that juvenile detention center? They must have brainwashed you or something." Ed threaded his fingers behind his head and shifted his body weight from one leg to the other. The notion that I'd gone cold turkey with my drinking was something he couldn't comprehend and was unwilling to accept.

"Don't tell me you went and got all religious on me." Ed was truly hurt by my news.

"I'm a new person, Ed. Can't you tell?"

"No. You look the same to me." Ed looked into my eyes. "Okay, the whites of your eyes are white and not red. I did notice that, but you look so much better with red eyes. You looked cooler and you were more at ease. The old Wesley wouldn't talk all the nonsense you're talking. All you need is a quick hit and you'll be fine. I want the old Wesley back. You need to drop the choirboy act."

I smiled because he honestly thought his speech was enough to turn me back into the person he liked.

"I'm not going down that road again, Ed. The Wesley you knew was not the person that I am. That was someone else. That was someone who was very unhappy. This is who I am," I said to him. Ed looked at me as if I'd just wrecked his brand-new car.

"What has gotten into you? What's next, you're going to start getting good grades?"

"Yeah, that's one of my new goals," I said to him, feeling confident.

"You're dumb, Wesley. Just like the rest of the school. You're one of us, not one of the book nerds who join the math or debate team. You'll never fit in with them. They won't accept you."

"Ed, I'm not looking to be accepted by anyone. If who I truly am upsets you, then I'm sorry but that's just the way it is now." Ed was speechless. "Look, I'll catch up with you some other time, Ed. I have to get to my science class," I said as I closed my locker, and headed toward the classroom.

Throughout that first day I went around to all of my so-called friends and let them know that I wouldn't be hanging out with them anymore. They all thought I'd gone crazy but I didn't care. Eventually I heard that Liz Lloyd began spreading rumors around about me having some kind of mental breakdown while I was locked up, but I didn't care about that either. She could say whatever she wanted to.

I was such a poor student when I was drinking. I didn't care about what grades I got or turning in assignments on time. Now that I was sober and could think straight, I saw how ignoring my schoolwork was a monumental error. I was behind in every class I had. I was even failing gym, which anyone can get an *A* in as long as they participate. But it's hard to run laps around a track or play flag football when you're dealing with a hangover. After I saw where I was academically, I made a promise to myself to get my act together. I studied harder, listened in class and participated more than I ever had. I freaked several of my teachers out because they couldn't believe the transformation that had occurred.

"You're like a completely different person," Miss Eisner told me one day as I was leaving her second-period science class. "Keep up the good work," she said as I exited the room. I often arrived at school early and did extra-credit work or studied at the school's library. For the past several weeks I'd noticed a girl studying and working just as hard as I was. She was very cute. Okay, well, maybe better than cute, she was beautiful. She had gorgeous eyes, pretty caramel skin and a strong presence about her. I never saw her smile though. She always has a very determined look on her face. Sometimes I wanted to approach her and say something witty to make her laugh, but I feared that she might snap on me. I wondered if she remembered that I said hello to her before. A few times I've sat on the opposite side of the room and allowed my eyes to dance all over her. I was hoping that she'd feel me ogling her, but she didn't. She focused on her work and had no clue that I even existed.

twelve

Keysha

After my initial altercation with Liz I didn't see her for two days. I'd heard through the grapevine that she and several of the kids from her crew were cutting school as an act of defiance against her teachers and the educational system in general. The fact that Liz decided to cut school for a few days irritated me to no end, because regardless of the promises I'd made to my father to stay away from her and avoid another big quarrel, I found myself obsessed with confronting her another time. When I did see her again, it was on Thursday morning just after Mike had left me to head to football practice. I was on my way to the school library to work on an essay I had to write. I spotted Liz in the parking lot gossiping with several girls from her crew. The moment I saw her, I slung my book bag on the pavement and ran toward her. I couldn't help it. Racing toward her, I was like an animal chasing down its prey. I was so focused on Liz that a student who was trying to park her car almost nailed me. The person driving blew her horn at me but I ignored the loud noise.

"Liz!" I yelled out her name as I approached her. "We need to talk." My voice was filled with fury.

"Well, I don't want to speak to you, jailbird," she insulted me, and I felt my blood boiling over.

"Liz, I am not playing with you, girl," I said, clenching my fists repeatedly.

"See, girls, this is what happens to you when you can't handle the drugs you're taking." Liz was filled with attitude and spite, I could hear it in her words and see it in her body language.

"Keysha is the poster child for the word 'stalker.'"

Liz and the girls laughed at me and that really ticked me off.

"What did you just say?" I asked as I clenched my jaw tightly. I was doing everything within my power to keep from committing a homicide in the school parking lot.

"Oh, come on, Keysha. You know you've been stalking me like some lovesick girl who can't get over the fact that her lover has dumped her."

"I am not some lovesick girl and you know it." Liz was really trying my patience. "I'm here to talk about the drugs you planted on me and I want some answers. I also want you to confess that you're the one who set me up!" I was now shouting at her.

"Who are you raising your voice at?" Liz snarled at me.

"You!" I barked back.

"You know what, jailbird, if I were you, I'd leave before something bad happens to you."

I couldn't help it. My rage consumed me and I was ready to pull out her spiked raven-black hair and scratch her face with my fingernails until it became covered with blood.

"Move out of my way." She pushed my shoulder and that

did it. I swung at her and connected with a solid slap right on the jaw. Before Liz or any of the other girls could react, I was cocking my arm back for a second shot. I swung and missed, which gave Liz enough time to recover and grab a handful of my hair. She began pulling it hard, causing my neck to jerk. I somehow managed to get a hold of her shirt and began tugging at it until it started to rip. I heard the fabric tear.

"This is a new blouse, you—"

"Why did you do it, Liz?" I interrupted as I continued to rip her blouse away from her body.

"Let me go!" I shouted but Liz continued to violently yank on my hair. Her shirt was almost completely off of her body, so she released me and I let her go, as well.

"Are either one of you two sluts going to help me?" Liz shouted out for help from her girls. I knew that I was about to get a beat-down because I was outnumbered. But I didn't care. Turning my fingers into talons, I lunged for Liz, screaming like a madwoman. I clawed her face several times before her goons could make a move. They tried to grab me but I was swinging my fists like a lunatic. I began fighting them, as well. I took a few hits but I gave out some as well. A crowd of students formed around us and began encouraging us to fight dirty. Someone punched me in the back and then slapped me. I swung back and connected with a slap on the ear. At that very moment I heard Mike's voice.

"Hey, break it up! Stop it!" I could tell that my brother was charging toward me. He'd broken through the crowd and began pushing me away to safety.

"No," I yelled. "I'm going to keep fighting her. She can't ruin my life like this."

"Your life was already screwed up!" Liz howled at me. I spit on her and nailed her right between the eyes. She spit back and hit me on the neck.

"Come on, Keysha, just walk away, let it go." Mike grabbed me and was pushing me farther away from her.

I fought Mike off of me. And rushed at Liz once again. She landed a punch on my lips, but it didn't matter because I'd locked my fingers around her neck and started choking her. Mike once again pulled me off of her.

"Come on! Let's finish this right now, Liz. You think you're bad but you're not." I was fired up. "Come on! I'm waiting."

"Your day is coming Keysha! I swear, you are going to regret this."

"Does it look as if I'm scared of you? Huh?"

"Keysha, shut up!" Mike kept pulling me away.

Since I wanted to get in the last word, I gave Liz the middle finger.

"Same to you, Keysha!" she barked out as she tried to adjust her torn clothing.

"Bring it on, Liz. I'm not afraid of you. You may have those other girls afraid of you but I'm not. Anytime and anywhere." I pointed my index finger at her. "I hate you!"

"The feeling is mutual!" Liz howled out.

"Let me go, Mike. I'm not done with her." I tried to break free of his grip.

"No. That's enough," Mike said. "You're just a little hellcat, aren't you?" he said as he continued to move me farther way.

"Okay, I'm done with it," I said. "Now, let me go." Mike looked into my eyes to see if I was telling the truth.

"It's okay, I'm cool," I said. He let me go.

"What the hell was all of that about, Keysha?" Mike yelled at me.

"How did you get to me so quickly?" I asked.

"I told you. I have friends all over this campus. Someone called me on my cellular phone just as I was about to change into my gear and told me that you and Liz looked as if you guys were about to throw down. I knew right then I needed to run like the wind to get over here." We reached a bus bench and sat down.

"Keysha, that's the second time I've had to break up a fight between you and that girl."

"It probably will not be the last either," I said to him.

"Keysha, I know you hate the girl but people like her never win. Liz is poison. I probably should have told you that instead of making you feel unwelcome." Mike stroked down my hair.

"Your hair is all jacked up," he said.

"I must look like something out of a horror movie," I said as I tried to pat down my messy hair.

"I've seen worse. You're so lucky that her girls didn't do more damage. You could've really gotten hurt."

"I didn't care, Mike," I said.

"Yeah, but I do," he said.

I paused because I wasn't expecting to hear that from him. I stared at Mike for a moment.

"You really do care, don't you?" I asked.

"Of course I do." Mike took in a deep breath and then slowly let it out.

"Hey, I'm sorry about all of the mean things I said to you. I didn't really mean any of it," I admitted.

"That's good to know. Because I'm not going to keep coming to your rescue if you hate my guts."

"I don't hate you, Mike. I envy you but I don't hate you."

"Look, the bell is going to ring in about fifteen minutes and I need to get all the way back to the other side of campus to get my books and stuff. Are you going to be cool? No more fighting?"

"Yeah, no more fighting. I'm cool now. I've gotten it out of my system. Liz is just a low-down, evil snake in the grass. I need to learn how to pick better friends."

"I told you that Liz was a real nutcase. I think the girl is bipolar or something."

"You could be right," I said. "I'm going to go pick up my book bag. It's in the middle of the parking lot. You head on back to the locker room. I'll catch up with you after school, okay?"

"Cool," Mike said, then stood up and sprinted back toward the other side of campus.

There was an unwritten agreement between Liz and me to avoid each other at all costs. I didn't want to run into her any more than she wanted to run into me. After I realized that I wouldn't be able to get Liz to admit to her wrongdoing, I decided to listen to what my father said and let Asia handle my case. I gave her Liz's name, phone number and address so that she could serve her with a subpoena to appear in court. I spent the next several weeks at the school library focusing on pulling up my grades and proving to Jordan and myself that I was a much better person and student in spite of what my grades and quandary seemed to say.

thirteen

Wesley

"wesley, it's time to get up." My dad entered my bedroom and hovered above my body. He shook my shoulder a few times to make sure I was awake. "Come on, get up, I've already let you sleep for a few extra minutes."

"Let me sleep a little longer," I whined as I pulled my blanket around my body tighter.

"No, you need to get to the library so you can locate some books about Henry Ford. I want the paper you have to write on him to be completed long before it's due."

"Dad, I have four weeks to write that paper," I complained. My dad wasn't having it so he walked over to the wall and hit the light switch.

"Get up, Wesley, you don't have time to be horsing around." My dad left my room and headed for the kitchen.

"What's for breakfast?" I called out behind him.

"Cereal and milk," he shouted back.

"I'm tired of eating cereal and milk for breakfast," I grumbled as I sat upright on my bed. Placing my bare feet on the floor, I took a long stretch. I stood up and shuffled my way into the bathroom so that I could prepare for my day.

Once I was dressed my dad and I sat down and ate together. He was drinking his morning cup of coffee and eating a bowl of Cap'n Crunch while watching the morning news. There was a story about teens, their independence and drug usage. News reporter Angela Rivers was in the field doing an investigative report on the subject and offering tips for teens and their parents on how to deal with the issue.

"A driver's license is a teenager's rite of passage, a gateway to greater freedom as they move toward adulthood. However, for countless teenagers that journey toward independence can sometimes turn into tragedy. Automobile accidents remain the number-one killer of teens, a dilemma that has defied the efforts of parents, educators, lawmakers and law enforcement." Footage of a car accident that happened last week popped up on screen. The accident had been major news because three teens had gotten injured.

My dad turned up the volume on the television. "Let's watch this together," he said. I positioned myself in front of the television and listened.

"This year alone thirty-five local teens have lost their life through recklessness and driving under the influence of alcohol. Law enforcement authorities say that many teenagers don't have to go through the hassle of getting a fake identification card in order to purchase alcohol. Many of them only have to go as far as their parents' cabinet to find a variety of choices." The camera panned to a grim-faced police officer. "It's the parents' job to guide their children through their teen years. I would recommend that parents dispose of or lock up any alcoholic beverages in their home that teens have direct access to," stated the police officer. The serious expression of his face conveyed that he had seen a fair amount of tragedy. "Experts recommend keeping an open line of communication with your teenager, as well as taking a positive and active role in their life. Learn who their friends are and keep a close eye out for any sudden unexplained changes in behavior and attitude. It could be an indication that something has gone wrong. Teens are most vulnerable to making a bad decision when they're hanging around their friends without the supervision of an adult. Responsible parents may want to consider making their home a safe place where teens can hang out and still have their privacy," Angela Rivers concluded. My dad lowered the volume on the television.

"New rule," he began. "I realize that there may come a time where you find yourself in a situation where your friends are doing things that you're not in agreement with. If you ever find yourself in a bad situation, I want you to call me. I'll come and get you from any place at any time. No questions asked," he said.

"What do you mean by 'no questions asked'?"

"It means that I will not ask questions and I will not preach to you. It means that my main concern would be for your safety and well-being. When you're ready to talk about whatever the situation was, I'll be here for you. What I'm driving at here, Wesley, is that you have options. You're in control of your own actions and not your friends'. If you're ever in a jam I'll always be the person you can count on."

"Dad, as far as I'm concerned you've already proven that to me," I said. My dad smiled at me warmly.

"So, how is school going?" he asked.

"Okay. I had to get rid of some friends. One guy named

Ed Daley thinks that I got brainwashed while I was locked up. He didn't want to believe that I'd gone cold turkey and stopped drinking."

"Let me guess, he said that he liked the old you better, right?" my dad asked.

"Yeah, how did you know that?" I was curious.

"Misery loves company. It sounds as if Ed is miserable and now he has to either change his life or find someone new to be miserable with."

"Knowing Ed, he is going to find someone else to be unhappy with. I also stopped hanging around the crew that I used to hang with. In fact, they kind of disowned me now so I really feel like a loner."

"Give the new you some time. You'll find new friends who have the same interests."

"Trust me, I don't mind being a loner. It doesn't bother me one bit. There is a certain type of freedom that comes with being a loner," I said. "I don't have anyone influencing me and it keeps me out of trouble."

"Well, don't become too much of a loner because you will have to interact with people. You just have to be a little more selective and hang around students who are positive and who make you feel good about who you are. You don't want to select friends who belittle you."

"I feel what you're saying," I answered as I chomped on my cereal.

"Have you talked to your mother?" he asked.

"No," I answered dryly.

"Has she tried to contact you at all?" he asked.

"No," I answered again.

"Wesley, regardless of everything she has done, she's still your mom."

"I know that, but right now, I'm enjoying not being around her. I'm not ready to see her or talk to her." My words were cold and icy but that was the way I felt.

"Well, it's time for me to head off to work." My dad decided not to push the issue. "I'll be home around 4:00 p.m. to see how you're doing with your paper."

"Okay, see you later," I said, before changing the channel. *The Simpsons* was on so I turned up the volume.

"Don't be late," my dad said as he walked out the door.

"I won't," I answered as I laughed at Homer Simpson guzzling beer and then belching loudly.

I placed my duffel bag on one of the wooden tables at my school's library. Walking over to the card catalog, I found the drawer for the letter *F* and thumbed through the index until I found several cards that listed books about the life and legacy of Henry Ford. I wrote down the reference numbers on a scrap of sheet paper that was sitting atop the card catalog. Then I walked to the other side of the library to search the shelves for the books I thought would provide me with good information. As I began searching the shelves I saw her again. Man, she's pretty, I said to myself. I remembered that her name was Keysha but that's about all I knew. She sat down at one of the computer stations and began tapping the keyboard with her two index fingers. It was clear to me that she needed to learn how to type and I was willing to help her learn, if she'd allow me to. I had to make myself stop staring at her as if I were some pervert with nothing better to do. Locating the book I'd been searching for, I made it a point to walk past her. I hoped that she'd notice me but she didn't. I wanted to make eye contact with her so that I could introduce myself. The last thing I wanted to do was approach her and catch her off guard. If I did that, I just knew she'd say, "Why are you bothering me?" or "I don't want no scrub so get away from me." Deciding to go back to the other side of the library, I brought my belongings closer to where Keysha was working. I figured at least I'd have a chance to look at her and drool. I positioned myself so that I was facing her. I studied her flawless skin, her full lips and the way she softly tapped her index finger on her lips when she was thinking about something. Keysha gathered up her belongings and moved to a table in front of me. She was now in my direct line of sight. Just looking at her inspired me to write a poem to express how I felt. I'd never written a poem in my life, but for some reason, my untamed attraction to Keysha demanded that I put my feelings down on paper. I removed my spiral notebook from my bag and began.

I am fascinated and captivated by your mystery and secrets. I want to know who you are and what part of heaven you came from. I want the combination to your heart so that I can place your emotions next to my own and feel the warmth of your spirit. You have enchanted my thoughts with the sweet melody of your mystery. My heart dances for you, my soul sings for you and my mind is consumed with thoughts of us being—

I stopped writing for a moment and focused my attention back on her. That's when I noticed that Dorothy Pam

Pinkerton and two other members of the girls' basketball team had surrounded Keysha.

"You remember me, don't you?" I heard Dorothy whisper loudly. She had invaded Keysha's personal space. Keysha looked up at her and wrinkled up her nose. I deduced that Dorothy's breath had a rank odor.

"No one in this school likes you, Keysha! And I can't wait for the day the cops come and drag you out of here for good. This school doesn't need weeds like you. You need to go on back to the ghetto and make a bunch of ghetto babies and live off of welfare. I heard that you and your mama were welfare queens."

I couldn't believe what Dorothy had just said to her. That ticked me off, so I know it had to have ticked off Keysha.

"You say one more thing about my mother and I will stomp you into the ground."

"Come on, I've been waiting to beat the crap out of you." Dorothy backed up and waited for Keysha to stand on her feet. Keysha was brave and fearless. She was outnumbered three to one and yet she stood up and prepared to defend herself at all costs. I quickly scanned the room for one of the librarians before their conflict got out of control. However, I didn't see one. *Figures,* I said to myself. *Whenever you're sitting and gossiping with your friends, a librarian will pop up out of thin air and tell you to be quiet. Now, when I really need one, I can't find one.* I glanced back over at the girls and saw Dorothy anticipating Keysha's next move. Keysha was keeping a close eye on Dorothy while making sure the other two girls didn't attack her by surprise. Keysha quickly positioned her chair between her and the other two girls.

"Come on, do something." Keysha encouraged Dorothy to make her move.

I looked around for other students, but since it was still early, no one else was in the library.

"Ahhhheeemm." I cleared my throat and walked toward them.

"Dorothy, why don't you get out of here and leave her alone?" I said, positioning myself between Keysha and Dorothy.

"Wesley, if you don't get your narrow wine-headed behind out of my business I'm going to kick your—"

"I don't need your help," Keysha interrupted Dorothy. "I can take care of this myself."

"I'm sure that you can," I said to Keysha, "but just in case, I thought I'd help even up the odds a little."

"What? You're into beating up on girls now, Wesley?" Dorothy asked.

I looked Dorothy up and down.

"Last I heard, you were more of a man than your own father," I barked at Dorothy. She and I had some history of conflict that dated back to grammar school.

"Why are you even over here? Shouldn't you be drunk or high by now and sitting on the floor nodding in and out of reality?"

I hated Dorothy for bringing up my past addiction problems in front of Keysha. Her words hurt me a little more than I thought they would, but I didn't let it show.

"And shouldn't you and your trolls be somewhere dribbling a basketball and assaulting the air with your body funk?"

"Who are you calling funky?" Dorothy got loud.

"You!" Keysha got in on the action. "Your breath smells as if you've been licking the buttocks of a gorilla!" Dorothy's teammates laughed at Keysha's comment.

"Am I right, girls? I mean, come on. You had to have noticed that sister girl is just a little on the hot side when it comes to her breath?" Dorothy's teammates laughed a little harder.

"Shut up!" Dorothy was even louder now. "Ya'll are not supposed to be laughing at that," she scolded her girlfriends.

"Shhhhh!" Finally, a librarian appeared. It was Miss Haskey, who was a no-nonsense type of person. "What is the matter with you, Dorothy? You're shouting so loud that I heard you all the way in the bathroom." Miss Haskey approached us. "What's going on over here?" she asked, sensing that something was afoot.

"Nothing," I answered Miss Haskey.

"Dorothy?" Miss Haskey looked at her. Dorothy stomped her foot and appeared to be contemplating a violent outburst.

"Dorothy, are you in here causing trouble?" Miss Haskey asked.

"No," she answered. "Everything is cool."

"Good, now disperse and go on about your business." Miss Haskey ordered Dorothy and her teammates to leave. Keysha plopped down in her seat and exhaled.

"I hate this retarded school," Keysha complained.

I took that as an invitation to a conversation, so I sat down on the opposite side of her table.

"Hi, my name is Wesley Morris." I extended my hand for a handshake.

"Keysha," she said, shaking my hand. "So, why aren't you hating on me too?" she asked.

"Hating on you? Why would I do that?" I was confused.

"Why not? Everyone else is."

"Why do you have so many haters?" I inquired because I genuinely wanted to know.

"It's a long story," Keysha said as she picked up her pencil, and began tapping it on a nearby book cover.

"I like long stories." I smiled at her. She looked at me as if she were perplexed by something.

"Who are you?" she asked.

"I told you, my name is Wesley."

"No, I mean, why did you get involved?"

"I don't know. It seemed like the right thing to do."

"So, what are you? Some choirboy on a crusade to save the world or something?" I could tell that Keysha was trying to analyze me.

"Trust me. I'm no choirboy." I laughed. Keysha wasn't laughing so I stopped.

"Relax, the fight is over. You don't have to fight me." I wanted my words to comfort her.

"I have to fight everybody," she said.

"Why?" I asked.

"Why do you want to know?" she countered.

"Whew, are you always this tough to talk to?" I asked.

"Stop avoiding my question and answer it." Keysha wasn't letting up.

"I'm just curious. I mean, why do you have to fight so much?"

"Because that's just the way it is," she answered.

"That's not an answer," I said.

"Yes, it is."

"No, it isn't. That's a cop-out."

She paused for a moment and studied me. I could tell she was making all types of assumptions and determinations about me.

"What did Dorothy mean when she called you a wine head?"

"Oh, man. That's a long story," I answered.

"I like long stories," she countered.

"You can't use my own words against me," I complained.

"I just did." She stood her ground and I liked that. I was attracted to her robustness and strong will.

"Do you really want to know?" I asked.

"I'm all ears." She stopped tapping her pencil and folded her arms across her chest and leaned back in her seat.

"You don't trust me, do you?" I asked.

"Should I?" Her words were as sharp as a surgeon's blade.

"Whew, hello, it's me. The moron who tried to protect you from a major beat-down. I'm not the enemy." I placed a silly expression on my face. "See, I'm very friendly." I finally cracked the ice and got Keysha to laugh.

"Stop that. You look like a lost puppy begging to be let inside from a cold storm."

"Ruff, ruff, ruff," I barked quietly. She laughed some more. I was about to do my Scooby Doo impression but then Miss Haskey walked past us and gave me the evil glare.

"Okay, Wesley, you have my attention." Keysha smiled.

"You know, that is the very first time that I've seen you smile. I see you in here often but I've never seen you smile.

You have a pretty smile. You should let people see who you really are more often."

"So, are you a sophomore or junior?" she asked.

"A junior, but if I don't get my grades up, I may be a junior for life," I admitted.

"Huh, you and I both. I'm new here," Keysha said. "When I first arrived at the beginning of the semester, I had a difficult time making friends. Then I hooked up with this crazy girl named Liz."

"Not Liz Lloyd. Please tell me you didn't befriend her."

"Why?" she asked before answering the question.

"I know Liz Lloyd. I know her very well."

"What, did you guys used to date or something?"

I could tell Keysha was once again on the defensive and, if I didn't clear the air, she'd shut down on me again.

"No, not really. Listen, Liz is like a virus. She infects everyone she comes in contact with. She's sneaky, two-faced and is not to be trusted."

"How do you know all of this about Liz?" she asked.

"Like I said, I'm no choirboy but I'm working on bettering myself. I had to turn my life around because I was so unhappy. I used to hang with Liz and her crew." I paused in thought because I didn't want to frighten her off with my history. "Let's just say I'm not proud of who I was."

Keysha leaned forward and rested her elbows on the table. She captured my gaze and looked at me intensely.

"Liz Lloyd has screwed me over so bad that, whenever I see her, I want to kick her ass. I don't like her one bit," Keysha said with absolute conviction.

"Well, neither do I," I responded.

"Then you and I have something in common." Keysha repositioned herself in her seat. "So, tell me your story, Wesley Morris. From the beginning. I want to know everything." Keysha smiled at me once again.

"Everything?" I smiled mannishly.

"In vivid detail." She smiled at me as I opened the windows to my soul and invited her inside for an enlightening conversation about who I am.

fourteen

Keysha

wesley was hot. I don't mean just cute hot. I mean, he was so fine that he made me want to scream out his name at the top of my lungs. He kind of reminded me of the Jamaican rapper Sean Paul. He gave me goose bumps whenever I was near him and, when he looked into my eyes, he melted my heart. The way he studied me and talked to me made me feel as if destiny brought us together. It had been a week since he came to my rescue and introduced himself to me at the library. I'd talked to him every day since and I couldn't stop thinking about him. It was hard to believe that he and I had so much in common. We both had mothers that didn't have our best interests at heart. Our fathers rescued us both from problematical situations and we both hated Liz Lloyd. I got all excited when I was near him and he had taken it upon himself to protect me against anyone who tried to harm me. Wesley was nothing like my ex-boyfriend, Ronnie. In fact, Wesley was much nicer than Ronnie ever was. Ronnie was always making me feel stupid and worthless. Wesley, on the other hand, listened to me. He cared about what I'd been through and praised me for weathering all of the hardships I'd endured. He was a dream come true.

When the 3:45 p.m. bell rang, I leaped up out of my study-hall seat and rushed out into the crowded hallway toward my locker so that I could grab my homework. Wesley was meeting me at my locker so that he could escort me to the football field where I had to wait for Mike to finish practice. As he'd promised, Wesley showed up around 3:45 p.m., trying to look stylish.

"We need to hang out at the mall one Saturday afternoon," I said as I closed my locker.

"I don't like malls that much," Wesley said.

"Why not?" I asked.

"It's just never been my thing," he answered.

"Well, you'll be with me, so that will make it fun," I said.

"Oh, you got it like that, huh? You can just turn anything into fun for me." Wesley smiled.

"What, do you think that I can't?" I placed a little playful authority in my voice.

"Girl, as far as I'm concerned you make the grayest sky blue, make it rain whenever you want to and make a ship sail on dry land."

"Wow. You make me feel as if I can do anything in the world," I said.

"That's because you can," he assured me as he held the exit door open for me. We stepped outside and began our journey around the school and toward the football field.

"I want to take you shopping so that we can pick out some better clothes for you," I said.

"What's wrong with what I have on?" he asked.

"You need an upgrade, boo. The color in that blue shirt you're wearing has completely faded. Who does your laundry?" I asked.

"I do," he answered.

"Do you know how to separate your clothes?"

"Separate them." He laughed. "I just throw them all in the washing machine together. They all get washed the same way, right?"

"Oh, Lord, you're a typical male." I chuckled.

"And what's that supposed to mean?"

"It means that you're normal. Maybe one day I can come over and show both you and your dad how to do laundry. Especially if his shirts and stuff are faded like yours."

"Yeah, they are."

"You guys just need a woman in your lives." I wanted to say a woman like me but I didn't push it.

"My dad dates a little but he doesn't really have anyone in particular that he's real serious about. He likes his simple and uncomplicated life."

"That's good. If you guys are happy, then that's great. But you still need to learn how to do your laundry properly."

"Whatever." Wesley laughed. "I'll let you show me how it's that important." We maneuvered our way past a cluster of school buses and began walking across the school's vast parking lot.

"I've been meaning to ask you, how could you stand to be with a guy who constantly put you down?" Wesley asked.

"I don't know. Sometimes I listened to him and sometimes I didn't. Either way, I'm glad that he's out of my life for good," I said as I adjusted my backpack.

"Here, let me carry that for you." Wesley helped me remove my backpack.

"This is heavy," he whined.

"I'll carry it. Don't worry about it," I said, reaching for the backpack.

"Relax, I was just teasing you." Wesley smiled at me and I playfully punched him on the arm.

"So, what about you and your girlfriend?" I asked. I wanted to know his history as much as he did mine.

"I used to date this girl named Della Turner. It didn't work out between us."

"Why not?" I asked.

"I don't know." He shrugged his shoulders.

"Yes, you do. Come on, tell me. You can trust me." I wanted him to know that I was a loyal kind of person.

"The truth is she came from a wealthy family and I didn't. Her father was the president of some big advertising company downtown. Her dad played golf with other executives. Anyway, her parents made her break up with me."

"That's not fair," I said.

"Believe me when I say they did me a favor. I learned that she was cheating on me anyway, so the breakup was no big deal."

"So you haven't had a girlfriend since that time?" I asked.

"Pretty much. Although, I had a few minor dates, but nothing serious." He shrugged again. "I mean, I've tried but I seem to like girls who are out of my league. Whenever I got rejected or humiliated by them, drinking alcohol reduced the sting of embarrassment. Eventually alcohol became the only way I dealt with my problems. But I'm better now," Wesley said. "The therapy sessions that I had to go through really helped a great deal. I feel stronger than I ever felt before and, now that I live with my father, I just don't have the problems I had with my mother. Speaking of mothers, have you been in contact with your mom?"

I exhaled loudly. The thought of my mother gave me chills.

"You don't have to talk about it if you don't want to," Wesley said, sensing my uneasiness.

"No, it's cool," I said. "I heard from my mother a few times. We've talked on the phone. She talked about her court case, which she thinks she's going to lose. Then she talked about the possibility of having her baby while she's still locked up and how she's going to have to turn it over to child services if she delivers while she's behind bars. She also continually asks me to send her money, which I don't have. That's about it. I can only talk to her for so long because she upsets me."

"I know that feeling." Wesley understood where I was coming from because of our similar experience. We arrived at the football field and I was hoping that Wesley would say he'd sit with me for a while.

"Well, here we are," he said. We were standing behind the concession stand out of the sight from the football players.

"Yeah, here we are," I repeated. I had butterflies in my stomach.

"Well, here. Let me give you your backpack." He handed it to me.

"So, can I call you later?" he asked.

"You better," I answered.

"Cool." He paused for a moment, then reached out to touch my hand. He wrapped his fingers around my hand and we looked at each other for a long moment. I knew he wanted to kiss me and I had to determine whether or not I was ready for that. I mean, I was definitely ready but I didn't want to get hurt if things didn't work out. I also wanted to know what the kiss would mean.

"Do you want to kiss me?" I asked nervously.

"Only if you want to kiss me," he responded. I paused and bit my lip and began to contemplate the moment. I exhaled.

"I don't want to get hurt again. I've got enough problems in my life." I tossed up a roadblock.

"Do you think I'm a problem?" he asked, staring at me with his warm eyes. He'd just blown through my roadblock.

"No," I answered softly.

"Do you think I'd ever hurt you?" he asked.

"I don't know."

"I won't," he said. "I'd never hurt you, Keysha. You can trust me."

"Are you sure?" I asked.

"Yeah," he said, and I wanted to believe him so I did.

"One kiss and that's it, okay?" I swallowed hard. Wesley leaned toward me slowly. I lowered my eyes and awaited contact. When our lips met, he cupped his hand and caressed my right cheek. The stroke of his hand was very gentle and nurturing. I felt my heartbeat begin to race wildly, and my body was giving in to him way too easily. When my knees started buckling beneath me, I pulled away.

"Whew," I exhaled. "I've got to go."

"What's wrong?" he asked, concerned that he'd done something wrong.

"Nothing." My voice and lips quivered because they were filled with passion.

"I'll call you later, okay?"

"You had better," I said, and rushed away from him so that I could get a grip and pull myself together. There is nothing as sweet as the first kiss, I thought to myself as I found a spot to sit down.

During the walk home from football practice Mike complained about how sore he was from being tackled repeatedly.

"I swear, everything hurts on my body," he groaned as we walked back across the student parking lot. I wasn't really paying attention to him because I was still floating on air over the kiss that Wesley and I had shared. I wanted him to ask me to be his girlfriend. I wanted to be everything to him because, as far as I was concerned, he was the brightest spot in my life and I was hoping he realized that.

"Keysha," Mike yelled out. The loudness of his voice startled me out of my daydream.

"Dang, girl, get your head out of the clouds. A car almost hit you. Didn't you notice that we reached the corner stoplight?" Mike glared at me as if I were retarded.

"No. I didn't notice it," I answered him. I didn't like the expression on his face and for some reason I felt as if he had an issue with me but I didn't know what the issue was.

"Well, duh! Pay attention," Mike said sarcastically.

I felt as if he was trying to belittle me and I got defensive. "Give me a break, Mike. I was just daydreaming a little. Is that a crime?"

"No, but if you keep hanging around with that burnout Wesley Morris, crime and more trouble will certainly show up."

"What are you talking about?"

"You know what I'm talking about, Keysha."

"No, I don't, Mike." I suddenly got mad at him for trying to question my relationship with Wesley.

"Wesley is not good for you, Keysha. He's trouble. He has a very bad reputation and is known for getting completely wasted. I've heard all types of crazy stories about him."

"Stories like what, Mike?" I was really getting angry now.

"I heard that he and his goons got some young girl completely bombed so she could be taken advantage of. I also heard that he was arrested for auto theft, did time at a juvenile detention center and is in rehab."

"That's not the Wesley I know. That's the old Wesley," I fired back at him. I wasn't about to let him talk about my friend in a bad way.

"Keysha, open up your eyes, Wesley will get you in trouble. All he probably wants to do is get you wasted so that he can have his way with you."

"Shut up, Mike. I don't want to hear it."

"Well, you're going to hear it because you need to. He's the wrong guy for you. When are you going to start trusting me, Keysha? I know what I'm talking about. I told you about Liz but you didn't believe me until it was too late. Now I'm telling you about Wesley before something major happens."

"He doesn't do that anymore, Mike. He's been through rehab and is much better now. Besides, it's not your right to judge a person. You should also really take the time to get to know him and understand what he's been through before you criticize and attack his character."

"You are utterly impossible, Keysha. I don't know what it's going to take for you to see people for who they truly are."

"I know who Wesley is and who he is not," I said.

"Whatever," Mike said as he placed the key in the front door.

"Yeah, whatever," I said, feeling uneasy as I followed him inside and hustled up the stairs to my room.

fifteen

Wesley

On Saturday Keysha and I rode the Pace Bus to the Lincoln Mall in Matteson, Illinois. During the ride she began asking questions about incidents that had occurred during the time I was addicted to alcohol. She didn't sugarcoat any of her questions, she flat-out asked some very serious questions. I felt as if I were being interrogated.

"Wesley, have you ever gotten a girl drunk and taken advantage of her?"

"Wow, where did that question come from?" I asked, feeling uneasy about telling her the truth.

"You said it yourself, you're no choirboy."

The tone in her voice made me uneasy. I was at a crossroads. I wanted say no, but that wouldn't have been completely accurate. Or I could tell the truth and be as open and as honest as I could and hope that she'd understand that I'd made a big mistake. I took a deep breath and then exhaled.

"What had happened was—" I paused. "No, the truth of the matter is, an incident happened at this house party about a year ago. It happened one day when there was no school. That particular day I was hanging out with my friend Ed Daley. We were sitting in his front yard drinking some booze that his twenty-one-year-old brother, who happened to be a bartender, had gotten for us. Some schoolmates rode by on their bikes and said that there was a major house party going on three blocks over. Ed and I were bored out of our minds so we were all for crashing a party. We gathered up our six-pack, got on our bikes and went to check out the party. As it turned out it was the party of the century. It seemed as if every student from our district's high schools were there. Ed and I got in because we had alcohol and decided to get more of it by calling his brother back. Ed and I took up a collection and came up with two hundred dollars to spend. Ed's brother showed up with a few of his buddies and they made a liquor run. They came back with all types of alcohol and Ed's brother began mixing up really strong drinks for everyone. Everyone thought we were so cool for scoring some alcohol and a bartender. Then Ed called up Liz Lloyd and told her where the party was and to bring some Ecstasy. Liz and a few members of her crew showed up about thirty minutes later, and for those who wanted to take their experience to the next level, she supplied them with the pill, at a good price, mind you. She made a lot of money that day.

"Before long a number of people were either buzzed, bombed out or well on their way to being smashed. The music was good too. Everyone was dancing close to each other, grinding on each other with wild, horny energy. Then Liz hooked up with this young girl who was completely wasted but wanted to have sex."

"Wait a minute. Some girl was walking around asking for it?" Keysha needed clarification.

"Yeah."

"Who was she?" Keysha asked.

"You don't know her. She doesn't go to our school. But her name was Felicia Wilson. Anyway, Liz took Felicia by the hand and began dancing wildly with her in the middle of the living room where people could see them. Liz was all over Felicia but she didn't seem to mind. One thing led to another and Liz did her."

"What do you mean?" Keysha wanted me to spell it all out for her.

"She did her. Right there on the living room floor in front of everyone."

"You mean to tell me that people watched?"

"Everyone wanted to watch, especially the guys."

"Where were you when all of this was happening?"

"I was on the sofa, watching. Felicia was looking directly into my eyes as the whole thing went down. She kept mumbling something but I was too smashed to understand what she was saying. I just drank my liquor and watched the entire thing go down."

"So Felicia basically got raped by Liz."

"It's sounds so horrible when you put it like that," I said.

"I say it like that because Liz tried to do the same thing to me. She wanted to cover up the crime by calling it a good time," Keysha said with disgust. "She tried to dope me up so that she could take full advantage of me." Keysha huffed, "Liz just makes my skin crawl."

I agreed with her. "She makes the skin of a lot of people crawl."

"So, what happened next?" Keysha asked.

"I got so smashed that I passed out on the sofa. Ed woke

me up by slapping my face a few times. Ed said that we had to get out of the house because the home owners would be back soon and they were not going to be happy with their son for throwing such a wild and crazy party. You should have seen the place. It had gotten completely trashed."

"So, what happened to Felicia?" Keysha asked.

"I don't know. When I woke up, she wasn't there any-more."

"So how did the rumor about you taking advantage of Felicia even get started?"

"I have no idea but that's why they call them rumors, I suppose." I lied. I knew who started the rumor.

"I don't understand. You didn't try to put the truth out there. You let the rumor grow into something that it shouldn't have."

"Keysha, if there is one thing that I've learned it's that people are going to believe whatever they want to. I tried to detach my name from the rumor but I couldn't."

"Do you even know who started the rumor?" she asked.

I chuckled. "Liz Lloyd started it. She spread the word around that I'd gotten the girl drunk so that she could be taken advantage of."

"But that's not true," Keysha pointed out.

"Well, I didn't pour the alcohol down her throat. But had Ed, his brother and I not showed up with the alcohol that may not have happened."

"Well, I don't blame you for that. Felicia had a choice and she chose to drink," Keysha said, and then was silent for a long moment.

"So, do you hate me now?" I asked.

"No," she said as she threaded her fingers between mine. "Thank you for being honest."

"I'll always be honest with you, Keysha," I assured her.

"I like knowing that," she answered, and then kissed me on the cheek.

Keysha and I spent the entire afternoon at the mall. I really enjoyed being with her and spending time with her. I enjoyed sharing my food with her and watching her try on clothes and watching her help me determine what looked good on me and what didn't. During our bus ride back home she shared with me her love of reading and suggested that I read a book called, *Makes Me Wanna Holla,* by journalist Nathan McCall.

"It's a really good book about this guy who hung around the wrong crowd and eventually ended up in jail. Then when he got out he turned his life around and now actually writes for the *Washington Post* newspaper."

"Are you serious?" I asked because it sounded like a book I'd like to read.

"Yes, I'm serious. Go online and Google his name for yourself if you don't believe me."

"I'm not much of a reader, Keysha," I confessed.

"Well, if you're going to hang with me, you've got to read. That's not an option."

"Why do we have to read? What's that all about?"

"We have to read so that we'll have different subjects to talk about. I mean, you can't just sit around telling me how good I look all of the time. That would get boring. I need conversation. I need to know how you think. I need to know what kind of brain you have. Don't you know that a guy who can communicate well is a big turn-on to girls?"

"No, but now I do. I guess reading a book or two for pleasure won't hurt me. I mean, I do dabble in a little poetry from time to time but nothing serious."

"See, reading may help you with your poetry. That's all the more reason you should read. Besides, you don't want to be the guy who is too cool to read or who thinks reading is only something girls do. Guys like that are so lame." Keysha was passionate about her feelings toward reading.

"Okay, I get your point but I'm a slow reader," I said as I slung my arm around her.

"A slow reader is only an indication of a person who isn't reading enough. I know because I used to be a very slow reader. In fact, I used to hate reading because it put me to sleep. But my eighth-grade teacher, Ms. Shaheen, was a writer and she let me read her manuscript for a young-adult book she was working on. It was about this nerdy high school girl who wanted to hang out with the popular girls. In order to prove that she was cool enough to hang out with them, they dared her to take a fake gun into a convenience store and rob it. She did it and got away with a few hundred dollars. Anyway, what she thought was just a onetime initiation thing turned into something else. The girls decided that it would be cool to go around robbing places so that they could get money for clothes and stuff. Well, then it got real messy because one of the girls got shot by an off-duty police officer who was in the store."

"Man, that sounds as if it could be a movie. Did she ever get the book published?"

"I don't think so. I've been keeping an eye out for it, but so far I haven't found anything. After reading her manuscript, I developed a love of reading and I haven't been able to stop."

"So now you want to turn me into a book junkie, as well."

"Hey, there are worse habits to have." Keysha chuckled as she reached down into the shopping bag that was between her legs and pulled out the Phat Farm shirt she'd picked out for me. She held it up close to my body to make sure she still liked the way the shirt looked.

"You are going to look so hot in this," she said.

I smiled at her as I leaned back in my seat. For the first time in ages I felt really good and I knew Keysha was a big part of why I felt the way I did. She didn't judge me or preach at me and I liked that.

"There is something I've been meaning to ask you," I said.

"What's that?" Keysha asked.

"Well, it's like this." I stopped to think about how to phrase what I needed to say. I began to wring my hands because I was edgy. "I mean, will you be my girl?" I asked.

Keysha put the shirt back in the bag and locked her gaze upon me.

"Are you serious?" she asked.

"Yeah," I answered, wondering why she thought I was joking.

"Well, it's about time you asked. You had a sister waiting and wondering what the real deal was. I mean, honestly after our first kiss you should have come back the next—"

I cut her off by kissing her passionately. When I pulled

away, her eyes were still closed and she was enjoying the euphoric moment.

"So, are you going to be my girl or what?"

Keysha opened her eyes and said, "Yes."

sixteen

Keysha

WeSley, Wesley, Wesley! Ooo, I liked the sound of his name. It was so masculine and tough like a ruffian who can kick butt, take names and still be gentle enough to treat a lady right. Needless to say, after Wesley asked me to be his girl, the only thing on my mind was him. I am floating on cloud number nine. I felt he was sent to protect me and to make sure that everything in my life turned out harmonious. I'm not saying that I couldn't hold my own, but it's nice to know that I could call backup reinforcements if I needed to.

In order to spend an entire day with Wesley I had to tell Jordan and my stepmom, Barbara, a little white lie. I told them that I was going to the library to do more research for one of my papers. I even went as far as to let Jordan drop me off at the public library. Although I did check out two books that I needed, I didn't read them. Instead I waited for Wesley to arrive. He had to tell the same white lie in order to get out of the house. Once he was there, we headed over to the bus stop for our grand day of fun, romance and shopping.

"Keysha," I heard Jordan call out my name from the bottom of the staircase.

"Yeah," I answered.

"Come on down for dinner," he said.

"I'll be right there," I said. I got up from my bed, went into the bathroom to wash my hands and then headed down to dinner.

"What's for dinner?" I asked Barbara who was placing silverware on the table.

"Baked chicken, rice pilaf and biscuits," she said as she moved between the kitchen and the dining room.

"Let me help set the table," I said as I followed her into the kitchen. Once the table was set, we all held hands and Mike blessed the food.

"So, how did it go at the library?" Jordan asked as he carved a small portion of chicken to eat.

"It was okay," I answered, giving very few details. I figured the less I spoke, the less likely it would be for me to slip up.

"What were you doing research on?" Barbara asked. She and I got along much better than we had before. I didn't look at her as my mother or my girlfriend. She was more like an additional mentor to me.

"Well, I picked up two books about the women's rights movement. I haven't really gotten into it yet, though. I spent time reading other periodicals on the subject," I lied a little.

"That's an excellent and important subject to write about," said Barbara. "Do you have to give a speech for it?"

"No, I just have to turn in a ten-page paper on it. I still have some time before it's due."

"So, how do you think you're doing with your classes?" she asked. I had to give it to Barbara and Jordan. They stayed on me when it came to my schoolwork. Barbara also made herself available in case I got stumped or needed additional help.

"I am doing so much better with my classes. I'm confident that my grades are going to be much better. I'm also doing any extra-credit work that I can to help me improve."

"More like extracurricular activities," Mike mumbled.

I shot daggers at him with my eyes. I couldn't believe he was being so childish.

"When do you think you'll have a first draft of the paper completed?" Barbara asked.

"I'm not sure," I answered.

"Yeah, but you're certainly sure about other things." Mike once again uttered a nasty remark. I tried to kick his leg from beneath the table but I couldn't reach him.

"Mike, stop it with the negative comments." Barbara got on him. Mike looked at his mom as if she'd betrayed him.

"Cut it out." Barbara held her ground.

"She likes this boy at school," Mike blurted out, and I could've died right where I sat.

"Boy?" was all Jordan heard.

I started talking quickly so that Mike wouldn't twist everything around.

"He's just a friend," I quickly said, not wanting to tell the full truth. This was entirely new territory I was crossing. When I lived with my real mom, Justine, she didn't care who I dated or what I did. But Jordan and Barbara questioned everything.

"You can't date," Jordan said with absolute finality. I glanced at Mike, who was grinning at the drama he'd just started.

"I'm not dating. He's just a friend." I tried to soften my relationship with Wesley. "I am allowed to have friends, aren't I?"

"Boy, and you know how to pick really good ones." Mike blurted out another nasty comment. He kept fanning the flames I was trying to put out. I swear, if I had a gun at that moment I would have shot him dead.

"Now, wait a minute," Barbara chimed in. "She's sixteen years old and it's age and developmentally appropriate for her to have a male friend as long as it's innocent." When Barbara said that, she basically chose a side, and the expressions on Jordan's and Mike's faces were priceless. They looked as if Barbara had just nailed them both in the face with a yellow snowball.

"No." Jordan raised his voice. "She is too young to deal with boys. We have way too much going on in this family right now to add another layer of complication. We have to worry about the pending court case, the cost of the attorney and our family name. So no."

"Jordan, you can't lock her up and not expect her to live. I think she has proven that she has some sense of responsibility and knows the difference between right and wrong. At least in my mind she has."

I was speechless. I don't mean just quiet, I mean, absolutely shocked by Barbara's willingness to go out on a limb for me.

"The court case is going to work itself out. If there is one thing I know for sure, it's that Keysha is neither a drug abuser nor a distributor and our name will be cleared. I think that as long as she's responsible and stays away from trouble, there is no harm in her having a male friend."

"What about that girl?" Jordan was talking fast and couldn't remember Liz's name. He popped his fingers when he remembered. "Liz. She had an altercation with her."

"I've haven't seen Liz in a while. Besides, we stay away from each other now." I defended myself and tried to downplay the fight I'd had with Liz.

"Keysha got into a fight with Liz." Mike once again fanned the flames of conflict. I gave him yet another warning glare. He just smirked at me.

"Fight? What fight?" Jordan was getting upset.

"It wasn't a fight," I lied again. "We just had an argument that got very heated. I wanted her to own up to what she'd done."

"Well, I can't blame Keysha for trying to straighten things out," Barbara said.

"But fighting isn't the way to do it," Jordan argued.

"I know," I said, "and I see that now. I stay away from Liz as much as possible. I'm not looking to trade blows with her." I once again defended myself.

"Here is what I propose. Invite the young man over. We can meet him, talk to him and learn more about him before we automatically assume that he's trouble," Barbara stated.

"We'd better lock down the liquor cabinets," Mike uttered. A vicious streak of evil flowed through me as I lowered my eyes to slits and focused on him.

"What did you just say, Mike?" Jordan asked.

"He didn't say anything," I cut Mike off before he had a chance to ruin everything.

"Good, it's settled, then. Keysha." Barbara looked at me.

"Invite him over tomorrow afternoon for brunch. You guys can hang out over here."

"Okay," I said as I tried to relax and calm my nerves down. No one said a word during the rest of our dinnertime together. The silence among us was unnerving. Once dinner was finished, I helped Barbara clean the table and wash up the dishes. As I stood at the kitchen sink with my hands submerged in soapy dishwater washing a plate, Barbara came over and stood next to me.

"Hey," she said.

"Hey," I answered.

"Dry your hands and let's have a little girl talk for a minute, okay?"

"Okay," I said as I reached for a paper towel to dry my hands with. I followed Barbara out to the exercise room above the garage. I took a seat in one of the chairs that was up there. Barbara took another chair and positioned it so that she could face me as we talked.

"Okay, you know that I went out on a limb for you in there, right?" she asked.

"Yeah, I know. Thank you," I said.

"No need to thank me. I was sixteen once and I know how hard it is for a father to come to grips with the fact that his daughter wants to have male friends." Barbara was silent for a moment. Then she leaned forward in her seat and cupped her hands. "Give me your hands," she said. I gave her my hands as we made eye contact. "This boy that you like, what is his name?"

"Wesley," I answered.

"Is he your boyfriend?" she asked.

"He asked me to be his girl, and I said yes. But that's it."

"Are you active with him?" she asked.

"Active?" I needed her to be a little clearer.

"Intimate? Are you having or considering an intimate relationship with him?"

I thought about the question for a moment before I answered. Wesley and I hadn't gotten to that level or even talked about being intimate with each other.

"I don't think I'm ready for that again," I answered her honestly. "We haven't talked about that at all and he isn't pressuring me in any way and I like that about him."

"Do you think that'll change?" Barbara asked another tough question.

"I don't know. I suppose at some point it will come up."

"What will you say if it does?" Barbara softly caressed the center of my hand with her thumbs. Her movements were soothing and comforting. I felt as if I could trust her.

"I don't want to be pressured into doing it. But I don't want him to think that I don't like him if I don't. Guys can be so confusing at times."

"You don't have to do anything that makes you feel uncomfortable, okay? If you feel at any point you're being led down a path that you don't want to go down you have the power to change your own destiny and direction. Do you understand?"

"Yes," I answered.

"Let's talk about a few girl rules."

"What are girl rules?" I asked.

"They're a few rules that my mother put in place when I was a young woman your age. The rules are like safety nets. My sister hated the rules but eventually she learned why we needed them. Rule number one. If Wesley or any other boy tries to force himself on you, fight. You fight him until you can't fight him anymore and then you still fight. That's about self-defense. Rule number two. If you ever need a ride home, just call. Jordan and I will come and get you. Anytime and anyplace, no questions asked."

"Really?" I was completely awestruck by that one. No one had ever offered that to me before. If I ever got in a jam, it was either walk home or catch a bus.

"Yes, really. Rule number three. Always remember that someone cares. Always remember that you are loved." Barbara's comment made me feel very special.

"I have one suggestion that may help me if I get into a sticky situation. If you guys get me a car, then I'd be in control and boys wouldn't have the power to kick me out. Since I'm taking driver's ed next semester, the timing would be perfect," I said, uncertain of the reaction I'd get. Barbara laughed.

"Good try but we'll cross that bridge when we get to it." She chuckled. "So, tell me about Wesley." Barbara once again connected with my eyes. That's when I became nervous. I didn't know how much I should tell her. I didn't know if I should tell her everything or just a few things. Barbara must have read my thoughts.

"So he's a bad boy." She read my thoughts effortlessly.

"Well, he sort of is and he sort of isn't," I answered.

"Well, it's okay. It's not uncommon for a girl to be attracted to a boy who is a little rough around the edges. There is a certain amount of mystery to a man who is a renegade.

But there has to be boundaries set. A boy shouldn't hit you or anything like that."

"No. Wesley isn't like that," I said. "He's more of a renegade with a bruised heart that is pure. Like mine. He's had some problems dealing with emotional abuse from his mom, as well as alcohol abuse, but he's doing much better now." I decided that I could trust Barbara and tell her everything.

"Go on, I'm listening," she said. So I continued to tell everything I knew about Wesley. I even surprised myself and told her about the magic of our first kiss and she didn't scold me for it.

I phoned Wesley late Saturday evening and asked him to come over for brunch. He was excited about the idea of seeing me again but wasn't too thrilled about meeting my father and stepmother.

"I don't know about that one, Keysha," Wesley said nervously.

"Why not?" I asked.

"Because, what if they don't like me or think that I'm all wrong for you?" Wesley voiced his concerns.

"It's okay. I had a really good and long talk with my stepmom and she knows everything," I said with both pride and confidence.

"Everything?" Wesley questioned.

"Well, she doesn't know that I spent all Saturday afternoon with you at the mall, but she knows about your struggles and your mom and how you're living with your dad now."

"And she was cool with that?" Wesley asked, not fully believing me.

"To my surprise, yes, she was. It's like my grandmother

Katie told me. She said that Barbara and I have more in common than I think. Barbara even told me about this motorcycle bad boy she dated when she was eighteen. So trust me, compared to all of the sneaking around she was doing with him, you're tame. Besides, she said that she didn't want me to feel as if I had to sneak around. She wants to meet you."

"Okay," Wesley said hesitantly.

"Be here at my house by 1:00 p.m. tomorrow. Oh, and wear the shirt I picked out for you," I said.

"Okay, I'll see you then," he said, and hung up the phone.

seventeen

Wesley

I sat down next to my dad, who was lounging around on the sofa down in the basement where the home theater and entertainment systems were. He was watching *The Matrix,* which he'd rented for the weekend. He was at the point where the characters Neo and Trinity entered an office building, shot up all of the guards and blew up the elevator shaft all in an effort to save their friend Morpheus.

"Dad, I have a question for you." My dad pressed Pause on the remote.

"This is a really good movie," he said. "Have you seen it?"

"Aah, yeah, Dad. It's been out for a while now," I answered.

"You know that I don't go to the movies much. The girl at the video store said that I'd like this and she was right."

"Well, just so that you know, they're making part—"

"Don't tell me." He cut me off. "Don't tell me anything right now about it. I just want to finish it. So, what's going on?"

"Remember how I was telling you about the girl I liked, named Keysha?"

"Yes. The one that is kind of feisty and likes to read. Didn't she invite you over to lunch or something?" he asked.

"Yeah, the lunch thing is today. I'm going to head over there but I'm not sure of what to expect. I mean, I've met the parents of other girls before, but I got a feeling this time things are going to be a little different."

"Don't expect anything. Just be yourself," my dad advised me.

"But her father, what if he doesn't like me?" I asked the question that I really wanted to know the answer to. My dad smiled at me.

"Oh, I see, this is really about meeting her father for the first time."

"Yeah, it is," I said.

"Tell you what. Why don't I drop you off at this young lady's home and then that way we can both meet her parents. It'll take a lot of the uneasiness out of the situation."

"No," I said quickly. "Then I'll look like a baby."

"Well, where does she live, Wesley?"

"A few blocks over. I wrote down her address and phone number and left it on the kitchen counter like you asked me to do. I'm worried about her parents' approval of me."

"There is nothing wrong with you, Wesley. You're a nice and respectful young man. You've just run into a few wrinkles in the road, that's all."

"I know, but what do I say to her father? What if the guy is a real jerk?"

"Okay. A few rules for you. When you meet him, be very respectful. Address him as sir. When you enter his home, listen to his direction. If he asks you to have a seat on a particular chair, make sure that's where you sit. Then, when he asks you questions, be honest and truthful. Meeting fathers is never easy, especially the first time. Her father was your age once and he's probably thinking that if you are anything like he was at the age of sixteen, the only thing your brain is filled with is having sex with his daughter."

"Aah, well—that would be true, I have thought about it but I haven't brought that up to her. I'm not putting her under any pressure or anything like that." At that point my father turned the television completely off.

"Are you still a virgin, Wesley?" my dad asked out of the blue. I suddenly felt mortified that he'd asked such a personal question.

"Yeah," I answered, suddenly wanting to end our conversation.

"There is nothing wrong with you being a virgin at your age. In fact, it's a good thing that you are because having sex is a major step and it's a lot of responsibility."

"We don't have to discuss this right now. It can wait," I said, wanting to end our conversation.

"No, I think it's a good time to have it. We've talked about everything else but this. I know that you must have some very strong urges. So let's talk about it."

I felt numb. Talking about sex with my old man was like trying to talk about a wet dream with my mother. It was just odd.

"You do have urges, don't you?" my dad asked.

"Yeah, I do—" That was all I could say but I could tell that my dad wanted to know more.

"It's okay to have those feelings," he said, "but you have to be in control. You can't allow yourself to go around trying to hump every girl you meet. It's unhealthy, it's irresponsible and you could get a reputation that you may not be very nice."

"Are you kidding me? Guys my age love having a reputation for getting down with a lot of girls. There are guys around my school who brag constantly about their conquests. One guy told the entire locker room about how he did some girl in his car and how bad she was. Another guy has tricked several girls into giving it up by telling a variety of lies from 'if you love me, you'll do it' to 'I'll go blind if you don't' and girls actually fall for it."

"Wesley, just because a young man claims to have had an intimate relationship with a young lady doesn't mean it's true. A guy that brags about his conquest to an entire locker room is a real jerk. Because now that young lady is going to be approached by those other guys looking for their own opportunity because she has a reputation of being active. And just because a guy has an intimate time with a number of girls it doesn't make him more of a man or a great lover. In fact, I'd be willing to bet that the young men who are bragging so much know very little about love, romance, compassion, respect and truly carrying for a person. Intimacy is much more than jumping up and down inside some young lady's belly for a few moments of pleasure. It is so much more than that. It sounds as if the guys who are bragging have removed their emotions from the relationship, which is why they don't care about what they're saying. When you're involved emotionally, you've made a commitment on a different level. I'd be willing to bet that the young ladies who are active believe that they are in an emotional relationship with the guys they've given it up to."

"Yeah, I think you're right because I do hear those same guys talking about how crazy some of the girls get when they dump them for another girl. The girls cry, they argue in public and some even fight the guy's new girlfriend. The boys I know get a kick out of it when girls fight over them. Oh, and one girl even had her male cousins beat up a boy for having sex with her and then dumping her the next day."

"Wesley, you don't want to be in a position where you slept with a stranger and then wake up with an enemy. Love is not about having intercourse. Loving a person is much deeper and there is a emotional bond that is formed when you love someone—I know that it's not easy when your body is sending out signals of desire. Sometimes the hunger for intimacy can cloud a man's judgment." My dad paused for a moment. "Do you have condoms?" he asked.

"No," I answered.

"Then I'll get you some to keep with you. I'm not saying go out and do anything, I'm just being a father." He paused again before speaking. "You're my son and you're a likable kid with a good heart. Keysha's father will see that," my dad said, and that made me feel a little more at ease.

"Okay," I said, glad to know that our conversation about sex was ending.

"Are you sure you don't want me to drive you over there?" he asked again.

"No, I'm cool. I'll walk," I said.

"I would let you take the car but you know that we have

to wait for the final paperwork releasing you from the care of the rehab center to reach the judge for approval."

"I know. I still can't believe that Judge Hill actually suspended my license."

"Well, I think it was a good thing that she did that. It keeps you from making an irreversible mistake. What time will you be back?"

"I should be back around 4:00 p.m. or 5:00 p.m. Before the weather turns too cold. Oh, on my way home I'm going to stop at the library and pick up a book Keysha suggested I read."

"You really like her, don't you?" my dad asked.

"Yeah, I do."

"I like her too and I haven't even met her. When are you going to bring her over?"

"I don't know. I haven't thought about it."

"Well, here is a word of advice from your old man. She's probably waiting for an invitation from you. So make sure you invite her over before she says something to you."

"Gotcha. What are you going to do this afternoon?" I asked.

"I'm going to install that ceiling fan sitting in the corner." He pointed to a box on the floor. "I'm going to remove the old light fixture above the sofa." My dad pointed toward the ceiling.

"Do you need any help installing it?" I asked.

"No, I can handle it. You go and have a nice time," he insisted. "As soon as this movie goes off I'm going to get that project taken care of."

"Cool. I'll catch you later," I said as he clicked the television back on and continued watching his movie.

When I arrived at Keysha's house, I was so nervous that I felt like puking. I rang her doorbell and waited for someone to answer it. I cleared my throat a few times in anticipation of greeting her dad. I heard the tumbler on the door turn and then finally it opened up.

"Keysha." I breathed a sigh of relief.

"Ooh, you said that as if you were expecting a dragon to answer the door."

"I'm just a little nervous, that's all," I whispered. "Here, I purchased a flower arrangement for you."

"Oh, they're so pretty," Keysha cooed as if the flowers were the best gift she'd ever gotten. "Come on in. My dad is sitting in the family room. My stepmom is on her way back from the grocery store with my brother."

"Oh, okay," I said nervously as I entered the house and kicked off my shoes so that I wouldn't track in any dirt from outside. I walked up several steps and entered the family room.

Keysha introduced us. "Dad, this is my friend Wesley. And, Wesley, this is my dad, Jordan."

"Hello, sir," I said as I approached him. Jordan was sitting on a chair, glaring at me as if I'd stolen something from him. I mean, honestly, Jordan looked as if a smile hadn't crossed his face in at least one hundred years. I immediately got a bad vibe from him.

"So, you're Wesley." He didn't sound pleased at all.

"Yes, sir." Jordan shook my hand but squeezed it so hard I swear it felt as if he'd shifted several bones in my hand around.

When he released me from his clutch, I had to shake my hand and fingers out to make sure they still worked.

"They used to call me the bone crusher," he said with a condescending grin on his face.

"What are you talking about?" Keysha asked. It appeared to be the first time she'd ever heard him say such a thing. Her father ignored her request for additional information.

"Have a seat." He pointed to a chair and I sat down. Keysha came over and sat next to me. She placed my hand in hers. I know she did it as a way to ease my nerves. Heck, I wasn't as uneasy when I had to go into juvie as I was now. Jordan didn't like the fact that Keysha was so close to me. I could see the distrust in his eyes.

"So, what do you want to do with your life, Winston?" Her father didn't remember my name.

"Um, my name is Wesley, sir," I politely corrected him. I glanced at Keysha and I could see her murdering him with her eyes.

"Oh, my bad." Her father tried to sound hip but it seemed so out of character for him.

"I haven't thought about what I want to do yet as far as a career goes," I answered him truthfully.

"Why haven't you thought about it?" he asked as if I was a complete idiot for not having a plan mapped out.

"I don't know." I shrugged my shoulders. I felt my heart beating about four times faster than normal. I felt as if I was blowing my first encounter with him.

"He's going to go to college, Jordan." Keysha jumped in the conversation. "He's going to do great things with his life. I just know he is." Keysha smiled at me.

"What kind of job do you have now?"

"He's not working right now but I'm sure he'll find a job over the summer. Isn't that right, Wesley?" Keysha asked.

"Yeah," I agreed.

"Can't he speak for himself?" Jordan cut Keysha off. I could hear Keysha's breathing getting heavier. I knew that she was upset with her father for grilling me so hard.

"So, what do you plan on doing with my child?" he asked, but I didn't know what he meant.

"Excuse me, sir?" I asked.

"You know, why don't we cut straight to the chase, Wesley?"

"Okay," I said, not certain of what he meant.

"I don't like you. And I probably never will."

"Jordan!" Keysha yelled at him. "That's not fair and you know it. Why are you acting like this?"

"It's okay, Keysha," I said.

"No, it isn't. You haven't done anything to him so he has no right to treat you like this."

Jordan leaned back in his seat and just glared at me. His eyes were filled with fire and I didn't know why.

"I think I should leave," I said.

"But you just got here. Barbara planned on cooking for us."

"No, Keysha," I said, rising to my feet. "It's time for me to go. Your dad just said that he didn't like me."

"You can stay," Jordan said, but I could tell that his words were empty and didn't mean anything.

"I can't believe you're behaving like this, Jordan," Keysha scolded her father.

"Look, I'll just catch up with you later, Keysha. Maybe this is just a bad time or something," I said, and made my way toward the door. I quickly put on my shoes and exited the house. Just as I stepped out into the sunlight I saw a blue Volvo pull into the driveway.

A woman got out of the car. "You must be Wesley. I'm Keysha's stepmom, Barbara."

"Hi," I said.

"Where are you guys going? It will not take me long to whip up something to eat."

"I'm walking Wesley home," Keysha said. "Jordan is being a real big jerk!" she said it very loudly. The smile fell from Barbara's face.

"What did he do? Was he being mean-spirited?" Barbara seemed to know her husband very well.

"Mean and evil," Keysha said. "Ooh, I can't believe he acted out like that."

"He was like a big bully, wasn't he?" Barbara asked.

"Yeah," Keysha said. At that moment I glanced in the passenger seat of the car and saw Mike with a sinister smile on his face and wondered what that was all about.

"I'm going to walk him home. Is that okay with you, Barbara?" Keysha asked.

"Wesley, you're really welcome to stay. Jordan isn't going to bother you. I promise."

"Thanks for offering but I really should get back. My dad needs help installing a new ceiling fan anyway."

"Wesley's phone number is sitting on my desk in my room in case you need it. I won't be gone long," Keysha informed Barbara.

Barbara sighed. "All right, then. Let me go in there and straighten Jordan out. Oh, and for the record, I apologize for Jordan's behavior."

"Don't worry about it," I said, and began walking past the car.

"Are you sure you don't need a drink, Wesley?" Mike asked. At that moment Keysha realized that Mike must have had something to do with the way Jordan was acting.

"What did you say to Jordan?" Keysha snapped at him.

"I told him what he needed to know," Mike answered.

"You just wait, Mike. I'm going to make you regret this."

"Whatever, Keysha." Mike wasn't worried about the verbal threat from his sister.

Keysha and I continued down her driveway and noticed a fire engine and an ambulance racing by.

"Those sirens are so loud," Keysha complained. "I hate it when they rush past, especially during the evening hours."

"Yeah, the sounds of those sirens are earsplitting. I've always wondered if the drivers go deaf after a while," I said.

"I'm sure they do— I'm really sorry about the way my dad behaved. He really isn't like that. Lord only knows what Mike told him to make him act so bad."

"Don't worry about it," I said, trying not to make her feel bad.

"I mean, he switched from Jordan to Evil Jordan in a matter of moments."

"He's probably just being protective," I said, blowing the entire unpleasant encounter off. "You know Halloween is coming up. Do you have any plans?"

"No," Keysha answered.

"We should do something together. Maybe we could go see a movie."

"I'd like that," Keysha said. As we were making our way past the library I had Keysha stop inside with me and pick up the book she suggested that I read. We then made plans to go back to my house and listen to some music and just chill out.

"My dad will not grill you," I said jokingly.

"I know he won't. He's going to meet me and instantly adore me," Keysha said with absolute certainty. I chuckled because I knew that she was right. My dad would treat her like a member of the family and I knew it.

My house was only one block from the library. As we turned the corner onto my street, Keysha noticed that my street was buzzing with activity. I hadn't noticed anything immediately because I was reading the back cover of the book I'd just checked out.

"Say, isn't that your house that the fire truck and ambulance are parked in front of?"

I looked in the direction of my house.

"Oh, damn!" I dropped the book and took off running down the street toward my home to see what was going on.

eighteen

Keysha

I sprinted down the block behind Wesley and when I caught up with him, he was panic-stricken. His home had caught on fire. There were cords of fire hoses and streams of water all over the ground. Firefighters were hosing down a rear portion of Wesley's home.

"What happened? Where's my dad?" Wesley rushed up to one of the firefighters, whose face was covered in blackness. I was right behind him, ready to offer my support.

"Who are you?" I heard the firefighter ask.

"I live here," Wesley quickly explained. "My dad… Where's my dad?" Wesley pleaded with the firefighter for answers.

"We pulled someone out earlier. They're being worked on in the ambulance." Wesley and I both made a quick dash over to the ambulance.

Wesley pounded on the back door of the vehicle like a deranged man.

"Open up!" he shouted. "Open up the door now!" One of the paramedics opened the door.

"Is my dad in there?" Wesley asked as he tried to look past the paramedic.

"Who are you?" he asked.

"I'm his son. Is that him with the oxygen mask on?" Wesley was about to leap inside the cab.

"Hold on. He's being worked on."

"What happened to him? What's wrong with him? Where are you taking him?"

"We're rushing him to the Metropolitan Hospital now," said the paramedic.

"I'm riding in with him." Wesley ignored the paramedic and leaped inside the cab. I wanted to go with. I wanted to be there for him, but I knew that there wasn't enough room for me. One paramedic closed the cab door and the other rushed to the front of the vehicle and took off with the siren wailing. Standing in the middle of the street, I felt helpless. Totally upset. My heart pounded so hard I thought bombs were exploding in my chest. I was about to cry but didn't want to break down in the middle of the street. I moved out of the way of the firefighters, who were still working, and joined the crowd of neighbors who'd come out to watch the drama unfold. I looked at Wesley's home, which was soaked in water and charred with blackness. I felt so bad and so useless. There was nothing more I could do so I began to head back home.

As I made my way back down the block I saw Liz Lloyd drive past me in her dad's convertible P.T. Cruiser. She then made a quick U-Turn and zoomed back toward me. *Damn*, I thought to myself. *The last person I want to see right now is Liz Lloyd*. She cruised up to me and slowed down.

"Hey, girl," she said. I stopped walking and turned to

look at her. She was in the car along with several people from her crew.

"Liz, just leave me—"

Before I could even finish my sentence, Liz yelled, "This is for ripping my shirt!" and then Liz, Brittany and Courtney slung cups filled with soda at me. One cup hit me on the face and exploded all over me. Another one hit me on the arm and a third one nailed me in the chest. I stood in shock as Liz and her crew laughed at me and then sped off. I felt completely humiliated and was so angry that I screamed out at the top of my voice. As I rushed home I could only think about all of the harmful things I wanted to do to Liz. I wanted to get a few bricks and smash out her car windows or get a can of paint and pour it all over her and her car. Once I got home, I rushed inside. I marched through the family without saying a word to Jordan or Barbara. I ran up the stairs, went into the bathroom and locked the door. I sat on the edge of the bathtub, placed my face in the palms of my hand and began sobbing. I didn't know what to do. Just when I thought things were looking brighter they got worse, all in a matter of moments. I heard a light knock at the door.

"Are you okay?" It was Jordan. He now wanted to sound concerned.

"Go away," I said. "I don't want to talk to you."

"Open the door, Keysha. Let's talk about this." He sounded regretful but I didn't care.

"Go away, I don't want to talk," I said as I continued to cry.

"I'll be here if you need anything. I'm sorry," he said,

and walked away. About ten minutes later there was another knock at the door.

"What? Why can't I just be left alone?" I asked.

"It's me, Barbara. Can I come in?" she asked. I wanted to say go away but I didn't.

"Keysha?" she called to me again. "Just open the door and let me see you."

I exhaled, stood to my feet and walked over to the door. I unlocked it and Barbara came in. Once she was in, she closed the door behind her and locked it. I sat back down on the edge of the bathtub and she lowered the lid on the toilet and sat.

"What happened?" she asked. Before I could stop myself, I began crying again. I couldn't help it. I was so emotional.

"There was a fire." My voice trembled.

"A fire!" Barbara raised her voice. "What fire? Where?" She began firing questions.

"Wesley," I said. "When I walked him home, the fire department was putting out a fire at his house. His dad was still inside."

"Oh, my God." Barbara came over and draped her arm around me. Once again there was a knock at the door.

"Can I come in for a moment?" It was Jordan again.

"Go away, Jordan," Barbara yelled at the door. She turned back to me. "Is his dad okay?"

"I don't know. It all happened so quickly. When he saw the fire trucks in front of his house, he took off running. By the time I caught up to him he was leaping into the rear of the ambulance so that he could ride to the hospital with his dad. I didn't know what to do. I felt so helpless," I said.

"Oh, my. That is horrible. Do you know what hospital they went to?" Barbara asked.

"Metropolitan," I said.

"Come on. Pull yourself together. We're going to head over to the hospital with a care package for Wesley and offer our support."

"What?" I looked at her, confused.

"It's what a good neighbor does when something like this happens," Barbara said as she stood up and opened the door.

"Are you just going to sit there and cry, or are you going to do something to help?" Barbara surprised me yet again.

"I want to help," I said.

"Well, clean yourself up, put on some dry clothes and meet me downstairs in ten minutes. Why are your clothes wet anyway?"

"That's another complicated story. We'll talk about that later," I said as I rushed into my room to find some dry clothes to put on.

nineteen

Wesley

I paced the floor of the emergency room to keep myself from completely losing it. My nerves were completely shot. I needed a drink to calm myself down and get my mind off things. My body was craving alcohol so that I could relax and mellow out. Dealing with the reality right now was too difficult. I had no one. My dad was my world. If I lost him, I didn't know what I'd do. I didn't plan on calling my mother, but when I arrived, the hospital staff insisted that I contact her, since I was a minor. I kept exhaling all of the anxious thoughts that had consumed my mind. *Please don't die,* I kept repeating to myself over and over again.

"Wesley," someone called. When I turned around, I saw Keysha rushing toward me. We embraced each other.

"Oh, I'm so happy to see you," I said. "I'm so glad that you came."

"I couldn't let you go through something like this alone," she said as I hugged her tighter.

"How did you get here?" I asked.

"My stepmom, Barbara, brought me here. She's parking the car right now."

"This is so messed up, Keysha," Wesley said.

"Hello, Wesley." Barbara came up to us. "I'm so sorry that we're meeting again under such difficult circumstances."

"Thanks for coming. It means a lot to me," I said.

"Keysha and I brought you a care package of necessary items you may need." Barbara handed me a bag filled with fresh towels, toothpaste, canned goods and other items.

"Wow, thank you so much," I said, really appreciating their kindness.

"Why don't we have a seat?" Barbara suggested.

"Wesley, how is your dad?" Keysha asked.

"I don't know. When I got in the ambulance, they were working on him. He was unconscious. I do know that he's alive but I don't know much else."

"As long as he's still with us that's a good sign," said Barbara.

I exhaled away my anxiety once again. I ran my fingers through my hair and then stood up. *Man, I need a drink,* I thought to myself. I began pacing the floor once again.

"You know, if he doesn't pull through this, and I have to go back to living with my mother, I don't know what I'll do."

"Where is your mother, Wesley? Does she know you're here?"

"Yeah, the hospital staff insisted that I contact her. She's on her way over here now."

"Do they know how the fire started?" Keysha asked.

"I heard something about faulty wiring in a ceiling fan and inadvertent electrocution, but I'm not certain what it all means." I paused. "I'd just left him in the family room before I came over to your house. He was watching *The Matrix*. He said that he was going to put up a new ceiling fan when the movie went off. I should've stayed to help him. This would not have happened had I stayed with him."

"Oh, there you are. I've been looking all over this damn place for you, boy!" My mother walked over to where we were sitting. I studied her for a moment. She had on way too much eyeliner. It appeared as if she'd been drawing on her face with a crayon. She was sporting yet another big-hair wig. And the way she was dressed wasn't much better. She had on a hot pink jacket, an old faded Air Supply concert T-shirt that should have been thrown out years ago, a hot pink mini skirt with matching pink leg warmers and white tennis shoes.

"So you finally drove your daddy so crazy that he tried to kill himself. I told him you were too much to handle. I told him you'd put him in his grave with that nasty attitude of yours." My mother smelled like a distillery and she was filled with negative energy.

"Well, is he dead yet, because I still have insurance on him?" she asked.

I couldn't take her and all of her madness. I blew up at her. "Why did you even come here? I told you that you didn't have to! You should have just stayed where you were, drinking yourself into a coma. I don't need you! My dad doesn't need you!"

"Who in the hell are you shouting at?" she roared at me. "I mean, if he's sick and all, he can't take care of you so that means you'll be living right back in the house with me. That's a good thing because I really need that child-support money."

"Mom, just—just—leave! Okay?" I expressed my anger with my hands.

"Honey, I'm here for you. Whether you like it or not, I'm your mother. And that's what moms are supposed to do." She paused. She got close to me and whispered, or at least she thought she was whispering, "You need a drink? 'Cause if you do, I got a little something down in my purse." She winked at me.

"Hi, I'm Mrs. Kendall," Keysha's stepmom introduced herself.

"Who the hell are you?" My mother gave her a nasty look.

"I'm Wesley's neighbor. He and my daughter are good friends." Barbara pointed out Keysha, who waved at my mom.

"She's kind of a homely looking girl, isn't she, Wesley?" my mother said, without regard for discretion.

"She's been drinking. You'll have to excuse her," I apologized to Barbara.

"You don't need to make any excuses for me, boy. I speak my mind and I don't care who hears it."

I placed my hands in my face and moved away from her. I found a seat on the opposite side of the room and sat down.

"Hey." Keysha came over to me and rubbed my shoulders.

"It's going to be okay," she assured me.

"She's given me a massive migraine headache," I said. "I feel as if I'm in a bad dream."

"Wesley." Barbara came over to where Keysha and I were sitting. "The doctor is looking for you. He's talking to your mom now." I took my hands out of my face and exhaled. "I'm sorry about my mom," I apologized to Barbara once again.

"It's okay," she said. "Go see about your dad."

twenty

Keysha

"HIS mother is crazy!" Barbara said as we walked to the car. I wanted to stay and be there for Wesley but Barbara insisted that I come back home with her.

I pleaded my case to her. "You know she's crazy. That's why he needs me. He can't deal with her all by himself, Barbara. She'll drive him mad. Trust me on this one. If there is one thing I have experience with, it's crazy mothers."

"Keysha." Barbara stopped walking and looked at me. "Let's get in the car first before I say what I have to say." We continued to the car. Once we were inside, she fired up the motor. "Sweetie, I know you want to be there for Wesley, but right now is not the proper time." Barbara began backing out of the parking space.

"I can't believe you're worried about what is proper and what isn't! How could you be like that? He's hurting, you saw that with your own two eyes. How could your heart not feel that?"

"Keysha, I know he's hurting but you can't go sticking your nose in their business. His relationship with his mother is something we can't get involved with. I don't want you getting mixed up in that drama."

"I'm already mixed up in it!" I snapped out. "I care about him."

"I know that you care." Barbara was silent. I could almost hear her thinking. "He knows that you care."

"Then let me go back," I said.

"Keysha, I'm going to have to say no. You may not agree with my decision, but I am truly looking out for your best interests and your heart. Stay away from Wesley for a little while. At least until things settle down. Wesley and his family have a lot of old emotional wounds that need to heal." Barbara paused again. "Wesley and his mother really need to see a therapist."

She continued to babble about how a desperate woman like his mother could do or say anything just for attention and she didn't want to draw any more attention to our family especially with a case pending against me. I folded my arms across my chest and mentally shut down. I didn't want to hear anything more that Barbara had to say.

When we arrived home, I ran into my room, slammed the door shut, crashed on my bed and cried into my pillow.

On Monday morning I rushed out of the house so that I could get to the school library. I was hoping that I'd run into Wesley. I walked all around the library searching for him but didn't see him. I sat down at one of the tables and tried to manage my feelings of frustration and anger, but it wasn't easy.

"Hello, Keysha," I looked up and saw Miss Haskey standing in front of me.

"Hey," I responded dryly.

"Sugar, can I ask you a question?"

"Miss Haskey, I don't have any late or damaged books. I—"

"No, baby. Did you burn down your boyfriend's house?" she asked.

"What?" I couldn't believe she'd asked such a question. "No! Where are you getting your information from?" I glared at her as if she'd lost her mind.

"Well, I was in the bathroom and overheard some girls talking about how you were trying to cook something for him and ended up setting his house on fire. I caught a clip of the news this morning and heard something about a house burning up, so I thought—"

"Miss Haskey." I stopped her midsentence. "That's a rumor."

"Well, you certainly have a lot of rumors about you floating around."

"Who were the girls you heard talking about this?" I demanded to know.

"No, forget it. As long as it's a rumor, I'm going to let it go."

"Wait a minute. Tell me who was saying this so that I can set the person straight!"

"No." She flat-out denied my request. "You're not going to start a fight off of something I said," she explained. "Just relax and do your studying like you nor-mally do," she said, and walked away.

There was no way I could study after hearing that, so I got up and left. As I made my way to my locker, I could hear people whispering about me, but I couldn't make out exactly what they were saying. I felt paranoid because it appeared as if everyone was staring at me. I stopped at my locker and began working the combination. The next thing I knew, a hand slammed against the locker next to me. The noise startled me. I looked up and saw Ed Daley, a former friend of Wesley's.

"So you burned down my boy's house. What kind of crazy chick are you? Why would you set his house on fire?"

"I didn't set his house on fire!"

"That's not what I heard. Everyone around the school is talking about it. They say that you set his house on fire with charcoal lighter fluid because he was about to break up with you."

"That is a damn lie!" I snapped at Ed. "Get away from me."

"Where's Wesley?"

"In his skin," I barked at Ed.

"It's because of you, isn't it? You're the reason he changed. You're the one who has been filling his head with ideas about being a good student and staying sober. Well, let me tell you something, sister savior! Wesley is an alcoholic and will always be one. You'll see. I know Wesley better than anyone. Now that you've burned him out of his house, he's going to need a drink to help him get through it. And trust me, when he starts drinking again and gets back to his old self, he's going to kick you to the curb."

"Get out of my face, Ed!" I said as I clenched my teeth.

"Hey." He put his hands up and began backing away from me. "It is what is," he said, then began singing an old song from the 1980s just to annoy me. "The roof—the roof—the roof is on fire—" Ed said as moved farther away from me.

The entire day at school was messed up. Everyone thought

I'd burned down Wesley's house, and it was driving me crazy because I couldn't figure out who'd started the rumor until I saw Liz Lloyd during lunch.

"Liz!" I hissed to myself. "She's behind all of this, I should've known." The moment I saw her, I became consumed with rage. Besides, I owed her another beat-down for splashing soda all over me. I dropped my book bag on the floor in the middle of the cafeteria and rushed over to Liz and her crew. I didn't plan on saying a word to her because I was through talking. It was my intention to walk up to her and just let my fists go. Curling my fingers, I made the tightest fist that I could. I was about to crush every bone in her face. I was a few steps away from Liz when Mr. Sanders, my guidance counselor, stopped me.

"Keysha, there you are. I've been looking for you again."

"What do you want now?" I was as angry as a fire-breathing dragon. Liz heard the sound of my voice and looked up from her plate of food. She placed a look of defiance on her face and then stuck her tongue out at me. That did it. I tried to push Mr. Sanders out of my way but he stood planted like a tree.

"Hey, slow down." He grabbed my arm just above my elbow. "What's the hurry?"

"Mr. Sanders, you have no idea of what I'm going through at this school."

"Well, that's what I'm here for. Do you want to talk about it?" he asked.

"No, I can handle it on my own," I snarled.

"Well, answer this question for me."

"What?" I focused on him briefly.

"Do you know a person by the name of Justine Wiley?"

"Justine." I paused. "That's my mother. She's in jail, though."

"Well, I think she may be out because she called here asking all types of questions. She says that she's being denied her right to see you. Is this true?" he asked. At that moment the bell rang and the students began to exit the cafeteria. Mr. Sanders kept talking but I tuned him completely out. I focused on Liz. She stood up, winked at me and then gave me the middle finger with both of her hands. Liz walked out of the door and blended in with the crowd.

"Can I go now?" I cut off Mr. Sanders midsentence. I needed to run back to pick up my book bag and then catch up with Liz so that I could beat her down.

"Sure, but if you want to talk about this, you know where to find me."

"Whatever," I said, and rushed over to my book bag, which was being kicked around. I finally picked it up and rushed out into the hallway, which was thinning out. I didn't see Liz so I started running toward my next class, but the late bell rang.

"Dang it," I hissed. I had to turn and walk in the other direction toward the office so that I could pick up a tardy slip.

When I got out of school I dodged my brother so he wouldn't force me to go sit at the football field. Instead I exited the school through another door and headed over to Wesley's house. When I got there, no one was home and several of the windows that had been busted out during the fire were now boarded up. The black charcoal scars on the house were a painful reminder of what had happened. I tried to call Wesley but his house phone was disconnected and I couldn't get through to him on his cell phone. I felt as if I was losing my mind. It was driving me crazy not knowing what was going on with Wesley.

twenty–one

Wesley

It's been two days since the fire. My dad was injured pretty badly in the blaze but he'd recover although it was going to take time. He suffered from smoke inhalation and some burns. Smoke from the fire contained poison gases that were hot enough to irritate his throat and airways, which have caused him to have breathing problems. He also sustained burns to his hands and arms, but luckily his wounds would heal with time, treatment and some surgery. The fire department said that it appeared the fire was caused from faulty wiring in a ceiling fan. I was happy to learn that my dad was going to recover from his injuries, although the road to full strength wasn't going to be a short one. When he finally became fully alert and aware, we talked about what had happened.

"The movie I was watching had gone off," he said. I was sitting next to his hospital bed. He had breathing tubes in his nose and his arms and hands were completely wrapped in white bandages so infection wouldn't settle in. "When the movie went off, I decided to wire up the ceiling fan. I didn't trip the circuit breaker like I should've and I accidentally electrocuted myself. The power of the shock not only burned me but it knocked me out and sparked a fire."

"Thankfully the house security system triggered phone calls to the police and fire departments when the smoke alarms tripped. The fire department got there fast enough to pull you out," I said.

"God, this hurts like hell," he said. I felt bad because there was nothing I could do to make him feel better.

"The house," he asked, "how badly is it damaged?"

"Some windows had to be smashed out. There are black stains around the building and the family room is pretty charred. Most of the damage is smoke-and-water-related. The house smells like a chimney." My dad began coughing uncontrollably. Once he stopped, he looked me in the eye.

"I need you to take care of business for me," he said.

"What do you need me to do?" I asked.

"You need to contact the insurance company and my job," he said. "Let them know what has happened. The insurance company will send out an adjuster and provide money for clothes and other necessities." My dad began coughing wildly once again.

"Don't talk anymore," I said. "I'll take care of everything. I've already boarded up the windows. I got the plywood from our neighbors. It's going to be okay."

"Well, look at what you've done to yourself." My mom walked into the room, hovered over my dad and began filling up the room with attitude and spitefulness.

"I hope you don't think that I'm going to take care of you now, because I'm not. And don't even think you're going to come live with me while you're recovering." She laughed at him and then opened her purse and pulled out a cigarette and a lighter. She spun the wheel of her lighter a few times until the flame jumped up. She then lit her cigarette. The smoke filled the room and my dad began coughing once again.

"What's the matter? Is my smoke bothering you?" She expelled a long trail of smoke from her lips and blew it in his face.

"Would you please put that out?" I asked her through gritted teeth.

"What for? This smoke isn't hurting him." She fanned the smoke away with her hand.

"You're not supposed to smoke in a hospital!" I raised my voice at her. "Hello! Does that make any sense to you?"

"Watch your tone of voice with me, boy. I'm your mother whether you like me or not!" She took another drag from her cigarette and blew a long cord of smoke in my face. "I'm the only thing you've got left."

"No, you mean, he's the only thing you've got left. You're as evil as ever," my dad said to her.

"What about your insurance?" she asked my dad. She didn't care about what he'd just said to her. "You do know how to milk the insurance company for all of the money you can get, don't you?"

"Leave," my father said as he began coughing again. "Get out!"

"Make me." She shifted her weight from one foot to the other and blew more smoke in his direction.

"This is ridiculous," I said, and pressed the button for the nurse. A few moments later the nurse walked into the room.

"Hey, what are you doing?" the nurse snapped at my mom.

She was a full-figured woman who looked as if she didn't play around when it came to the health of patients under her care.

"Nurse, can you make her put out her cigarette?" I pleaded.

"Are you crazy?" the nurse snapped at my mother. "You don't come into a hospital room and smoke around sick people!"

"I can do what I want to, honey." My mom continued to smoke, ignoring her.

"You've got three seconds to put that cigarette out." The nurse folded her arms across her chest and took an authoritative stance.

"And if I don't?" My mother blew smoke toward the nurse.

"Oh, it's like that?" The nurse walked over to the nightstand situated next to my father's bed and picked up the telephone. "I've got something for you. You've picked the wrong nurse to mess with." She dialed a number and requested security to come up to my father's room.

"I know my smoking really isn't bothering him," my mother said to the nurse as she took one final drag before extinguishing the cigarette. The security guards suddenly appeared in the doorway.

"She needs to be escorted out of this room," the nurse said to the two men.

"I've put the damned thing out! Why do I still have to leave?" my mom snapped.

"Guys, please escort her off the property," the nurse said.

"Sure," said one of the guards. My mother hissed and cursed as she left the room with the guards and the nurse close behind.

"I know this is a really bad time to bring this up but I can't live with her," I said. My dad began coughing again and I could see pain carved in his face. I felt bad for mentioning my problem to him.

"I'll do what I have to do to get along with her, okay?" He nodded his head. At that moment I saw him press a button so that some pain medicine could be released and pumped into his bloodstream. It wasn't long before the drugs made him drowsy.

I did everything my dad needed me to do. I contacted his job, as well as the insurance company. Cards and flowers from his friends and coworkers began arriving and a few of his coworkers came by to see him. On Wednesday, three days after the fire, an insurance adjuster came out to the house and did an estimate on the damages and began the process of getting a contractor to come and repair the house. The adjuster also placed a sizable amount of recovery money into my dad's bank account. My dad gave me his account information and password so that I could make sure that the bills got paid. As soon as my mother learned that I had access to his account, she began working on me to get a cut of the money. I wasn't about to start giving her money, though, no matter what tactic she used.

I didn't go to school for one full week. However, Friday I finally caught up with Keysha after school. She was walking down the sidewalk, headed toward the football stadium. There was a game going on between our school and our crosstown rival.

"Yo, Keysha," I shouted out as I waited for traffic to clear so that I could cross the street. "Wait up."

"Wesley, where have you been?" she shouted at me as I rushed across several lanes to get to her. Once I reached her, I tried to embrace her but she placed her hand on my chest and stopped me.

"What?" I asked. "I'm happy to see you. Aren't you happy to see me?"

"Wesley, I have been walking around in circles worried sick about you. You didn't call me to let me know what's been going on with you."

"Girl, don't even do this to me." I tossed up my hands. "I've been through too much these past few days to deal with an attitude."

"What? Like I haven't been going through stuff?"

I got the impression that she wasn't as happy to see me as I was to see her.

"You know what. I don't have time to be out here fighting. I'll holla at you later." I turned to cross to the other side.

"Wesley, wait a minute." Keysha came up to me from behind and hugged me. "I'm sorry. I just didn't know what was going on. I wanted to be there for you but I didn't know how."

"You're here for me now, right?" I asked.

"Of course I am. How is your dad doing?" she asked.

"He's going to make it," I answered. "It's going to take some time but I'm glad I didn't lose him."

"Well, I'm happy to hear that he's expected to make a full recovery," she said as she pressed her cheek into my back. "I've missed you."

"I've missed you too." I unlatched her fingers and turned to face her. I caressed the side of her cheek for a moment.

"That feels nice," she admitted. "You had me so worried."

"I didn't mean to make you worry. It just hasn't been easy dealing with my mom and all of my dad's business."

"Yeah, what was up with your mom at the hospital?"

"I told you, Keysha, my mother is real a whack job. I'm amazed that I'm as sane as I am." I looked away toward the football field because I heard the sound of a whistle and the roar of the crowd.

"Did you want to go to the game?" I asked.

"Not really. I'd rather be with you," she answered.

"Come on, walk with me," I said as I took her hand into my own. We walked back to my burned-out house. I wanted Keysha to see some of the damage so I opened the door and we went inside.

"Oh, it smells all charred out in here." She gagged a little.

"We can go back out if you want to," I quickly said.

"No, I'm okay. I just have to get used to the smell."

"Follow me into the basement and I'll show you where it started." I led Keysha through the living room and into the kitchen. I grabbed a flashlight off of the countertop and then opened the door that led down to the basement. I hit the switch for the flashlight so that we could see.

"Oh, the smell is really strong down here," she complained.

"I know. This is where it began." I flashed the light toward the ceiling so that she could see the melted ceiling fan.

"What's that humming noise I hear?" she asked. I illuminated a dark corner of the room.

"That's the sump pump that the contractors are using to pump out all of the water from the fire hoses. Come on, let's go upstairs. It doesn't smell so smoky up there." I walked Keysha upstairs to my bedroom and opened up my room window so that fresh air could circulate. Keysha sat down on the edge of my bed and I sat down next to her.

"So, what's been going on with you?" I asked.

"Well, besides being worried about you I almost got into a fight with Liz Lloyd. You won't believe this, but she went around and spread a rumor that I burned down your house."

"You're kidding me?" I was completely blown away by what she was saying.

"I wish I were. Everyone at school thinks I'm some sort of psycho. Even Miss Haskey heard about it and asked me if I did it."

"Man, someone has to give that girl a dose of her own medicine," I said.

"Oh, and then your friend Ed Daley came up to me, talking crazy. He—"

I cut Keysha off midsentence by kissing her. "I've been wanting to do that for a couple of days now," I admitted to her.

"Whew," she said. "Okay, let's just slow it down a little bit."

"I'm cool. I'm not trying to go there like that. At least not yet anyway."

"Well, good. That makes me feel better," she said. "I picked up your homework so you wouldn't fall behind. I even did a few assignments for you."

"Really, you did that for me?" I asked, feeling rather special.

"Yeah, I didn't want you to fall behind. I know how easy it is to do when you have other stuff going on."

"See, that's why I like you. You truly and honestly look out for me."

"Of course I do. You're my boo."

"And you're my boo," I said.

"I also wanted to invite you over to a Halloween party my family is throwing next weekend."

"Are you kidding me?" I asked. "After my first meeting with your crazy father, I'm not coming anywhere near him."

"You let me worry about Jordan. All you have to do is come over and hang out with me. I assure you it will be much better than hanging out with your mom or sitting around this smoked-out house."

"You have a point there," I said.

"Then come on over. We'll have fun. There will be lots of food. It will help get your mind off of things."

"Do I have to wear a costume?"

"No, you can just come."

"Are you going to wear a costume?"

"I don't know, I may put on a little makeup and turn myself into a cat but that's about it. I'm not putting any serious effort into it. It's just a party he hosts every year for close friends and stuff."

"Okay. I'll be there," I said.

"Good, now, let's get out of here. I can't take the burned-out smell anymore. We can hang out at the pizza parlor. I'll buy you a slice along with a tall cup of pink lemonade."

"That sounds like a plan to me," I said with a smile, and then kissed her once more before getting up to leave.

twenty-two

Keysha

I was standing at the stove waiting for the right time to flip over the pancakes I was cooking for everyone. On the countertop next to me was a glass bowl with several eggs that I'd cracked opened and whipped up along with a can of biscuits and a box of sausage. I suppose I was starting to feel as if I belonged to a real family even though Jordan and Mike didn't like my boyfriend and Mike seemed to enjoy getting on my nerves. However, I came to the conclusion that it was just their way of showing that they cared about me and I couldn't blame them for that. Everyone was still in bed, but I knew that it wouldn't be long before the scent of food wafting through the house would make all of them spring up. A short while later, just as I was taking the warm sausage patties out of the oven, Jordan walked into the kitchen.

"Man, that smells good, Keysha," he said as he walked over to the stove to see what I'd prepared. "What's the occasion?" he asked.

"Nothing," I said. "I just wanted to cook for everyone. Do you have an issue with that?"

"No. None at all," he answered. Jordan went into the bathroom that was situated near the kitchen to freshen up. When he came out, he sat down at the kitchen table.

"Are you ready to eat now or do you want to wait?" I asked.

"No, as good as that smells, I can't wait," Jordan said. At that moment, Barbara walked into the kitchen.

"I know you were not about to eat without the family," Barbara scolded Jordan.

"Um, yeah, I was," he answered.

"Well, now you can wait for me and Mike," she said as if he had no choice in the matter. Ten minutes later all of us were seated at the kitchen table eating the breakfast that I'd prepared. They all enjoyed what I'd cooked and that made me feel really good.

"So, how is your friend doing?" asked Barbara.

"Who?" I played dumb because I wanted her to say his name.

"Wesley."

"He's okay," I answered vaguely, because I wanted her to probe more. I wanted to get to the point where I could ask if I could invite him to the Halloween party Jordan was hosting.

"What about his dad? How is he doing?" she asked.

"What happened to his dad?" Jordan finally got curious.

"Well, after you kicked him out last week—"

"Hey, for the record I didn't kick him out. He left on his own," Jordan said in an attempt to not sound like the bad guy.

"Sure you didn't," I said condescendingly. Jordan allowed my sneering remark to slide for the moment.

"Anyway, as I'm sure you all have heard, with the exception of you, Jordan, as I was walking him back home last week we were both horrified when we saw that his house had caught on fire."

"Wait a minute, Wesley's house caught on fire?" Mike asked.

"Duh, where have you been?" I mocked him. "If I sneeze too loudly in the hallway, one of your spies tells you. I'm surprised you didn't hear about this."

"Whatever, Keysha." Mike didn't argue with me.

"Get to the point, Keysha. How is his dad doing?" Barbara had grown impatient.

"He's going to make a full recovery but it's going to take some time."

"Well, I'm sorry to hear that the young man is going through hard times. If there is anything this family can do to help, let me know," Jordan said.

"Well, there is one thing that may ease some of the stress he's dealing with," I said. "I would like to invite him to the Halloween party. I think it would be good for him. It would just help him get his mind off of his situation for a little while." I looked at Jordan and tried to read his facial expression. I knew that I'd just put him between a rock and a hard place. I could tell that he really wanted to say no but then he'd really look like a bad guy. Jordan released a large sigh.

"How is dude going to come kick it at a Halloween party and he doesn't have a place to live?" Mike asked.

"He's staying with his mother until the contractors repair his house."

"Whew, I feel sorry for him. His mother is truly one of a kind," Barbara said.

"Keysha." Jordan looked at me. "It's not that— How do I put this?" Jordan paused.

"He can come over, Keysha." Barbara once again stepped in. She then looked at Jordan. "There will be plenty of adult supervision, so I don't see what the harm is in allowing her friend to come visit her."

"But—"

"Jordan, you need to be thankful that she's even asking and sharing the important things in her life. Some kids don't talk because they're afraid to and that can lead to a whole lot of sneaking around. And I know you don't want anyone in this house sneaking around. We've already gone through that, remember?"

"But—" Jordan said again.

"But nothing. When he comes over, I want you to be nice to him," Barbara said, and then ended that conversation by starting another one. I looked at her and smiled. I was so happy that she'd helped me to persuade Jordan.

"He's a really nice guy, Jordan," I said to him.

"Yeah, when he's—"

"Mike, if you make another snide remark about Wesley, I'll make you regret it." I glared at him as if I were committing homicide with my eyes.

"Whatever, Keysha," he said, and then remained silent. He knew I was serious and didn't want to risk my swinging a broomstick at him again.

"Fine, he can come but I'll be keeping a close eye on him," Jordan said. "Now that we have that out of the way, let's talk about what needs to get done around here in order to prepare for the party."

"Whew, would you look at the time," said Mike. "Boy, I'm stuffed. I think I'm going to go lie down for a minute." He tried to excuse himself.

"Park it, player!" Jordan ordered him to remain seated. "You're not going to weasel your way out of doing some work. Okay, Barbara and I have come up with a theme for this year's party."

"Wait, we're doing a theme? I thought we were just having a regular party. I told Wesley that he didn't need a costume."

"And he doesn't," said Jordan. "I don't need him hiding behind some mask. I need to know exactly where he is at all times."

"Jeez, you act as if you're going to be on him like white on rice," I said. "What's the big deal? Would you act the same way if Mike brought a girl as a guest?"

"Yes, I would," Jordan said boldly.

"No, you wouldn't," Barbara corrected him. "Keysha, he's just being a typical man. My father was the exact same way. It didn't matter how nice a guy was. When I brought a date around my father, he instantly caught an attitude. Do you remember how my father treated you when you first met him, Jordan?" Barbara asked.

"We're not talking about me." He got a little sensitive.

"Keysha, my father met Jordan at the door and refused to allow him to come inside. He spoke to him through the screen door and the first thing he said to Jordan was 'Did you know that my daughter has decided to go into a convent? You might as well give up now and go home.'" Barbara began laughing.

"That wasn't funny." Jordan began pouting.

"Keysha, you should have seen the look on Jordan's face. He looked as if he'd been shot with a sack of spit and left hanging to dry."

"Eww." I cringed at the thought of that.

"Okay, enough. I get your point. Be as nice as I possibly can to the boy," Jordan said.

Barbara winked at me and I smiled back at her.

"Mike, I'm putting you in charge of the decorations. That means you'll be carving the pumpkin, stuffing the scarecrows and putting up the spiderwebs on the outside. Our theme this year is famous singers. I brought home some posters and other fun stuff from the radio station to help liven up the house. Now we all have to choose who we're going to be. Barbara, who will you be?" asked Jordan.

"Tina Turner," Barbara said, laughing.

"Keysha, who do you want to be?" Jordan asked.

"Um…" I had to think a minute.

"I'll be Alicia Keys," I said.

"You wish you could pull that off," Mike uttered.

"Shut up!" I snapped at him.

"Mike, who will you be?" Jordan asked.

"Ludacris," he said proudly.

"You can't fake the swagger," I snipped.

"Can so," Mike protested.

"You wish."

"Okay, that's enough, you two."

"What singer did you decide to be?" Barbara asked Jordan.

"Prince," said Jordan.

"Oh, I know you're not going there," said Mike. "Purple is not your color."

"Now, that's going to be funny," I said.

"What? You guys don't think I'm hip enough to do Prince?"

"Nothing about you says Prince," I added.

"Ya'll are just hating on me," Jordan said, trying to sound cool.

"Okay, enough already." Barbara interrupted our bickering.

"Keysha and I will handle all of the cooking and Jordan will take care of making sure the house is spotless and sending out the invitations."

"Cool, can I go now?" Mike asked.

"Yes," Jordan and Barbara said simultaneously.

The following Saturday the house was festooned with Halloween decorations. It was filled with guests and friends of Barbara and Jordan's, and there were also a few guys from the school football team who came over. As soon as they arrived they all rushed up to Mike's room to play video games. I was standing at the window waiting for Wesley to arrive. My patience was running out because he was late and hadn't called. I was starting to think that he'd blown me off. I turned my attention away from the window and looked at all of the adults standing around looking ridiculous. There was a very large and round man dressed up like Michael Jackson. His one glove and short black pants with white socks were enough to make me scream. The lady he was with was dressed like Janet Jackson but she looked more like Missy Elliot to me. As I scanned the room I noticed a woman dressed like Lil' Kim trying to dance in shoes that appeared to be killing her feet and another man was dressed like Flava Flav complete with a big white clock chained around his neck. At that moment, my father decided to get real crazy and play the song "Thriller" by Michael Jackson. That caused everyone in the room to shout and try to do the dance moves from the video. Watching them awkwardly bump into each other and step down on each other's toes was comical.

I focused my attention out the window once again and finally saw Wesley walking up my driveway.

"Finally," I said to myself. I maneuvered my way through the crowd and over to the front door. Before Wesley could ring the bell I opened the door.

"Hey, you," I greeted him.

"What's up? You look nice," he complimented me. "I didn't get a costume. I had a really bad day today. I hope that's okay."

"Yeah, of course it is. Don't even worry about it. The adults are too busy drinking to notice anyway."

"Are you going to invite me in? It's kind of chilly out here."

"Come on in, silly. You're the one standing there like a rooted tree."

"Are you sure it's okay for me to be here? I mean, I don't want any trouble with your dad."

"Yes, I'm sure. Speaking of fathers, how is your dad doing?"

"He's doing a little better. His burns are pretty bad, though," Wesley said.

"Well, I'll keep praying for him," I said. "Come on, follow me and I'll fix you a plate of food." I took him by the hand and led him to the kitchen.

"Hello, Wesley," said Barbara the moment she saw him.

"Hi, Mrs. Kendall," Wesley greeted her politely. "You look very nice. I mean, Tina Turner has nothing on you," he said.

"Do you really think so?" Barbara soaked up the compliment as she tried to strike a quick pose.

"Yeah, I'm serious, you look like all of that." Wesley smiled at her.

"Hello, Wesley." Jordan entered the kitchen.

"Hello, Mr. Kendall."

"I'm sorry to hear about what happened the other day," Jordan said.

I was glad that he was trying to be nice to Wesley.

"Come on, Jordan. Leave them in here to eat and talk," Barbara said as she took Jordan by the arm and led him back into the family room where the other adults were. I began preparing Wesley's plate. I made sure he had a sampling of everything before I sat his food before him.

"What took you so long to get here?" I asked as I opened up the door to the refrigerator to get him something to drink.

"I've had a really, really bad day," Wesley said.

"Tell me about it," I said as I placed a can of soda before him and then sat down.

"I'm very depressed, Keysha." Wesley sounded as if he'd just lost his soul.

"What's wrong?" I asked, touching his hand.

Wesley swiveled his head from right to left several times. "My mother. We had a major fight before I came over here."

"What did you guys fight about this time?" I was concerned because I saw a look in Wesley's eyes that I'd never seen before.

"She wants me to give her access to my dad's money and I refuse to."

"Why is she tripping like that? Your dad is sick and re-covering. Why does she want you to give her access to his account?"

"She claims that she needs money to pay a lawyer to help her fight a DUI case."

"She needs to get her own money for that," I said quickly.

"I know. But she doesn't see it that way. All she knows is that my dad got a large sum of money from his home own-er's insurance policy and she wants her cut."

"Did you give her any money?" I asked.

"No. And because of that, she's put me out of the house."

"What?" I couldn't believe my ears.

"You heard me, Keysha. I said that she put me out on the street. But knowing her she'll freak out, call the cops and report me as a runaway. If the cops catch me, back to juvie I go."

"Well, let's not wish for that," I said. "How can she do that? You're her son!" I'd gotten very upset and raised my voice.

"She just did. She took my duffel bag filled with clothes and tossed them out the door."

"Ooh, I could just strangle that woman!" I felt so bad for Wesley. I wanted to ask him what he was going to do, but he placed his face in his hands to hide his pain. I got up and stood behind him to rub his shoulders.

"It's going to be okay," I whispered in his ear.

"Hey. What's going on in here? Why are you touching him like that?" Jordan rushed into the kitchen as if he'd caught us doing something foul.

"I'm just rubbing his shoulders, Jordan." I snapped at him for thinking that something was going on.

"Where's the bathroom?" Wesley asked.

"Right here." I pointed to the one just off of the kitchen, but the door was closed, which meant someone was inside. "Go into the basement, there is no one down there," I said. Wesley got up and walked down the basement steps.

"No touching," Jordan said as he rejoined his guests. I rolled my eyes at him. I wanted to tell him to get over it, but I didn't because I was too worried about Wesley. I sat back down at the kitchen table and began to think of how I could explain Wesley's situation to Barbara and get permission for him to stay with us for the night.

"Your friend still hasn't come back from the bathroom yet?" Jordan said as he placed a few glasses in the sink. "He's been down there for about twenty minutes."

"It hasn't been that long," I said.

"Um, yes, it has," Jordan said, and walked toward the basement. I followed him. We walked to the bathroom but Wesley wasn't there.

"Where'd he go?" Jordan asked, puzzled.

"I don't know," I said. "Wesley?" I called out. Jordan and I began to search for him. Jordan opened up his office door and flipped on the light switch. "What are you doing in here?" Jordan yelled at him. I quickly marched up behind Jordan and when I saw Wesley I was completely shocked and hurt.

He'd sneaked into the refrigerator that was in the basement and removed a wine cooler and was standing in the dark drinking it in Jordan's office.

"Get out of my house!" Jordan snapped at him.

"Wesley?" I couldn't believe what I'd seen. He looked at me.

"I—I—" Wesley couldn't get his words to form.

"Get out of my house before I throw you out!" Jordan howled at him again.

Wesley put down the wine cooler and rushed past Jordan and me. He ran up the steps and out the door.

"He made a mistake, Jordan! You didn't have to yell at him!" I lashed out at him. I tried to hold back my tears but they started flowing in spite of my wishes. "He's going through a lot of pain right now and he just made a mistake."

"Keysha. Mike told me about his problem. He's no good for you. And I don't want you to ever see him again. End of story!"

I couldn't take the pain in my heart or the rage in Jordan's eyes. I ran out of the basement and up to my room. I slammed the door shut, locked it and collapsed to the floor and cried.

twenty-three

Wesley

I rushed away from Keysha's house as quickly as I could. I was so angry, irritated and annoyed with myself. I didn't understand why my thirst for alcohol was strong, but it was. In Jordan's office, I had stood and sucked down a wine cooler like water going down a drain. There was a longing deep inside me that I couldn't control. I thought I had my cravings completely managed but apparently I had a relapse. Feeling as if I were fighting against a monster that knew me better than I knew myself scared me.

A sense of relief washed over me when I finally made it to my charred home. I used my door key to gain access. The house still had a smoky odor to it that was pungent, but at that moment I didn't care. I was just happy to be indoors. Thrilled to have a place to stay even though it was barely inhabitable. I locked the door and made my way up to my bedroom. Opened my window so that fresh cold air could come in. I went to my closet and grabbed all of the blankets I could find and spread them across my bed. When I finally got situated on my mattress, I pulled the blankets above my head and cried, but only for a moment. I hated the fact that I was so emotional. I cried just enough to release my initial pain and then made myself stop. I swallowed down all of the pain I was feeling until I was able to contain it. Once I got my emotions in order, a sense of loneliness came over me. Then came my sense of confusion and hopelessness. In order to rid my mind of those demons, I said a little prayer and then drifted off to sleep.

I awoke to the sound of construction workers unloading equipment from their trucks. Tossing back the blankets, I exposed myself to a room that was so cold I could see the smoke of my breath escaping my lips. When I got up to close the window, I noticed crystal-white frost covering the lawn. After I closed the window, I went into the bathroom to get myself ready to head to the hospital to see my dad.

When I arrived at the hospital to see him later that day he was looking much better. He was sitting upright in his bed and being spoon-fed by one of the nurses.

"You look like you're feeling better today," I said as I entered the room and sat down on a nearby chair.

"Yeah, I'm feeling a little bit better every day," said my dad as the nurse encouraged him to finish up the Jell-O he was eating. Once the nurse was done feeding him, she left the room to go check on her other patients.

"What's wrong? What happened?" my father asked.

"Nothing," I answered with a phony smile.

"Wesley—" he gave me a serious look "—what's going on?" he asked again. I was trying to figure out how to tell about my relapse but I couldn't bare to tell him.

"I know you better than you know yourself, Wesley. Now tell me what happened."

I was finding it very difficult to share my demons with him because I feared that I'd disappoint him and that's the last thing I wanted to do.

"Did something happen at the house?" he asked.

"No," I answered.

"Did something happen at school?" he asked. I could tell that he was going to go through the process of elimination in order to get to the truth.

"Did something—"

"I had a relapse," I finally blurted out. My dad was silent for long moment. He just looked at me with a blank stare. I couldn't tell what he was thinking but I knew whatever it was, it wasn't good.

"How did it happen?" he finally asked.

"I don't know." I paused in thought. "Mom kicked me out of the house because I refused to give her money out of your account. When she kicked me out, I guess that hurt me and depressed me to the point of a relapse." I was silent for a long moment. I expected my dad to say something but he didn't. He just listened to me. "I have trouble dealing with stress," I admitted. "When I'm feeling overwhelmed the urge to drink consumes me and this time I lost control over the urge. I would like to start going back to the therapy sessions so that I can become stronger."

"You're a good son, Wesley," my dad assured me. "You're responsible, you're caring and you're honest. The fact that your mom has tried to manipulate you is not only upsetting but it's sad. I'm sorry that you have to go through that."

"I thought you'd be mad at me," I said.

"I'm not mad at you, Wesley. I am concerned about your

well-being, though. I think that continuing on with therapy is an excellent idea." At that moment the nurse came back into the room with a small container of pills and a cup of water.

"Okay, it's time to take your medicine," she said. My dad grumbled. I knew that he didn't like taking the medication. After the nurse left my dad focused his attention back on me.

"The medicine makes me very drowsy," he said. "The doctor will come through later on to unwrap my hands and forearms. It will be the first time I've seen my hands since the accident. I hope they still look normal." He looked at his bandaged hands for a moment.

"It doesn't matter what they look like," I said to him. "What matters most to me is that you're okay."

"I'm going to have to go through physical therapy to get the strength back in them."

"And I'll be there to help," I reminded him.

"I know you will." My dad paused in thought. "So, where are you sleeping?" he asked.

"At the house. It's not so bad. A little smoky but I can deal with it," I said.

"Pick up the phone and dial your mother and then hold the phone up to my ear," he said. "I'll straighten this thing out about her putting you out of the house. I swear, some of the things she does are absolutely crazy."

"If it's all the same to you, Dad, I'd really rather just stay at the house. For real, it's not that bad. Besides, that way I can keep an eye on the progress of the reconstruction."

"I'm not sure about that, Wesley."

"Dad, trust me. I'm not going to do anything crazy. I can handle being there unsupervised. Please, just let me stay."

He locked his gaze upon me for a while before speaking. "Okay. But let's get some rules put in place."

"Let me guess. No houseguests."

"Yes," he said. "And be responsible, Wesley."

"Dad, I'm not going to let you down," I said.

"Okay." We talked for a little while longer before he drifted off to sleep.

I left the room and headed downstairs to the gift shop where I purchased a copy of the local community newspaper. Then I came back to my father's room, sat down and began reading. Flipping through the pages, I came across an article about two sisters who were sent to youth court for videotaping a fight they'd gotten into with another girl and then posting the video on a computer. I began reading the article.

Two Sisters Accused for Assaulting a Student

Three teenagers from Harvey, IL, were arrested and sent to the judge after a video showing them assaulting a fourth teen was posted on the Internet. The three attackers are sisters who assaulted a fourth girl who was walking home from school. According to authorities, the three sisters followed their victim for several blocks before attacking her in a small city park. Police reports indicate that the reason for the attack centers on the victim spreading false rumors around their high school campus about one of the sisters being HIV-positive.

The video clip showing the attack had been downloaded to a particular computer at their high school and then subsequently posted on the Internet. When school officials became aware of the video they contacted the police, who, with the help of other students, quickly identified the attackers. The mother of the three attackers explained that she doesn't understand why her children resorted to violence to resolve their conflict. In the juvenile hearing, the assistant state's attorney asked Judge Nancy Hill to send a clear message that violence in our communities will not be tolerated.

"Assault is a serious offense for adults, let alone teenagers, and the fact that they videotaped it is even more disturbing," said Judge Hill, who sentenced the girls to sixty days at a local juvenile detention center.

I stopped reading the newspaper because Keysha and her situation were consuming my thoughts. The article had sparked a brilliant idea. I quickly began forming a plan in my mind. The more I thought about it, the more I realized that, if properly executed, it would work. I put the newspaper down and began pacing the floor. I continued formulating my ingenious plan. When it all finally came together I clapped my hands. I'd just figured out a way to turn the tables on Liz Lloyd and get Keysha out of trouble at the same time. Now all I had to do was hope that she'd forgive me and give me a chance to make everything up to her.

twenty-four

Keysha

I felt sick to my stomach on Sunday morning. My stomach was doing continuous summersaults and refused to stop. I was stressed out beyond my wildest imagination. I was upset by what Wesley had done. I didn't understand why he'd do such a stupid thing at my house. Yes, I knew that he was upset about his mother, but still, drinking wasn't the answer to his problem. I refused to get out of bed because I was so ashamed and embarrassed by what had happened. The only thing I truly wanted to do was disappear into thin air so that I wouldn't have to face criticism from Jordan. Around 8:00 a.m. Mike knocked on my door.

"Keysha, breakfast is ready," he said.

"I'm not hungry, Mike," I answered.

"Are you okay in there?" he asked.

"Leave me alone, please. I don't want to be bothered."

"Okay," he said, and actually left me alone. That was a shocker. Around 10:00 a.m. Jordan knocked on my door. By that time I had decided to sit at my desk and work on some extra-credit work for school.

"I'm coming in, Keysha," he announced. I was about to

tell him to leave me alone because I didn't feel like dealing with his brazenness.

"I know that it hurts," he said to me as he sat on the edge of my bed. I had my back turned to him and my face buried in the page before me. "Sometimes people are not what they appear to be. What you see is not always what you get." Jordan's voice was surprisingly calm and soothing. He sounded as if he was just as remorseful about what had happened as I was.

"I don't want to talk about it," I said, wanting him to leave my room so that I could wallow in my misery.

"Keysha, I will admit that I don't care much for Wesley. But it's because I felt threatened by him."

That comment caught my attention. I turned around in my seat and looked at him.

"You felt threatened by him?" I was perplexed.

"Yeah, I felt threatened by him."

"But why?" I asked.

"Because, as silly as it sounds I didn't want you to like him more than you liked me. You just arrived here, Keysha, and we're really starting to relate to each other and I didn't want anything or anyone to come between that. Wesley, in my mind, was a person who was going to take you away from me before we had a chance to really bond and I had an issue coping with that."

"Wesley wasn't going to pull me away from you," I assured him. "He's my friend. I like him. We come from similar backgrounds. He has a mother from hell and so have I. He has a father who rescued him from a hopeless situation.

Just like me. We just relate to each other well, that's all. It has nothing to do with him pulling me away from you."

Jordan took a deep breath and then exhaled. "It's nice to hear you say that, Keysha."

At that moment, I felt the strangest urge. I felt the urge to hug him but I felt kind of strange about making the first move. I captured his gaze and held it for a moment. Then I thought, *What the heck?* I stood up, walked over to him and gave him a gigantic hug. I held on to him tightly. He did the same and we rocked back and forth for a moment before I finally released him.

"You know I still don't like him, don't you?" said Jordan.

"But why?" I asked. "Trust me, what happened yesterday was a bad mistake that he made."

"I'm your father. It's my job to dislike all of your boyfriends. Just like it's Barbara's job to dislike any girl who is brave enough to admit that she likes Mike," Jordan said jokingly. I laughed with him for a moment.

"Keysha." Jordan paused. "Our court date has been set. We'll be appearing before the judge in three weeks."

"Oh," I said. My good feelings suddenly plummeted into the dump.

"It's okay, relax," he tried to assure me. "Asia will be coming by sometime this week to discuss the case and update the family."

"I didn't do anything." I was frustrated again. "Liz Lloyd, this girl at school, set me up. I know she did," I said.

"I know. Asia has already forwarded a summons for her to appear in court."

"That girl has caused me so much drama." I exhaled a

frustrating sigh. Jordan was silent for a moment. "I'm sorry," I said.

"No need to apologize. I just wanted to let you know that we're getting down to the wire, okay?"

"Okay," I answered.

"Your food is still on the stove if you want to eat," Jordan said as he stood.

"I'll be down in a little while. I just want to finish my extra-credit worksheet." Jordan exited my bedroom without saying anything more.

On Monday morning during my walk to school with Mike, Wesley ran up on us.

"Yo, Keysha and Mike, wait up," he said, slowing down as he approached. I almost started to tell Mike we should run away from him but I didn't. However, I did keep moving.

"Yo, I said wait up," Wesley hollered out again. Mike and I didn't stop. We just kept moving. By the time Wesley caught up to us he was clearly out of breath.

"Dang, why are ya'll tripping like that?" he asked.

"Get away from us!" Mike snapped out at Wesley.

"What?" Wesley wasn't the least bit intimidated by my brother.

"She doesn't need you," Mike barked at him. Mike had become extremely protective of me and was willing to do whatever it took to make sure that I was safe.

"Mike, hang on a second." I called off his attack. "Wesley, what you did is inexcusable. How could you do that to me? Do you have any idea of what I had to go through just to get permission for you to come over?"

"Look, I know I messed up. I had a relapse but I'm going

to go back to therapy for help. I spent all day with my dad yesterday. I told him about my setback and how I wanted to go back to therapy for it."

"Dude, then come back once you've got your act together. Right now, Keysha just doesn't have time to babysit you, dog."

"I don't need a babysitter," Wesley fired back. "I'm not perfect, okay? I'm human so cut me some slack."

"Why should we?" I asked, even though I was happier than a bird soaring through the sky to see that he was okay. I just didn't want him to think that what he did was cool.

"Because I've figured out a way to get the charges against you dropped." Wesley looked at both of us and awaited our reaction to his statement.

"Come on, Keysha, this fool has been drinking again." Mike pulled my arm and I continued to walk with him.

"Wait a minute!" Wesley placed himself directly in our path. "Come on, guys. I'm trying to help. And for the record I didn't drink this morning."

"Wesley, what can you do that our lawyer can't do?" asked Mike.

"Get a confession out of Liz," Wesley stated boldly.

"And how are you going to do that? I can't even get her to spill her guts," I said.

"Liz trusts me. Or at least the old me. She knows that I'm not a snitch. I can get her to talk about how she set you up."

"Even if you could get a confession out of her, if you're called as a witness, your character is going to be called into question because of your record. This isn't a joke, Wesley, it's real," said Mike.

"Don't you think that I know that, Sherlock?" Wesley snarled back. "Just hear me out for a moment."

"Wesley, I'm really glad that you're—"

"Keysha, please. Just hear me out. I'm trying to make things right." Wesley looked at me with sadness. His sincere expression went directly to my heart.

"Okay, we'll hear you out," I said.

"Good. Because we'll need Mike's help and connections, as well."

"Oh, no, you're not including me in your scheme." Mike tried to remove himself from the plan.

"Look, do you want to help her or not?" Wesley asked.

Mike was silent for a moment before he answered yes.

"Okay. The Tricked Out Nightclub has a surveillance camera at the door. We need to get a copy of the tape from the night Keysha and Liz were there. Mike, can you talk to your DJ buddy at the club to get access to it?"

"Maybe, but how is that going to help?"

"It's going to prove that Liz was there on the same night. Mike, I also need you to get some recording equipment from your DJ friend."

"Dude, you're asking for a lot," Mike said.

"No, I'm not. You're one of the most popular kids on campus. You know how to get people to work for you. Get me a small tape recorder and a microphone. I'm going to wire myself up so that when Liz gets to talking, I'll be recording her."

"Yeah," Mike suddenly chimed in. "If you can get her to admit that she drugged Keysha at the nightclub, as well as supply the videotape placing her at the nightclub on the same night that the bad batch of Ecstasy came out, it would be easier for the police to at least consider Liz as a possible suspect."

"But isn't this something Asia should be doing? I mean, why can't we just go to the police and tell them this?"

"Because they want to nail someone and they're looking for a scapegoat. These guys found a smoking gun on you, Keysha. They're not going to waste man-hours searching for additional evidence. To them this is a slam-dunk case," said Wesley.

"That's true," said Mike.

"So, what do you guys think?" asked Wesley.

"Do you really think you can pull this off?" I asked.

"Yes!" Wesley said with absolute certainty. "We don't have anything to lose, but everything to gain."

"He's got a point there," Mike said. "I can get you the recording stuff by tomorrow."

"What about the access to the videotape?" Wesley asked.

"That's going to take a little longer, but I think I can get it."

"Good. I'm going to go catch up with Ed Daley so that I can find out what Liz is doing these days. I'm not going to hang around with you guys while at school because I don't want them to get suspicious."

"Meet me at the community center tonight around 5:00 p.m.," said Mike. "I'll have the recording equipment by then."

"Cool, I'll holla back," Wesley said, and was about to depart from us.

"Hey, wait a minute," I said to him. "What am I supposed to do?"

"Just let me be your hero." He kissed me on the cheek before continuing on.

twenty-five

Wesley

"It's about time you came around to your dang senses." I was dribbling a basketball while standing beneath one of the hoops in the gymnasium. I'd just asked Ed Daley to let me know the time and location of Liz's next party. "I thought they'd completely fried your brain. You were really creeping me out talking about how you'd changed. At one point you got on my nerves so bad that I was planning on kicking your—"

"Whatever, man," I interrupted Ed midsentence. "You can just call it temporary insanity or something. I really want and need to party. I'm all stressed out."

"I'll bet you are. I heard about that girl Keysha setting your house on fire. What kind of crazy chicks are you hooked up with?" Ed asked. I wanted to correct him, but I decided not to, especially if he honestly thought Keysha set my house on fire. I could use his ignorance to my advantage.

"Yeah, man. That's why I need to get high. I need to just forget about that crazy girl and what she's done. My dad is talking about pressing charges against her," I lied.

"Really?"

"Yeah."

Ed leaned in closer to me and began to whisper so no one would hear him. "Well, you should because according to Liz, Keysha's attorney has summoned her to court. Keysha is trying to say that Liz planted the drugs on her. Can you believe that?"

"No, that's hard to believe," I lied.

"Well, believe it. Liz is highly ticked off about it. She says that she plans on destroying and humiliating her in front of everyone." I was silent for a moment as I processed what Ed had just said. I was also thinking of ways to use it to my advantage.

"How does she plan on humiliating her?" I asked.

"I don't know. You know Liz is creative. She'll come up with something that's brilliant."

"Has Liz been asking about me since I was gone?" I asked.

"Now, you know that she has. She's all irritated that you won't party with us and she's been calling you a Goody Two-shoes and a punk ever since you started hanging with that Keysha chick."

"A punk." I didn't like being considered a punk.

"That's what she's been calling you," Ed reiterated.

"Well, when I see Liz, I'm going to let her know that the old Wesley is back. And if she calls me a punk while I'm standing in front of her, I'll make her regret it." I was bluffing but Ed understood where I was coming from. "So, when are we going to celebrate my return, Ed? I want to do something wild like get completely smashed and then go out in my dad's car and smoke the tires by doing doughnut circles in the school parking lot. We need to get back to doing all of the fun stuff we used to do," I said, filling my voice with enthusiasm and using my hands to express how much I wanted to do something reckless.

"That's what I'm talking about." Ed knuckled up his fist and lightly punched my shoulder. "The old Wesley is back."

"Yeah!" I said, shouting out. "I just want to party and release all of my pent-up stress and anxiety. I know Liz has to have something coming up."

"Yeah, she does." Ed smiled. "And I know for a fact she'd love to see you come and hang out."

"Well, stop being so secretive, man. Give me the details. When is the party and where is it at?"

"Calm down. You sound like some eighth grader who has never been to a party before," Ed teased me.

"Shut up!" I flinched as if I were about to punch him out for calling me an eighth grader.

"Okay, here is the real deal. You remember Neophus, don't you?" Ed asked.

"Yeah, that's Liz's contact, right?" I wanted to make sure that Neophus was the person Liz got all of her drugs and alcohol from.

"Yeah. He's throwing a birthday celebration for himself at his house in two days. He's asked Liz to make sure that there were plenty of clients who wanted to have a good time, if you know what I mean."

"Yeah, we're going to be partying like a rock star, dog!" I behaved as if I were superexcited. "Come on, Ed, get me hooked up, man." I slapped Ed's chest with the back of my hand.

"Nope. You've got to hook your own self up on this

party," Ed informed me. "I know Liz wants to party with you again because she's said it. So what I suggest you do is find her and ask her for all of the details. I'm pretty sure she'll be glad to hook you up, but since this is something big for Neophus, you need to go directly to her. She may want to do a different party with you."

"Okay, that makes sense," I said. "I know I'll see her at some point later on today. I'll pull her to the side and talk to her at that time."

"Oh, one more thing. Don't let her know that I told you about the party. She's only telling certain people about it."

"Cool," I answered just as the bell rang.

I had a permission slip to travel through the hallway from my English class to the resource center where I was planning to take a make-up test. As I exited the hallway, which was lined with blue lockers, I ran into Liz as she was coming out of the bathroom.

"What's up, Liz?" I said as I walked up to her.

"What's going on, Wesley?" She looked at me suspiciously. "I didn't think I'd ever see the day you'd start talking to me again."

"What are you talking about?" I played dumb. "You're my girl. How is your mom doing?"

"She hasn't changed. She's never around— You haven't been acting like your old self lately. I heard you were spending time at the library trying to get all bookwormed out."

"I was suffering from temporary insanity." I downplayed my frequent visits to the library.

"So, what's up with that twisted and demented girl Keysha I've seen you around with?" Liz asked.

"Nothing," I answered.

"Yeah, right." Liz didn't believe me.

"Hey, there isn't anything between us. She's just some girl I was tying to kick it with, but she isn't giving it up like I thought she would." A sinister grin formed on Liz's face.

"So you couldn't get it either?" She laughed and I felt a chill wash over me.

"Nope. She has her stuff on lockdown. Maximum security—you know what I'm saying?" She laughed again.

"So, why are you suddenly talking to me again, Wesley?" Liz captured my gaze and I knew what she was waiting to hear.

"Come on, you know why." I continued to play dumb.

"No, I don't, boo." Liz wanted a direct answer from me.

"You know being locked up in juvie kind of messed up my head a little bit. They had me sitting with counselors trying to get me to talk about my feelings and why I was locked up. It was so damn lame but I had to play the role in order to get out. Because if I didn't the judge would've kept me detained and I just wasn't feeling that."

"What was it like for you in there?" she asked.

"Jacked up," I answered honestly. "The officers were constantly trying to get inside my head."

"So they got to you?" Liz asked.

"They tried but I outfoxed them."

"Oh, okay," Liz said, seeming to understand.

"Say, now that I'm back to my old self—" I leaned toward

Liz so that my voice wouldn't carry "—do you have something on you right now?" I asked. Liz snickered at me.

"No, fool." Liz quickly searched our surroundings looking for any hall monitor that might be approaching.

"Liz. It's me. Your boy, Wesley. I need something bad. I'm back to my old self and I need to get my head back to where it was. Those people in juvie had my thinking all twisted up in knots. Now everything is cool and I'm telling you that I need something to get me through the rest of the afternoon."

"I told you. I don't have anything on me."

"No wine cooler, no small bottle of gin? No Ecstasy?"

"Dude, I'm telling you. I don't have anything like that."

"Okay," I said, not pressing the issue. I gave her a look of disappointment

"I tell you what. There is an intimate gathering in about two days. I'm only allowing certain people that I know and trust to come to it."

"How many people will there be?" I asked.

"Trust me, there will be enough people."

"So, are you going to let me in on this great secret or what?" I asked. Liz smiled at me.

"You are so cute." She caressed my face with the palm of her hand. "When are you going to stop fronting and start expressing your true feelings for me?"

"Liz, you know that I've always liked you," I lied again in order to gain her trust. That was the trust connection between Liz and me. At one point we were both attracted to each other and shared some special moments.

"Do you remember the time that you and I drove into the city and took a stroll along the lakefront?"

"Yeah, I remember. It was you, the entire crew and I. We had a good time."

"I'm not talking about the crew, Wesley. I'm talking about how you and I shared a little time together. I liked the way you kissed me." She placed her index finger on my lips. "Do you remember that kiss, Wesley?"

I wanted to forget that we ever shared an intimate moment but I couldn't.

"Yeah, I remember that," I said.

"Our kiss was electric. No one has ever kissed me the way that you did."

I licked my lips. I got a charge out of hearing that. Liz was stroking my ego and I couldn't help but get excited about my kissing prowess. My body was suddenly deceiving me by sending out signals of readiness.

"So you were feeling that kiss?" My ego was now talking and it was clouding my judgment.

"Yes, do you think I can get another one?"

I licked my lips again. "Yeah, we can make that happen."

"I want you to kiss me now." She stepped closer to me and wrapped her arms around my neck. She craned her neck toward me and I felt myself going with the moment.

"I've missed you, Wesley," she whispered.

In my mind I didn't want to kiss Liz, but my body was aching for attention and it didn't care where it came from. I justified the desires of my body by telling myself that I needed to play along with her in order to get her to trust me enough to tell me about how she'd set up Keysha.

"Kiss me like you mean it," Liz said as more of a demand than a request as she pressed her body against me. Just as our lips were about to meet, we were interrupted by Mr. Sanders, one of the guidance counselors.

"Don't you two have some place you should be?" he asked.

"Yes," I quickly answered him.

"Damn, he is everywhere. You owe me," Liz whispered as we gathered our composure.

"We can discuss it over a pint some time," I whispered back.

"Check your e-mail later tonight. I'll send you an address, a date and time to a party in two days. Make sure you're there," she said, and then continued on her way.

twenty-six

Keysha

I was standing outside the community center with Mike, waiting for Wesley to show up. Mike had gotten the necessary recording equipment from his weirdo DJ friend who liked to order spy and surveillance equipment online.

"Why in the world does your friend order equipment like this?" I asked.

"Who, Derek? He's always been inquisitive like that. He gets it honestly. His dad is a detective and Derek wants to be just like him."

"Oh," I said, looking at Mike strongly.

"What?" he asked.

"What do you guys do with the spy and surveillance equipment?" I asked, not really wanting to know.

"All kinds of stuff," he said, laughing.

"Okay, just answer me this. You guys aren't the type who'll drill a hole in the girls' locker room wall in order to peep inside, are you?" I was concerned because I knew Mike didn't have a girlfriend and I feared that testosterone might have flooded his brain out and caused it to short-circuit.

"No, I haven't thought of that one, but it sounds like something I need to try. Thanks, sis."

I rolled my eyes at him. At that moment I spotted Wesley walking toward us.

"There's my hero," I said to Mike

"He isn't all that."

I could tell Mike was a little jealous.

"Hey, guys," Wesley said. "Let's go inside the lobby so no one sees us standing together."

The three of us went inside the lobby. Before I allowed Wesley to speak I gave him a big hug.

"I've missed you," I said to him.

"I've missed you too," he answered.

"Are you two going to stand here and make out or are we going to get down to business?" Mike didn't understand the necessity of our open display of affection. I ignored Mike and kissed my man.

"Ooh, I love the way you kiss," I whispered. "You'd better not be kissing anyone else the way you kiss me," I said to him as I studied his eyes. I could tell that he seemed to be worried about something.

"Is everything okay?" I asked, suspicious of the odd expression on his face.

"Yeah," Wesley answered, but I felt as if he was hiding something from me.

"Hello, can you let him go, Keysha, so I can show him how to use the wire tap?"

"Dang, boy. Relax," I admonished Mike, who had become very annoying.

"Let me see how this thing works," Wesley said as I unlatched myself from him. Mike explained how the small microphone and mini tape recorder worked.

"What about the surveillance video from the nightclub?" Wesley asked.

"My friend and I are still working on that. He's going to dub the tape so it's going to take a little time."

"Cool," Wesley said.

"How do you get people to do stuff for you, Mike?" I asked because I was curious as hell.

"What, you haven't figured that part out yet?" Wesley chuckled.

"What?" I asked, confused.

"Your father works at a radio station and has access to all types of promotional materials, concert tickets and other stuff," said Wesley. "Your brother trades goods for services."

"How do you get stuff from Jordan, Mike?" I asked.

"If I told you that, you might decide to cut in on my business." Mike was dead serious about protecting his interests. Since he was so sensitive about it, I dropped that conversation.

"Okay, here's the deal." Wesley began to talk more about his plan. "Today, I got Liz to trust me enough to invite me to a secret party. Only certain people are invited."

"So, what did you have to do to get invited?" I asked.

"I had to convince her that I was my old self again and charm her a little," Wesley said. I wanted to ask him exactly what he meant but I didn't.

"Okay, in order for me to really get Liz to open up I have to arrive at the party smelling like alcohol."

"Why?" I asked.

"Because the old Wesley always arrived at a party half smashed."

"But you can't go and start drinking again. I won't let you!"

"I know that I can't start drinking again and I don't want to. I just need for them to believe that I'd been drinking. I can act drunk, that's not a problem. The trick is going to be getting them to think that I'm half-baked. Any suggestions?" Wesley asked.

"I have no idea of how you can pull that one off without actually drinking," Mike said.

"Keysha, do you have any ideas?"

"You just need to smell like you've been drinking, right?"

"Yeah," Wesley answered.

"Spray the alcohol on your clothes, like you would perfume. That should work. Just pour some alcohol in a spray bottle."

"That's a good idea," said Mike. "I don't see why it wouldn't work."

"I knew my boo would come up with something brilliant," said Wesley, who made me feel good about my suggestion.

"Have you figured out how you're going to bring up a conversation about me?" I asked.

"I'm going to charm her," Wesley answered.

There he goes with the word "charm" again, I thought to myself.

"What exactly do you mean by charm?" I asked. The only thing running through my mind was the conversation I'd had with Grandmother Katie about boys using their charm and wit to get a girl to lower her guard so that they could trick them into agreeing to sex.

"Just making her feel comfortable around me."

I read Wesley's facial expressions and knew that the subject of his charm and Liz made him uncomfortable.

"You've done Liz before, haven't you?" I asked flat out.

"No, Keysha, I haven't," he answered. "We—"

"Do we really need to deal with this soap opera right now?" Mike asked. "Next thing you know I'll hear a thunderous voice saying 'tune in next week to find out if Wesley will tell Keysha about his sex-change operation.' Give me a break! Come on, Keysha, work with us here," Mike said sarcastically. "Girls charm guys all the time to get what they want. Wesley is just going to turn the tables on her. Do you get it?"

"No." I got upset. "I don't want him flirting with Liz. That's disgusting to me."

"Look, I'm not going to cross any lines, okay?" Wesley tried to reassure me. "I'm just going to be the old Wesley for a moment. Liz loved talking to the old Wesley. By the time I'm done, I'll have everything recorded."

"What if she doesn't believe you? What if she wants you to prove that you're really back? What if she wants you to drink in front of her to prove it? What if she wants to drug you up and have sex with you?" I asked.

"Keysha does have a point, Wesley." Mike tossed a little support my way.

Wesley exhaled. I knew that he was trying to think.

"I don't want to have sex with Liz. I'm not going to do that," he said.

"Keysha made a few valid points. What if she wants you

to drink in front of her? You could get busted if you screw this up," Mike said.

"I'm thinking," Wesley said, and was silent for a moment.

"Bring your own alcohol bottle." I finally provided him with an answer to the dilemma. "Just pour out the real stuff and replace it with sweet tea or some other dark color drink."

"Good thinking, boo," said Wesley, who then kissed me on the forehead.

"You just make sure that you don't do anything that's going to upset me," I said.

"I won't, I promise. I'm going to hang around Liz and the rest of the crew over the next two days. I'll call you once I have the information we need."

"You'd better not mess this up, Wesley. I've got a lot riding on this," I said.

"I won't. I promise," he said.

"Oh, one more thing," said Mike. "As far as the equipment goes, if you break it, you just bought it. Are we clear?"

"We're clear," Wesley said as we all walked out of the community center and headed in separate directions.

twenty-seven

Wesley

Ed Daley and I had just parked his car in front of a very large white house. The curtains were drawn shut and there was no loud music emanating from the dwelling.

"Are you sure this is it?" I spoke slowly as if every word I said held importance.

"Of course this is it," Ed said. "Whew, man, you smell like a straight-up wine head. How much did you drink? I'm getting buzzed just smelling you."

"I'm just making up for lost time, dog," I said, half laughing.

"Do you need help walking up to the door?" he asked.

"I'll be happy to remind you that I have two feet, which have specialized party radar built right into my toenails. They can sniff out any party on the planet and keep me balanced all at the same time."

Ed cracked up with laughter.

"You're so stupid," he said as we continued laughing and snorting in unison.

We got out of the car and made our way up to the front door. Ed rang the doorbell and a very tall and sinister-looking man opened it. His eyes were blazing red and his eyebrows were pinched into an expression of anger and irritation.

"What do you two fools want?" he asked.

"Neophus, it's me, man. Ed Daley." Ed attempted to break the ice.

"And?" Neophus asked.

"Liz invited me and my boy, Wesley. She said that this was an exclusive party."

I leaned my shoulder against the side of the house pretending I could barely stand. I stuffed my hands in my pockets and pretended to cough violently. While my hands were in my pockets, I clicked the button on the recorder.

"This boy looks like he can barely stand up. And he smells like he's been hitting the bottle already."

"This is Wesley. I know you remember Wesley, man. He's the guy who I said could drink tequila and chew jalapeno peppers at the same time."

"Yeah, I remember him. The crazy one," said Neophus. "Come in here and go sit down. Don't walk around in this house. You might see too much and that wouldn't be good for your life expectancy."

"Cool, man. We got you. We just came to party, right, Wesley?" Ed slapped his hand on my back.

"Yeah, I came to get my head right," I said, talking slowly.

"Liz is sitting over on the sofa with the rest of the crew," Neophus said as he stepped aside and allowed us to enter. The house was rather dark and had a chemical odor that was wafting through the air. Ed and I made our way over to the crew, who were sitting near the glowing red flame of the fireplace. There were two very large black leather sofas situated on both sides of a glass cocktail table that was filled with pills, alcohol, marijuana and condoms. I sat down on the end of the sofa, close to the fireplace. I thought Ed was going to sit next to me but he didn't, instead he kneeled down in front of the glass table and began searching for the perfect pill to take. Neophus walked over and stood in front of the fireplace. He looked like pure evil. Everything about his presence and body language said *hell-raiser*.

"I want everyone in here to sample something from this table. If I don't see everyone try something, I'm going to crack open your skull," said Neophus.

At that point I became very nervous and paranoid. If I didn't participate, I'd have hell to pay. My heart began racing as I started searching the room for the exit. I wanted to get out of there because I'd bitten off more than I could chew. There were about twenty kids in the room and the girls outnumbered the guys. Most everyone was on their hands and knees taking up the offerings that were before them.

"What's wrong with you, fool?" Neophus snarled at me.

"I'm cool," I answered him, hoping that he'd let me off the hook.

"No you're not! Now either you sample something or I'm going to beat the daylights out of you and your friend. So make a choice, right now? Try something or get your ass kicked!"

"Wesley, dude, try one of these pills." Ed offered me something but I didn't know what it was. "Come on man, this is what we came here for, bro." I reluctantly moved toward Ed. Neophus stalked my every move as if he was hunting for my soul.

"It's good for you, bro," Ed said. "You'll feel as if you're floating like a cloud in the sky, baby. The feeling is spectacular! Trust me."

I took the round red pill from Ed's hand. I put it in my mouth, picked up a glass filled with water that was sitting on the table and took a gulp. I opened my mouth to show Neophus that it was empty. He seemed satisfied. However, I didn't really swallow the red pill. I'd maneuvered it around so that it was positioned between my cheek and jaw. Neophus turned his back and I was about to spit the pill out but Liz came over and pulled me down to the sofa. I certainly couldn't get rid of it while she was sitting so close, especially if I wanted her to trust me enough to open up about what she'd done to Keysha.

"Hey, babe." She smiled at me. I trapped her gaze and studied her features. Her hair was raven black and resting on her shoulders. She had on black eyeliner, a black turtleneck and a black skirt. Her skin appeared to be a little more pasty than usual but her goth style of dress suited her well. Liz ran her fingertips through my hair.

"Hey," I answered her back trying to contain the large amount of saliva that was rapidly building up in my mouth. I swallowed hard and I could tell that the pill had begun to dissolve.

"I'm glad to see you," she said. "And it smells as if you're in a partying mood." She inhaled the air around us. "You've been drinking scotch," she said.

"Yeah," I answered, still playing the role of an alcoholic.

"The scent of alcohol excites me. Did you know that?" she asked.

"No," I answered her, feeling extremely uneasy. I swallowed again and could taste some more of the dissolving pill.

"I want to pick up where we left off in the hallway." She leaned close to me and spoke purposely in my ear. She clenched my earlobe with her teeth and lightly tugged on it. A bolt of electric energy shot through my body and formed goose bumps on my skin. I started to feel strange and couldn't tell if it was the pill or because I was aroused. Either way, I knew I had to get rid of the pill.

"Did you like that?" Liz asked. I knew that she was tempting and manipulating me all at the same time.

"Do you want something more to drink?" she asked.

"No," I said, "I'm good."

"Come on, Wesley, I know you can handle more." She traced the edge of my ear with her tongue. I shivered with anticipation. "Have a drink with me and I'll do something that will blow your mind."

Another sensual bolt of electricity plucked every nerve in my body.

"Is he the one, Liz?"

I glanced over my shoulder and Neophus was standing nearby.

"Yes, this is Wesley," she answered.

"Bring him back to my office," Neophus ordered her.

"What's going on?" I asked.

"Neophus and I want to chat with you for a moment about something."

"What? Did I do something?" I was nervous and afraid. And I immediately felt that getting back with Liz and the crew just to save Keysha wasn't such a grand idea after all.

"Come on." Liz pulled me to my feet.

"Hey, Ed, I'll be right back," I said, hoping that he'd come with me. Ed couldn't have cared less. His mind was already flickering between reality and the unknown. Liz pulled me along and I trailed behind her. I covered my mouth with my free hand and blew out the pill. It was almost completely dissolved. I walked into an office where Neophus was sitting behind a desk that had piles of money stacked up on it. There were four other men in the dark room who were sitting at a table packaging various types of pills into Ziplock bags.

"Sit down," said Neophus. I sat in a chair in front of his desk. Liz stood behind me and began rubbing my shoulders. "Relax, babe. You're so tense. You shouldn't be so tense smelling as if you've been on a four-day drinking binge. Plus the pill you took should have kicked in at least a little by now."

"I feel as if I'm floating," I said. My statement was partially true. I felt a sense of euphoria, but I wasn't completely out of it yet.

"Tell him about the mess you've gotten us into," said Neophus as he leaned back in his seat. His gaze upon me was like an eagle about to kill its prey.

"First of all, I want you to know that Neophus and I need your help."

"Help?" I asked nervously. "What kind of help?"

"Well, you see." Liz tried to position her fingers on the inside of my shirt, but I stopped her because I didn't want her to feel the recording wire I had taped to my skin.

"A bad batch of Ecstasy ended up on the streets from my operation," Neophus said. "Some kid ended up with brain damage because of it. I failed chemistry so my science isn't perfect." He laughed and so did the other men in the room.

"The police were looking for someone to blame," said Liz. "So I told Neophus that I knew someone who the police could target."

"Who?" I asked.

"Someone you know," Liz said. "Someone who should not have rejected my advances toward her." She continued to rub my shoulders.

"Relax," she said. "It's okay."

"I don't understand," I said.

"Keysha, Wesley. I placed a very large quantity of the bad Ecstasy in Keysha's locker."

"And the police and media just happened to receive several anonymous tips about where the pills could be located," said Neophus. "I wasn't about to allow my operation to sink over a few bad pills."

"But why did you pick Keysha?" I asked. "Why not someone else?"

"I told you. I wanted her and she rejected me." Liz nibbled on my earlobe once again and then spoke directly in my ear. "And no one rejects me."

"She's such a sinister little hellcat, isn't she?" Neophus asked. "I've taught her well," he said with pride. "Keysha just happened to be in the wrong place at the right time, you know what I mean?"

"Yeah, I understand," I said. "But what does this have to do with me?"

"Well, Wesley darling." Liz walked in front of me and squatted down. She looked directly into my eyes.

"She's now trying to haul me into court to say that I set her up. I need a favor from you. Wait, scratch that. Neophus and I need a favor from you."

I swallowed hard. I instantly realized that I was just like Keysha. I was in the right place but at the wrong time. I also realized that Liz was playing me just as much as I was playing her.

"We want you to help us assassinate her character. When I return to school, I'm going to have on some tattered clothing. I'm going to head to the principal's office and make up a story about how Keysha Kendall attacked me. Brittany and Courtney will confirm my story. However, the icing on the cake will come from you. I want you to come to the office and make a report about how Keysha plans to shoot me with a gun she's brought to school."

"Wow," I said as I listened to Liz's twisted plan.

"Then Dorothy Pam Pinkerton is going to rush into the office pretending to be upset because Keysha has threatened her with a gun. In addition to that Neophus and I want you to plant more drugs and a gun in her locker. Ed Daley has been spying on her and has copied down her combination. Once this is done the school will be forced to check her locker. Then they'll call the police and our problem should take care of itself. Keysha will have a difficult time explaining all of the accusations and evidence against her. So, what do you say, Wesley? To be a part of this crew you have to be willing to get a little dirty."

I swallowed hard again and then asked another question. "Do I get any money for doing this?" Everyone in the room laughed.

"Hell to the no!" Neophus yelled at me and I damn near leaped out of my skin. "But you will get to walk out of here alive."

"Give it to him," Neophus said to one of his goons. I was handed a large brown bag. "Make sure the contents of this bag end up in her locker. Don't touch it unless you want the police to find your fingerprints. Ed will give you the combination. The moment the evidence is planted, contact Liz and we'll take care of the rest. Do you think you can handle that?" asked Neophus.

"Yeah, I can handle that," I said. I peeked inside the bag and saw a gun with some Ecstasy pills.

Liz kissed my lips but I didn't like the taste of her. My stomach started doing flips and I felt as if a vomiting episode would be arriving soon.

"The prize that you get for doing this is me and I'm worth the risk," Liz whispered.

"Oh, and just in case you're thinking of crossing me or not participating in our plan. I'd hate to see your daddy have a setback while he's recovering in the hospital. Have I made myself clear?" Neophus stared me down.

"Yeah, it's all good. I know where you're coming from," I answered.

"Good," he said, and then dismissed both Liz and me.

"Where's the bathroom?" I asked Liz as we walked out.

"Over there," she pointed. "Hurry up now, I have things I want to do to you." My stomach did another flip. I rushed into the bathroom and dropped to my knees before the toilet and vomited. Once I was done I felt much better. I rinsed my mouth out then exited the bathroom.

I walked back toward the fireplace to find Ed. He and some girl were dancing in their underwear in front of the fireplace. They both appeared to be completely doped up and hallucinating.

"Dude, when did you get here on Mars?" Ed asked.

"Mars?" I repeated.

"The alien chicks love us, bro." Ed continued to speak as if we were on another planet.

"There you are," Liz approached me from a dark corner of the room. She took me by the hand and led me to the sofa. She pushed me down and then straddled me. She placed my face in her hands and forced me to look into her eyes.

"You've always wanted me, haven't you?" she asked.

"Yes," I answered her. I wasn't sure if I was lying or telling the truth.

"What is it that you like about me?" she asked.

My mind went blank when I didn't have an answer for her.

"Bro, you're getting busy with an alien. Her skin is green man. You're getting down with a green alien, that's wicked." Ed's mind was fully submerged in his fantasy.

"You like me because I'm hot, don't you?" Liz put words in my mouth.

"Yes." I just agreed with her to keep things from spiralling out of control. Liz kissed my forehead, then my eyelid, then my cheek.

"Unlatch my bra," Liz invited me to explore her body. "The latch is right here, in the front." I suddenly found myself at an odd crossroad. Some twisted part of me wanted to be intimate. A dark selfish part of me had surfaced was telling me to take my opportunity. I listened to that dark voice and began pulling Liz's shirt from inside of her skirt. Liz exhaled sensually in anticipation of what was about to go down. My hands were now underneath her clothing. I began stroking her back as she continued to plant kisses all over my face. I was being seduced by her in a way that I never thought possible.

"Hey, Liz. You need to do a drop right now," Neophus interrupted her. "Come back to him later. I doubt he's going anywhere." Neophus tossed a package to her and she caught it.

"The address is inside the package. They're waiting on it."

"Damn," Liz hissed. "I have to go. When Neophus wants something done, I have to do it."

"Who is he to you anyway?" I asked.

Liz chuckled. "He's my mom's boyfriend." Liz winked at me when she saw a boatload of questions come across my face.

"It's a long story. I'll tell you about it later. Right now I just want you to wait here for me, okay?"

"Okay." I once again agreed with her but my mind was still processing the fact that she was doing all of this madness with her mom's boyfriend. *What's that about?* I thought to myself.

"I promise, you are going to enjoy what I have in mind. It will be well worth your wait," Liz said as she got up and followed Neophus toward the back door. I gathered my wits and stood up.

"Ed, let's go," I pleaded with him.

"Dude, I'm on Venus now, doing an alien named, get this, Venus." Ed laughed at his own joke. "You should come to

Venus, bro, the ladies are off the chain," Ed said as he began swirling his arms around like an octopus swimming.

"Ed, we should get out of here." I tried to convince him once more. I wanted to save him from his self-destructive behavior.

Ed ignored my plea and continued kissing the girl he was dancing with earlier. I looked around the room and noticed that everyone was either completely bombed or sprawled out on the floor or making out. Muffled moans, drugs and bare skin were everywhere. I decided right then and there that my opportunity to escape had just presented itself. The temptation to stay and participate was no longer there. Consuming drugs, hallucinating and getting down with strangers just wasn't who I was or what I was about. There was no need for me to try and save Ed if he didn't want to be so I discretely walked over to the front door, opened it up and slipped away into the night.

twenty-eight

Keysha

"This is Angela Rivers reporting to you live from outside the county jailhouse where Neophus Trinity, a notorious drug lord, is being held without bond."

My family and I were sitting in the family room, watching the breaking news story. I was also on the telephone with Wesley, who was watching the news with his father from the hospital.

"A few days ago a court order was issued that gave local narcotics agents the authority to raid Neophus's home, where it was suspected that he produced mass amounts of the drug Ecstasy. It is reported that Neophus recruited teens from several area high schools to help him distribute the popular drug. At this time authorities are saying that not only did they seize mass quantities of Ecstasy but they also confiscated over eighty thousand dollars in cash, several bags of marijuana and a number of unregistered handguns and assault rifles. Neighbors in the quiet suburban community were stunned when the raid took place and are still reeling in shock and disbelief. Authorities have also confirmed that several other teens have been arrested on various drug-trafficking charges. One of those teens, named Liz Lloyd, is also being charged in connection with framing one of her classmates, Keysha Kendall. Keysha Kendall was originally charged

with distributing the drugs, but as a result of new evidence in connec-
tion with this case, all charges against Keysha have been dropped."

Jordan, Barbara and Mike all began clapping.

"What's that noise I hear in the background?" Wesley asked.

"That's my family clapping for me," I said, beaming with joy.

"Here is more on Liz," said Wesley.

"Liz Lloyd has been taken into custody and will remain in a juvenile holding facility until she has to appear in court on several charges ranging from drug selling to blackmail."

"She's going to hate that place," Wesley said.

"Good," I replied. "I hope she rots in there."

"Keysha, don't say that. The girl needs help," said Barbara.

I glanced at her and said okay out of respect, but as far as I was concerned I really, really wanted Liz to rot.

"Let me speak to Wesley," said Jordan, getting up from his seat. I handed the cordless phone to him.

"Hello, Wesley," he said. "I just want to say thank you again for what you've done. I misjudged you on so many levels and I truly apologize for being such a jerk. For you to risk your life and well-being to clear Keysha of the charges against her is nothing short of phenomenal." Jordan paused and I heard Wesley's muffled voice. "I know that I don't have to thank you again but I can't help it. You're a very bright and smart young man and you've most certainly earned my respect. What's that?" Jordan paused and listened to Wesley. "I know, I won't forget that you couldn't have done any of it without the help of Mike and Keysha."

"That's right," Mike shouted. "We're a crack team of investigators."

"Okay," Jordan said, "I'll let you talk with Keysha again." Jordan was about to hand me the telephone. "Oh, Wesley, you're still coming by for dinner this evening, right?... Good, I'll see you then."

"What's up, boo?" I said as Angela Rivers wrapped up her news story.

"So, have I made up for my mistake?" Wesley asked.

"Now, you know that you don't even need to ask that question." Wesley laughed.

"Okay, just checking."

"You know you're my hero," I said. I heard Jordan clear his throat at my comment. "And you too," I said, which made him feel better. I didn't really mind that he was all up in my conversation because everyone in the house was so relieved.

"I still can't believe what you did for me. I mean, going into that house, dealing with that crazy man and all of those people doing drugs. I would have taken one look at everything that was going down and turned right around and walked out the door."

"I really did do it for you," Wesley said once again. "When I got home I became violently ill because of the Red Pill that I partially swallowed. I thought I'd gotten it all out of my system when I puked in Neophus's bathroom but I hadn't."

"I am so glad you came through all of this unharmed. This was so dangerous."

"I'm not afraid of danger, especially when it comes to you," Wesley said. I felt butterflies dancing in my tummy when he said that.

"Thank you, boo. It's nice to have man who has my back. So what happened with Ed Daley?" I asked.

"Rehab," Wesley said. "He really needs it because he's was out of control."

"Well, I hope it helps him," I said.

"So do I," Wesley answered.

"How is your dad doing?" I asked.

"He's okay. His arms and hands are healing up well. He still has to keep them wrapped to fight off infection but he's able to move them more. He'll be coming home soon."

"I walked past your house earlier today. It looks as if the workers are really moving along."

"Yeah, they're working a little harder since they know I have to stay there. They're real nice guys. They're going to show me how to put up drywall over the weekend. I think it will be cool to learn how to do that."

"What about your mom?"

"What about her?" Wesley asked.

"Is she behaving any better?"

"You know, my mom is my mom. I know I have to respect her to some degree, but for the most part we just don't get along and the less contact I have with her, the better."

"Okay, I just thought I'd ask."

"Keysha, let me call you back. My dad's food just came and he's going to need a little help eating."

"Okay, call me back when you can." I hung up the phone and asked if there was anything additional that I missed in Angela Rivers's report.

"No," said Barbara. "Now it's just a matter of due process," she said. "I got the local newspaper to print an apology letter for all of the stress they caused us."

"Oh, really?" said Jordan.

"Yeah, they pretty much crucified Keysha and this family and I didn't like it one bit."

"Ooh, I'm just glad all of this drama is over with," I said.

"You can say that again," Mike chimed in. He stood up and headed upstairs.

"Where are you going?" I asked.

"To my room to read."

"What are you reading?" I asked.

"Some book called *Indigo Summer* by Monica McKayhan. My English teacher met the author at some book signing and read the book. She thought it was so good that she had the school order it for the class."

"What's it about?" I asked.

"So far it's about a girl named Indigo Summer. She's in high school and is trying out for the school dance team. I haven't gotten that far into the book. What about you? What are you reading?"

"*Can't Stop the Shine* by Joyce E. Davis. I just picked it up from the school library but I haven't started it yet."

"Well, let me know if it's any good," Mike said, and then continued on to his room.

"I think I'm going to follow Mike's lead, guys," I said to Jordan and Barbara. "I'll be in my room if you need me."

"Okay," they both said simultaneously. I got up, went to my room and relaxed on my bed. It was so cool to not have any drama going on in my life. My grades had improved, my family cared about me, I no longer had a court case hovering over my head, plus I had a new boyfriend who truly cared about me. What more could a girl ask for? At that moment I thought about my grandmother Katie, whom I hadn't talked to in a while. I decided that before I began reading, I'd give her a call and share all of my good news with her.

The following Saturday morning I woke up before anyone in the house. I walked downstairs and into the family room with my book. I opened up the shutters so that the sunlight could come inside. I placed my book on the end table adjacent to the sofa and then went into the kitchen to pour myself a tall glass of orange juice. As I walked back into the family room I noticed a raggedy and loud burgundy car creeping up the driveway.

"Who in the world is coming by this early in the morning?" I uttered to myself. The car paused for a minute.

"Oh, they must be lost," I whispered to myself but then realized that the car had actually stalled out and the driver had to fire it back up. The engine snarled, rattled and growled as it came back alive.

"Oh, this guy is definitely a gold-card member of the hoopity ride club." The car pulled around to the rear of the house and stopped.

"Jordan." I called out my father's name but he didn't hear me. I rushed toward the front of the house and knocked on the master bedroom door.

"Jordan?" I called out again.

"Yeah." I heard his voice come alive.

"Someone just pulled into our driveway."

"Who is it?" he asked.

"I don't know," I said. At that moment the doorbell rang.

"Go see who it is," he said. "I'm right behind you."

I walked back through the house and toward the door. The doorbell chimed again before I could reach it. I went to the door and looked through the peephole and who I saw made my heart stop beating for a few seconds. The doorbell chimed again. I began hyperventilating. The doorbell chimed yet again. I unlocked the door and opened it.

"Well, it's about damn time, girl. You shouldn't leave your mama standing outside in the cold like this." It was my pregnant mother, Justine. I was horrified and speechless.

"I told you we were related." I looked at who was with her. It was her friend Simon, the man with the hideous scar on his face. "Open up the screen door and give your cousin a big hug." He spread his arms out for me to step into his embrace, but I didn't move.

"Why are you looking like that?" my mother asked.

"Look at you," I uttered. She was a mess. She was wearing bright red sweatpants and a purple sweatshirt that was too small. Her pregnant belly was poking out like a beach ball.

"I know, girl. I'm fine and sexy even though I'm pregnant." She spoke so loudly.

"Is my cousin Jordan home?" asked Simon.

"Yes—he's coming. Why are you here?" I asked.

"Why do you think? It's time for you to come home with me."

Everything around me began to spin around. I felt light-headed and dizzy.

"I got a new one-bedroom apartment in the hood for us to live in, so you can start packing your bags."

I threw a horrified look at my mother. I wanted to tell both her and Simon to go away, but my words couldn't form fast enough.

"Hurry up and go get your things," Justine ordered me but I refused to move. "Come on now, stop playing around. I'm going to have this baby soon and I need you back in the house with me to take care of it." I couldn't believe what I was hearing. I couldn't believe that my mother was actually out of jail and demanding that I return home with her.

"Keysha!" she called. I tried to respond but everything began to spin around. "Come on, girl. You can't live the lifestyle of the rich and famous. I won't let you." Her voice was filled with hostility. "Keysha!" she yelled. I felt my legs buckle beneath me just before I fainted.

Reading Guide Questions

1) Why do you think Wesley turned to alcohol as a way of dealing with his parents' divorce?

2) Discuss why Wesley became infatuated with Keysha the moment he met her.

3) Discuss some of the lessons about friendship that both Keysha and Wesley learned.

4) What are the reasons you feel Liz turned against Keysha?

5) Who do you think trusted Keysha more, her stepmother, Barbara, or her father, Jordan?

6) Why do you think Wesley was so bitter toward his mother?

7) Discuss why the rumors about Keysha and Wesley were so easy for the students at their school and the community at large to believe?

8) Have you personally spread or shared a rumor about an-

other person at your school? If so, what was it, was it true and why did you spread it around?

9) Why do you think Liz was able to persuade so many students to believe everything she said?

10) If you had a friend who was in Keysha's or Wesley's situation, discuss how you would help them cope with their circumstances.

11) Do you think Keysha had justification for attacking Liz and trying to get the truth through violence?

12) Why do you think Wesley's relationship with his father was so strong?

13) Everyone has dealt with drama or conflict at some point. Discuss an uncomfortable situation that you were confronted with and how you resolved it.

14) Discuss the lesson Jordan learned about judging an individual before getting to know him or her.

15) Why do you think Keysha's mother, Justine, has resurfaced?